STOLEN

Rebecca was born and raised in Redcar where she still lives. She has a degree in Film and Media and an MA in Creative Writing. She has lived and worked in Holland and London, and travelled across America on a Greyhound bus in 2002. She won a Northern Writers' Award in 2010.

Stolen

REBECCA MUDDIMAN

MOTH
PUBLISHING

First Published 2013 by Moth Publishing an imprint of Business Education Publishers Limited.

Reprinted 2013.

Paperback ISBN 978 1 901888 86 7

Ebook ISBN 978 1 901888 90 4

Cover design by **courage**.

Printed and bound in Great Britain by Martins the Printers Ltd.

Moth Publishing
Chase House
Rainton Bridge
Tyne and Wear
DH4 5RA

www.mothpublishing.com

FOR STEPHEN WITH LOVE

You don't know what it feels like to have something stolen from you. The one thing that means more to you than anything else. One minute it's there. The next it's gone.

Think of your most prized possession. Think of the one thing you love more than anything else. Think of the one thing you would die for. And then think of losing it.

Think of the words of comfort given by others and how useless they are. Think of how the world keeps going on and on but how yours would stop, just like that. Think of the emptiness and the gaping hole where love once was.

Maybe you feel numb. Maybe it hurts too much to even contemplate. Maybe you cannot bear to think about it and so you bury your head in the sand and pretend everything is okay.

I cannot do that. I can't let it go. I can't grieve and move on. I don't want to face the rest of my days with that emptiness. I choose to do something. I choose to be a mother. Her mother. I choose her. I will not stop until I have a daughter again.

2005

CHAPTER ONE

Abby Henshaw's foot tapped as she glanced at the clock again before turning to her daughter, Beth, who was playing on the floor. A man with a little girl came out of the doctor's office. He picked the girl up, swinging her under his arm until she giggled. Abby's phone rang. She pulled it out of her bag, attracting the stares of the other people in the waiting room, and looked at the screen, cursing her husband for calling when he should've known she'd be at the doctor's.

'Hey. How did the doctor's go?' Paul asked.

'We haven't been in yet,' Abby said.

'What time was your appointment? I thought it was early,' Paul said.

'It was. Things got a bit behind schedule.'

'Your fault or theirs?' he asked.

Abby wanted to say theirs but she knew that wasn't strictly true so she ignored the question. 'So what's up?' she asked. 'You sound tired.'

'I'm alright. I just didn't sleep very well.' He paused. 'Anyway I just wanted to check-in.' She could hear him moving about, probably shuffling books around shelves. 'What's on your agenda today?' he said.

'Once we see Dr Evans we're going to see Auntie Jen, aren't we?' Abby looked down at Beth and ran her fingers through her daughter's feathery hair.

A nurse came to the door leading to the clinic rooms and shouted, 'Martin Savage, please?' A man with crutches stood up and hobbled towards the nurse.

'Jen?' Paul said. '*You're* driving up to see *her*?'

'Yeah, I told you that the other day.'

'I don't think you did,' he said and Abby opened her mouth to argue but Paul cut her off. 'Anyway that's not the point.'

'What *is* the point?' Abby asked.

'Why can't she come here?'

'Don't start, Paul.'

'I'm not starting. I'm just asking why she can't come to you.'

'She said she's got builders in. She doesn't want to leave them unsupervised.'

Abby heard Paul snort. 'She's such a...' He stopped. Since Beth had been born Paul had curbed his swearing and rarely lapsed. Abby wasn't quite as restrained. 'She should come to you, Abby,' Paul said. 'You're the one who's just had a baby.'

'I'm the one who had a baby *eight* months ago. Anyway, she came here last time.'

'That's not the point. If she wants people to go to her she should live somewhere near civilisation. I mean what does she *do* up there? As far as I can tell, the only reason to move to the country is if you're being punished for something.'

'She writes,' Abby said.

6

'Jen doesn't write. She lives the life of an *artiste*,' he said. Abby could almost see quotation marks in the air.

Abby looked down at Beth and realised she was watching someone sitting behind her. Abby turned and saw a red-haired woman pulling funny faces. Abby dragged the pushchair closer towards her and turned her attention back to Paul, who was still complaining.

'I'm just saying, I think she should come here. You'll get lost,' Paul said.

'I will not,' Abby said.

'I spent half an hour on the phone to you last time trying to get you out of *Deliverance* country.'

'I'll be fine.'

'Okay,' Paul sighed. 'Have it your way.'

Abby knew that his opposition to the visit had less to do with the inconvenience of the drive out there and more to do with his feelings about Jen. Some people thought it was odd Abby was such good friends with her husband's ex but Abby found it amusing more than anything else. The idea of them ever having been together was so hard to believe that any jealousy she felt would be ridiculous.

'Anyway, I'd better get back to it,' he said. 'There's a huge delivery here to sort through.'

'Okay.'

'What time will you be back? If you don't get lost.'

Abby smiled. 'I don't know. About five, six maybe.'

'Okay, see you then. Give Beth a kiss for me.'

She disconnected and bent down to Beth, kissing the top of her head. The man with the crutches came out and the nurse stood with a clipboard, scrolling down her list. Beth was staring behind her and Abby turned to see if the woman was still making faces at her. The woman caught Abby's eye but Abby turned quickly back around. She didn't want to get talking to her. She could sense that broody look on the woman's face and she really couldn't be bothered with her 'let's compare baby stories'. She prayed that one of them would be called in next.

'Helen Deal, please,' the short blonde nurse called. The woman stood up and walked towards the smiling nurse.

Abby got Beth settled into her car seat and sat staring out at the people rushing about the supermarket car park. She wondered how many of them were actually happy with their lives. Is anyone? She'd once read something like you can have *anything* you want but you can't have *everything* you want. She'd thought that pretty wise at the time. She could do anything but she couldn't do everything. Not at the same time. Not if she wanted things to end well. She knew that now, that something will always break. Hopefully she'd learned in time, before anything or anyone was hurt too much. Things weren't perfect, she wasn't totally happy, but she was content. And as long as she could keep juggling everything it'd be fine. Fine was enough.

She pulled out her phone and dialled, watching Beth in the mirror. After a few rings the answerphone cut in.

'This is Simon Abbott. I'm away in New Zealand until the 28th of September. Leave a message and I'll get back to you as soon as possible.'

Abby hung up. She thought he was leaving tomorrow. Not that it mattered. What would she say to him anyway? She felt that horrible weight in her gut again. A feeling she couldn't even remember being without. Why was she risking everything? Why didn't she stop?

Because she couldn't. Not now. It was too late. She'd gotten herself into it and now she was stuck. She thought about Paul. She loved him, she truly did. So why had she risked everything? She looked back at Beth. Why had she risked her family?

Abby looked down at the phone in her hand and dialled Jen. It rang several times before cutting off to voicemail. Abby hung up. She searched through her phone for Jen's landline and tried again. No doubt she was too busy flirting with the builders.

Another answering machine. She sighed and waited for the beep. 'Hi, Jen, it's me. I'm running a little late so I'll be about forty minutes, an hour if I get lost. I don't know where you are but you'd better be there when I arrive.'

As she pulled out of the car park and onto the main road through town she wondered whether today should be the day. So many times she'd wanted to share her secret with Jen but she kept bottling out at the last minute. Her friend was no angel herself and what she'd been told, reluctantly by Paul, less so by Jen, was that their relationship had been brief and passionate, and based more on a love of arguing about writers than any great feeling for each other. But something stopped her. Maybe there was still some kind of loyalty there. It just wasn't worth the risk.

As she reached the junction off the main road and headed out towards the countryside, Abby tried to forget her problems. She wanted to focus on the here and now; the road signs and not getting lost. She listened to the noises of Beth gurgling her way to sleep in the backseat and wondered where Jen had got to when she said she couldn't leave the house all day.

CHAPTER TWO

Abby slowed down by the pub on Loftus High Street, a queue of traffic ahead. She craned her neck to try to see what was causing the holdup but a lorry in front blocked her view. She watched as two cars turned around. Whatever was causing the delay clearly wasn't moving. Abby crawled forward, edging out slightly to see past the lorry before she rummaged in her bag for the directions she'd printed off. She traced her finger along the map, trying to work out where she was. She had two options. Left or right.

Abby indicated and pulled out past the lorry. From the pub car park a white van took her place in the queue. She looked at the map again before turning right, then glanced in the rear-view mirror. Beth was sleeping soundly.

When she finally came to the end of the track the daylight was a welcome relief from the endless canopy of branches. She paused at the junction before turning into the narrow country road.

After hitting several potholes Abby looked back at Beth and marvelled that she was able to sleep through the turbulence. After a few hundred yards the last of the few houses disappeared and the trees cut out the light once more. Abby carried on straight ahead. As she looked in the mirror again she was surprised to see a white van was now behind her. She turned her eyes back to the road in front of her and opened the window a crack to let some air in. Looking back into the mirror to check on Beth she noticed the van getting closer. Her stomach tightened. The speed limit was sixty and, okay, she was only doing forty but she refused to speed up. Not on this road and not with Beth in the car. The van edged closer.

'Arsehole,' she muttered, wary of disturbing Beth.

Begrudgingly, she moved to the left to let the van pass. It made no move to overtake, continuing to tailgate her.

'For God's sake,' Abby muttered. 'Even I could get it through there.' She rolled her window down further and waved for the van to overtake. For ten seconds or so it stayed right where it was, Abby becoming more and more uncomfortable until it eventually sped up and pulled out to pass her. Abby watched in her wing-mirror as it moved alongside her. 'Finally,' she said, her fists unclenching.

She looked up to the van's passenger window to try to get a look at the idiot behind the wheel. Her eyes widened as the van swerved towards her. Instinctively she swung the wheel to the left and braked hard as the van scraped against her wing-mirror. The van jerked away from her and sped past as Abby tried to control the car. Bushes along the side of the road scratched loudly at the passenger window as the car bounced along, half on the road, half on the grass verge before it ground to a halt. Abby caught her breath and pulled her seatbelt off, scrambling around to check on Beth, her heart pounding.

'Oh my God.' Abby leant over the seat to her daughter. Beth looked at her with wide eyes. 'Are you alright, baby?' Abby checked Beth over, although she knew that she was okay. She raised her hand to her mouth and stifled a cry, feeling stupid for letting her eyes fill up. Beth watched her mum and then started to cry. Abby wiped her face. 'No, it's okay, baby. It's alright.' She leaned over to unbuckle Beth from her seat but she couldn't quite reach. She turned back around and went to open the door when she noticed the white van parked just up the road ahead of her. A man stepped out of the passenger-side door and was looking in her direction. She could see he had a phone pressed to his ear. Overtaken by fury, Abby shoved the car door open and strode towards him. He hung up the phone and slid it into his pocket.

'What the fuck were you doing?' Abby said to him, stopping as the man approached her, his hands up as if to apologise. 'I've got a baby in the car; you could've killed her. You could've killed both of us.'

'I'm sorry,' he said in a heavily accented voice.

'Sorry isn't good enough,' Abby said glancing back at Beth. 'I'm going to report this–'

The man's fist slammed into her face, snapping her head back. Abby staggered backwards and fell to the ground, fear coursing through her. She stared up at the man in disbelief, her heart racing. Gravel dug into her palm as she tried to push herself up. She lifted her other hand to her face and felt blood dripping down from her nose. She swallowed hard and crawled away from him. Getting to her knees, she searched the road for someone, anyone, to help her. She reached back for her car door and started to pull herself up. The man grabbed her hair from behind and yanked her away. Abby could hear screaming. Beth, she thought. Oh my God, Beth. The man lifted Abby to her feet, one hand still in her hair, the other twisting the back of her jumper into a tight knot, dragging her backwards. She could see Beth in the car, her face placid and untroubled.

It was then that Abby realised that the screams were her own.

CHAPTER THREE

Abby turned and clawed at the man's face, pushing him, trying to pull away. She was aware of her own voice, a cacophony of screams for Beth and pleas to let her go. A second man appeared from the driver's side of the van; a baseball cap pulled down low over his face. He walked quickly towards them, looking around. He shouted something to his friend and the first man nodded towards Abby's car.

'Leave her alone,' Abby screamed, watching as the driver peered into her car at Beth. The driver turned and ran back towards them, shouting something she couldn't make out, in a language that might have been Russian.

The man dropped her to the ground as he tried to open to the van's back door, still arguing with his friend. She squirmed away from him, stumbling her way onto her hands and knees, frantically trying to stand and run. His foot pushed down on her back, forcing her face down into the dirt.

The driver bent and pulled Abby up to her feet, holding her tightly by her wrists, while the first man opened the doors.

She struggled against the driver, swinging an elbow up, catching his face. He shouted at her and pulled her wrists up behind her back, forcing her arms upwards, making her scream out in pain. The first man jumped into the back of the van and held his arms out for Abby. The driver tried to lift her, bumping her forward with his hip, but she caught her foot on the edge of the van and pushed herself away. The man inside the van grabbed her feet and she kicked out at him, causing him to curse at her. The driver stepped up into the van, still holding Abby by the wrists, and threw her to the floor. She scrambled on hands and knees towards the door but she was pulled back into the corner. The driver stepped out, closing one door. He looked around from under his hat and said something to his friend who stood over Abby, keeping her cowed in the corner. It sounded like they were arguing. Abby wondered if she could get past the one in the van but he turned back to face her before she could make a move, laughing as he looked at her.

Abby looked to the driver, still watching from the doorway. He looked less sure than his partner, less willing. His eyes shifted away from Abby's, looking back at her car, back at Beth, and as he closed the other door darkness took over and the world fell into silence. Abby realised she'd stopped screaming and now all she heard was her own breathing. She could barely see in the murkiness of the van. The engine shuddered into life and the man struggled for balance as they moved off. For a few seconds he just stared at her.

'What do you want?' Abby asked. 'I've got money, you can have it; please, take whatever you want. Just let me go. My baby needs me. She needs me.'

The man stared at Abby, seemingly unmoved by her words. She didn't even know if he could understand her.

'Please,' Abby begged again and felt hot tears on her face. As her eyes adjusted to the gloom she tried to make out his features, trying not to wonder why he wasn't wearing a mask to hide his identity.

He bent down, his face now inches from hers, and she let out a whimper. She looked into his eyes, tried to memorise his features. His skin was pock-marked, making Abby think about when she had chicken-pox as a child and her mum told her not to scratch. The memory faded as he leaned closer and Abby blinked, flinching, trying to pull herself away from his hot, fetid breath and black, empty eyes.

He moved back and tried to stand, stooping slightly beneath the low roof. He kicked something aside and leaned over to pull a sheet out of the way. The man turned back to her and said something. She looked to him, as if she could make out his meaning by his face alone. He indicated the space he'd just made. Abby looked back down and understood what he wanted. Abby's body shook; she couldn't breathe. On the floor on the other side of the van was a mattress, aged with use and covered with dirt, torn in several places. The man pointed again, his voice insistent. Abby felt vomit burning in her throat. She tried to disappear into the corner. The man came towards her unsteadily and she cowered. He grabbed her wrist and pulled.

'No,' Abby said, pulling away from his grip. 'No, no, no...'

The man grabbed her with both hands, dragging her by the arm across the cold metal floor. Abby screamed and lashed out at him with her free hand. He dropped her onto the filthy mattress but she pushed herself up again, trying to get away. He raised his fist and Abby covered her face just as it slammed into the side of her head. She cried out as he repeated the blow again and again. Abby curled up in a ball and covered her head, crying into the dirty fabric of the mattress. She listened to the man's heavy breathing and prayed for it to stop. She focused on the stench of the mattress beneath her, trying not to gag. Her ears started to ring and she realised he'd stopped. His breath was loud and heavy and she could smell the stinking animal-like sweat on him as he leaned in closer to her. He spat on the floor by her head.

'Good girl,' he said. Abby uncovered her face slightly so she could see him. He started to unzip his jeans and she let out another cry and tried to scramble away. The man grabbed both her arms and squeezed tightly, forcing them above her head, pinning her to the mattress. He shifted position so that he was straddling her thighs, his weight making it impossible for Abby to lift her legs. 'Good girl,' he repeated and released one arm, his hand moving down Abby's body to the buttons on her trousers. Abby started to breathe so fast she felt like she'd pass out. As he adjusted his position and pulled at her trousers, she prayed that she would.

Abby rocked back and forth with the motion of the van. She started to hear her mother's voice singing 'Rockabye Baby'. She wasn't sure her mother had ever sung that to her, but there it was anyway. She could smell vomit somewhere in the van. There was something wet in her hair. Her naked legs felt the cold breeze sneaking in through the doors. She wondered if she was nearly home.

The van slowed down to a stop. She heard footsteps on gravel somewhere close to her. As the van door opened she saw the silhouette of a man. She hoped Paul had come to get her.

The driver stepped into the van and leaned over her. He pulled her up gently by the shoulders until she was sitting. He wouldn't look her in the eye.

'Where's Beth?' she asked him but he wouldn't look at her, wouldn't answer.

She noticed the other man crouching in the corner of the van, smoking a cigarette. He stared at Abby and blew smoke towards her, making her cough. The driver helped her up and stepped backwards out of the van. He beckoned Abby. She stood, her legs rubbery. She used the side of the van to steady herself and moved towards the open door, the sudden daylight overwhelming her. She squinted up into the sky as the driver held his hand out to help her down. He looked down at her bare legs. Abby followed his glance and stared at her legs for a long time.

They looked dirty. She rubbed at a mark but it wouldn't come off. The driver leaned into the van, pulled her trousers and shoes towards him and held them out to Abby but the other man scuttled towards him and snatched them away, shouting something incomprehensible. He threw the clothes back in the van and climbed out, pushing Abby and his friend aside before slamming the back door closed. He shouted again and shoved the driver towards the side of the van. He stalked round to the passenger's side and got in.

Abby watched as the van quickly disappeared down the long, deserted road. She looked down at her shaking hands with surprise. She didn't feel that cold. She felt dampness between her legs. She looked down at the trickle of blood on her thigh and the world started spinning. An image of her daughter, alone, frightened, flashed into her mind as she hit the floor.

CHAPTER FOUR

Miklos Prochazka's hands gripped the wheel. His chest felt tight. He lifted his cap and wiped the sweat from his brow. Beside him his cousin Damek lit up another cigarette.

'Open the window,' Miklos said and Damek rolled his eyes before rolling down the window.

Miklos looked in his mirror. There was no one behind him. There'd been no one behind or in front of him since they'd dumped the woman at the side of the road. He was expecting to see a stream of police cars, sirens on, lights blazing. But nothing. Not a thing.

Damek hung an arm out of the window and spat. The wind caused remnants of his spit to cling to the window and he muttered. Miklos watched him, his eyes moving quickly between the road, the mirror and his passenger.

'What?' Damek said and leaned forward to turn on the radio.

Miklos just stared at him. He wished he could stop the van and dump Damek at the side of the road. Drive away and never see him again. He knew what Damek was like, knew what he was capable of, and yet he was in shock.

'What?' Damek repeated and flicked his cigarette butt out of the window. 'What's your problem?'

'My problem?' Miklos said and dug his fingers into the wheel. 'My problem!' He slammed his palm against the side of the van. 'What were you thinking?' He turned his eyes back to the road. 'What was I thinking?'

Damek shook his head. 'You got paid didn't you?' He fiddled with the radio again and sat back after he finally settled on a station.

Miklos leaned over and turned it off. His mind was racing. This wasn't supposed to happen. Not like this. He should've walked away. He shouldn't have gone through with it. Shouldn't have stuck with Damek. He shook his head, thinking, 'no more'.

'She was nice,' Damek said and grinned. 'Beautiful. Shame about the baby.'

Miklos felt bile at the back of his throat. He wasn't told about the baby. The baby wasn't supposed to be part of it. They weren't paid for that. He felt his breathing start to speed up and gulped air, trying to fill his lungs. He swerved to the side of the road and stopped.

Miklos scrambled from the van, dry heaving by the side of the road. He wiped his face and leaned against the van, trying to breathe. He heard Damek slam his door and walk around to the driver's side. He stopped in front of Miklos and lifted his head up, looking him in the eye.

'Pussy,' he said and laughed. He pushed Miklos aside and climbed into the driver's seat. Miklos stood watching him before checking behind them once more. The police could be on their way. He wiped his face again and got back in the van. Damek pulled away before he'd even closed the door.

19

Miklos stared at Damek again. 'Did you know?'

Damek just shrugged and Miklos asked again. It wouldn't surprise him if Damek had known. It was all the same to him.

'Didn't ask the details,' Damek said and turned the radio back on.

CHAPTER FIVE

Abby opened her eyes to a fly buzzing around her head and the dry, dead grass on the verge scratching at her face. She sat up quickly and wished she hadn't. Pain shot through her skull causing her to squeeze her eyes shut again. She lifted her hand to her head and then pulled it away. Her hair clung to it, damp and sticky, and she wondered what the hell she'd been lying in. She was suddenly aware of the sound of a car on gravel, somewhere close by. Her first thought was that she should hide; she didn't want anyone to see her in this state.

Her second thought had her scrambling to her feet and running.

'Beth,' Abby said through her heavy breaths. 'Beth, Beth!' She started to scream. She stumbled, the gravel tearing into her bare feet. She suddenly stopped and looked around. Where the hell was she?

Where was her car? Where was Beth? Abby turned around again and again, looking for something familiar, until she was dizzy. The car was getting louder; closer. She ran towards the sound. A blue car appeared from a dip in the road, swerving wildly as Abby ran towards it along the centre of the road. Her palms thudded into the bonnet as the car came to a stop. Through the windshield the startled faces of a middle-aged man and woman stared back at Abby. The couple exchanged alarmed glances before Abby ran around to the passenger side, her eyes pleading with the woman.

'Please, have you seen her? Have you seen Beth?' Abby said. She heard a door open and the man ran around to Abby's side. He reached out to put a hand on her shoulder and she recoiled from his touch. 'Have you seen her?' she pleaded. Her head darted between the two of them, her breath shallow.

'Okay, love, calm down. Tell us what happened. Has somebody hurt you?' the man said, again reaching out to Abby but quickly pulling back. His eyes drifted to her bare legs before darting back to her face. He turned to the woman who slowly climbed out of the car.

Abby glanced around her and started to walk back down the hill, back the way the car had come. 'I need to find her,' she said, wiping her face with an unsteady hand. 'I need to find her.'

The man jogged to catch up with Abby. 'Who do you need to find, love? Who've you lost?'

'Beth!'

'Who's Beth?' he asked.

'My daughter. My little girl.' Abby stopped and turned to the man. 'You must've seen her. Or heard her. She'd have been crying for me.' Abby started to shake with her sobs. The man shrugged his jacket off and held it out for Abby but she ignored the gesture. 'I have to find her.'

'I know,' the man said and steered Abby back towards the car as gently as he could manage. 'We'll find her.' He opened the passenger-side door and sat Abby down. He turned back to the woman. 'Give me your phone.'

22

The woman stared at Abby for a second, before turning her attention back to the man. 'What?' she asked.

'The phone, woman, give me the bloody phone!' he snapped, hand outstretched.

The woman rummaged around in her huge handbag and pulled out a phone. The man grabbed it from her and dialled. He looked back to Abby momentarily and then turned away.

'Hello? Police, please,' he said. He started to walk along the grass verge away from Abby until she could no longer hear him. The woman crouched down in front of Abby, clumsily taking her hand and murmuring unhelpful platitudes.

The man hung up and walked back towards the car. 'The police are on their way, love.'

Abby looked up at the man. 'Have they found her?'

The man cleared his throat. 'They'll sort it out. Won't be long now.'

Abby shook her head. 'No, I can't wait. I need to go. I need to find her.' She stepped past the man, and the woman moved out of her way.

'For God's sake, Andrea,' the man said as he pushed past her. He caught up with Abby again. 'I think we should wait, love. They won't be long.'

'I can't wait,' Abby said. 'What if something's happened to her? What if they hurt her too?' She made a move to walk around him but he grabbed her by the shoulder. Abby cried out and he dropped his hand.

'I'm sorry,' he said. 'I'm really sorry. Look, I don't know what's happened to your little girl but the police can help you. They'll know what to do. Please. Come back to the car and we'll get this sorted out. I promise.'

Abby stared at the man and then started to walk around him again. As she passed him, a police car came up the hill. Bypassing Abby and the man, it pulled in on the grass verge behind the man's car. Two uniformed officers stepped out, approaching Abby.

'Could you tell us your name?' the female officer asked, pushing her dark hair from her eyes, before putting on her hat.

'Abby. Abby Henshaw,' she said, her voice croaky.

'Okay, Abby. I'm PC Lawton. This is PC Cartwright,' she said, indicating her colleague. 'Could you tell us what happened?'

'We were just driving out for lunch and she came out of nowhere. Almost hit her. She keeps talking about needing to find someone, her daughter. I could see she was hurt and she seemed distressed so I called yourselves,' the man said.

'Mr Walker?' Cartwright asked.

The man nodded and Cartwright turned his attention back to Abby.

'I just want to find Beth,' Abby said.

'Who's Beth?' Lawton asked.

'My daughter,' she said, swiping her hand across her forehead and brushing her sticky, sweaty hair from her face.

Lawton and Cartwright exchanged glances.

'Please, I just want my daughter back.' Abby rubbed her hand down the side of her face, smearing the blood that had yet to dry over her cheek.

'If you can tell us what happened, Abby, we can help you. We'll help you find your daughter.'

Abby stared at Lawton and then let out a breath, her frustration rising. The woman didn't even look old enough to be a police officer. How was she going to help? She looked at the others standing there watching her. Why wouldn't anyone help her?

Lawton ushered Abby towards the police car, trying to sit her down but Abby pulled away. 'Just tell us what happened, Abby.'

Abby squeezed her eyes shut. She didn't want to talk, she just wanted to find Beth. She didn't want to think about it.

'Abby?' Cartwright said.

She sighed. 'They took me. They put me in a van and hurt me and they just left Beth there on her own. She can't be on her own, she's only a baby.'

'Okay, Abby. Who took you? Did you know them?' Lawton asked, glancing at Cartwright. As he turned to walk away, Abby heard him say, 'Requesting CID and an ambulance.'

'No.' Abby's breath caught in her throat. 'Please, I don't care about me but I need to find Beth. Why won't you listen? She's on her own. She's not safe.'

'I am listening, Abby. But I need to know what happened so I can help you. Do you understand?'

'Ambulance is on its way,' Cartwright said.

'She was in the car. They left her in the car. It was right down there,' Abby said pointing back down the road. 'I'm sure that was the way I came. I was driving from town, from Redcar, and I think... It's a silver Corsa. You must've passed it. One of you must've seen it.' Abby looked from Lawton to Mr Walker. They exchanged a glance. 'You saw it?' Abby asked.

Lawton nodded. Walker looked ill.

'I saw the car. I thought someone had left it there, gone for a picnic or something. I didn't know...' Walker said and looked between Abby and the police. 'There was no one in it though, I'm sure.'

Cartwright rubbed his chin.

'But you might not have seen her. If you didn't stop, you wouldn't have seen her. She was in her car seat, in the back. She'll be frightened on her own, we need to go and get her.'

Cartwright beckoned Lawton. 'Wait here while I go back to check the car. And get a statement from Mr and Mrs Walker.'

Lawton nodded.

'I'm coming with you,' Abby said.

Cartwright started to argue but Abby climbed into the passenger seat. Lawton walked away, speaking into her radio. Mr and Mrs Walker stood huddled together. Cartwright started the car. As they drove back down the hill Abby's stomach turned, her nausea rising.

A few minutes later they saw her car on the side of the road. Cartwright pulled over and Abby was out the door before he'd even stopped the car. She ran across the road and pulled open the door.

She heard the sound, a guttural, hollow noise, and felt Cartwright's hand on her arm, trying to gently pull her away.

Beth was gone.

CHAPTER SIX

DI Gardner pulled up at the side of the gravel road and took in the scene. All he knew so far was that a woman had been attacked and dumped on the road and was claiming her baby was missing. Usually the kid turned up within hours, sometimes the parents were involved, and occasionally there was no child at all. He felt like he'd come across every kind of person there was in his line of work and yet cases kept coming up that proved him wrong.

Gardner watched as Dave Sanders, one of the SOCOs, who only ever spoke in scientific jargon, climbed out of his car with his bag of tricks. At least that was something. Sanders was one of the best. They'd worked together many times and Gardner knew he could trust him. If there was any evidence out there, Sanders would find it. He worked his team hard and got results.

He saw the paramedics standing beside the ambulance, talking to PC Craig Cartwright. That was all he needed, a little shit like Cartwright on the case. Cartwright looked up and nodded across the road. Gardner followed his stare and saw Lawton crouched down beside the woman. That was something. PC Dawn Lawton balanced things out. She was good. Would make a good detective one day.

Gardner shifted his attention to the woman. Clearly something awful had happened, but he hoped that her ordeal had confused her. It wouldn't be the first time a parent was convinced a child was lost when in fact the kid had been left at home or school.

Gardner let out a breath and opened the car door. As he walked towards Lawton he hoped that this would be an easy one.

Abby sat on the hard gravel road, her arms wrapped around her knees. She noticed the small, sharp stones digging into her flesh but felt nothing. PC Cartwright had given up trying to move her into the ambulance and was instead talking constantly into his radio, seemingly desperate for control over *something*. She saw his arms moving, fingers pointing to the cars that arrived and the people who climbed out. Yellow tape was unwound and fluttered in the breeze. Abby tuned out his words, desperate to cling onto unreality. This wasn't a police matter. Beth wasn't gone. Things were fine. But the arrival of more cars, more police, uniforms, equipment; they all conspired together and refused to let her keep believing in it.

Two pairs of feet arrived in front of her.

'Mrs Henshaw?' She recognised Lawton's voice and ignored her, hoping she'd go away, taking all of it with her. 'Mrs Henshaw?' Her feet shuffled and then the second pair moved slightly as someone stooped in front of her. She felt a gentle touch on her chin, manoeuvring her to face him. An older, more experienced face, wearing a concerned expression, looked down at her.

'Mrs Henshaw? I'm DI Gardner.' He looked back up at Lawton and then at Abby. 'Can you hear me? If you can hear me, just nod, alright?'

Abby paused, her brain struggling to comprehend. Eventually she felt herself nod.

'Good. Okay, we're going to take you to the hospital. Get you checked out, make sure you're okay and then we'll have a talk. Is that alright?'

Abby stared at Gardner and then nodded again. She felt like she wanted to speak but she couldn't think what it was she should say. What was there left to say? Beth was gone. Gardner moved back to let the paramedics in. They gave her a quick once-over and then helped her stand. As they walked her to the ambulance she looked around at the frenzy of activity. She felt like she was in a film where the hero stands still and alone as the rest of the world rushes around, unaware of the statue among them. PC Lawton got into the ambulance. Abby could hear her talking but couldn't make out what she was saying. She spotted Cartwright lurking by her car. Another man, wearing latex gloves, backed out of her car holding something. She watched as Gardner approached him.

'Definitely her car,' he said and handed Gardner some papers. 'ID in her handbag matches the registration. We've got a contact number for the husband, but haven't got hold of him yet. A uniform's on the way to try and pick him up.'

'Paul,' Abby muttered. What about Paul? How was he going to feel? How would she tell him what'd happened? That Beth was gone?

The paramedic nearest to her helped her into the ambulance and went to close the door. Before he did she heard one last thing from the man with the gloves.

'No sign of a baby in there though. No car seat, no nappies or whatever. No picture in her wallet. Nothing.'

CHAPTER SEVEN

'Okay, Abby, we're all done here. Sit up in your own time and when you're ready you can use the bathroom. If you need anything just let me know,' Doctor Rosen said, her voice soothing and even.

Abby watched her as she peeled off her gloves and disposed of them. She looked up, giving Abby a slight smile, comforting and professional. There was no pity in her words or actions. Abby wondered how long she'd done this. Was this all she did? Day after day, taking care of victims. She wondered how the woman felt when she went home at night; unclean and angry, or like she'd done something good? Maybe both. Abby looked down to Doctor Rosen's left hand but saw no ring. She must be in her late-fifties at least. Abby wondered if she'd never married; perhaps her job had marred her opinion of men. Maybe she just didn't wear a ring for work.

'Abby?' She realised the doctor was speaking and looked up into her eyes. 'Do you want to get up now?' Doctor Rosen asked.

Part of Abby wanted to stay put, listening to her gentle voice forever. She wanted to hear that everything was okay. If she were to tell her that, Abby was sure she'd believe her. But she didn't. Not once had she told Abby that things were fine. She hadn't told her that she was okay. She hadn't promised that Beth would be safe. Maybe it was this honesty that inspired trust in the women who came through her doors.

Abby sat up and felt the room spin. Doctor Rosen put a steadying hand on her shoulder. After a couple of minutes she gave Abby's shoulder a slight squeeze.

'Ready?' she asked.

Abby nodded and slid off the table, glancing from side to side. She stood still, unsure of what to do and where to go. Doctor Rosen held her arm out beside Abby, guiding but not touching.

'Just through here,' she said, gesturing to a door with her other hand. 'There are clean towels and a change of clothes. Just leave the gown on the floor.'

Abby stepped into the bathroom, which was blinding in its whiteness. Doctor Rosen closed the door behind her and for the first time in hours Abby was alone. She could hear her own breaths quietly echoing off the pristine tiles. She stepped forward to the sink, keeping her head down to avoid looking into the mirror above it. After a few deep breaths she raised her head. Abby stared at herself. Blood stained her face and was caked in her hair; the red reminded her of the time she stole her mother's lipstick and smeared it across her seven-year-old face. Bruises covered a good portion of her face and her lips were swollen and torn. She went to touch her cheek and realised her hands were behind her back, gripping the hospital gown, keeping it closed, keeping the cold out, keeping anyone from seeing her. She looked behind her at the closed door and gradually let go of the thin, papery costume. It drifted apart, exposing her goose-pimpled skin to the harsh overhead lights.

Abby reached up to her sad clown face and traced a line down the dried blood on one side. She reached her chin and then started again from the top, drawing patterns round the edge of the bruises, trying to make shapes.

A noise from outside the room made her jump. She turned away from the mirror and looked at the pile of white hotel-folded towels on the shelf next to the bath. She panicked for a moment, thinking she was going to get blood on them, and then decided that Doctor Rosen probably didn't care. She wondered if they re-used the towels or if they disposed of them like plastic gloves. It seemed a waste, but she couldn't help feeling sick at the thought of other women, other girls, wiping away their own blood on those same towels.

On the chair was a pile of clothes, again folded neatly and professionally. Abby brushed her hand along the edge of the pile. Bra, knickers, socks, T-shirt, tracksuit bottoms, jumper, and slip-on trainers; the kind you see in the Sunday supplements. She wondered if she needed all those clothes. She didn't remember it being that cold.

Another noise from the other side of the door made her move. There could be someone else waiting to come in, a factory line of victims. Examination – wash – questioning. Abby looked around for another door that would lead her to the next stage but saw none. She'd have to go back the way she came. But what if there was someone in there? The next victim? Do you wait until you're called or knock on the door to come out? How were you supposed to know?

Abby turned back to the bath. Behind the curtain was a shower. She wondered which she was meant to use. A shower would be quicker if there was a queue. She turned the taps and a violent flow of water shot out of the showerhead. Abby held her hand underneath the stream and then stepped under it. The hot water stung her face and burned as it heated up. She felt heavy and constricted. She ran her hands down her body and her skin felt like it was pulling away from her bones. She looked down and realised that she was still wearing the gown. Stepping back, she struggled to unfasten the gown; the cord too wet and tight to un-do. She clawed at it but it was too strong. Abby felt her chest tighten with the effort. She pulled at the front of the gown and felt tears burning in her eyes. She slid down the tiled wall until she was sitting at the bottom of the bath, the hot water just about reaching her, steam beginning to fill the room and blank her out. Safe in the knowledge that the water would drown out the sound, she let go.

Abby turned off the shower and stepped out, leaving a trail of water across the floor. The soaked gown clung to her body. She pulled it up over her head and dropped it to the floor with a heavy splat. Her chest hurt, her throat felt raw. She wondered how long she'd been in there and if Dr Rosen had been hammering at the door like her father used to. She'd missed the sound of his voice after he'd gone, wished he could yell at her just one more time.

She picked up a large white towel and wrapped it around herself, no longer caring if she made a mess. She threw the pile of clothes onto the floor, watching water seep into the T-shirt, and sat on the vacant chair, her hair dripping down her back. She looked at her arms, red from the heat of the water, and thought about that summer Paul fell asleep in the garden and got sunburnt all over the front of his body. She wondered if Paul had been told yet; if he was waiting out there somewhere. Maybe he was sitting out there right now with Beth on his knee, thinking how she always spends too long in the bathroom.

Abby got up and dried herself. She examined each item of clothing before putting it on. The bra: slightly too small and fraying on one cup. The knickers: large and comical. The T-shirt: peach and bland. The tracksuit bottoms: too long and too nylon. She questioned putting on the blue jumper, but felt like it must be there for a reason and so slid it over her head. Finally the socks. The socks were OK. She slipped her feet into the Sunday shoes that were a little too big and clip-clopped slowly across the floor back to the mirror. She took one last look at herself before going out to face the world. Reaching up again to her swollen face she touched a bruise and pressed her fingers into it. She let out a whimper and pressed harder. It didn't hurt enough.

CHAPTER EIGHT

'Alright, thanks. Bring him up.' Gardner put down the phone and rubbed his eyes. The husband had arrived. Abby Henshaw had already been brought in after being examined. Fortunately she'd suffered no serious injury, he'd been told. *Fortunately*. That was a joke. Cuts and bruises were the least of her trouble. The woman had been raped. Her daughter was missing. If he was going to pick one word to describe Abby Henshaw it wouldn't be 'fortunate'.

Gardner started to walk out to meet Mr Henshaw when DC Don Murphy and PC Cartwright walked in. Murphy had a face like a slapped arse for a change.

'What's wrong with you?' Gardner asked him.

Murphy shook his head, making his jowls wobble. 'My knee's killing me. Walking up and down that bloody road all afternoon.'

'So you're done?' Gardner asked, looking between Murphy and Cartwright.

'SOCO's still out there,' Cartwright said when Murphy didn't bother. 'Sanders said he'd call as soon as he found anything.'

'And what about you?' Gardner said.

'I spoke to a couple of dog walkers who saw nothing. The couple that found Mrs Henshaw gave a statement but know nothing useful. Like I said, SOCO's found nothing so far. Some blood that's probably hers. A few cigarette butts, a few bottles; nothing useful,' Cartwright said, with a shrug. 'Waste of time.'

Cartwright was a cocky little shit. Ambitious too. Had an eye on the boss's job. Thought actual police work was below him. Gardner glared at him before turning to Murphy.

'There's a few footwear marks but no clear ones,' Murphy said and leaned back so far in his chair Gardner thought it would break. 'We've got an eye out for the van but as she doesn't know what make it is or a licence plate, it won't be easy. Unless of course you want us to bring in every white van on the bloody roads. There's nothing out there.'

'What about door-to-doors? What about searching for the kid?'

Murphy shrugged. 'What doors? There's nothing out there but cows.' Murphy rolled his eyes when Gardner opened his mouth to speak. 'There's a pub and a few houses way back. They've covered it all. No one saw anything. No one heard anything. No one knows anything. There's a team searching the fields nearby but how likely is it that a bloody baby is going to be crawling around out there? It's a waste of time.'

'I'll decide what's a waste of fucking time,' Gardner said and Cartwright looked down at his feet. 'I want to know every CCTV camera, every speed camera, on the road from when she left Redcar to the scene. I want to know that every last possible witness has been accounted for. Are you listening?'

Murphy stopped with his hand in his snack drawer. Lawton walked in but started to edge towards the door as Gardner yelled at his team. 'Hang on,' Gardner said to her and she stopped. 'You,' Gardner said, pointing at Murphy. 'Get your fat arse out of that chair and get back out there. When you've checked every last inch of that road, when you've stopped and checked every single car, and when you've looked under every last cow, then you come back here and tell me it was a waste of time. You,' he said, pointing at Cartwright, 'go with him. Start knocking on doors yourself. And carry his fucking snacks for him.'

'But...' Cartwright started. Gardner glared at him. 'I thought I could sit in on the interview.'

'No. Lawton's doing it. I need a female officer in there with me. You know that.'

'I thought I could speak to the husband,' Cartwright said.

'No,' Gardner said. 'I want you back out doing door-to-doors.'

'But I never get to interview,' Cartwright said.

'Is there something wrong with you?' Gardner asked him. 'This isn't about your fucking career, Cartwright. It's about her,' he said pointing towards the door.

Cartwright let out a sigh and shrugged like a sullen teenager. 'Sir,' he muttered.

'Now shut the fuck up and get out. Both of you,' Gardner said, looking to Murphy.

Murphy sat there for a few seconds. 'Get out!' Gardner said and Murphy scuttled away after Cartwright. 'Jesus,' Gardner said. 'Who's in charge here?' He rubbed his temples and let out a breath. 'Right,' he said. 'Lawton, follow me. Any luck with the mug shots?'

'No, sir,' Lawton said, looking up at him. 'I left her with the sketch artist. That could give us something useful,' she said, walking quickly, trying to keep up.

'I'm not holding my breath. She can't remember much, a couple of vague details. From what she's said so far there were two men in a white van. They had accents which could've been Russian or Eastern European. One had a scarred face, someone could recall seeing him.

But like Tweedle-Dum said, she didn't notice a licence plate, didn't notice a make. I'll take the husband to see her before we get started. Go and find Wilson and ask him to make a start on finding anyone in the system who could be our guys. Meet me back upstairs in five minutes.' He pointed to a room at the end of the hall. 'In here?' he asked her and Lawton nodded as he walked down the hall to meet Paul Henshaw.

Gardner wished he had more answers. He knew that was what people wanted. The relatives. The mothers, fathers, husbands, wives. That was all they wanted from him. Answers. But right now he didn't have any.

Abby sat in another new room, alone. The sketch artist had gone. She'd tried her hardest to remember their faces, she thought she had, but nothing seemed right. Nothing he put in front of her seemed right. All she remembered were the pock-marks on his face. Nothing else.

The hard, plastic chairs were uncomfortable and there was a stale cigarette smell that caught in her throat. She wished she was at home in her own bed, and then felt guilty for wanting comfort. Was *Beth* comfortable? She stood and walked to the window, trying to push the thoughts from her mind. Where was she? Why would someone want to take her daughter? She wanted her mum. More than anything she wanted her mum. More than Paul, more than Simon. She closed her eyes, blinking back tears, and pressed her forehead against the cool glass. Detective Gardner said he'd be right back but that was thirty minutes ago. He'd tried to answer Abby's questions but it seemed like he knew nothing at this point. No, they hadn't found Beth. No, they hadn't found anyone who'd seen anything. And no, there hadn't been any demands or anything to indicate that it was 'a simple' kidnapping.

She wanted to see Paul. She needed him to tell her it'd be alright.

The clock on the wall ticked loudly. She hated it reminding her with each stroke it was another second that Beth was missing. Another second Abby was not being her mother.

Voices in the hallway caused Abby to turn. She recognised Paul's voice; angry, upset, demanding answers. She moved over to the door as the voices approached. The door swung open and Gardner almost walked into her. He stepped back as Paul pushed past him. He took one look at Abby and froze. The colour drained from his face and his eyes glazed over with tears.

'Abby,' he said, his voice catching.

Abby felt herself start to cry again and took half a step closer to Paul. He reached out to her and then dropped his hand, as if he was afraid to touch her.

'What did they do?' he said, his voice thin and lifeless. 'My God.' He moved towards her and threw his arms around her. She could feel his whole body shaking. She buried her face in his chest and as his fingers curled into her hair she felt her own body shudder as she cried.

'They took Beth,' Abby said into Paul's body. 'I let them take her.'

He shook his head. 'It's not your fault, Abby. Please, look at me.' He pulled back to look her in the eye. 'This isn't your fault.' He shifted his glance to Gardner who was staring at the floor. 'Please, tell me you're going to find who did this.'

Gardner cleared his throat. He looked between Abby and Paul. 'We're doing everything we can but at this point we need to speak to Abby to get a better idea of what–'

'Is anyone even out looking for her?' Paul asked.

'We have officers looking around the local area but due to Beth's age it's clear that someone must've taken her.'

'Jesus.'

'We have a description of the men who attacked your wife and of the van. That's a start but we need to speak to your wife again to fully understand the situation. And it's quite possible that someone saw your daughter in the car alone and took her for her own safety–'

'So where the hell is she then? Why haven't they brought her back?'

'We're checking with local stations and hospitals.'

'But what about the men who... the men who took me?' Abby said. 'They must have something to do with it?'

37

'We'll look into all possibilities but we need to take a statement from you.'

Abby nodded and Paul ran his fingers through his hair. 'Can I at least stay with her while you talk to her?' he asked.

'No, I'm afraid not. We need to take yours and your wife's statements separately.'

'Mine? I don't understand,' Paul said. 'You need a statement from me?'

'Yes.'

'Why? I don't understand.' Paul glared at Gardner. 'You think I kidnapped my own daughter?'

'It's a formality, Mr Henshaw. Just so we can get some background info.'

Paul released his stare and let out a slow, deep breath. 'Right. Of course. Whatever you need to do.' He looked across at Abby. 'Will you be okay?'

Abby nodded and turned back to Gardner.

'Okay, Mrs Henshaw, if you'll come with me,' Gardner said and opened the door. 'If you'll wait here, Mr Henshaw,' he said indicating the plastic chairs against the wall. 'Can I get you anything?'

Paul gave a short shake of his head and dropped into a chair. He slumped forward, head in hands.

CHAPTER NINE

Abby felt claustrophobic in the small, square interview room. The overhead light was dim and the only window was high up on the wall. She sat opposite Gardner and PC Lawton. Lawton smiled, softly, each time Abby looked towards her. Gardner turned on a video camera and made the formal introductory statements. Abby glanced at the lens and swallowed. She hated being on camera. On more than one occasion she'd threatened Paul with divorce if he didn't get his camcorder out of her face.

She watched DI Gardner scribble the date - Monday 19th September 2005. She hadn't taken much notice of the date that morning when she left the house - she barely knew what day it was anymore - but she'd remember it now. It'd be etched into her brain forever.

'Okay, whenever you're ready,' Gardner said. Abby looked at him, unsure what to say or where to start from. She looked from Gardner to Lawton for a prompt.

'Would you be more comfortable speaking to another female officer?' Gardner asked.

Abby shook her head. 'No, it's just...' She looked Gardner in the eye and he nodded.

'Just start by telling me what happened.'

Abby nodded. As she took a breath it caught in her throat. The image of that man looming above her, his hot breath on her face. She closed her eyes but it only made it worse. When she opened them, both Gardner and Lawton were staring. She knew she had to speak. The only way she would get Beth back was to tell them what happened out there.

After she recounted every detail, Gardner poured a glass of water and pushed it towards her. Abby gulped it down and watched him write some more notes.

'Do you want to take a break?' Gardner asked.

Abby paused before shaking her head. How much longer would she have to sit there? What else could she tell them?

'Okay. So you were going to see your friend Jen?' Gardner said.

'Yes. Jen. Jennifer Harvey.'

Gardner asked for her address and made a note as Abby dictated.

'Was it planned?' he asked.

Abby looked confused for a moment. 'What?'

'Had you and Jen arranged the visit in advance or did you just decide this morning to go out there? Did Jen know you were coming?'

Abby nodded. 'It was planned. We arranged it last week, I think.'

'So apart from yourself and Jen, who else knew you were going?'

Abby ran her fingers through her hair, flinching as she did so. 'Paul, obviously.' She shook her head. 'I think that's it.'

'You told no one else, no other family members?'

'We don't have any other family.'

Gardner looked at her. 'None at all?'

Abby shook her head. 'My parents died in a car crash when I was eighteen. I've got an aunt but I haven't seen her for a long time. She lives in America. Both mine and Paul's parents are dead.' She paused. 'Paul's mum killed herself.'

Gardner waited but Abby didn't continue. 'And his dad?' he asked eventually.

'He died,' Abby said.

Gardner looked like he was about to query this but just nodded again and moved on. 'Okay, no other family? Brothers, sisters?'

'No,' Abby said.

Gardner nodded again. 'No other friends who might've known? Nobody from work you could've told?'

Abby shook her head. 'I'm on maternity leave.'

'What about Jen? Would she have told anyone?'

'I don't know. Maybe.'

'But as far as you know no one else knew you'd be going out there today except you, your husband, and your friend Jen?'

'Right,' Abby sighed.

'How long have you known Ms Harvey?'

Abby thought about it. How long *had* they been friends? It seemed like a long time but that was an illusion created by Jen's knowledge of her past, or at least her husband's past. 'About four years,' she said. Gardner remained silent, compelling Abby to continue. 'We met at a work party.'

'So you know her through work. Would you say you were close?'

'Yes.' Abby paused. 'What's this got to do with finding Beth?' Gardner said nothing. 'You can't think Jen had anything to do with this? Why would she?'

Gardner cleared his throat again. 'I just need to fill in as much background as I can. I'm not suggesting your friend had anything to do with what happened but I need to know as much as possible. The details are usually what help the most.'

Abby sighed again, her mind racing. *Should she tell him?* She looked down at her raw hands as she spoke. 'I've known Jen for four years but

Paul has known her a lot longer.' She sensed Gardner shift in his seat. 'Paul and Jen were at university together. They used to be together.' She looked back at Gardner who didn't even try to conceal his surprise. Abby suddenly felt embarrassed, wondering what Gardner and Lawton were thinking.

Was this some kind of love-triangle, Mrs Henshaw?

'Is there any chance that your husband and Ms Harvey...?' Gardner made a gesture with his hand.

Abby stared at him for a few seconds. 'Paul and Jen?' She looked at Lawton who sat with her Mona Lisa smile. 'Believe me that would never happen.'

'They didn't get on?'

'No. Well, yes. Sometimes they'd bitch about each other but not seriously. I think it made Paul uncomfortable knowing his wife and ex-girlfriend were friends.'

'So Paul wasn't keen on Jen being around. What about her?'

Abby shrugged. 'She just, I don't know. She likes to tease him. She knows she can always get a rise out of him.'

Lawton shot Gardner a quick glance before looking back to Abby. 'Did you ever get the feeling that Jen was jealous? Maybe still had feelings for Paul?'

'No,' Abby said. 'She didn't even know I was married to him until a few months after we'd been friends.'

'How did she find out?'

'She just mentioned one day that she used to go out with someone called Henshaw and we realised it was Paul.'

'And it didn't bother you?' Lawton said. 'I don't think I'd like to know my friend used to go out with my husband.'

'No. Me and Paul had already been together for four years. I just found it funny that they'd ever been together. I couldn't imagine them as a couple. Still can't.'

'And what about Paul? How did he react?'

'He was surprised. She was a blast from the past. He asked if she was still a nutter and that was it really.'

'A nutter?' Gardner asked.

'He just thought she was a bit mad, you know. They're so different. That's why I thought it odd that they'd ever been together.'

Gardner scratched at his ear and made some final notes. Abby tugged at the sleeve of her jumper.

'Is any of this actually helping?' she asked.

'We need to make sure we cover everything,' Gardner said.

'But Jen didn't take Beth. She didn't hurt me.' She took a deep breath and felt the tears burning her eyes again. She swiped at her face with the sleeve of her scratchy jumper. 'I'm sorry. I just want to find my little girl.'

'I know,' Gardner said. 'And we will. I know this is hard. I can't imagine how you're feeling right now but I need you to keep going. Just answer my questions, even if they might seem stupid. Okay?'

Abby swept the hair from her face behind her ear. She nodded at him.

'Okay. You didn't tell anybody else you'd be going to see Ms Harvey?'

Abby closed her eyes. She knew there was no one else. Who else would she tell? Then she had a thought. Her eyes opened.

'I was at the doctor's,' she said. 'Before going to Jen's, I went to the doctor's. I was on the phone to Paul and we were talking about it.' Abby felt sick. She tried to remember who'd been there, who was listening. The receptionist? The man with the crutches?

Gardner made a note. 'Which surgery?'

'Kirkleatham Street,' she said.

'In Redcar?' he asked and Abby nodded. 'Okay, we can check,' he said but Abby didn't know what that meant. He could check if any rapists or kidnappers had made an appointment that morning on the off chance? 'Okay, let's go back. Let's start with this morning before you left to go to Ms Harvey's.'

Abby told him about having breakfast, about losing her keys and running late. About the visit to the surgery and the drive up the narrow country roads. Gardner took notes and nodded in the right places. He stopped and asked questions to clarify and confirm. After what seemed like a long time he finally put his pen down and folded his hands on the table top.

'Okay. Is there anything else you can think of? Anyone out of place? Anything suspicious? Maybe it wasn't even today, maybe in the last few days? Maybe further back. Anything at all?'

Abby started to shake her head and then thought of something she'd ignored at the time as nothing more than an inconvenience, perhaps a malicious act by bored teenagers.

'Someone slashed my tyres,' she said.

'When was this?' Gardner asked.

'January, I think,' she said. 'Maybe the beginning of February. Not long after Beth was born.'

'Did you report it?'

'No,' she said, shaking her head. 'I had no idea when it was done. I didn't use the car for a couple of weeks so when I noticed it could've been done the night before or days before. I just thought it was kids or something. I had better things to worry about.'

Gardner nodded but she thought he seemed a little disappointed by her response. 'Okay,' he said. 'Was that an isolated incident? Nothing else happened around that time or since then? No one you can think of that might have reason to harass you?' He stared at her and she felt her mouth go dry. 'Anything at all?'

She could feel her chest tighten, her breathing beginning to labour. She wondered if Gardner saw right through her. If she told him, part of her felt like it would be for nothing. She knew Simon would never have done this; knew he wouldn't have slashed her tyres. Abby felt the weight of Gardner's stare and knew she had to make a decision. If she told him about Simon, that would be it. The truth would be out. She would lose Paul. But she needed to tell him. If it was a choice between Paul or Beth, she knew what she'd choose.

Tears began to form in her eyes again but she blinked them away, ignoring the pain, ignoring her throat constricting. She swallowed hard and met his gaze.

'This is my fault,' Abby said. She could feel Gardner watching her, waiting.

'Why is it your fault?' he asked.

She shook her head, unable to say it.

'Abby?'

'Simon,' she said.

'Excuse me?' Gardner glanced at Lawton and back to Abby.

'Simon Abbott.' Abby felt her voice catch in her throat and looked back down at her hands, pushing them under her thighs to stop them from shaking.

'Who's Simon Abbott?'

Abby licked her lips. 'He's the man I had an affair with.'

CHAPTER TEN

Gardner splashed his face with water. He gazed into the mirror as he dried off with a scratchy blue paper towel. God, he was tired. He couldn't decide if this new information would make things more simple or more complicated. It certainly added a whole other layer of possibilities. Abby claimed the affair was over, had been for a long time, and yet they were still in contact. Simon Abbott told her he was going on a work trip tomorrow and yet his answerphone said he'd already left; Gardner had just tried it himself. He'd dispatched an officer to Abbott's house to check just in case but that didn't necessarily mean anything. The man could've left, paying someone to hurt Abby while he was gone. What better alibi than to be on a plane headed for New Zealand at the time of the attack?

Abby had insisted he wouldn't have been involved. He wasn't that kind of man. That was a joke. No one was that kind of man until he was. And for now there was no one else, no other possible suspects, no one with any reason to hurt Abby. Abby denied that Simon and Jen knew each other, even knew about each other. There was no way Jen could've told him Abby was visiting.

His initial feeling had been that Abby was genuine, that she had no involvement in her daughter's disappearance, and he was sticking to that. For now anyway. But, the woman had had an affair. No, she didn't deserve to be punished for that, certainly not like this, but what Annie had done to him still hurt. He didn't think about her much these days, but when he did it brought back everything else that happened back in Blyth – the affair, Wallace, Wallace's kid and her face as she watched the coffin being carried from the hearse. Maybe that was what really hurt. Gardner shook his head. He'd hated Annie for what she did, for everything that happened because of one stupid decision she'd made. You can't imagine how much it'll tear you apart until your own wife tells you she's been sleeping with someone else. That's when you realise what heartbreak really means. And now he had to go and face Abby Henshaw's husband. He stared at himself in the mirror. According to Abby her husband had no idea about her affair. She'd begged him not to say anything. She'd lost her daughter; she didn't want to lose her husband too. Gardner knew he'd find out eventually. It would be impossible to keep it from him. But for now he decided to withhold the information. Paul was the only person she had to lean on. He looked at himself in the mirror, let out a breath and walked back out into the corridor.

'Lawton,' he said and the young officer turned. 'Any luck with Simon Abbott?'

'PC Copeland's been to his home address,' she said. 'No one there. He's on his way to Abbott's photography studio in Saltburn now. I'm trying to confirm his flight status.'

'Good.' Gardner nodded towards the room where Paul Henshaw was waiting. 'What do you think of him? First impressions?'

'He seems to be in shock,' she said after a moment.

'And?'

'Upset.'

'He say anything that seemed strange to you?' Gardner asked and Lawton shook her head. 'What was your gut instinct? Involved?'

'No,' Lawton said, looking in at Paul. 'No, I think he's devastated.'

'What were you thinking in there with Mrs Henshaw?' Gardner asked. 'You think Jen Harvey has something to do with it?'

Lawton looked like she wanted to speak but held back. She was too timid at times and that wasn't going to get her anywhere.

'I don't know,' she said. 'Something about the husband and the friend bothered me.'

'You think they're involved again?'

'No,' Lawton said. 'But maybe the friend isn't what she seems. Maybe when she saw him again something clicked and she remembered what she was missing. She could be jealous of what Abby Henshaw's got.'

Gardner thought about it. 'You think she could be jealous enough to do something like this?'

Lawton frowned. 'I don't know.'

'We'll speak to the husband first. Then we'll see about Jen Harvey.'

Lawton nodded and they walked into the interview room. Gardner looked at Paul Henshaw and wondered if he'd be able to answer his questions, if he really knew his wife at all.

CHAPTER ELEVEN

'Sorry about the wait,' Gardner said and pulled up a chair opposite Henshaw, who gave a half-hearted shrug. He seemed exhausted, his eyes red and damp. His hands rested on the table, clenching and unclenching.

'Shall we start?' Gardner asked, waiting for Lawton to set up the camera.

'Has there been any news?'

'No, not yet. I'm sorry,' Gardner said and took out a pen. He looked at Paul. He was shaking. In many ways he looked worse than Abby did. 'Can I get you something?' he asked, hoping that the man wasn't about to pass out. 'Water, maybe?'

Paul shook his head and let out another sob. He covered his face and Gardner had to look away. Jesus, the man was a wreck. He knew how embarrassing it was to be the crying man. He'd been there. And he'd had much less reason for it. He understood how humiliating it was so kept his eyes down and scribbled some notes that meant nothing.

'God, this is my fault,' Paul said.

Gardner looked up but Paul wasn't looking in his direction. He was staring up as if he was actually praying. 'Mr Henshaw?'

Paul closed his eyes and muttered, 'I should've been there.'

'Mr Henshaw?' Gardner repeated and Paul finally looked at him. He shook his head and apologised.

'I'm sorry,' Paul said and wiped his eyes, trying to compose himself. 'I'm sorry.'

Gardner nodded. 'That's alright.' He paused. He wanted Paul to continue. Sometimes the best information came from an emotional rant. But Paul was quiet. He decided to lead him gently back in. 'It's not your fault, Mr Henshaw,' he said.

Paul just stared for a while and then nodded. 'But I should've been there.'

'Where?'

'With Abby. With Beth. Maybe if I'd gone this wouldn't have happened,' he said. 'I should've told her not to go. I should've stopped her.' He took in a shaky breath and looked at Gardner. 'Please tell me you'll find her. You'll find the bastards who did this.'

Gardner nodded. 'We will,' he said and hoped it was true. 'Are you okay to start?' he asked and Paul nodded. 'Okay, let's start with this morning. Can you tell me what happened?'

'When?' Paul asked and rubbed at his eyes.

'This morning before you and Abby left the house. Talk me through what happened.'

Paul swallowed. 'We had breakfast. Me and Abby and Beth.' His voice caught as he said his daughter's name. 'Same as usual. I was in a hurry.'

'A hurry for what?'

'I had to get to the shop. There was a delivery,' Paul said.

Gardner nodded and indicated he should continue.

'I went to the shop. Opened up. I called Abby a little later. She was taking Beth to the doctors. I wanted to see how things went.'

'Is that all you talked about?'

Paul frowned but Gardner couldn't tell if he was trying to recall the conversation or whether he was irritated at what he thought was a pointless question. He waited for a response anyway.

'She hadn't been in, she was running late.' Paul squeezed his eyes. 'Then we talked about.' He shrugged. 'I don't know.' Gardner waited. 'She mentioned Jen. We argued-'

'About what?' Gardner asked. Abby hadn't mentioned an argument.

'It wasn't serious. I just didn't want her to have to drive up there, she got lost last time.' Paul stopped and let out a breath. 'Why didn't she listen? She shouldn't have gone,' he said, his voice catching again.

'So you didn't want her to go. Did you tell her that earlier? Before today?'

'No. I didn't know before today.'

'So that was the first you knew about the visit to Jen's?'

'Yes,' Paul nodded. 'She said she'd told me earlier but I don't think she did. I don't know. Maybe I forgot, maybe she was mistaken. Things have been a bit crazy.'

'In what way?'

'With the baby,' he said. 'Having a baby kind of makes your brain stop functioning as well as it normally does. No sleep, you know.'

Gardner nodded. 'So you found out she was going to Jen's and you fought about it?'

Paul shook his head. 'Not fought. It was just a silly argument; nothing really. I asked why Jen couldn't come to her and said she'd end up getting lost again but she insisted. And that was it.'

'So you left it on good terms?'

'Yes. Of course we did.'

'Do you argue often?' Lawton asked.

'No.'

'Isn't that unusual for a married couple?' Gardner asked, wondering what caused Abby to cheat on her husband. His ex-wife claimed he didn't pay her enough attention; he was distant, too caught up in his job. That'd be why she fucked off with another copper then.

Paul looked at the floor. 'Well, yes we argue. But not a lot. And it's never serious, never important. Just the usual stuff. Money, whose turn it is to wash up, stupid things.'

'What about Beth?'

Paul looked up. 'What about her?'

'Did things change after she was born? Did it change your relationship with Abby?'

'Of course it did. But for the better.'

'You'd been having problems before Beth was born?' Lawton asked.

'No.' Paul leaned back in his chair. 'I always wanted kids but Abby wasn't so sure. I wanted us to be a family. So when she got pregnant, when she had Beth, it was the best thing in the world. And yes it's hard. And sometimes I feel left out. Sometimes it's like you're on the outside looking in. But it's all I ever wanted.' Paul held Gardner's gaze. 'And now it's gone...' Paul wiped his hand across his face.

Gardner looked away. 'Did you and Abby have any other problems?'

Paul shook his head. 'What do you mean?'

'How long have you been married?'

'Five years,' Paul said.

'And you've never separated, never had any indiscretions?' He watched Paul and saw something like anger flash across his face. 'Either of you?'

'No, of course not,' Paul said. 'We love each other. We're a family.'

Gardner nodded to Lawton. He saw her hands curl into a ball like they always did when she was put on the spot.

'Tell me about Jen Harvey. What was your relationship with her?' she said after a while.

Paul cleared his throat. 'She's Abby's friend.'

They waited but Paul stayed quiet. 'Abby mentioned that you and Jen knew each other previously. That you went out at university.'

Paul's fists clenched. 'We did. But we're not seeing each other behind Abby's back if that's what you're asking. It wasn't serious. Not really. I'm surprised we lasted as long as we did.'

'Why was that?' Lawton said.

'She's just...' Paul shook his head. 'She's totally different to Abby. Jen's spoilt. She's the kind of woman who expects things to be done for her. High maintenance.'

'Sounds like you don't get along.'

Paul shrugged. 'We don't see that much of each other.'

'Jen knew that Abby would be driving up to see her this morning,' Gardner said.

Paul frowned. 'Yes.'

Gardner waited for Paul to get what he was hinting at. He didn't really think this woman was involved but he wanted to gauge Paul's reaction and find out who he thought might've done it without prodding too much. Without mentioning Simon Abbott for now.

Paul let out a little laugh. 'Jen? You think Jen did this? That's ridiculous.'

'Why?'

'Firstly, she would never do anything to hurt Abby, never. She might be hard work but she's not a bad person. And secondly what the fuck would she do with a baby?' Paul caught himself and raised his hand in apology. 'She can't even look after herself. And anything that took the limelight away from Jen would be a no-no.' Paul shook his head again. 'No way. Not a chance.'

'Okay,' Gardner said. 'What about someone else you or Abby know? Is there anyone you can think of who'd want to hurt either of you?'

Paul was shaking his head. 'No. Why would anyone want to do this?'

'Abby mentioned an incident that happened shortly after Beth was born. Her tyres were slashed,' Gardner said.

Paul's jaw tightened. 'Yes,' he said. 'Three tyres.'

'Any idea who might've done that? Why someone would do it?'

'No. Drunk kids probably,' he said before frowning. 'Why? You think that has something to do with this?'

'Probably not. It's probably like you said, drunk kids.'

Gardner looked down at his notes and wondered how to proceed. He was pretty sure that Paul knew nothing about Abby and her affair. If he did, surely he'd be pointing fingers by now. Despite his better judgement he didn't want to rock the boat until he'd spoken to Simon Abbott and made a decision on whether he'd had any involvement.

'You work in a bookshop, is that right?' Gardner asked, changing tack.

'I own it, yes.'

'How's business?'

'I do alright. Look, what's this got to do with anything?'

Gardner made a note to check the Henshaw's finances. Paul said they'd argued about money. 'What time did you say you got to the shop this morning? Did you go straight there after leaving the house?'

'Yes. I got there around eight thirty. I had a delivery to sort.'

'Were you alone?'

'Yes. I'm always on my own until lunchtime.'

'No one else works there?'

'Laura Pullman. She does afternoons.'

Gardner made a note. 'What about customers? Were you busy this morning?'

'I had a couple of people in, browsing. Not anyone I recognised.'

'What about the delivery? Did you speak to the driver?' Gardner asked.

'Yes.'

'Okay, we'll need the details of the delivery company,' Gardner said. 'No one else can verify you were there?'

'The CCTV can.'

'Okay, good.' Gardner stopped and made a note. 'And you're sure there's no one you can think of. No one who might've had a reason to hurt Abby or take your daughter?'

'No. Nobody.'

Gardner closed his notebook and stood. 'I think we can leave it there for now.'

CHAPTER TWELVE

Abby pulled her knees to her chest and held on to them as tightly as she could. She stared at her phone. She had no idea how long they'd been talking to Paul; he was gone when she came back to this room. She wondered if Gardner had told him about Simon. She wouldn't blame him if he did. She didn't deserve his help, didn't deserve Paul's love. She knew that when Paul found out what she'd done he'd be devastated. No, more than that. It was the worst kind of betrayal, especially for Paul. Knowing everything she did about his parents. About what they'd done. How could she hurt him this way?

She suspected she'd be taken back to the interview room again soon. Gardner would want to know more. She wondered why he didn't press her for more details about why she decided to ruin her marriage for a man who was never there. Maybe that stuff didn't matter. Or perhaps he understood. Perhaps he'd fucked up his life too.

But what did all that matter now? Beth was missing and that was all that was important. If she didn't get Beth back, then what? She closed her eyes, trying to shake the thoughts from her mind. She refused to even imagine it. Part of her hoped that Simon had taken her. That he wasn't the man she thought he was. At least then her daughter would be back. She'd be okay. It would be over.

She scrolled down to Simon's mobile again and dialled. The voicemail came on once more and she wondered if she should leave a message this time. But what could she possibly say? She guessed Gardner would've been trying to find him by now anyway, what else could she do? Warn him? Tell him the police wanted to talk to him regarding a rape and abduction? Abby closed her eyes. Just thinking those words made her shake. It all felt like a nightmare that she couldn't wake from.

She opened her eyes and looked at the phone. It was recording dead air. She wetted her lips, wanting to speak. In her heart she knew Simon couldn't have done this. He wouldn't have. She *knew* him. After Paul he was the person she knew best in this world. He wouldn't hurt her.

The door clicked open and Abby looked up, snapping her phone shut. Paul followed a uniformed officer in and took a seat next to her. He reached over and placed his hand on hers. The officer closed the door and his footsteps echoed down the corridor, leaving them alone. Abby looked Paul over. He was deathly pale with dark bags circling his eyes.

'Are you okay?' she asked.

Paul turned and pulled her towards him and they fell into each other. Abby dug her fingers into his back, clinging on to him for dear life. He rocked back and forth. 'She'll be okay, Abby. She'll be okay.'

Abby held onto him and cried into his shoulder, knowing it could be the last time she'd be this close to him. How she had ever been so stupid to risk what they had? Maybe if she'd told him from the start they could've worked things out. But now? Not now. He'd blame her for Beth. And maybe he'd be right.

Abby wiped her face and turned so that one cheek rested on his shoulder. 'What did they ask you?'

Paul seemed to be lost in his own thoughts, staring straight ahead. 'Paul?'

He sighed. 'He asked where I was this morning, if I knew anyone who'd want to hurt you or take Beth. How long I'd known Jen.' He shook his head. 'They're even checking the CCTV from the shop to make sure I was really there.'

Abby nodded, feeling gratitude to Gardner. He hadn't told him. Paul pushed Abby's hair from her face. 'Does it hurt?' he asked as his fingers traced the bruises on her cheek.

Abby shook her head but tears formed in her eyes. 'I'm okay.' She reached up and brushed her fingers across his face. 'I'm okay.'

For a moment he looked at her, unspeaking, and Abby wondered if he knew; if Gardner had said something or if he had come to his own conclusion. Or whether he just blamed her for losing their daughter. In that split second she contemplated coming clean, telling him everything. Then Paul bent down to her and took her face in his hands. Leaning his forehead against hers he closed his eyes.

'We'll get through this Abby. I promise. We'll be okay. Beth will be okay.' Abby nodded but her chest ached. She didn't know if she could make herself believe him.

CHAPTER THIRTEEN

Gardner blew out a breath and slumped back in his chair. He now had confirmation that Simon Abbott had in fact boarded a plane in Manchester to New Zealand via Dubai and Brisbane shortly before nine that morning. Of course that didn't rule him out completely; he could've been involved. Unfortunately his flight status meant that getting hold of him was impossible for the time being and Gardner's best lead was at a standstill.

He wanted to speak to Abby again, get more details on her and Abbott's relationship, but that could wait until the morning. He'd made a start looking into the Henshaws' lives. Their finances, their family and friends, their work, their marriage, phone records. He was working on getting hold of the CCTV from the doctor's surgery, to see if anything, or anyone stood out. He'd dispatched officers to speak to the Henshaws' neighbours, partly to see if they'd seen anyone or any white vans hanging around, and partly to find out what the Henshaws were really like. So far all reports he'd had back were that they were nice. A lovely couple. So cute. The baby was adorable. None of it useful. He'd got the ball rolling on their finances. The fact that both of them had consented to him accessing their accounts made him think he wouldn't find anything, but he still had to check. As much as he hated to say it, it wouldn't be the first time a family struggling financially had used their kid as a way to earn a bit of cash. Though Paul had insisted the bookshop was fine, Gardner couldn't imagine it was *that* good. Not these days. He'd be surprised if the Henshaws were involved in the disappearance of Beth but he'd learned a long time ago that you could always be surprised in this job. You never knew for sure. What bothered him most in that scenario was the attack on Abby. Even if you were going for authenticity, that was overkill. He'd make sure he checked every avenue but he doubted this was about paying the Henshaws' mortgage.

Dozens of officers were now involved in the search and he was working to get more. They'd checked the few local houses and the pub but no one saw a thing. So far there'd been nothing on the van or the two men. The lack of registration number made it tricky. And he doubted that the men would've hung around. They were long gone.

What bothered him was the fact that the men took Abby and left Beth. If this was about kidnapping, why take Abby and leave Beth behind? Why not hurt Abby there and take the baby and disappear? Probably because Abby would've called for help immediately, one way or another. But if the baby was what they were really after, then why the rape? Why go to such extremes? And the fact they didn't cover their faces, didn't make any attempt to hide trace evidence. Other than taking Abby's clothes, of course. But even an idiot must've known that was pointless. That was more about power than actually trying to get away with anything.

Earlier on he thought maybe the attack was the primary goal and that Beth was incidental. Possibly a random attack, possibly not. He'd checked for any other reports of rapes or attempted rapes in the area or by two men in a van but nothing had come up.

Abby couldn't say for sure how long she was in that van, how long she was away from Beth. Maybe someone had seen her at the side of the road and taken her for her own good. He'd hoped that was true. It seemed possible a few hours ago. But now? She would've been brought back by now. That Beth was still missing wasn't right.

But then none of this was right. And Gardner felt stuck, like he was treading water. He was itching to speak to Simon Abbott and then maybe he'd have some answers.

Abby sat curled up on the hard plastic chair, her head against the wall, her eyes closed. Paul sat beside her staring into space as Gardner entered, closing the door quietly behind him. Abby opened her eyes and jumped out of the chair. Paul slowly stood.

'Have you found her?' Abby asked.

Gardner shook his head and watched as Abby deflated. 'There's something I want you both to take a look at,' Gardner said. 'We have some CCTV footage of the doctor's surgery from this morning. If you could take a look, see if anyone sticks out, anyone you know or have seen before.' He led them into a room where a TV was set up. Abby and Paul stood in front of it and Gardner pressed play.

Abby watched the scene in front of her; saw herself walking into the waiting room with Beth. She felt a tug and wondered if she'd be allowed to keep the video. A souvenir of the last few hours she had with her daughter. She could see Gardner watching her from the corner of her eye. She recalled the people from earlier that day – the rude receptionist, the woman who'd been sat behind her pulling faces, and an elderly couple she hadn't noticed while she was there. She let out a breath. What was she expecting? That those men would've been sat there, waiting for her?

Beside her Paul shifted and Gardner pressed pause. 'You recognise someone?' he asked and Abby looked at her husband. For a moment he just stared at the screen and Abby looked back at the frozen frame trying to see what he could see.

'No,' Paul said and looked from Abby to Gardner. He stepped forward and pointed at the screen. 'That man,' he said, pointing to the man with crutches. 'I thought I recognised him. But no. Sorry,' he said.

Gardner let the tape run until a few minutes after Abby left the doctor's. 'I checked footage from outside the surgery. No one follows you out,' he said and turned the TV off.

'What now?' Abby said.

Gardner indicated for them to take seats again and he pulled another chair around in front of them. 'There've been no reports of a baby being found; no one has taken her into a hospital or police station. We're going to do an appeal. We're looking for witnesses who may have seen Beth and also the men in the van.'

'So you don't think someone took her for her own safety anymore?' Paul said.

Gardner paused, considering his words. 'It's still a possibility. We're going to use that as the basis of the appeal. Like I say, it's possible someone took her and thought they were doing what's best for her. But, it's also a possibility that someone took her deliberately, and that the attack on Abby was planned as part of it. As there hasn't been any kind of contact or ransom demand we have to assume that whoever took Beth took her because they planned to keep her.

'That said, if we appeal to them, show them that Beth has a family, a good family. Show them the consequences of what they've done, use her name and yours, make the situation real to them; there is a possibility that they will return her. At this point we're appealing for witnesses as much as to the person who took Beth.

'We need you, both of you, to appear on camera. Someone will talk you through it beforehand, but if either of you want to make a statement yourselves we can go through that with you.' He looked at them both.

'It's up to you if you want to speak.'

Abby and Paul searched each other's faces for the right answer. 'Does it matter?' Paul asked. 'I mean does it make a difference. Will they be more likely to bring her back if we say something?'

Gardner rubbed his chin. 'To be honest, I don't know. I know that having you there on-screen helps. But if you do decide to say something, you need to work it out with us first. Depending on the person who has Beth, depending on the reason they took her... you have to choose your words carefully.' Abby went to speak but Gardner put his hand up. 'I know Beth is your baby, and you just want her home and that's the only real message you want to send to this person but if this person took her for a specific reason, say they thought you weren't good enough for Beth,' Gardner said, 'or they think they deserve her for whatever reason. You have to be very careful not to make this person angry, make sure you don't reinforce something they already believe.'

'But how do we know what they believe if we don't know who they are?' Paul asked.

'That's why we keep it general. Show them that you're hurting, that there are consequences to their actions. Show them you're good parents. And just ask them to bring Beth back. Don't make any judgements about them, don't say they're a bad person or that they're hurting Beth.'

Abby glanced at Gardner before looking down at the floor. 'What if they are?'

CHAPTER FOURTEEN

'Where are we?' DCI Atherton asked the room from his place by the window. He stood with his hands behind his back like a character from Trumpton. Gardner had never seen him sit down. He didn't know why. Maybe it was an authority thing, maybe so he'd always be ready to move. Maybe it was piles.

Gardner stood up and wished he'd had something other than coffee in the last twenty-four hours. 'Abby Henshaw, thirty-one, her car was forced off the road,' he said.

'I know this,' Atherton said. 'We all know this. What I asked was where are we? Meaning what have you done since yesterday and where has it got us?'

Everyone turned to Gardner. Atherton raised his eyebrows and left them hanging while Gardner counted to ten. Atherton was a pain in the arse. He had the people he liked and the people he didn't and a way of making those he didn't feel like they were idiots. It just so happened Gardner was in the latter group. Atherton knew what happened in Blyth, but if that was why he hated him, who knew? Atherton made judgements about people for all kinds of reasons – where you were from, where you were educated, what kind of shoes you wore. What happened up there had never been mentioned since he moved down the coast to Middlesbrough but the silence didn't mean anything. He knew people talked about it behind his back. Gossip had a way of following you around. It didn't matter that it'd been almost ten years. Gardner wasn't likely to forget about it, why would anyone else?

He got to ten and looked Atherton in the eye.

'A search of the area produced nothing. Nothing useful anyway. The only blood at the scene was from the victim. I'm expecting results this morning regarding the semen taken from the examination but I'm not holding my breath that we'll get a match from anyone in the system. Despite the fact our guy made a point of holding onto the victim's clothes, I seriously doubt he's unaware we'd get trace evidence from her. Not unless he's a complete idiot. So I'm assuming he either knows there'll be no matches or he just doesn't care.

'We have nothing on the van except a colour and a vague description. No licence plate so an APA is going to be fruitless. The location produced little in the way of witnesses. The pub and businesses in Loftus gave us nothing, same with the few houses along the stretch of road. Mrs Henshaw gave us a description of the men who attacked her. We've shown the sketch around, so far it hasn't sparked anything but we'll keep trying. The teams will continue the search this morning including inside properties around the area. We've issued an All Ports Warning and alerted all police forces to be on the lookout but-'

'But all babies look the bloody same so we've got no chance,' Murphy said and raised a few sniggers.

Gardner ignored the comment but couldn't help but think the idiot had a point. To most people one baby looked the same as every other baby. They'd be inundated with sightings of every single baby in the region, if not the whole country.

'We're looking into the Henshaws' finances. They gave consent so it's unlikely we'll find anything of interest. I want to look at Simon Abbott too but as he's God knows where at present, consent isn't happening.'

'Court order?' Murphy asked.

Gardner shook his head. 'Not yet. If Abbott refuses or if we don't get hold of him soon then we'll take it to a magistrates but we don't have enough yet.'

Gardner continued but could see Atherton starting to sway. Every so often one of the team piped up and Gardner couldn't help but notice Atherton seemed more interested in what they had to say. Even Murphy.

'So,' Atherton said when he'd finished, 'basically what we have is absolutely nothing. And when I go down there to brief the media I'll have to tell them we have absolutely nothing?'

'We've got the appeal which is nationwide,' Gardner said.

'Anything come out of that?'

Gardner shook his head. He knew what Atherton was getting at. Although appeals often produced results in some form or another by digging up witnesses and refreshing memories, they were often used as a tool to pile pressure on the family and friends of victims who were potential suspects. It often worked but Gardner couldn't help feeling it was a cynical ploy, especially when those family members were innocent.

'We're looking into several angles, including child trafficking,' Gardner said. 'We're liaising with Interpol regarding any known trans-border gangs.'

'Good,' Atherton said. 'Is that it?'

'One more thing,' Gardner said as people started moving. 'As you should all know, the details of Mrs Henshaw's attack have not been released. She's requested that the rape not be made known to the media.

So far it's been kept under wraps, let's keep it that way.'

'Right, people, let's get on with it. And let's try to actually get something done today.'

Gardner turned away from Atherton and found Lawton staring at him. She gave him a smile that made him feel worse.

'Cartwright,' he heard Atherton say behind him. 'Good work.'

'Thank you, sir,' Cartwright said and Gardner tried to walk faster but the stairs were clogged with people making their way out of the briefing. 'I just wish I could've done a bit more. I'd like the opportunity to lead an interview. Or at least sit in. But it wasn't possible yesterday.'

'Well, we'll see what we can do about it.'

'Thank you, sir.'

As Gardner turned on the stairs Cartwright caught his eye and grinned. Little prick. If he sucked up any harder he could quit his job with the police and start his own vacuuming business.

'So I'll see you tomorrow night then,' Atherton said to Cartwright over his shoulder.

'Wouldn't miss it, sir. The big five-oh.'

Gardner tried to swallow down the bile he felt creeping up his throat. It was probably just the coffee.

CHAPTER FIFTEEN

Abby looked down at Beth's empty crib. She held the small, pink fleece blanket against her face, letting the tears soak into the fluffy fabric. She sensed Paul was behind her but didn't turn. He stood a few feet away, trying to decide what to do.

'Maybe you should lie down, Ab, try and get some rest,' he said.

Abby kept her face pressed hard into the blanket. She hadn't slept at all after coming home from the police station. They'd arrived home to pitiful glances from neighbours and some flowers on the doorstep that reminded Abby of when her parents died. But no one was dead this time. She couldn't be.

After standing by Beth's crib for a few hours, Paul had led her into the bedroom and made her lie down in his arms. Sometime around three he had fallen asleep. Abby felt a combination of jealousy and outrage. Part of her wished she could sleep too. That if she slept long enough she'd wake to find everything back to normal. The other part, the larger part, felt anger at him for being able to sleep while Beth was out there somewhere with a stranger. At around five she'd got up and made a cup of tea, which had been on the kitchen table all day.

Paul sat watching the TV, re-runs of the appeal. Abby couldn't bear to watch it. She hadn't even changed, she was still wearing the clothes she'd put on after being examined. A smart-looking woman had briefed them and Abby agreed to speak the words the woman had prepared for her. But as they filed into the room in front of the cameras and microphones, she couldn't speak. Thoughts of the bastards that hurt her, that took Beth, coursed through her mind. She wanted to scream. She wanted to beg. She tried to focus on the words in front of her, determined to stick to the script. The words swam in and out of focus. Abby reached for her face to check she had her glasses on. Finding them where they should be she realised that the tears were the cause of the blur. She felt like she was reading underwater. Her daughter's name came out of her mouth but it sounded wrong. She looked up into the bright lights of the cameras and tried to remember the words she was supposed to say. Under the desk she felt Paul's hand on hers and then realised he was speaking. She looked down to the script and noticed it was gone.

Then it was over.

The people beside her were moving. A hand was around her arm, lifting her from her seat. She could hear her name being repeated until it faded out and she was in the car on the way home.

So now she stood next to Beth's crib. She had no idea what time it was. When was the last time she'd eaten? Slept? When was the last time she'd seen her daughter? She'd heard the door a few times. Heard the voices of neighbours they rarely spoke to, friends they hadn't seen for years. The phone rang constantly. She heard Paul mutter thank you over and over. She heard him answer a few questions and then say 'no comment' again and again like some well-rehearsed politician. She could hear noise outside and guessed there were reporters out there. But she stayed where she was, beside Beth's crib. She knew she shouldn't leave Paul to deal with everything but she was too tired, too scared to do it herself. Listening to it all made her head hurt. If she let her mind drift from the thought of Beth sleeping peacefully in her crib she felt the pain of realising she was gone. She saw the hatred in the eyes of the man who raped her. Could smell his breath. She gripped the side of the crib and dug her fingers into the wood.

A creaky floorboard reminded her of Paul's presence and she turned to him. 'In a while,' she muttered although she couldn't remember what he'd said. Paul stroked her fingers lightly with his and then turned and went back downstairs to watch their performance over and over on the news.

Abby pulled her mobile phone from her pocket, staring as its silence mocked her. She knew she should call Simon but had no idea how to start. She wondered if Gardner had found him, had told him.

She looked down at the phone again, clicked her way into the pictures folder, bringing to life the last photo she'd taken of Beth. She caressed her daughter's pixelated hair with her thumb and tried not to think about what was happening to her at that moment. She stared into the phone for an answer when the ringing of the doorbell shook her out of her reverie. She heard Paul answer and this time he didn't say, 'no comment.' She could hear his voice but not the conversation.

Abby raced down the stairs, her heart pumping out of her chest, praying that it would be Gardner holding Beth in his arms. Paul stood with the door half-open, whispering to someone, his face twisted in anger. Abby's foot on the creaky stair made him stop. He turned to Abby and then walked wordlessly back to the living room. Abby squeezed herself between the stairs and the open door to find Jen on the doorstep. The sight of her friend looking so deadly serious, so completely out of character, was too much for her. Jen stepped forward and took Abby in her arms. Abby ignored the shouts from outside.

'God, Abby, I'm sorry.'

Abby clung to her friend and tried to rein in her tears. After a while she stepped back and Jen closed the door. Abby led Jen through to the kitchen.

Abby glanced around, looking for something to do. She picked up the cold cup of tea and poured it down the sink. 'Tea?' She stared down at the bowl in the sink, still showing traces of the banana Beth had eaten yesterday morning. She ran her finger over the edge of the bowl. She felt Jen come and take her by the elbow, guiding her to the kitchen table.

'I'll do it,' Jen said. Abby took a seat and laid her palms flat on the patchwork tablecloth to stop them from shaking. Jen didn't say anything and the only noises were from the filling and boiling of the kettle, the cups being dragged from cupboards and the scraping of spoons around the ceramic.

When she finally took a seat next to Abby she took her friend's hand. 'How are you feeling?' Abby looked into Jen's eyes and gave a slight shake of her head. How could she describe how she was feeling? Jen shook her head. 'Sorry, that was a stupid question.'

Abby took a deep breath and made an attempt to smile. She knew if the circumstances were different and she was the one trying to provide comfort she would've opened with the same question, banal as it was.

'I just can't believe it. I keep thinking that it's a mistake. That Beth's fine, tucked up in bed and it's someone else who's...' Abby bit at the loose skin on her lip. 'I keep checking, going up and looking in her crib thinking she'll suddenly appear but she doesn't.'

'I know,' Jen said stroking Abby's hand.

Abby watched as Jen's eyes filled with tears. She held back a sob and her friend squeezed her hand before letting go. She hadn't told her friend what had happened to her. What those men had done. She couldn't. She couldn't say it out loud.

'What have the police said?'

Abby rubbed her hands over her face. 'They have no idea. They thought that maybe someone just took her because she was alone, but if that was true they would've brought her back by now, wouldn't they?'

'I guess...'

'No one has come forward. No one saw anything, or heard anything.' Abby let her hands drop. 'They'll want to speak to you.'

'I've spoken to them.'

Abby paused. 'When?'

'Yesterday. This morning. They came by yesterday and told me what'd happened. Had a look around. Asked me loads of questions. I wanted to come by last night but...' Jen said as she pushed her hair back behind her ear. 'I spoke briefly to that detective, Garner?'

'Gardner,' Abby said.

'Right. And then I went to the station this morning and spoke to someone else. A fat bloke?' Abby shrugged. 'Anyway, they just asked me how long I'd known you, what our relationship was like. They wanted to know who I told about you coming up yesterday.'

'They asked me that too.' Abby watched Jen, unsure whether to say what she was thinking.

'What?' Jen asked.

'Did you tell anyone?'

'No. Who would I tell?'

Abby shrugged.

'So that's it? No leads?' Jen asked.

'No. Not yet,' Abby said folding her hands around her hot cup. The warmth felt good, it was such a relief to feel something else, something different to the pain. She rocked the cup and the tea swirled around making mini whirlpools. 'Where were you yesterday when I called?'

Jen froze with her cup midway between her mouth and the table. 'Do I need a solicitor present?' she said, smiling slightly.

'Of course not, I just wondered where you went. I tried you on both phones.'

'I went out to the shop for more milk and tea. Those bloody builders are drinking me out of house and home.'

'Builders?'

'Yeah.' She looked at Abby, puzzled. 'What? What's wrong?'

'Where are they from?' Abby said.

Jen shrugged. 'Someone recommended them to me, I don't know if they're in the book.'

'No. Where are they from? Are they local? Are they foreign?'

'The boss is from London I think. I suppose that's foreign.' Abby just stared. 'The other two, I don't know. One never speaks. The other, maybe he's foreign, I don't know. I never really paid them that much notice. I just tell them what I want doing and take them cups of tea. Why?'

Abby stood and went to the phone. 'Did they know?'

'Know what? What's going on?'

'Did they know I was coming out to see you?' she said while dialling, her voice raised with anxiety.

Paul stepped out of the living room. 'What's going on?' Abby asked for Gardner then moved the phone from her mouth while she waited.

'Did they know, Jen?'

Jen shrugged. 'I don't think so. They could've heard me on the phone I suppose but...'

Abby moved her mouth back to the phone. 'Detective Gardner? It's Abby Henshaw. I need to see you.'

CHAPTER SIXTEEN

Miklos stared at the small TV in the corner of the room. The curtains were closed giving the room a strange orange glow. At least it disguised the shit-brown carpet and the flea-bitten quilt. Damek was lying on the other bed, cigarette in hand despite the no-smoking sign by the door.

Miklos licked his lips and glanced at his cousin. He wasn't even watching. He looked like he didn't give a shit. Which Miklos knew was probably true. He turned back to the TV and watched the police giving details about where it'd happened. They mentioned the van, the road. If anyone saw anything...

Then the woman. The woman was to speak. Miklos swallowed hard. She stared out, her eyes glassy. Beside her the woman's husband slid a sheet of paper from in front of her and started talking. Miklos didn't really listen to what he said. He was looking at the woman. The woman he'd taken yesterday. He knew her name now. Abby Henshaw. He hadn't been told that before. He wasn't sure if Damek had known but *he* didn't know. But then he didn't know a lot. Hadn't been told lots of things. Like the baby. He hadn't been told about the baby. And now the baby was gone.

The news moved on to something else and he switched it off. He turned to Damek who stubbed out his cigarette on the table beside the bed.

'Are you hungry?' Damek asked. 'I could eat.'

Miklos just stared at him. He didn't care at all. Didn't care about that woman. About the baby. He didn't care that they could be caught. He didn't care about anything. He watched as Damek stood and pulled his trousers on.

'We have to do something,' Miklos said.

'About what?'

'About that,' Miklos said and pointed at the TV. 'About what we did.'

Damek sat down and started pulling his shoes on. He didn't even turn around. 'We got paid, didn't we?' He pulled on the other shoe. 'Where do you want to eat?'

'Listen to me,' Miklos shouted. 'The baby was taken.'

'So?' Damek shrugged. 'Not our business.'

'They think we took her.'

'So?' Damek shrugged again. 'Think what they like. We don't have a baby. They don't even know who we are. They're looking for a white van,' he laughed. 'How many white vans are there?'

'They had our pictures,' Miklos said and walked round to stand in front of Damek. 'They could find us.'

'It didn't look like me,' Damek said and stood up. He patted Miklos on the shoulder. 'Not handsome enough,' he said and grinned.

Miklos thought about the sketches the police showed. Damek might be wrong about many things but he was right about the pictures. They looked nothing like them. But that wasn't the point. 'We have to do something. We could call and tell them what we know. We don't have to say our names.'

Damek slapped Miklos on the side of the head. 'Don't be stupid,' he said. 'Besides we don't know anything. We don't have the baby.' Damek slipped on his jacket. He stepped up close to Miklos, bent down to look him in the eye, and put his hand on his throat. 'And we don't know who does, right?'

CHAPTER SEVENTEEN

Abby was relieved when the doorbell finally rang and raced to the front door. DI Gardner frowned at her as they listened to the sound of the raised voices coming from the kitchen.

'You've always been a selfish cow. If she hadn't been driving all the way out there to see you none of this would've happened,' Paul said.

'That's not fair,' Jen said.

'I'm sorry, have I hurt your feelings? Are you feeling a little bit sorry for yourself? Or is it guilt that's getting to you?'

'Fuck you, Paul. Where were you then? Why weren't you there to take care of your wife and baby?' Jen said.

'Alright, enough,' Gardner said. Both Jen and Paul looked around like naughty children, suddenly noticing his presence. Paul turned away and grabbed the edge of the table, knuckles whitening, his breathing heavy. Jen folded her arms across her chest.

'Sit down,' Gardner ordered.

Jen pulled out a chair and sat. Paul lifted his head and shook it. 'I can't do this now.' He brushed past Abby and grabbed his car keys from the table by the door.

'Paul,' Abby called out as he slammed the front door. Abby turned to follow but Gardner took hold of her arm.

'Let him go. Give him some space.'

Abby looked back to the door, letterbox still fluttering, and then turned back into the kitchen and allowed Gardner to usher her towards the table. Jen's arms and legs were crossed.

'Do you want to tell me what's going on?' he asked.

Abby glanced at Jen and then back to Gardner. 'Jen had builders at her house for the past week or so.'

'Yes, I believe one of my team spoke to them yesterday.' He looked at Jen and she nodded.

'They might've known I was going there.' Abby tried to make eye contact with her but Jen kept her face turned away. Abby couldn't tell if it was because of guilt or anger. 'They might be foreign,' Abby said, and even as the words came out of her mouth she felt embarrassed, like she should be handing out leaflets for the BNP. A foreign builder? Of course he did it.

Gardner took in a deep breath and let it out slowly. 'They *might* be foreign?'

Abby and Gardner both looked to Jen but she remained quiet. 'Jen said one was from London but the other two could've been... foreign.'

Jen lifted her head. 'I said I didn't know. They could be from Middlesbrough for all I know,' she said.

'Are they still there?' Gardner asked. Jen nodded. 'Did they leave at all yesterday?'

'No,' Jen said, this time looking at Abby. 'They were there from half eight to about five, I think.'

Abby felt her face burn. She hadn't even considered asking if they had an alibi. It hadn't even occurred to her to ask Jen whether they'd left her house. She closed her eyes.

'I still want to speak to them again. You think they would have used the same road as Abby to get to your house?' he said to Jen, who shrugged. 'It's possible they saw the van. It could've been hanging around there all day, or even another day.'

'I suppose,' Jen said and stood, scraping her chair across the kitchen floor. 'We can go now. They're still there.' Abby opened her eyes once more, surprised to see Jen looking back at her. 'Do you blame me too, Abby?' Jen asked.

Abby shook her head and stood. 'Of course I don't. I'm sorry. I just want Beth back.'

Jen relaxed and moved around the table. 'I know,' she said and hugged Abby. 'You'll get her back, babe, you will.'

CHAPTER EIGHTEEN

Helen Deal stared at the TV screen, her hands gripping her knees, her fingernails making half moons in her skin. A police officer was speaking on screen, asking for witnesses to come forward, but Helen's eyes were on the woman. Her heart was beating fast. She had been there yesterday. She had sat there behind her in the doctor's surgery. She had been there moments before this had happened. Should she go to the police? Should she tell them she was there, that she saw Abby Henshaw? That she saw the baby? What for? What good would it do anyone? She was panicking. She took a breath and turned to her daughter, fast asleep in the Moses basket. She looked so peaceful. So beautiful. She was everything to her. The thought of her being taken away was too much to contemplate.

The officer introduced Abby Henshaw. She stared into space. Her mouth opened and closed but nothing came out. *Why isn't she screaming? Why isn't she begging for someone to bring her baby home?* Beside her, Paul Henshaw pulled a sheet of paper towards himself and started to speak. His voice reedy, wavering, making the appeal his wife couldn't make. Helen watched as his hands shook, his long fingers clinging to the paper. She wondered what was going through his mind. He looked like he could fall to pieces at any moment. But he couldn't. He had to be strong. One of them had to be. For the sake of the child.

Helen turned down the sound and looked at the basket once more. She was sleeping so soundly. Helen reached out and touched her cheek. Her skin was so soft, so untouched. She knew she should leave her to sleep but she couldn't help it. She needed to feel her, needed to hold on to her. Helen scooped her up and she made a soft groan before waking fully into a scream. Helen soothed her until she stopped but she didn't really care. She appreciated every scream, every cry. At least it meant she was still there. She was alive.

The knock at the door made her jump. She gently put her daughter down and walked to the window, pulling back the net curtain just enough to peek outside. A policeman in uniform stood at the door. Helen dropped the curtain, switched off the TV and went to answer the front door, closing the living room door behind her.

'Yes?' she said, opening the front door. The officer stood up straighter before speaking.

'Helen Deal?' he said and she nodded. 'I'm PC Cartwright. I'm just making some enquiries about an incident yesterday. Do you mind if I come in?'

Helen glanced over her shoulder before opening the door to let him in. 'Of course not,' she said. She led him through to the kitchen. 'Would you like a cup of tea?'

'No, thanks,' Cartwright said, looking around as they walked through the house. As he glanced up the stairs he tripped on a child's car seat. 'This shouldn't take long.'

'It's about that woman and the baby, isn't it? I saw the news,' she said, moving to stand by the sink. 'I wondered if I should call the police but I didn't want to waste anyone's time.'

'How do you mean?' Cartwright asked, taking his notebook from his pocket.

'Well, I saw her. At the surgery. I didn't know if you'd need to know about it.'

'Did you see anything? Did you speak to Mrs Henshaw?'

'No,' Helen said. 'We didn't speak.'

'And you don't know her?'

'No,' Helen said. 'I've never met her before.'

'Did you see anyone else at the surgery, in the waiting room or outside? Anyone who seemed like they shouldn't be there?'

Helen shook her head. 'No, sorry.'

'What about a white van?'

Helen shook her head again and PC Cartwright nodded. 'What about when you left? Did you see Mrs Henshaw then? Was she with anyone?'

'I didn't see her leave,' Helen said. 'I went in to see the nurse and when I left I don't recall seeing her again. I don't think she was in the waiting room but I wouldn't swear to it.'

'Okay, Ms Deal. That should do it,' Cartwright said, walking to the door. 'If you think of anything, please don't hesitate to get in touch. Sorry to have disturbed you.'

'I'm just sorry I couldn't help,' Helen said.

Helen watched the officer walk across the street to his car. She waited until he was driving away before she closed the door. She went back into the living room and stared down at her daughter, fast asleep, once again. She wished she hadn't been in the surgery yesterday. Wished she hadn't seen Abby Henshaw. But as she brushed her fingers along her daughter's chest, she realised how close she'd been to losing her and just how lucky she was.

CHAPTER NINETEEN

After Gardner and Jen had left, Abby closed the door behind them, leaning her head against the glass. In the silence of the house she felt utterly alone. The truth was that part of her did blame Jen. A small part of her agreed completely with Paul. If it hadn't been for Jen, she would still have her baby. If she hadn't been driving out there to see her friend, maybe none of this would've happened. If only...

For the next few hours Abby was alone. Almost. While Paul was gone she'd answered the phone once and quickly regretted it. The reporter had bombarded her with questions. Abby screamed at her. Why wouldn't they leave her alone? She wasn't naive enough to think that would go untold to the baying public but she didn't much care. All she cared about was getting Beth back.

Two neighbours from across the street, women Abby couldn't recall ever speaking to, came to the door bearing gifts of soup and flowers. Abby felt like she was in a bad American film, that a pile of casseroles would be discovered on the doorstep in the morning.

Amy from work called her, promising to drop by, giving her condolences. Her boss, Jason, dropped in and talked for almost an hour, wanting every detail, pretending he was concerned. Abby had never known Jason to be concerned about anything or anyone other than himself and his company. But she thanked him and was grateful when he left.

Laura from the shop arrived soon after with enough tears that anyone would think she was the one who'd lost her child. That she was the one who'd been raped. Abby told her that Paul wasn't there and thankfully the girl took the hint and left soon after arriving. Abby only answered the door because she was hoping it was Gardner. That he was back with news, that he'd found the men who'd done this. That Beth was safe and sound.

CHAPTER TWENTY

Gardner watched as the builders slammed the van doors and disappeared down the drive. He got the feeling Ms Harvey might be needing to find new builders. They'd been polite enough when answering his questions but if looks could kill, Jen Harvey would currently be laid out in a body bag.

The boss was from London – Brixton to be precise, a place Gardner knew well from his early days on the force. The other two were Scottish and not exactly comfortable with eye contact. Gardner suspected they had something to hide but he was sure it wasn't anything to do with Abby Henshaw and her daughter. At first he'd thought, alright, so none of them are Russian or Eastern European, but then maybe the guys in the van weren't either. Mrs Henshaw couldn't have known for sure. A fake accent might've been picked up under normal circumstances but if you're being shoved into the back of the van you're hardly going to be listening out for consistency. But he'd checked with the neighbours and both sides had confirmed that the builders and their van hadn't left Ms Harvey's all day. As one old guy put it, they hadn't stopped with their 'bastard banging and whistling all bastard day'.

Gardner turned from the window as the van disappeared and found Jen sitting at the kitchen table lighting a cigarette. She held the packet up for him but he shook his head.

'So, they're off the hook?' she asked and inhaled deeply, tossing the lighter onto the table.

'Probably,' Gardner said. He'd look into them further, check if any of them had a record, but he doubted it would lead anywhere.

'Can I get you anything? Tea? Coffee?' Jen asked without getting up.

'No thanks. I should be getting back soon.'

She nodded and took another drag. 'You think you'll find her?'

Gardner looked out the window. 'I hope so,' he said and turned back to Jen. 'You mind if I take a look around?'

'Feel free,' she said and stood up, stubbing her cigarette out. 'You know they had a look round yesterday though.'

Gardner nodded and pointed through a doorway covered in plastic sheeting. Jen walked over and pulled back the sheet. 'Nothing but rubble,' she said and Gardner stuck his head through. Tools were scattered about amongst the debris but that was all. He moved back into the kitchen as her phone started ringing. She glanced at the screen and answered. 'Go ahead,' she said to Gardner and then turned away, her attention with whoever was on the phone. 'Hey, babe.'

Gardner walked out through the hall and into the living room. The house was a beautiful, old stone building. A perfect country cottage from the outside but Jen Harvey had butchered the inside, turning it into a minimalist shell. Plenty of white walls and Perspex furniture. He assumed the building work was to get rid of the remaining character left in the house. On the wall was a triptych of Jen. There were no more photos or paintings. There was barely anything at all. He moved on to the next room which he assumed was her study. On a small white desk was a laptop. The lid was closed, covered in dust. On the shelves were dozens of books, several with her name on. He took one from the shelf, glanced at the pink cover and flicked through it.

'That was my first,' Jen said and Gardner turned to look at her. 'Sold it for a small fortune. Shame no one else bought it.' She walked over and took it from his hand. 'But it paid for this place,' she said.

'What about the others?' Gardner asked, nodding to the other books on the shelf.

Jen shrugged. 'They just about pay the bills,' she said and put her book back in its place. 'Listen,' she said, putting her hand on his sleeve. 'That was my editor. I have to go. Do you need to see anything else?'

'No, that's alright,' he said and moved away from her. Gardner walked towards the front door. 'Thanks for your help. I'll be in touch.'

Gardner walked down the path and heard her close the door. He got in the car and waited for her to come out, wondering what could be so urgent. After ten minutes he saw her through the window, pacing up and down, her hands gesturing wildly. When she didn't come out after another ten minutes Gardner started the car and drove away.

CHAPTER TWENTY-ONE

Abby thanked Gardner for the update and hung up. There was nothing to report again. No sign of the van. No sign of the men. No sign of Beth.

No hope.

He'd called the night before to tell her there was nothing on Jen's builders. She'd sat down, her head in her hands. What had she expected? She didn't know what to say to him. Thanks? Thanks for what? For doing his job? For not finding Beth?

'Mrs Henshaw?' Gardner said when she hadn't spoken for a while.

'Yes. I'm here,' she said.

'There's something else. Are you alone?'

Abby felt sick. He didn't want her to be alone. Why didn't he want her to be alone?

'Is your husband there?'

'Yes,' Abby said. 'He's downstairs.'

'Okay,' he said, clearing his throat. 'I just wanted to let you know I've managed to contact Simon Abbott. I spoke to him this afternoon.'

Abby felt the breath slip from her. Relief that it wasn't bad news. Fear of... what? That Simon was involved? She closed her eyes. 'Is he back?' she asked.

'No, not yet. We didn't manage to catch him before he caught his connecting flight out of Dubai. He arrived in Brisbane in the middle of the night or morning, whatever it is over there. He's trying to find a flight home but I don't know how long that'll take. He said he'd try and get the next one out, he's on stand-by.'

'Did you tell him?' Abby asked. She heard Gardner sigh.

'I told him that... I told him Beth was missing,' he said.

'And?'

Another sigh. 'I told him you'd been hurt. I didn't...' Gardner seemed to be considering his words.

Abby put him out of his misery. 'What did he say? He must've asked questions, must've wanted to know what was going on?'

'I told him I needed him to return as soon as possible. He agreed. Let's wait until he gets here.'

Abby closed her eyes. She hated herself for even considering it. She knew it wasn't possible. But... 'Could he? I mean, what if he...'

Gardner paused, the dead air uncomfortable. 'Let's just see what happens when I speak to him.'

The phone rang downstairs, shaking Abby from her thoughts about Simon. She listened to Paul speak, his voice a monotone, repeating the same thing over and over again. She'd told him to disconnect the phone – the only call she wanted was from Gardner, who could reach her on her mobile – but then the media had found that number too so she'd reconnected the landline and let Paul deal with it all. Part of her wanted them to keep printing their stories, to keep showing Beth's picture. Maybe then someone would come forward, bring her little girl home. But she just couldn't bring herself to speak to them, to face their endless questions, to listen to their subtle accusations.

She felt guilty for managing to sleep a few hours the night before. Paul soothed her by telling her she needed to be rested when they brought Beth back. She considered changing the bedding on the crib so it would be nice and fresh for Beth's return but she just couldn't bear to wash away the smell of her little girl.

Abby walked into Beth's bedroom. Her hand grazed the wall and she thought of how she and Paul had spent hours decorating the room, how he'd smiled at her from across the room, paintbrush in hand, and how she'd blanked out her mistakes and told herself it was going to be fine. She'd let the excitement take over. She stood over Beth's crib and watched her tears fall and soak into the sheets.

Outside she could see a small crowd of people, mostly reporters, and a couple of news vans. Other people milled about looking at the house, wondering what was going on behind closed doors. A woman leaned against one of the news vans, smoking. Abby couldn't see any sign of a cameraman. She watched the woman take one last drag and then flick the butt across the street before looking up at the window. Abby ducked away. Downstairs the phone rang a few times before Paul answered. Abby moved back to the window. The woman was still staring but was now talking on the phone. Abby walked away and went to the top of the stairs. She could see Paul standing in the hall.

'Please, just leave us alone. Please,' he said and hung up. In the living room his mobile started ringing and he disappeared to answer it. Abby stayed where she was, trying to listen to his conversation but his voice was quiet, exhausted.

Paul came out and started to climb the stairs before stopping, noticing her there. 'I thought you might be sleeping.'

Abby shook her head. 'I heard the phone,' she said. 'Was it that reporter? The woman out there?'

Paul nodded. 'She wants to talk to you. I told her you were sleeping.' He looked down at his mobile, still in his hand. 'I have to go out,' he said. 'I need to sort some things at the shop.'

Abby wanted to say something. Ask what was so important it had to be done now. But she just nodded and sat down on the top stair.

'I can stay if you like,' he said. 'It's just Laura's going away. She said she'd stay but... there's no point...' He looked up at Abby again. 'I just need to sort some things out and then I'll be back.'

'Okay,' Abby said.

Paul turned to walk away before stopping and climbing the stairs. He bent over and kissed Abby on top of her head. 'I promise I won't be long,' he said.

Abby leaned against the banister and watched him go. She could hear the TV left on downstairs but the sound of being alone overwhelmed her. She wished he hadn't gone but knew it was a cover anyway; anything that needed doing could wait. He just needed time alone in his sanctuary. He didn't have the heart to open the shop. He'd just sit there, flicking through the children's books that he'd earmarked to give Beth when she was old enough. It was better than sitting in the house all day, listening to the phone ring.

She wondered why he didn't want to stay with her. Had she been too distant? Had she pushed him away when he was suffering too? She tried to talk to him but it felt forced. She knew it was wrong but she felt like the pain belonged to *her*, not him. This was her tragedy. She was the one who'd lost her daughter.

After a few minutes she went downstairs and turned off the TV. She walked through to the kitchen and stood a moment before returning to the living room, finally sitting down.

She tried not to think of anything but Simon came to mind. Where he was? Did he know? She hadn't tried to call him again. Didn't know what to say. He hadn't tried to call her. What did that mean? She wondered if he was finally on his way home. What would happen when she saw him?

Abby wondered how long this would go on, if Beth would ever be found. How long had it been? Two days? It felt like a lifetime. Would this be her life from now on? Walking from room to room like some kind of wraith. Unwashed and unfed. She wondered what would happen when Paul found out the truth. And he would, eventually. She planned to sit him down and tell him everything. All of it. Let him decide what to do. She couldn't imagine life would ever be right again anyway. But she couldn't do it.

She felt the tears well in her eyes and tried to fight them, tried to stand. But the tears came and she couldn't stop. The disbelief, the denial, of Beth's disappearance had finally slipped away, replaced by the realisation that Beth was gone. She was gone. Abby slid down from the chair and curled up on the floor, covering her face with her hands. She screamed but in her mind it sounded like an animal. Her face burned, her throat closed up. She felt like she was dying. For a moment she wished she was.

She lay there on the floor, slowly starting to breathe again, feeling her chest rise and fall. She hiccupped the last few tears and then was silent. The floor was hard but she felt she could stay there forever. Or at least until this was over.

Abby didn't know how long she lay there. The light changed outside. Paul hadn't come home. She wanted someone to come and pick her up. She needed someone.

Slowly she pulled herself from the floor and reached for the phone. She dialled Jen, needing to talk to her.

'Hello?' Jen said.

'It's me,' Abby said and heard a man's voice in the background. 'Jen?'

'Abby? Hang on.' Abby listened to Jen mumble something and heard a door slam. 'Abby? What's up? Has something happened?'

'No,' Abby said. 'No, I just...'

'Are you alright?'

Abby nodded. 'I'm okay. I just wanted... DI Gardner told me he'd spoken to your builders. I'm sorry.'

'Don't worry about it,' Jen said. It sounded like she was smoking. 'Listen, I'm just in the middle of something. Can I call you back?'

Abby deflated. She knew her friend could be petty at times but she didn't think she'd hold a grudge, not now. 'No, it's fine. I'll speak to you later,' Abby said and hung up before she started to cry again.

Abby held the phone against her chest. She needed to do something. Why wasn't she out there looking for Beth? Why wasn't she banging on doors? She looked at the phone in her hand. She could call Gardner. She ran her fingers over the phone. Her finger stopped over the buttons and before she changed her mind she pressed 1471. She listened to the number and pressed 3. Someone picked up straight away.

'Hannah Jones.' Abby said nothing. 'Hello?'

'Is this..? It's Abby Henshaw,' she said. 'I want to talk to you.'

CHAPTER TWENTY-TWO

Abby opened the door to the reporter, Hannah Jones. She hadn't expected the two men standing with her, one holding a camera, the other a microphone.

'I just want to talk to *you*,' Abby said.

The reporter looked like she was going to argue but instead nodded over her shoulder to the two men. 'Give us a minute,' she said to them.

Abby opened the door wider and let Hannah in, ignoring the looks from the other people outside. She saw the cameraman roll his eyes and he and his mate walked over to the wall and sat down. Hannah closed the door behind her. Abby led her to the living room.

'I don't want to talk on camera,' Abby said. 'Can you do that? Can you just write something?'

Hannah looked around the room. 'I'm a TV reporter but I guess I can do that.' She smiled at Abby. She didn't look very old, maybe mid-twenties, but she seemed confident, like she knew what she was doing. 'But TV reaches more people, you know,' she said and shrugged. 'It's up to you.' She walked to the window and picked up a photo frame. 'Is this Beth? She's beautiful.'

Abby took the photo from her and wondered if she was doing the right thing. 'What do you want?' she asked.

'You called me. I thought-'

'No,' Abby said. 'I mean what do you want me to do? How does this work? Does it help? Have you ever reported on something like this-' Abby stopped. She was asking the woman all these questions but she didn't even know what *she* wanted from it.

Hannah walked to the settee and sat down. 'I can't tell you what to do. I can tell you that if you want to do this to get your message out, then the best way is to give me an interview on camera. More people watch TV than read the paper. We can record something; it's not going to go out live.'

'You think it'll help?' Abby asked again.

'Yes,' Hannah said, pressing her lips together. 'I think it will. The more people who see this, the more likely Beth will be found.' She leaned forward and smiled at Abby. 'I know you did a press conference with the police but they won't keep showing that. It sucks but you need to keep giving them something new or else people lose interest. It's sad but true.'

Abby ran her hand across her forehead.

'So?' Hannah said. 'Should I bring the guys in?'

Hannah thanked Abby and walked to the door, telling her to call her anytime if she wanted to talk again. Abby felt sick. She didn't want to believe what the woman had said to her, but why would she make up something like that? Throughout the interview she wished someone would come in and tell her she was doing the right thing, or even that she was wrong and put a stop to it. She wished Paul would come home or Jen would call her back. She wished Gardner would show up and tell her he'd found Beth. But no one came and Hannah asked her question after question while the two men stood there looking uninterested.

Hannah tried to shake her hand again but Abby ignored her and as she closed the door she heard one of the guys say, 'It would've been better if she'd cried.'

CHAPTER TWENTY-THREE

'It was revealed this afternoon that police would be using divers in the search for Beth Henshaw, suggesting that hopes for finding her alive are fading. I spoke to Beth's mother, Abby Henshaw, earlier in what was an emotional interview.'

Helen watched the scene cut away to Abby Henshaw. She sat with her hands on her knees. The reporter's voice, off-screen, was soothing but it sounded fake. Abby's eyes darted around. She looked nervous. She looked awful.

'What went through your mind when you realised Beth had gone?' the reporter asked.

Helen shook her head. It was a stupid question. This woman

clearly wasn't a mother. Helen knew what she would feel. She knew she wouldn't be thinking, she'd just feel her heart being torn out.

Abby sat there without speaking for a few seconds, she glanced at the camera for a split second and then looked away again. 'I just...' she started. 'I didn't...' Another look at the lens. 'I didn't believe it. I didn't want to. I thought maybe I was wrong. That I was confused. I wanted to be wrong. I couldn't understand it.'

'And how do you feel now? What's gone through your mind over the past day?'

Abby shook her head. 'I feel guilty,' she said. 'I feel like I should've stopped it. I keep thinking is it my fault?' She looked at the reporter. 'I just wish that...'

'Wish what, Abby?'

'I wish... I just want her home. I just want Beth home. Whoever has her, please, just bring her home.' Abby closed her eyes.

'The police have been searching throughout the area, they've appealed for witnesses to come forward but so far no one has provided them with anything. No one has seen Beth. There've been no sightings, no witnesses. Do you think the police are doing enough?'

Abby looked confused. 'Yes, they've been... I'm sure they're doing everything they can-'

'I've been told the police are going to start searching local rivers and waterways, that police divers are being brought in. Do you think this is an indication of where they think the investigation is going? Have they suggested to you that they're changing the focus of their search?'

'What?' Abby asked and looked around her at the people off-screen. 'What are you talking about? The police are still looking for my daughter. Beth is still alive. Someone out there has her and they're going to find her.'

The scene cut back to the reporter standing outside the Henshaws' house. 'An emotional scene, I'm sure you'll agree. Since I spoke to Abby Henshaw a few hours ago, police have confirmed that as well as the police divers, they *will* be continuing their search on land of local areas with a team of over a hundred police officers, as well as having the cooperation of forces across the country. So perhaps not all hope is lost yet.'

The picture cut back to the studio. 'Hannah Jones, in Redcar. In other news...'

Helen switched off the TV. She wondered if the police really thought the baby was dead and how long they'd keep searching. She wondered how that reporter could sleep at night. And she wondered why Abby Henshaw hadn't cried once.

Paul was still gone when Gardner finally called Abby back. She wasn't sure how many times she'd called him. How many messages she'd left.

'Is it true?' she asked, before he could say anything. 'You're checking rivers. You're looking for her body? Is it true?'

She heard him sigh. 'Yes,' he said. 'We've started a search using police divers but that doesn't mean we think she's dead. We're just covering everything we can.'

Abby's anger finally broke and she started to cry. 'Why didn't you tell me? Why did I have to hear it from that fucking reporter?'

'I'm sorry,' Gardner said. 'I really am. The information wasn't officially released.'

Abby wiped her face with her sleeve. 'Have you found anything?'

'No. We're still canvassing the local area. We're still working with forces across the country. We haven't stopped looking. We won't stop until we find her. Remember that.'

CHAPTER TWENTY-FOUR

It was early on Thursday morning when Gardner arrived at the Henshaws'. Paul answered the door and let him in without a word, leading him into the kitchen. He took a seat as if he was waiting for the all too familiar speech to begin. No leads, nothing new to report, hang in there.

Gardner wondered why Abby hadn't run down the stairs like she usually did. Perhaps she was finally sleeping. He hadn't spoken to her since the incident with the reporter. Why would anyone suggest to an agonised mother that her baby was likely to be dead? He knew why. Ratings. To get a reaction from Abby that would make good television. The media were the scum of the earth. And yet part of him couldn't help admit she'd been right. Most of his team had lost hope. It had only been three days but in most cases like this, forty-eight hours was the window of hope. After that things usually didn't turn out so well. And by bringing in the divers perhaps he was making a statement to the world that he agreed with them. The truth was he'd brought them in as a formality, to cover all bases, but he hadn't given up hope himself. Someone out there had taken Beth Henshaw and he didn't believe they'd taken her to kill her. It didn't make sense to him, didn't feel right. But now he was there to tell Abby what they'd found. And his hope was drifting away.

Paul motioned for Gardner to sit down but he remained by the door.

'What is it?' Paul asked, his fists clenching. 'What? Has something happened?'

'Is Abby here?' Gardner asked, looking around the room, wanting to see anything but the eyes of the man in front of him.

'She's asleep.'

Gardner opened his mouth but closed it quickly and moved towards him. 'You should go and get her,' he said.

Paul frowned. 'Why? What's going on? Tell me.'

Gardner rested a hand on Paul's shoulder, cleared his throat and exhaled loudly. 'There was a body found this morning,' he said.

CHAPTER TWENTY-FIVE

Gardner watched as Paul's face froze for a second and then what seemed like all of his breath came rushing out. His eyes darted around the kitchen, as if his mind was furiously trying to process the information.

'She appears to be about the right age,' Gardner continued and took a seat across from Paul. 'According to preliminary results she's been dead over a week, which would suggest it's not Beth but...' Gardner stopped. He didn't need to go into details now. Didn't need to tell the man that a body in the water will decompose at a different rate to one found outside. 'There've been no reports of another missing child of that age in the area so to be sure we need to do a DNA comparison.'

Paul raised his hand to his mouth and swallowed hard. Gardner stood and found a glass in the cupboard beneath the sink. Filling it with water, he handed it to Paul. Paul took it from him with shaky hands but didn't attempt to lift it to his mouth. Gardner sat next to him and folded and unfolded his hands.

'I know this is hard. But I think you should get your wife.'

Paul dropped the glass onto the table, spilling the liquid across the tablecloth. 'Can I see her?' he asked.

Gardner shook his head. 'No.'

Paul looked directly at him and gave him a questioning look. Gardner licked his lips and wished he'd gotten a glass of water for himself. 'I'm afraid a visual identification would be impossible. The child was found in the river.'

'Jesus,' Paul said and rushed to the sink, dry heaving over the dirty dishes. Gardner stood and moved closer to Paul. Paul turned back to Gardner, his eyes red and wet. 'You need a DNA sample?'

'I really think you should get your wife. I don't want her finding out about this from anyone else.'

Paul shook his head. 'No. I don't want Abby to know unless she has to. If you need DNA, I can do it.'

Gardner's jaw clenched. 'That won't be necessary, Mr Henshaw. I know it's not my place but I really think you should tell your wife.'

'No,' Paul said again. 'No. She doesn't need to know yet. It'll kill her. Let me do the test. Let me do it and then if it's not Beth Abby never needs to know. Hasn't she been through enough already?'

Gardner blew out a breath. 'I realise that you just want to protect Abby-'

'So why won't you let me?' Paul said. 'Why won't you let me take the test?'

They both turned when they heard Abby walk into the room.

'Because you're not Beth's father,' she said.

CHAPTER TWENTY-SIX

Simon Abbott closed his eyes and ignored the stewardess' questions. He hoped if he kept his eyes closed he'd be able to go to sleep, God knew he needed it, but it was unlikely. He'd been in Brisbane barely an hour before he got the call from the police. He had planned to keep his phone turned off and just sleep for as long as possible before his next flight to Auckland. But habit, or the fear of missing something, a symptom of modern life, made him turn it on. He had a couple of missed calls - from Abby and an unknown number, the police he guessed - and a message urging him to call a DI Gardner as soon as possible. The mention of Beth's name caused him to panic. Receiving a message like that from the police was bad enough, but the fact that no one knew that Beth was his daughter, or no one except for him and Abby, made it even worse.

The stewardess moved on and Simon opened his eyes. He was desperate for a cigarette. He had no idea what was waiting for him when he got home. All the copper had said was that Beth was missing and Abby was hurt. That was it. No details, no hint that he was a suspect. And why would he be? He was a mile high when it happened. But he wasn't stupid. In situations like this it was usually the father who was under suspicion. And then of course there was his past. It had nothing to do with this but he'd bet they'd have dragged it up by now.

He wondered what Abby would've said to them. How much she'd told them. He wondered if her husband knew yet, if the shit had totally hit the fan.

Gardner had said Abby was hurt. That was it. He'd explain more when they talked in person. At that point Simon's heart had stuttered. He had images of Abby's body laid out on a slab – 'Abby's hurt' being a euphemism for dead. But he realised she must've been okay. How else would they know about him? Abby was the only person who could've told them. But why? Was it just so they could bring him home or did they actually think he was involved?

He rubbed his eyes as the plane took off. He couldn't decide what was worse right now: the not knowing what was waiting for him when he finally got home or the fact that he'd spent ninety-percent of the last few days on a plane. Manchester to Dubai, Dubai to Brisbane; a brief break spent sitting waiting in the airport on stand-by, worrying himself to death, and then back again. Flying out hadn't been too bad, he'd managed to sleep a little; it was just the jet-lag he had to contend with. But there was no chance of sleeping this time. Part of him thought that all of this was some weird nightmare. That he was actually in his hotel room and the travel had got to him in a seriously fucked up way.

He really wished he would wake up.

CHAPTER TWENTY-SEVEN

The two men turned and looked at Abby standing in the doorway, her arms wrapped tightly around herself. Paul's face was frozen in shock. Gardner thought she probably shouldn't have told him like that, with him in the room. Her husband deserved better than that. But what was more important now? He'd bet Beth was all that mattered to her.

'I'm sorry, Paul,' Abby said. 'I'm so sorry.' She turned to Gardner. 'You found something?'

'Yes, we found-'

'You knew,' Paul said, interrupting.

Gardner looked up at Paul but didn't speak. He wondered why that was his first question, that someone else knew first. Maybe it was humiliation. Maybe it was shock.

'This isn't right,' Paul said. 'Please Abby, tell me this isn't right.' Abby stepped closer to Paul and reached out to him. 'Tell me!' he shouted.

Abby closed her eyes. 'I'm sorry, Paul,' she said.

Gardner looked at Abby, thinking back to that first day, to the interview when she'd told him about Simon, revealed he was Beth's father. She was sitting about as far away from him as she was now, the same pained expression on her face.

'Who's Simon Abbott?' Gardner asked.

Abby licked her lips. 'He's the man I had an affair with,' she started, her voice cracking. 'I'm sorry. It's such a mess. I know I should've said something before. But I didn't want to lose Paul. I just wanted to keep my family together but I've messed it up. I'm sorry. I'm so sorry.'

He sank back into his chair, sighing. 'Why did you bring up Simon's name now, Abby?' he asked.

'I told you. I had an affair with him.'

'Had. As in past tense?'

Abby nodded. He waited, expecting her to expand on the subject. To tell him how it had ended badly, that he was insane, that he was the one who'd done this. But she didn't. She didn't say another word. He looked at Lawton. She looked like he felt. Shocked.

'Do you think he could've done this?' he asked.

Abby shook her head. 'No. No he wouldn't do this. I know him. He wouldn't hurt Beth.'

Gardner felt that unsettling feeling in his stomach. It was likely that the answer to his next question would be the key to all of this. He knew how these things went. 'Abby, is Simon Abbott Beth's father?'

Abby squeezed her eyes shut and took a deep breath. When she opened them she still wouldn't look at him but she nodded. 'Yes,' she said her voice barely more than a whisper. Gardner opened his mouth but Abby cut him off. 'He didn't do this,' she said, finally looking at him. 'He wouldn't.'

'Statistically, most abduction cases are committed by non-custodial parents. If Mr Abbott couldn't get access to his daughter.' Gardner stopped and looked Abby in the eye. 'Was he aware that he was Beth's father?'

Abby nodded. 'Yes. But he didn't need to... He has access. We meet every couple of weeks when he isn't working. He works abroad a lot of the time.'

Gardner studied Abby, trying to understand what she was implying. 'So you were still having a relationship with him?'

'No. Not like that. We ended it when I found out I was pregnant.' Abby tugged at the sleeves of her jumper. 'Paul wanted children and I never wanted to leave him. It wasn't like that. When I got pregnant, Simon and I agreed that we'd stop seeing each other. That Beth would be brought up as Paul's but he would see her regularly.'

'And he was fine with that? Another man bringing up his child?' Gardner asked, trying to get his head around it. What kind of person would just agree to something like that?

'He knew that's what I wanted and he agreed to it.'

'That's very noble of him,' Gardner said. 'How long had you known Mr Abbott?'

'About eleven, twelve years,' she said. Gardner's eyebrows rose. 'We used to go out a long time ago. He was my first proper boyfriend. After my parents died he was everything to me. We were together for two years and then he left to work in Hong Kong. We kept in touch for a little while but...' Abby shrugged. 'A couple of years ago I ran into him again. He'd moved back to Saltburn so we met up a few times to catch up and things just...' She looked at Gardner for help, hoping he'd fill in the blanks himself. 'I never wanted to hurt Paul. And I've never stopped loving him, it was just...' Abby shook her head. 'I don't know. I suppose Simon and I never really finished things properly. I always thought he'd come back after a few months and we'd just pick up where we left off.' Abby looked back at Gardner and her cheeks burned. 'He wouldn't do this. He loves her.'

'Does your husband know?'

Abby shook her head. 'No.'

'Are you sure,' he asked.

'I'm positive,' Abby said.

Gardner nodded. 'I'll try and track down Mr Abbott.' He stood.

'Please don't tell Paul,' Abby said. 'Please. Not yet.'

Gardner opened his eyes again, the clock on the kitchen wall loudly ticked out the seconds that no one spoke. He looked at Paul bending over, his hands gripping the back of the kitchen chair. His breathing was laboured and for a moment Gardner thought the man might keel over. Abby turned to Gardner with a pleading look but he said nothing. What could he say? He wished he'd never involved himself in the lie. He'd been in Paul's shoes himself. Not exactly the same, thank God, but still. He'd been betrayed, been lied to, cheated on. Why had he taken Abby's side? His job wasn't to lie for her; it was to find out the truth. To find the men who'd raped her and who had taken Beth. That was it.

Abby walked over to Paul and put a hand on his arm. He didn't look at her. 'Paul,' she started. 'Please, look at me.' She waited but he didn't respond, didn't move at all. 'I'm sorry,' she said. 'I never meant to hurt you. I didn't-'

Paul's head snapped up. 'Who is it?' he asked.

Abby swallowed and shook her head. 'It doesn't matter,' she said.

'Of course it fucking matters,' he shouted. 'Of course it does. He's Beth's-' Paul stopped, clearly unable to say the word.

Abby looked at Gardner for help again. He knew there was a risk that Paul would go after Simon once he found out. That he'd want to go over there and break his legs, and who could blame him? But Gardner doubted it'd happen. Paul Henshaw didn't seem like the kind of man capable of breaking anyone's legs, whether they'd slept with his wife or not.

Gardner nodded at Abby and she turned back to Paul. She took a moment and Paul stared, waiting for her to talk.

'Is it someone from work?' Paul asked. 'Someone who's been published? Instead of me, the failed fucking writer?'

Abby shook her head. 'No,' she said.

'Then who?'

'His name's Simon,' she said quietly. 'Simon Abbott.'

Gardner watched Paul for a reaction but he just stared at her. If he had any idea about Simon, any idea about the affair, he was a damn good actor.

'We used to go out when I was a teenager,' Abby said. 'I hadn't seen him for years and we bumped into each other. We just...' Abby stopped, realising her husband probably didn't want the details.

'So what? You just picked up where you left off?' Paul asked. 'Never mind the fact you're married.'

'I'm sorry,' Abby said again. 'I never wanted to hurt you-'

'Well you fucked that up, didn't you?' Paul said.

Gardner looked at the floor. He didn't want to be there. He didn't need to hear this. To see their marriage fall apart. Both Abby and Paul had stopped speaking. He wanted to leave.

'Does he know?' Paul asked. 'Does he know he's Beth's father?' Abby just nodded and Paul pulled a face. 'So what? He didn't even want her so she got me instead? The consolation prize.'

'No it's not like that,' Abby said. 'We... I wanted you to bring Beth up. I wanted you to be her father.'

'But I'm not, am I?' he said. Abby closed her eyes to stop the tears. 'Why didn't he want her?'

'He did,' Abby started. 'He's not around. He works abroad a lot. He sees her sometimes.'

Paul took in a deep breath and a sob came out. 'So...' He looked at Gardner this time. 'So he took her? He wanted her back so he took her?'

Gardner opened his mouth but he paused before speaking. Abby had told him that her arrangement with Simon was amicable. That it'd been worked out to suit them both, that he was a good guy. Then there was the fact he was getting on a plane when it happened. But he still had doubts. He knew the statistics. He knew that people changed their minds. For the time being Simon Abbott was top of his list in terms of suspects but Paul Henshaw didn't need to know that.

'I need to speak to Mr Abbott,' he said. 'There's no evidence at this stage to suggest he was involved.'

Paul let out a desperate laugh and rubbed his hands across his face. 'I can't believe this,' he said. He stepped back and ran a hand through his hair, looking from Gardner to Abby. 'I can't deal with this,' he said and walked towards the door, pushing past Abby.

'Paul,' she called after him and started to follow. The door slammed as she got to there. She opened it to see her husband reversing out of the drive. 'Paul,' she shouted again but Gardner led her back inside, out of the way of stares from neighbours and calls from reporters.

'Let him go,' he said. 'He needs time.'

Gardner thought about when Annie had told him. He'd had no idea. Complete bolt of lightning. He'd stormed out of the house, driven off and then stopped at the side of the road thinking of all the things he should've said. The names he wanted to call her, the questions he wanted to ask. He stayed out all night and then managed to avoid her for two days after. By the time he worked up the courage to finally speak to her she'd already started packing her things.

Gardner waited a few seconds before speaking. 'You heard us talking earlier?'

She nodded. 'About DNA.'

'Did you hear the rest?'

Abby shook her head slightly and then she seemed to pale. 'Have you found her?'

'We found a body. A baby.'

'Oh God,' Abby said, her hands curling into themselves. 'Is it her?'

Gardner shook his head. 'We don't know. I think it's unlikely, the body appears to have been in the water for at least a week but,' he looked away, 'we need to make sure. We need to do the test so we can be sure.'

Abby nodded. 'Okay,' she said and stood up. 'I'll get my shoes.' She walked towards the front door and looked around like she was lost.

'No, it's okay,' Gardner said. 'We've got a sample already.'

Abby looked back at him and nodded, her hands were shaking and she tucked them into her pockets.

'I'm sorry, I should've been clearer. I only came because I wanted to let you know in person after what happened with that reporter. I'm sorry,' he said. 'I'm sorry about Paul.'

Abby just shook her head. 'When will we know?' she asked.

'Hopefully within twenty four hours,' he said. He'd be putting as much pressure on the lab as possible. He didn't want to wait either. He looked down at his shoes. He needed to go, needed to get on with finding Beth, but he felt guilty at leaving Abby alone.

As if reading his mind Abby turned to the sink, busying herself with rinsing out dishes. 'Thanks for telling me,' she said.

Gardner wanted to offer some kind of comfort but nothing seemed appropriate. He wondered if she'd be alright on her own. If Paul would come back. With nothing to say he pushed the chair back in to the table and walked to the doorway.

'I'll let you know as soon as I hear anything,' he said and watched Abby's head nod. He turned and walked to the front door and as he left he heard Abby crying.

CHAPTER TWENTY-EIGHT

Helen glanced over her shoulder at the TV as she folded her washing.

'*...From what I understand, the location in Stockton, close to the Tees Barrage, had not been a part of the police's initial search. It was in fact a tip-off from a member of the public that led police to the part of the river where the body was found. Police have not yet confirmed the body is that of eight-month old Beth Henshaw who went missing earlier this week but this could be a tragic end to what has been a massive search for the missing girl.'*

The reporter looked over her shoulder as a car pulled up. DI Gardner climbed out and walked quickly towards the station.

'DI Gardner,' Hannah shouted and jogged towards him. The camera

jiggled as her team followed. 'DI Gardner,' she said again to his back. 'Can you confirm that it's Beth Henshaw?'

Detective Gardner ignored her, along with the throng of other reporters, and headed for the door.

'Do you think it's her?' another reporter shouted and jostled Hannah out of the way of her own camera.

'Is there any suggestion that her parents could be involved? Is it true Abby Henshaw had an affair?' a man's voice shouted over the noise. The other reporters seemed to quiet down. Gardner turned around and glared in the general direction of the crowd.

Helen put the washing basket down and moved closer to the TV.

'The body of a child was recovered from the River Tees this morning. So far the identity of the child has not been confirmed. I'll make no further comment at this time,' Gardner said and walked away, letting the door slam behind him.

Helen stood, transfixed by the television, her arms around herself. A tear slid down her cheek and she wiped it away with the palm of her hand. That poor baby, she thought. That poor mother, losing her child.

Helen turned off the TV and walked over to the cot in the corner of the room where her baby lay so peacefully, so unaware of the tragedy in the world. Helen bent down and put her hand on her daughter's chest, feeling the life in her body.

'I will never let anything happen to you,' she said. 'I'll never let anyone hurt you.'

CHAPTER TWENTY-NINE

Simon got off the train in Middlesbrough and dragged his case behind him, trying to dodge the other passengers milling about. He wasn't sure whether he'd been expecting a police escort when he arrived but there didn't seem to be anyone waiting for him. He called the police station from the airport, letting them know he was back in the country, that he'd be home in a couple of hours. Someone promised to pass the message on to DI Gardner. He wasn't sure whether he was supposed to go straight to the station or if they'd arrange to speak to him later. His head was pounding. He'd managed to grab an hour or two's sleep on the plane but in the end he thought it'd made him feel worse. The desire to sleep was only defeated by the desire to find out what was going on.

He'd tried to call Abby from the train but it'd gone through to voicemail. He was about to try again when he realised he didn't know what was happening. Was Abby blaming him? Would she really think he'd taken their daughter? Gardner said she'd been hurt. Maybe she was in the hospital and couldn't answer.

He'd go to the police station, speak to Gardner, and find out what the hell was going on. Then he'd find Abby. God only knew if her husband had found about him, about Beth. But right now he didn't care. His daughter was missing. Screw Abby's husband.

Simon walked out of the train station and headed towards the police station. As he stood alone in front of the new building he felt all his muscles tense. He was about to find out what was going on. He hadn't heard anything since he was in Brisbane. That seemed like a lifetime ago. And a lot could happen in a lifetime.

He took a deep breath and walked into the station. He waited for the desk sergeant to come off the phone and then leaned on the counter.

'Simon Abbott,' he said. 'I'm here to see DI Gardner.'

He was told to take a seat and someone would be right with him. He collapsed into the nearest chair and tried to stop his eyes from closing.

'Simon Abbott?'

Simon opened his eyes and looked up at the man in front of him. He sat up straight. 'Yeah.'

'I'm DI Gardner,' he said and offered a hand. At first Simon thought he was offering to help him out of the chair and wondered just how terrible he looked, how many years all the flying had aged him. But then he realised he was supposed to shake it.

'If you'd like to follow me,' Gardner said and started walking away, holding a door open for Simon and his suitcase.

Simon looked at Gardner as they walked along the corridor, trying to gauge the situation from his face. But he couldn't tell. As he walked to the interview room he didn't know what to expect. If he was a suspect or not. If he was about to be told his daughter was fine or that she was dead.

CHAPTER THIRTY

Gardner looked Abbott up and down and immediately thought how different he was to Paul Henshaw. Clearly Abby Henshaw didn't have a type. Apart from both being tall, the two men were opposites. Where Paul was rake thin, Simon was broad. Paul wore glasses and had a bookish quality and Simon looked like he went mountain biking and worked with his hands.

He watched as Simon rubbed his eyes and settled into the chair. He looked exhausted. And who could blame him.

'Can I get you anything? Water? Coffee?'

Simon shook his head. 'No. Thank you.'

He looked back at Simon and wondered how to play it. There was the possibility that the man had abducted his daughter but then again it was possible he was as innocent as Abby had insisted.

'Can you just tell me what's going on?' Simon said. 'I mean, what happened?' He sat forward, suddenly animated. 'Have you found her? Have you..?'

'Your daughter's still missing,' Gardner said and watched as Simon paled. 'Abby Henshaw was attacked and Beth was taken from her car.'

'Abby,' Simon whispered and his eyes started darting around. 'Is she okay? Abby? Is she alright? What did they do to her?'

'She's okay.' Gardner wondered how much of a lie that sentence was. 'Her car was forced off the road. Two men forced her into a van and raped her.'

Simon made a noise and for a moment Gardner thought the man was going to be sick. He stopped and waited. Simon took a breath and his hands curled into fists.

'Have you got them? The men?' he asked.

Gardner shook his head. 'No. Not yet. We have descriptions from Abby but so far we haven't-'

'And what about Beth?' Simon said. 'What did they do to her?' He looked like he was going to blow any minute.

'Abby said the men left Beth in the car. When she returned to the car with a police officer Beth was gone.'

Simon frowned, the confusion etched on his face. 'So someone else took Beth? Those men didn't take her?'

Gardner looked down at the table. He wished he knew. At the outset he'd been optimistic that Abby's attack and Beth disappearing were unrelated. But that clearly wasn't the case. There *was* someone else. He looked back at Simon. 'We believe that's the case, yes,' he said.

Simon squeezed the top of his nose. 'What about Abby?' he said. 'I tried to call her earlier. Is she still in hospital?'

Gardner shook his head. 'No, she's at home,' he said. 'You haven't spoken to her at all?'

'No,' Simon said.

Gardner nodded. That was probably a good thing. 'I realise you must be tired and I know this will be difficult but I need to ask you a few questions.'

'You think I took her,' Simon said. A statement not a question.

Gardner looked back blankly. 'You were out of the country at the time of the incident. I know you were already on the plane when Abby was attacked.'

'But you still think I could be involved? That I wanted to get Beth?' Simon sat leaning forward, head in hands.

'Tell me about your relationship with Abby Henshaw,' Gardner said.

Simon looked up from behind his hands and sat back in his chair, his eyes barely open. Gardner had briefly considered waiting until Simon had slept before speaking to him. He couldn't imagine what the round trip to New Zealand would do to your head. But he figured the tiredness, the jet-lag, might make Simon more open, less able to bullshit him.

'She's the mother of my child. We dated a long time ago, hadn't seen each other in years, and then bumped into each other again a couple of years ago.' He shrugged. 'Things developed. We had an affair. Abby got pregnant and we decided it would be for the best if Beth was raised as her husband's daughter.'

'Why?' Gardner asked.

Simon looked away from Gardner. His jaw clenched. 'Work. I travel a lot for work.'

'A lot of parents work. And lots travel for work. They manage.'

Simon sat forward again. 'Do their kids manage though?'

Gardner gave him a half smile. 'So you decided Beth needed a stable environment with two parents?'

'Right,' Simon said and sat back again. 'Abby's dad was hardly ever around when she was young. She hated that. She didn't want it for Beth.'

'So how do you fit in? You see Beth regularly, is that correct?'

'As much as possible,' he said. 'Every two weeks usually. Sometimes less if I'm working away. Sometimes more to make up for it.'

'And you think that's more stable for Beth?'

'It works for us.'

'Does it?' Gardner asked. 'Does it work for both of you or just Abby?'

'I didn't take her,' Simon said. 'I don't need to steal her away. I see my daughter. She's a part of my life. I don't need to take her away from Abby.' He paused for breath. 'And I would never hurt Abby. Never.'

Gardner watched as Simon's eyes filled with tears and looked away, down to the notepad in front of him.

'If I'm being honest, it was more for Abby than for me. This arrangement we have. But I'm fine with it. I still get to see my daughter.' Simon stifled a yawn. 'I knew Abby would never leave her husband. I knew that from the start. And, yes, that hurt. And, yes, when she told me she was pregnant I thought maybe things would change but...' He shrugged. 'It was what Abby wanted, and it made sense. She wouldn't have gone through with it if I'd said no. We made the decision together.'

'And you still think you made the right decision?'

Simon sat for a few moments, looking past Gardner, caught up in his own thoughts. He gave a barely noticeable shake of his head. 'I don't know,' he said. 'It was the hardest thing I've ever done. I knew it'd be hard. Giving up Abby was one thing, but Beth.' He shook his head. 'When I found out Abby'd had her it was the best and worst day of my life. I knew that out there was this little girl who was mine but I couldn't see her. But when I saw her. The first time I held her...' Simon coughed and cleared his throat. 'I thought I'd made a mistake. I knew I'd made a mistake. But it was too late. I couldn't do that to Abby, I couldn't just go back on our decision.'

'Surely Abby would've understood? I'm sure anyone would understand a father wanting to be with his child.'

Simon shook his head. 'I promised her. And I knew I'd get to see her. Beth.' Simon smiled, sadly. 'We named her together.' He shook his head. 'I was convinced her husband was going to come up with something else. But he seemed to like it.'

Gardner nodded. He didn't know what he could say to the man. His alibi was airtight and he seemed genuine enough, but Simon Abbott had clearly regretted his decision to let Paul Henshaw bring up Beth as his own daughter. His love for Beth was evident. But for all that he and Abby insisted that things were fine, something wasn't right. Simon just admitted he'd made a mistake, he wished he could be a proper father to Beth. And if things were so right between him and Abby, why wasn't she answering his calls?

Gardner opened a file and then looked at Simon. 'You were arrested in 1994, a fight outside a club.'

Simon sighed and rubbed his face. 'Yes.'

'And then in 2001 you were arrested again. This time convicted of assault.'

'Yes,' Simon said again. Gardner waited, allowing Simon to explain it himself. 'The first one was nothing. A couple of kids fighting outside a nightclub. Some arsehole started mouthing off to Abby.'

'Abby was with you then?' Gardner asked, although he'd guessed that she was from the date. The report mentioned a girlfriend but didn't name her. 'So she knew you could be violent?'

'I'm not violent,' Simon said. 'Not with Abby. Not usually with anyone. This guy called Abby a bitch or something, I can't even remember, and I told him to shove off. He swung for me, missed, and then I hit him back. The guy was so drunk he couldn't stand. He fell over.'

'A witness report said you punched him repeatedly when he was on the ground. That your girlfriend had to pull you off him.'

Simon shook his head. 'That's not true. I hit him once. He fell over. Maybe he hit his head when he fell. I don't know. The police were there before I had a chance to do anything else.'

'So you would've done something else if they hadn't arrived?' Gardner asked.

'No,' he said and frowned. 'It was just a stupid childish fight. Nothing happened.'

'Okay,' Gardner said. 'What about the next time? The assault in 2001?'

Simon's jaw clenched. 'Look, I'm not going to pretend it didn't happen or that it wasn't my fault. It was. I was drunk, I was pissed off about something or other and the guy just got in the way. I know I was wrong. I know it was completely unacceptable to do what I did but that has nothing to do with this. You said yourself I was on a plane when it happened. I *couldn't* have done it. And I wouldn't.'

Gardner waited. Simon Abbott was clearly a man with a temper. He wasn't sure he was ready to believe he would've paid someone to hurt Abby like that in order to get to his daughter. But would he have been prepared for Paul Henshaw to be hurt? Maybe the wrong parent was in the car that day and whoever had been paid to get them out of the way so Beth could be taken had to improvise.

'What about Paul Henshaw?' Gardner asked. 'What was your relationship with him?'

'I don't have a relationship with him. I've never met him.'

'Never?' Gardner asked and Simon shook his head. 'Okay, what are your feelings about him? What do you know about him?'

Simon sighed. 'My feelings? I was sleeping with his wife,' he said and shrugged. 'I suppose at one point I felt guilty about that. Abby didn't say much about him but I gathered he was good to her. Why else would she want to stay with him?' He sighed again. 'And maybe I was jealous of him. He had what I wanted.'

'So you didn't know anything about him but you were willing to let your daughter be brought up by him?'

'Abby loves him. Beth's looked after. He seems like a good guy,' he said. 'Abby wouldn't be there if he wasn't. The only reason she chose to do it this way was because she wanted the best for Beth and I trust her to do that.'

'You reported a break-in earlier this year,' Gardner said. 'What happened there?'

Simon blinked and rubbed his face. 'I was away for a couple of days. When I got back the door was broken and the place was a mess.'

'Nothing was taken?'

'A camera. Not a very good one. There were others in the house, better ones. And there'd been some money in a drawer. That was gone,' Simon said. 'Police came and had a look but nothing came of it.'

'Any idea who could've done it?'

Simon frowned. 'No,' he said. 'Smackheads probably. They could've taken all sorts but they didn't.'

'And that happened when? February?'

'Yes, I think so.'

'You ever travel to Russia or Eastern Europe for your job?' Gardner asked and watched as Simon's brain tried to catch up with the shift.

'What?' he said. He seemed to struggle with the question. 'I think so. Maybe once or twice. Just to Prague.'

Gardner nodded. 'You have friends there? Any contacts?'

'What? No. I don't know anyone in Prague. Why?'

'The men who attacked Abby, she thought they were Russian, maybe Eastern European.'

CHAPTER THIRTY-ONE

Abby sat on the settee listening to Paul's footsteps move across the ceiling as he went from wardrobe to bed to chest of drawers and back again.

She'd woken up when the door slammed. She'd been trying to stay awake, wanting to be ready in case Gardner came back with the results. But the fatigue engulfed her, forcing her to drift off. And the nightmares made it worse. Since she'd been told about the body being found she kept seeing her daughter's face, all white skin and blue lips, staring up at her from the river. She couldn't risk sleeping. The nightmares were almost as bad as reality.

Climbing the stairs she found Paul pulling things from the wardrobe. She watched as he struggled to shove his clothes into a holdall. At one point she started to offer to help but he silenced her with a look. *Of course, darling, thanks very much for helping me pack my bags to leave after you cheated on me and ruined my life.*

After a few attempts to close the holdall he gave up and moved onto another small suitcase. He looked around the room and then walked towards Abby in the doorway. She held her hand out to him and begged him to stop and talk to her, but he pushed his way past into the bathroom and collected his few toiletries together as best he could in the crook of his arm, pressing them into his chest. Abby watched helplessly as he stomped back into the bedroom and tossed the plastic bottles and shaving kit into the case.

'Paul, please. You can't just leave. What about Beth?'

Paul stopped and gave Abby a look that could kill. 'Don't do that,' he said. 'Don't try and use her to make me stay.'

'I'm not,' Abby said, feeling like he'd slapped her. 'But you can't just go. Not now. Not while... We need to talk.' Abby moved closer. 'Where are you going to go?'

'I don't think it's your business anymore, is it?' He picked up his toothbrush, which had dropped onto the bed, and threw it violently into the case. 'You don't tell me that my child isn't my child and I don't tell you where I'm going. I think that's fair, don't you?'

Abby sank onto the bed. 'I never wanted to hurt you. You have to know that. I'd never hurt you intentionally. I made a mistake, I know that. But I thought I could make things right. I thought Beth could make things right-'

'You lied to me!' Paul grabbed her by the shoulders and shook her. 'Having an affair is one thing but you made me believe that Beth was my daughter! I loved her! And you... You broke my heart, Abby.' Paul dropped his hands as there was a knock at the door. Neither of them moved for a moment until Paul turned back to her. 'You should get that. It could be someone important.' After a few moments Abby stood and dragged herself downstairs.

Simon came out of the police station, dragging his case behind him, and lit a cigarette. He'd quit three times already this year but it never lasted.

124

Bad day at work? Just one cigarette to relax. Long flight ahead? Just a couple to settle the nerves. As he stood inhaling his second cigarette in ten minutes he decided that after this he probably wouldn't be quitting again.

He felt around in his jacket pocket for his phone and called Abby. After a couple of rings it diverted to voicemail and he hung up. He wondered where she was and how she was coping. Detective Gardner said she was okay but he'd also said that on top of being attacked and Beth being missing, her husband now knew everything. So he doubted that she was actually okay.

He tried her again but this time when he got no answer he started walking towards the taxi rank.

CHAPTER THIRTY-TWO

Abby pressed divert as she went to answer the door. She knew she'd have to speak to Simon eventually, and though she had no idea what she'd say to him, she wanted to, desperately. Beth was his daughter too. But for now what she wanted was to talk to Paul. To try and get him to stay even though she knew it was probably pointless, and more than that she knew it was wrong to even ask him to. She had no right to ask anything of him anymore. She'd given up that right the moment she started seeing Simon again.

Even while she was seeing Simon she knew that it was wrong. Not only morally, but because she didn't want to break up with Paul. There was nothing really wrong in her marriage. Paul was about as perfect as a husband could be and she loved him, absolutely loved him. She would come home from meeting Simon and just looking at Paul made her want to call Simon and tell him it was over. And yet as soon as she walked into the same room as Simon she didn't want to be anywhere else. She felt like a different person with him. And so it went on. She wondered what would've happened if she hadn't fallen pregnant. Would she still be seeing Simon? Would she have ever chosen between him and her husband?

Abby opened the door and her heart sank as she saw Jen standing there. She wiped her eyes.

'Hey, babe,' Jen said and walked in. 'I'm sorry I didn't call you back. I'm a terrible friend. It's just they dropped me. The fucking publishers dropped me. I can't-'

The sound of a bag dropping onto the wooden floor in the hallway startled them both. They turned to see Paul standing there. He stared at Abby before turning his attention to Jen.

'I guess you're here to cheer me off. Good riddance, right?' Paul said.

Jen looked at Paul before turning to Abby. 'What's going on?' she asked.

'Give it up, Jen. I know everything. I know she was fucking someone else. I know Beth isn't mine,' he said, his voice catching. 'You'll be pleased to know I'm going.'

Jen stared, open-mouthed. Abby looked at the floor. She couldn't say anything, she just wanted Jen to leave.

'Jesus, I always knew you were a drama queen. I didn't realise you were actually an actress too,' Paul said.

Abby looked up at Paul, her eyes red.

'You didn't tell her?' he said and looked at Jen again. 'Well, that's something. I wasn't the last to know after all.' Paul pulled his coat on.

'Paul.' Abby tried to think of something to say but knew that anything she said would be trite and meaningless. Instead she walked towards him and stood with her hands on his chest. He moved away and picked up his car keys. She could see his hands shaking.

'Will you be okay?' she asked.

'I'll be fine,' he said and picked up one of his bags. He opened the front door and took it to the car. She ignored the stares from the lingering media; ignored them as they shifted themselves, ready to pounce on her unravelling life. She watched as he opened the boot and threw the bags in before slamming the door down over it. He walked around to the driver's side door and stopped.

'You don't have to go,' Abby said, trying to ignore Jen standing beside her. Ignoring the click of the camera from across the road.

'Yes, I do,' Paul said after a moment. He dropped his chin to his chest and closed his eyes. 'Just call me if you hear anything. Will you do that?'

The sound of a car pulling up caused them all to turn. Simon stepped out of the taxi and looked at Abby. Her heart sank as she turned back to Paul.

'I'll let the police know where they can reach me,' Paul said, opened his car door. He got in and drove away without a single glance backwards.

Abby ran onto the street after Paul's car and watched as it disappeared around the corner. Another camera snapped. Someone called her name.

After a minute or so she felt Simon's hand on her shoulder, gently steering her off the road. For a second he glanced at Jen standing by the door. He turned back to Abby. She needed him to go. He wasn't the one she wanted there with her. She wanted to scream and blame him and hurt him. Instead she collapsed into his chest and sobbed.

She felt Jen's hand on her arm before she walked away without a word.

Sometime, minutes or hours later, she could no longer tell, Simon picked her up and carried her inside and she cried again until she fell asleep, utterly exhausted.

CHAPTER THIRTY-THREE

Gardner dropped the notes on his desk and leaned back in his chair. He'd been through Simon Abbott's bank accounts and there was nothing. No unusually large withdrawals. No transfers of money to private accounts. Just the usual mortgage and bills – similar to the Henshaws except Abbott had also purchased a hell of a lot of plane tickets. The guy must've had air miles coming out of his arse. There was nothing to suggest he'd paid anyone to steal his daughter. Gardner hadn't really expected to find evidence he had. Like the Henshaws, Abbott had consented to the search. He didn't get the gut feeling that Simon was guilty but there was still something that bugged him. Maybe it was because he had a lack of other leads, maybe it was that the father usually did it. Maybe it was just because he'd found the man slightly arrogant. That was probably down to the fact he'd just spent a few days flying non-stop; Gardner had to admit he wouldn't exactly be charming after that, but maybe it wasn't his jet-lag, maybe it was just him. Or his job. International photographer. Maybe it'd gone to his head.

Gardner heard the sound of ringing and looked around his desk for his phone, pushing piles of paper aside. The ring was muffled and he found it in his pocket.

'DI Gardner,' he said.

'It's Paul Henshaw.'

Gardner sat up straight. He hadn't expected Paul to contact him. He felt like Paul had partly blamed him for Abby's deceit. That he'd been complicit in her lies.

'Mr Henshaw, what can I do for you?' he asked.

Paul sniffed as if he'd been crying. 'I just wanted to let you know where I'd be staying in case you needed to contact me,' he said. Gardner waited. He thought there was no point questioning him, pretending to be surprised. 'I'll be at the White Cliff B&B in Redcar until I can sort something out. You've got my mobile number?'

'Yes,' Gardner said.

'Right. I just thought I'd better let you know,' he said. 'But I'd appreciate it if you didn't tell Abby.'

Gardner scratched his chin. He couldn't help feeling like he was caught in the middle of the Henshaws marriage and that Paul thought he owed him one. You kept secrets for Abby now keep one for me. He sighed. 'Okay,' he said.

'Thank you,' Paul said and then he was gone.

Gardner put the phone down and sat staring at the wall. Poor guy. His wife cheats on him, he finds out his daughter isn't his, and then he's the one who has to move in to a dive like the White Cliff.

He shuffled the papers in front of him and found the statements for the Henshaws' bank accounts. Like Simon Abbott's, there was nothing unusual there. But unlike Simon's he wasn't so much looking for large withdrawals but large debts instead. If the Henshaws were drowning, unable to keep up with mortgage payments, they might have a reason to stage their daughter's kidnap. But there was nothing to suggest that. All the bills were paid on time and there was always a little spare at the end of the month. Plus there was a savings account with a tidy sum in it, though this was just in Abby's name. He checked the date the account was opened and decided it was probably her inheritance. He'd considered money as a possible reason for Beth's kidnap. It wasn't a huge amount – twenty thousand – but to someone desperate it was probably enough to risk committing a crime for. The only fly in the ointment there was that there'd been no ransom demands, no contact from whoever was holding Beth.

He ran his fingers through his hair. The case was bugging him. Nothing was working. He didn't believe that it was only chance Abby was on that road, that those men just happened to be there, that Beth was left in the car by mistake. It was planned. Someone wanted Beth and planned to take her, planned to get Abby out of the way. He didn't believe that some stranger had just decided one day to run away with Beth Henshaw. He'd been thinking too much about the people who knew that Abby would be on that road that day – Abby, Paul, Jen. Jen's builders? Abby swore that she hadn't told Simon. Why would she? But maybe he was looking at it wrong. Maybe it wasn't anyone Abby had told. Maybe someone had been watching her, following her. Maybe whoever had slashed her tyres? He thought about the break-in at Simon's house. That was shortly after Abby's car was damaged. Was it connected? Or was he just trying to make it connect?

Gardner bit his thumbnail. It *was* possible that the person who had Beth didn't know Abby. That it was just chance in some way. They wanted a child. They saw Abby and Beth. They started following them, waiting for an opportunity. If it was a gang, that'd explain the men in the van. There were gangs who abducted babies, children, then sold them to desperate couples - or worse, sold them into prostitution or labour. They were pursuing that angle but so far hadn't found anything.

Gardner closed his eyes. What else did he have? *Who* else? He was sure he could rule out any involvement of Abby herself. Paul had an alibi. He was at the shop when it happened, the CCTV proved it. There was no evidence he'd paid anyone to hurt his wife or take Beth. There was no evidence from his phone records that he'd been involved with anyone else either – all his calls were to or from Abby; Laura, his assistant at the shop; suppliers and other business contacts; and his dentist. Laura said she'd never seen him with anyone: there were no regular customers that stood out, no one she'd seen Paul with. Simon Abbott was the most obvious candidate. He had a motive. He'd admitted himself that he'd made a mistake letting Beth go. He'd been to Eastern Europe, possibly had contacts there. But he wasn't convinced. If Simon had taken Beth, where was she now? It didn't ring true with other cases like this. If another parent had taken a child they would just try and keep hidden, they wouldn't come back.

Jen? He didn't like her for it. True, she'd previously been involved with Paul Henshaw. Maybe she was jealous like Lawton suggested. It could be Abby had everything Jen wanted for herself. But again she had an alibi. The builders confirmed she'd been there all day. She was only gone a few minutes to stock up on tea bags and milk. And from the little time he'd spent with her he had to agree with Paul Henshaw – what would she do with a baby? He got the impression she was the most important person in her life and that didn't leave much room for a baby. And even if she was jealous of the Henshaws' relationship, he doubted she'd go after Beth. She was more likely to just pursue Paul.

Gardner looked at the clock. Jesus, was it really that late? It was too late now but tomorrow he'd speak to Jen again, dig a little deeper into her feelings about Paul. He'd look into the gang angle. And he'd visit Simon Abbott at home. Maybe he could still bring Beth home.

He stood up, put on his jacket, and headed for his car thinking about the test results that should've been back the next day. As he closed the car door he slumped back in his seat. There was a chance he wouldn't be bringing Beth home at all.

CHAPTER THIRTY-FOUR

Abby sat hunched on one end of the settee, Simon at the other end. She'd already given him the ins and outs of what had happened, leaving a few details out for his benefit and her own. She'd filled him in on the investigation, such as it was. And now she waited for the hard part. The blame, the responsibility, the guilt.

'Why didn't you call me?' he asked.

'I tried,' Abby said, knowing that she hadn't tried hard enough. 'I tried to call you from the police station the day–' Abby stopped. She hadn't come up with a suitable euphemism yet. 'I tried but Paul was there and I didn't know what to say. How could I tell you that over the phone?'

'I should've been here,' he said and Abby wasn't sure if he was blaming her for not calling him and getting him back as soon as it had happened or if he was talking to himself.

'What if it's her?' Abby said.

Simon pulled her close to him. 'They said it looked like the body had been in the water a week, right? So it can't be Beth.'

'But what if they're wrong? They can't be sure, can they? What if...?' Abby dissolved into tears, turning her face into Simon's chest. She couldn't bear it. She couldn't bear the waiting, the thoughts that came into her mind every time she closed her eyes. How could she live if Beth was gone? Her throat was tight as she sobbed. Simon held on tighter.

Abby woke in the early hours and found herself curled up against Simon on the settee. Her hair was still wet against her face from the tears. Simon shifted beside her.

'Hey,' he said. 'I'm going to get a drink. You want anything?'

Abby shook her head and watched him walk into the kitchen. It was strange seeing him there, in her house. In Paul's house. She stood up and moved to the armchair by the window.

'This is my fault,' Abby said when Simon came back in.

Simon frowned and shook his head. 'What do you mean?'

'If I'd told the truth from the start maybe none of this would've happened.'

'Why?'

Abby felt herself stop short. She had no idea. She knew that deep inside it made no sense and yet she still felt like she was to blame for being a liar.

'Now the truth is out are they any closer to finding Beth?' Simon asked.

'No, but if I'd never been unfaithful to Paul then maybe it wouldn't have happened.'

'If you hadn't been unfaithful Beth wouldn't be here at all.'

Abby closed her eyes. 'I know that, but maybe this is some kind of punishment.'

Simon snorted. 'From who? God? Even if there'd been no us, even if Beth was Paul's, the fucker who took our daughter would've still taken her. The fuckers that hurt you –' He stopped and caught his breath. 'Nothing you did or didn't do would change the situation, Abby. Nothing. What we did has nothing to do with it.'

Abby closed her eyes. 'Maybe,' she whispered. 'But how could I have done this to him? How could I have hurt him like this?'

'People have affairs all the time,' he said. 'I'm not saying it's alright but it happens every day. And people get over it.'

'No,' Abby said. 'No. Not Paul. You don't understand. You don't know what he's been through. His parents-'

'What? They broke up? So what? Who doesn't?'

'No, it's different for him, for his family. His dad thought his mum was having an affair and tried to kill the guy,' Abby said.

'So what? You think it runs in the family? You think he's going to come after me?'

Abby stood up and went to the window. 'Don't be stupid,' she said. 'His dad went to prison. His mum killed herself a year later. Overdosed. His grandparent's brought him up.'

'So he's had a shitty life. A lot of people do.' Abby shook her head at him. 'But people don't go around deciding to have affairs because they think their husbands or wives can handle it or not. They just happen. Things just happen.'

Abby looked at Simon. He always was pragmatic. Taking the job in Hong Kong made sense for his career; they could always keep in touch. Letting Paul bring up Beth as his own made more sense; he was often away travelling. And now this – reassuring Abby that she had done nothing to hurt Beth or make things worse. Abby reached for his hand and took a deep breath.

'Did you ever regret our decision?' she asked.

'Every single day,' he said.

She hadn't expected that answer, not one so blunt anyway. Sure,

135

she knew he loved Beth and the time he spent with her, but she never actually thought he'd want to be a full-time dad. He'd never told her that he wished things were different.

'What? You thought seeing her once a fortnight was enough for me?' he said.

'But... You never said anything... We talked about it, we made the decision together. You didn't want it.'

'No, Abby, you didn't want me to.'

Abby felt a stab in her chest. Why was he telling her this now? Why hadn't he told her this before?

'But,' she said.

'*You* didn't want to leave Paul. *You* didn't want Beth to have a part-time dad. *You* thought it was better this way so I agreed. And yes, maybe I thought you were right about me not being here all the time but that didn't mean I didn't want to try.'

'But you agreed.'

'For you. For you and Beth because that's what you wanted. I love you,' he said before correcting himself. 'I loved you. I wanted what you wanted. If you'd told me you wanted for us to be a family then I'd have done it. But you chose Paul and I let you and Beth go.' Simon stood, his back turned to Abby.

Abby stood. She had no idea he felt that way. She felt nauseous, like she'd ruined another life. Maybe they were right to take Beth away from her.

Simon turned back to face her and she felt a sudden chill. She knew it was impossible. Or she thought it was but...

She took a deep breath. 'I already know the answer, but I have to ask,' she said.

Simon stepped away from her. 'What?' he said. Abby looked down at her hands and tried to find the strength to finish asking him.

'Are you asking me..? You think I took her?'

'No, I know you would never do that,' Abby said, her stomach tight.

'Then why ask me?' he said. Abby looked back at him and noticed the tears in his eyes.

'I just wanted to hear you say it. I need to hear it. I didn't know you felt like this... I just needed to be sure.'

Simon stumbled back and picked up his jacket from the chair. 'Jesus.'

'I'm sorry. I didn't mean it. I don't know why I asked. It was stupid.'

Simon walked away, opened the front door and stalked out, trying to slam it but Abby stood in the way.

'Please don't go, Simon,' she begged. 'I'm sorry.'

Simon walked to the end of the driveway and then stopped. 'Call me when you hear something,' he said wiping his face before walking away, leaving Abby alone on the doorstep.

CHAPTER THIRTY-FIVE

Gardner stood looking at the red front door of Simon's house, after knocking for a second time. He'd already spoken to Jen Harvey first thing. There was something strange about the woman. He was questioning her about the abduction of her best friend's daughter and the woman kept flirting. Sure, it could've been nerves. Some people react like that in stressful situations, but it pissed him off regardless. When she'd finally clicked that he was treating her as a potential suspect she'd gotten frosty and had basically repeated what Paul Henshaw had told him that day – what the fuck would she do with a baby? She also had no interest in Paul Henshaw whatsoever. If she was honest she thought he was a stuck-up prick and wasn't sure what she ever saw in him. She only played nice because of Abby.

He'd noticed the distinct lack of builders in the house and she explained they'd quit. Being questioned by police when all you were trying to do was earn a living apparently put some people off. He'd got contact details for them, just in case, and then left her to get on with finding replacements, saying he'd be in touch.

After a few moments he knocked on Simon's door again and then stepped back, looking up to the first-floor windows. In the larger window the curtains were closed; in the smaller a mobile with what looked like ducks hanging from it swung gently in the breeze from the window, which was slightly ajar.

Gardner shifted his attention back to the door as he heard the sound of a key turning in the lock. The door opened a crack to reveal Simon in his boxers, squinting out at the daylight.

'Mr Abbott,' Gardner said. 'Can I come in?'

Simon covered his eyes with his hand. 'Sure.' He rubbed his eyes and moved back, pulling the door wide open. As Gardner stepped into the hallway, Simon suddenly came to life. 'What's going on? Has something happened? Have you got the results?'

Gardner stood in the doorway and glanced around, listening for any sign that Beth was there. He turned back to Simon and his gut told him that he was looking at an innocent man. For starters, most kidnappers didn't answer the door half asleep and in their underwear. Simon crossed his arms across his naked chest. When it became obvious that he wasn't going to close the door and let him in properly until he knew what was going on, Gardner started to talk.

'No, there's no news yet. I just wanted to ask you a few more questions,' he said.

Simon nodded and closed the door. 'I'll just get dressed. Go through,' he said and pointed to the living room.

'You mind if I look around?' Gardner asked and Simon shrugged.

'Feel free,' he said and went back upstairs.

Gardner glanced around the hallway before following Simon. Each wall held dozens of framed photographs and Gardner wondered if they were Simon's own work or someone else's. At the top of the stairs there was one Gardner recognised, an arty picture of a street in Venice that an ex-girlfriend used to have in her bedroom. He wondered if that was an Abbott original.

The first door he came to led into the bathroom and it had no signs of a baby ever having been there; there were barely signs of anyone at all. Gardner wondered how much stuff babies would even have in the bathroom; he had no idea what they needed. He moved on to the back bedroom, which was being used as a studio. Innumerable pictures graced the walls and stood on and up against every available surface.

He was about to leave when one photo caught his eye. Abby and Beth smiled up at him from a beautifully framed picture. Beth looked maybe a couple of months old; he never could tell a baby's age. Abby looked happy; completely different to the Abby Henshaw he had seen. They say women glow when they're pregnant; he wouldn't know himself, but from the look of it they glowed afterwards too. Gardner heard Simon moving behind him and put down the photograph and left the room.

At the front of the house were two more bedrooms. In the bigger, darker room, its curtains closed to the light of the day, Simon pulled on his trousers. Gardner headed for the smaller room. The walls were painted a soft yellow, with outlines of ducks and rabbits stencilled around the tops of them. An empty cot sat in the centre of the room beneath the mobile he had seen from outside. Dozens of toys were piled up against the wall in one corner and a small set of drawers held several tiny items of clothes. Gardner wondered how often Beth stayed with Simon, how Abby would've explained it to Paul, and how Simon really felt about it. How would *he* feel if he had to step back and watch someone else bring up his child? If he had to wait weeks until he could see her? He doubted he'd feel very good about it.

He left the nursery and stood in the doorway of Simon's room. As Simon pulled back the curtains, he caught Gardner's eye.

'You manage to get any sleep?' Gardner asked.

'Couple of hours,' Simon said.

'Sorry. I should've thought. Come later in the day.'

Simon nodded and sat on the edge of the bed to put on his socks. Gardner took the opportunity to look around. This bedroom was much sparser, less personal than the other rooms. A bed with a cabinet on each side, a narrow wardrobe, a chair by the window with clothes thrown across it, and a bookcase whose shelves bent under the weight of too many books, placed haphazardly with no regard to order. Maybe that was the common link between him and Paul.

On the bedside cabinet closest to the door was a lamp with a Polaroid photo leaning against its base. Gardner leaned forward for a better look. A tired and sweaty-looking Abby held a red and wrinkled Beth. Gardner guessed that wasn't an Abbott original but would bet his life that it was one of his favourites. Simon caught him looking and picked up the photo.

'Less than an hour old,' he said, staring down at the picture. 'I didn't get to see her in person until she was nearly three weeks.' He looked back at Gardner and something flashed across his face. Gardner felt a sting of sympathy for the man and wondered just how much he regretted his decision to let Beth go.

Almost half an hour later Gardner left the house. He'd asked Simon more about his relationship with Abby and Beth and been told it was great. What Simon knew about Paul, which was the same as the day before: very little. What he knew about Jen, which was even less. He'd seen her for the first time the night before but they hadn't spoken.

And as he walked back to the car thinking that maybe his best lead was a dead end his phone rang. The results of the DNA test were back.

CHAPTER THIRTY-SIX

Abby looked at the clouds through the window. After Simon had left she'd climbed the stairs to her daughter's bedroom and sat on the floor amongst the stuffed animals feeling more alone than she had ever felt in her life. Even more than when she heard about her parents' death. She watched as the swinging cat's tail of the clock on the wall counted down the minutes until she would find out whether her daughter was dead or alive. She wondered if anyone would be there with her when she found out or if she was truly alone from now on. Was this how her life would be? An empty house surrounding an empty crib?

After a while she'd picked up the phone and called Jen.

'Why didn't you tell me?' Jen asked. 'I can't believe you didn't say a word all this time.'

'I wanted to but I couldn't,' Abby said. 'I thought because of you and Paul it'd be weird.'

'Me and Paul?' she said. 'I couldn't care less about Paul. You're my best friend. You should've told me.'

'I know,' Abby said, allowing a tear to run down her face. 'I fucked it all up. I love Paul. I really do. I didn't want to hurt him, I just... I wish I could change things.'

'I know, babe,' Jen said. 'Is he still there?'

'Paul?' Abby said.

'No, Simon. That was him, right?'

'Yes,' Abby said. 'He left. I fucked that up too. I basically accused him of taking Beth.'

'You think he did?'

'No,' Abby said. 'No. He wouldn't.'

'You want me to come over?'

Abby paused. 'No,' she said eventually. 'I'm okay.'

She looked outside. Everything seemed so still. The clouds appeared to be frozen in time and Abby was sure she was dead and sitting in a strange, empty Hell until the doorbell rang and brought her back to reality.

Abby ran downstairs hoping whoever was on the other side of the door would be the one to save her from this torture.

Abby opened the door to find Gardner standing there, looking tired, as if he hadn't shaved in days and slept in less. She let him in and hugged her arms tightly to her body as she waited for him to speak. A second, a lifetime, later, he spoke.

'We got the results back,' he said.

2010

CHAPTER THIRTY-SEVEN

Concerns grow for schoolgirl Chelsea Davies, seven, of Redcar, who has been missing for four days. Despite the efforts of over 150 police officers and dozens of volunteers from the local community, no trace of Chelsea has been found. Detectives have made door-to-door enquiries and searched over two-thousand homes and properties in the area using sniffer dogs. Over a thousand motorists have been stopped and questioned.

Last night Chelsea's mother, Jill Hoffman, made an emotional appeal for her daughter to be returned.

'I love my daughter,' Ms Hoffman said yesterday. 'I'll do anything to get her back. I'd die for her.'

Ms Hoffman raised the alarm on Wednesday night when Chelsea didn't return home. A search began, involving police from across the region, led by Detective Inspector Michael Gardner of Cleveland Police. DI Gardner, gave this comment today:

'We are very concerned for Chelsea's welfare. In cases such as this, with children or vulnerable adults, time is of the essence so we urge anyone with any information to contact Cleveland police immediately.'

DI Gardner was also in charge of the Beth Henshaw case in 2005. Beth, also from Redcar, was just eight months old when she went missing. She was never found.

Abby tossed the newspaper back where she found it on the cold stone wall. The image of Chelsea Davies was burned into her mind; she'd seen it so much over the past few days. You couldn't turn on the TV or look at a newspaper without seeing her face. When a reporter called her earlier for a comment, Abby's first reaction had been to hang up. They weren't interested in Beth; they wanted a quote about Gardner. And she wouldn't play that game. But then again... maybe they could help her. They could remind the world that her little girl existed.

She looked out across the beach at the groups of people; couples holding hands, teenagers daring each other to brave the cold North Sea; children chasing dogs chasing balls.

The sun, such as it was, was getting ready to give up for the day, along with the mums packing up the blankets and buckets and spades. She was starving, almost tempted to buy a burger from the van in the car park, but she didn't want to move until the beach had cleared. Until every face has been scanned she would keep her place and keep watching.

Abby reached into her pocket, her fingers brushing against the envelopes. She didn't need to look inside them anymore to know what they said. Not that it'd take much to memorise them anyway. They were brief, always the same. Three notes, one a year after Beth had gone, and then nothing. They stopped just like that. She didn't know what that meant.

Pulling her jacket a little tighter against the wind she squinted into the slight sandstorm. A family came towards her, the children charging ahead despite their mother's warning. Abby took in their faces, quickly dismissing the boy. His sister struggled to keep up. Abby leant back, sighing. Too old, she thought. As the boy passed Abby, the little girl cried out as she lost her balance. Hitting the ground she started to cry but her brother kept on running. Abby slid off the wall to the girl's side, pulling her up and inspecting her grazed knee.

'It's okay, sweetheart,' Abby said and pulled a tissue from her pocket to wipe sand away from the wound.

'Lauren,' the girl's mother said, coming up behind Abby. She took hold of the girl's arm and pulled her towards the car park, glancing at Abby before doing a double-take. 'I told you not to run,' the woman said and rounded up the boy, corralling them back to the car park.

Abby stood up and watched as the woman packed up her car before she and the bickering children disappeared from view. Abby turned back to the wall and pulled herself up onto it. The beach was clearing quickly. Dark clouds started to form out at sea and Abby knew there was a storm brewing.

When the last of the stragglers had gone Abby hopped down and started to walk away. About halfway home the rain started. Big, fat drops quickly formed deep puddles on the pavement. Cars splashed the dirty water from the gutter onto Abby's legs as she walked on, the hard drops stinging her face. She wiped her sleeve over her eyes uselessly, feeling desperately lonely, unable to tell if she was crying beneath the rain. She tried to remember the last time she had cried. It had been a while now. Relatively.

Turning the final corner she noticed his car outside the house. She didn't expect him to be there but part of her was glad she wouldn't have to spend another night alone. Though maybe she deserved to. She knew she was terrible company. She couldn't face the accusatory looks, the unasked questions about where she'd been and what she was thinking. Stopping, she stared down at the house that she didn't belong in. She didn't really live there. Not really. It wasn't a home. She couldn't remember feeling at home anywhere. The house she'd shared – shared happily – with her family seemed like such a distant memory she sometimes wondered if she'd imagined it.

Abby contemplated turning and walking away, finding a bed and breakfast for the night, but that wasn't a solution, not long term. Money was too tight and she knew she'd just have to come back tomorrow. After she'd sold the house to fund her campaign, he'd been there for her, offering a place to stay. At first she rented a small flat in town but barely used the place. Then came the bed-sits, B&Bs, and increasingly, his settee. Now it was home. Or as close as she was going to get. True, from time to time she needed the company of someone real but, more pragmatically, she needed a place for Beth to stay when she finally came home.

Across the street a car started, its grumbling engine shaking her from her thoughts. The car screeched as it pulled away on the wet road. Abby took a deep breath and as the rain dripped from her nose she walked towards the house.

She saw him through the window, sitting with his arm across the back of the settee. He turned and looked at her. Gave her *that* look and stood up. She walked up to the door and before she could get the key out he'd opened it. He stood and gave her an appraising look before stepping aside and letting her in.

'Hang on,' he said and ran into the kitchen before returning holding a towel. He tossed it at Abby and she dried her face and kicked off her trainers.

'Thanks,' she said. He leaned against the banister as she peeled off her jacket and jeans and dropped them in a pile on the floor by the door.

'Hi.'

Abby looked behind Simon and saw Jen standing there, a cup of coffee in her hand. 'What are you doing here?' Abby asked her.

'Well, you don't write, you don't call...' Jen smiled. 'Just thought I'd come and say hi.'

Abby looked at Simon who was staring at the floor. She suddenly felt exposed. 'I need to get a shower,' Abby said and started up the stairs.

'Wait.' Simon put his hand on hers before turning to Jen who nodded and looked for somewhere to leave her cup.

'I should be getting back,' Jen said. 'I should've called ahead.' She slipped her coat on and stood in front of Abby. 'Give me a call. We'll do something.'

Abby nodded and watched as Jen squeezed Simon's shoulder before leaving. She wanted to walk away but Simon's hand still covered hers. Standing in her underwear, she shivered and waited for him to speak. She could tell that he was weighing up the pros and cons of challenging her or just letting it go. She didn't blame him really. Sometimes she wondered herself if she'd lost it already or was just on the road to crazy. Was there any point to all this? Maybe not. But the lack of any other plan, of anything else to do, meant she just went on and on.

Finally he made a decision. 'Any luck?' he asked.

Abby shook her head and felt ridiculously grateful that he'd decided to play along. He stood up straight and moved towards her.

'You should've called me. I would've come and got you. I could've used an excuse to get her to leave,' he said with a smile.

Abby nodded and made a move to pass him to get upstairs. Instead he reached out and pulled her towards him. Abby didn't even bother to put up a fight. He kissed her on the forehead and then let her head rest against his chest, his arms warming her cold, rain-soaked body.

After a few moments he released everything but her hand. 'Go and get a shower. I'll make something to eat.'

Abby squeezed his hand and let go. Halfway up the stairs she stopped and, without turning around, she spoke. 'Simon?'

Simon looked up through the railings and waited. 'Thank you,' she said and disappeared up the staircase.

CHAPTER THIRTY-EIGHT

Abby sat on the edge of the bed, towel wrapped tightly around her. Barely noticing the water dripping from her hair down her back, she stared out of the window at the rain-drenched street and wondered how she'd got there. How had this become her life? It wasn't even a life. She felt like a ghost.

After Gardner had told her it wasn't Beth's body in the river she felt overwhelming hope that her daughter would be returned to her, safe and sound. But the weeks turned into months and months into years and finally it seemed as though everyone had given up except for her. There were times she forgot Beth was gone. She'd wake in the night thinking she could hear her crying. But when she arrived to pacify her there'd be no one there. Just another ghost.

After a few months the case was gradually given less time and resources. Other children went missing and other mothers demanded the police's attention. Abby understood that, she knew they were doing all they could, but it still hurt that no one seemed to care, that everyone had given up when it was all she thought about. She thought about the baby in the river from time to time. It had taken weeks before the mother had come forward. A young girl with drug problems, she'd found her daughter dead in her cot and panicked. The papers said people like her shouldn't be allowed to have kids. The papers said a lot of things.

She thought about Chelsea Davies' mother, how she would be feeling, if she felt as alone as Abby did. The reporter had asked if Abby had anything to say to her but what could she say? At least people were still interested in Chelsea, no one had turned away, turned against her mother yet. She could still hear the voices of those who blamed her. Who told her she was a bad mother, a whore, a liar. She still heard them, she still believed them.

She knew Gardner was still on her side. He encouraged her not to give up, but as time went on he seemed to become less hopeful. She saw it in his eyes. She knew that the case wasn't officially closed but she got the feeling that Gardner's optimism had worn away. Sometimes she thought he was reluctant to see her in case his hopelessness rubbed off on her.

She still called to give him a piece of information she thought could be relevant, still updated him every month. He always listened and took down the information, following leads even when they couldn't possibly lead anywhere. She knew for a fact he often used his own time to chase things up that his bosses would never deem worthy of on-the-clock police time. She loved him for that. He was the only one who had stuck by her. Apart from Simon, of course. Jen came and went. She had her own life to lead.

Abby listened to Simon pottering about downstairs, rattling pots and pans. They didn't have what most people would call a relationship. She couldn't imagine they ever would. They lived together. They slept together – if Abby instigated it – but those men had taken everything that day. She wasn't living, just going through the motions. She wondered if things were different, if Beth came back, would she still be here with Simon? She did love him, in a way. He'd stood by her through it all. When she'd finally given in to his offers of a place to stay he suggested moving his studio out of the second bedroom but she'd declined. His work was everything to him. His offer of Beth's room was quickly shot down too. Abby didn't want anything to be touched. She knew that if and when Beth came back she would no longer be a baby and the room, as it was, would be useless; but Abby refused to change anything, desperately hanging onto the last little reminders of her baby girl.

The door opened and Simon stood in the doorway. 'Grub's up,' he said. She looked at the clock by the bed. No wonder she was hungry.

Abby nodded and stood, throwing on some clean clothes and rubbing her hair dry. Simon stood watching and as she passed him he gently touched his fingers to her neck. She gave him a smile and he followed her downstairs.

They ate the spaghetti Bolognese and talked half-heartedly about Simon's latest trip to London. Simon dumped the dishes into the sink, grabbed the bottle of wine and glasses off the table and headed for the living room. Abby followed and gladly accepted the refill before sinking into the large armchair by the window. Simon sat on the settee, his arm stretched out along the back. He waited until Abby was settled before he started.

'So where did you go today?' he asked. Abby took a long, slow sip of wine and then lowered the glass. She was about to put it on the table but knew that she'd fidget without something to hold on to.

'The beach,' she said without looking at him.

'Busy?'

'Yeah.'

They listened to the rain pitter-patter on the window and avoided each other's eyes. A car pulled out of a drive across the road lighting up the living room briefly before the lights disappeared, the tyres screeching in the distance. Simon sighed and Abby met his eye.

'I know you think...' she started as Simon said, 'Where to tomorrow then?' They looked at each other, both unsure whether to continue. The silence hung heavy until Simon broke it.

'There's a fun-day in Locke Park tomorrow. I saw a banner as I drove past earlier,' he said.

Abby nodded. 'Yeah. I thought I might go.' She took another sip of wine and then finally put the glass down. 'Are you busy? You could come..?'

Simon looked at his feet. She knew he would say no. She knew he thought it was pointless and he was only humouring her when he asked about how she spent her days. There were times when she was out there surrounded by happy and not-so-happy families and her heart ached. She wished she could be one of those families. She wished she was there for fun. Her and Beth and... who? She had dreams of happy family Christmases and birthdays and it was always Simon who was there with her, not Paul. She tried not to let the irony of that get to her.

'You're busy. It's okay. It'll probably rain anyway,' Abby said and wondered why she was trying to sound cheerful. Why she was trying to make out like it was a normal family day out rather than a desperate search for a long-gone daughter.

'Maybe another day,' Simon said and they both pretended not to notice that he was lying.

Abby left Simon downstairs watching TV. She closed the door and opened the laptop, sitting cross-legged on the bed. As she waited for the page to load she wondered if Simon knew what she did up here. If he'd ever searched her browsing history after she'd gone out. Not that he'd find anything. She always deleted it afterwards. But he never asked what she did, why she never used the computer downstairs. Maybe he knew, maybe he was being kind.

She logged on and noticed how many new postings had been left since she last checked in. She scanned the messages, recognising the names of the writers, noticing some new ones. New members of their club. The club you never want to join.

Abby used to post messages, wanting to know that someone understood, that she wasn't alone, but she stopped when she realised nobody could understand. Maybe someone else had their daughter taken from them, but she'd never know, she'd never told them that. What if someone recognised her? She wouldn't be Gail01 anymore; she'd be Abby Henshaw, with her whole life spread across the internet. So she'd left that part out.

She'd tried other sites. There were a lot of spiritual forums, places for forgiveness, where survivors could move on. She respected that, had wondered if she should try it, but it didn't work for her. She couldn't find it in her to forgive anyone. Not yet. She'd tried the more militant sites where she could lay out her revenge fantasies and revel in suggestions from other members but in the end she was never going to get it in the real world so what was the point?

So she stuck to this one and she felt like she was part of something for a little while. She could feel for these other women, these other girls, for a few minutes before getting back to her own pain. She could feel a connection to something for once. But now she'd stopped posting, she wondered why she was still going there.

Abby scrolled through the comments and realised it was because she was hoping there'd be an answer one day. Something to make it go away. Maybe someone would tell their story and she'd recognise it as her own and have a clue to finding the fuckers that did this to her.

She closed the laptop.

She hadn't found it yet.

CHAPTER THIRTY-NINE

Abby looked to the corner, at their usual table. An elderly woman sat there with her shopping bags spread across the three extra chairs and a pile of change spread across the table. Abby looked around and spotted him at the other side of the cafe. She knew he'd already be there, he was always first to arrive.

Gardner stood when he saw her and smiled as Abby made her way over to him before they sat across from each other. Gardner already had his coffee and chocolate slice and he'd ordered her an orange juice and scone. They were nothing if not predictable.

'How are you?' he asked as she took off her jacket.

Abby nodded. 'Okay,' she said. 'You?'

He shrugged. 'Same as always.'

Abby started working on buttering her scone while he stirred sugar into his coffee. The silence was comfortable but she wished she had something to tell him, any kind of lead. She pressed her hand against her jacket pocket, a habit she couldn't break. Gardner watched her. He knew that she carried the notes around with her like some kind of talisman.

'How's Simon?' Gardner asked.

'Fine,' she said. 'He's just had a couple of photos published... somewhere.' Abby felt a twinge of guilt that she didn't remember where.

Gardner nodded as if he was impressed but Abby guessed he probably couldn't care less. Sometimes she gave Simon news about Gardner and Simon reacted the same way. He sometimes asked what she and Gardner talked about; he didn't understand their relationship. Which was okay because she didn't understand it either. It had started fifteen months after Beth had gone. She'd received the first letter in the December, three months after it'd happened. A typed note simply saying, *'She's happy. She's okay.'* Abby had taken it to Gardner and the investigation surged slightly, a tiny sliver of hope after months of nothing. But there'd been no prints, no DNA. Nothing that helped. A year later another note came. Exactly the same as the first but posted in another part of the country. Abby called Gardner and asked him to meet her at the cafe. She knew there'd be nothing on it again, nothing to help her, but she wanted answers, wanted someone to talk to. A few months later she'd seen a girl she thought was Beth and had again called Gardner asking to meet. This evolved into a regular meeting whether there was news or not.

There were times Abby didn't want to go, when the thought of coming back with nothing was too much. But mostly she enjoyed their talks. She felt comfortable with Gardner. She felt she could trust him, could be open with him. He already knew her secrets, knew about her pain. She could tell him anything. He was a sounding board for her. God only knew what he got out of it. She'd learnt a little about him from their talks but he never really opened up.

Abby took a sip of juice. 'A reporter called me yesterday,' she said and Gardner looked up, surprised.

'Chelsea Davies?' he asked and she nodded. 'Fucking vultures,' he said and looked into his coffee.

'She wanted to know how I felt when I heard she'd gone missing. If it dredged up memories,' she said and laughed. She didn't need to hear about another missing girl to be reminded of Beth. She lived with it every day.

'What did you tell her?' he asked, still not looking at her. She knew the case was bothering him.

'Nothing,' she said and he finally looked at her and nodded.

'Best thing to do,' he said. 'They shouldn't be calling you.'

Abby nodded. She didn't tell him what the reporter had said; she didn't want to hurt him, although the newspapers had already started down that road anyway. The link between Beth and Chelsea, that Gardner was in charge of both investigations and neither girl had been found. But, Jesus, Chelsea Davies had only been gone a few days. They hadn't given him a chance. Hadn't considered the number of cases he had solved. They didn't have a real bad guy to blame so they'd blame Gardner instead. Everyone got their turn. After the initial sympathy in the days after Beth had gone they'd turned on Abby. Blamed her. Dissected her personal life and found her to be a bad mother. And then they forgot all about her and Beth and moved on to something else. But now they wanted to know about her again. Her misery could help sell a few more papers so why not?

'I thought about it though. That if I talked to her maybe people would start caring about Beth again,' she said and moved a crumb around her plate. 'It'd refresh their memories.'

Gardner stood. 'I might get another drink,' he said and walked over to the counter.

Abby wished she hadn't said anything. What was she expecting him to say? Go ahead, give them what they want? She knew he must've read the papers, known that they were questioning his competence. But if she was going to say anything to them it'd be in support of him. No, he hadn't found Beth yet. But he hadn't ever stopped trying.

CHAPTER FORTY

Abby was wrong about thinking it was going to rain. The sun was blazing and the park was swarming with children and frazzled-looking parents. Abby started making her way through the crowds and wondered how she was going to be able to take it all in. It was impossible to see even half of the kids in the tents they were so tightly packed together. She made her way to the front of one where face painting was taking place. A small, shy boy was being coaxed onto the stool by his dad. The unnaturally chirpy face-painter asked what he'd like to be. The boy shrugged and kept his eyes on his dad.

'What about a tiger?' the face-painter asked with a growl. The boy shrugged again. His dad stood over him with his arms crossed. 'Or a bear?' she tried, with another growl suspiciously like the tigers, before looking to his dad for help.

'Just do the tiger,' he said and looked at his watch. The woman turned to her paints and picked up a brush.

'A rabbit,' the boy said quietly.

'A rabbit?' his dad and the woman said in unison. 'You can't be a bloody rabbit,' his dad continued. 'Do the tiger,' he said to the woman.

The woman looked from the boy to his dad and then went for the orange paint. The boy sat looking down, the woman struggling to see his face well enough to get the paint on. The dad got his phone out and Abby moved on. She wondered what animal Beth would've chosen. She could hear a Punch and Judy show going on somewhere behind her. She'd always found them creepy and decided that she'd never take Beth to one of those then wondered if that made her like the man at the face-painting stall, deciding what his son could and couldn't do. If Beth wanted to see Punch and Judy, she could.

Making her way towards the ice cream van she sat on the bench opposite. It was a good vantage point. Streams of kids lined up under the watchful eyes of their parents. Abby took them all in, judging them by sex and age, those that met the first few requirements were scrutinised more carefully. Occasionally she wondered if the other parents were aware of her watching. She often worried that the police would be called and she'd be hauled off and told she wasn't allowed within two hundred yards of any school, playground or anywhere else kids might be, but so far no one seemed moved by her presence. No one ever really seemed to notice her at all anymore. Not like they used to. They were too caught up in their own lives to notice that Abby's had fallen apart.

Beside her, two women plonked themselves down, waving three children off towards the ice cream van. One lit a cigarette and as the smoke drifted, the other got up and swapped sides. The smoker shouted at her oldest to keep hold of the youngest and he grudgingly obliged, grabbing hold of his sister's arm and dragging her behind him sulkily. The women exchanged glances and rolled their eyes. Abby tried to smile and got up and walked on. As she made her way through the crowd surrounding a food stand she tried to take in the faces of the kids but they were too close together, too many to process.

Abby squeezed past. A young woman with bright red hair approached her, looking bored. She held out a flyer and said, 'You should go,' before moving on.

Abby looked down at the flyer. A performance of *Wind in the Willows* the next day. It was worth a try. She smiled, tears forming in her eyes, thinking it was exactly the type of thing she would've taken Beth to. Abby wondered if Beth would be the clever, happy, outgoing little girl that lived in her imagination or if she was sad and withdrawn like the unhappy boy in the face-painting tent. She touched the envelope in her pocket.

She's happy. She's okay.

Abby went to put the flyer in her pocket when something stopped her. There was something written on the other side, the ink had pressed through. She turned it over.

She'll be there.

Abby's breath caught in her chest. She looked around for the girl who'd handed her the flyer but could no longer see her through the mess of people. She started to push through the queue for the food stand, ignoring people's complaints.

She squeezed through to the other side but she couldn't see the girl's red hair anywhere. She spun around searching for her.

Nothing.

She looked back at the flyer. *She'll be there.* That wasn't a coincidence. She closed her eyes. The girl didn't have any more flyers with her. She only gave one to Abby, she was sure of it.

She needed to find her.

Abby started running through the park, eyes scanning the faces. She slowed down and started asking people if they'd seen her, the girl with the red hair.

When she'd reached the other side of the park she stopped, sitting down on a bench. Who was she? How did she know where Beth was?

Abby felt tears stinging her eyes; her mind was racing trying to process it. So she didn't know who the girl was. Did that matter? She'd basically told her that Beth would be there tomorrow. She knew what she needed to do. Be there. If Beth was there, if she'd found her, did it matter who the girl was?

She looked at the flyer again and then pulled out the envelope, battered and curled from years of being kept in her pocket. She wondered if it was from the same person. If the girl had sent the notes to her.

Maybe she should call Gardner, let him know what'd happened. As she went to take her phone out of her bag it started to ring. She looked at the screen. Simon.

'Hi,' she said and wondered whether she should tell him. She wanted to. She wanted him to be there when she found Beth. But she knew he wouldn't believe her, would think she was crazy, imagining things she wanted to believe were true.

'Hi,' he said. 'I'm on my way home, just wondered if you wanted a lift back.' He paused. 'If you're done.'

Abby thought about it. Usually she'd have said no. She wasn't done. She wouldn't leave until everyone else had gone. Until every face had been seen. But there was no reason for that today. She knew Beth wasn't there. She would be there tomorrow. And maybe tomorrow she would get her daughter back.

CHAPTER FORTY-ONE

'I saw Gardner today,' Abby said as they drove home, her hand touching the flyer in her pocket.

'Yeah?' Simon said and glanced briefly in her direction but didn't meet her eye.

'Yeah,' Abby said. 'He asked after you.' She waited for Simon to say something but after a while she realised he wasn't going to and carried on. 'I told him about that reporter.'

'What reporter?' he asked and Abby tried to recall whether she'd told Simon or not.

'Some reporter called me and asked for a comment. About that girl, Chelsea.'

'Just called you out of the blue?'

Abby nodded.

'And? Did you tell him to go fuck himself?' Simon said.

Abby looked at him and wondered why no one else thought it was a good thing that the media were interested again.

'No,' she said. 'I didn't say anything. She was after a quote about Gardner.'

This time Simon looked at her properly. 'And?' he said.

'And I didn't say anything,' she said. 'She was basically making connections about the fact that they haven't found Chelsea yet and...' Abby paused, her hand still on the flyer in her pocket. 'She was after some bitterness, or blame or something.'

Abby looked at Simon but he still didn't speak. 'What?' she said. 'You think they're right? That this is his fault?' Simon glanced in the side mirror. 'You think he hasn't done his job properly?' Abby asked, turning in her seat to face him. 'You don't think he's trying?'

'No, he's trying,' Simon said and finally looked at her. 'He's very attentive.'

Abby stared at him and felt a familiar burn in her stomach but rather than say anything she turned away from him, wanting to get home. She'd left the park feeling hopeful, that maybe tomorrow things would change, that they'd have a family again. But he was taking that away from her.

They stopped at the lights and Simon lit a cigarette. Abby wound down her window.

'Jen came by again today,' he said.

Abby turned to him. 'Why? I don't see her for months and then suddenly she's there every day?'

Simon shrugged. 'You made her leave before she got to see you yesterday.'

Abby snorted. 'Maybe it's not me she's coming to see.'

Simon pulled away from the lights and flicked ash out of the window. 'Well, it wasn't actually,' he said and Abby opened her mouth to say something but he cut her off. 'She came to ask about Paul.'

'Paul?' Abby said. 'What about him?'

'She wanted to know if you were seeing him again,' he said.

'What?' Abby said. 'Why?' Abby couldn't understand why she would ask that. She hadn't seen her husband – ex-husband – since he'd walked out the door five years earlier. Despite her many attempts to see him, Paul had avoided her completely after that day he'd left; allowing his solicitor to do all his talking for him.

'She thought she'd seen him yesterday,' he said. 'She just wondered if you were back in touch.'

'She's wondering or you're wondering?' Abby asked.

The car stopped and Abby realised they were home. Simon turned off the engine and looked at her. 'Are you?'

'No,' she said. 'And if I was I would've told you.'

'Would you?'

Abby unbuckled her seat belt. Throwing it off, she opened the door. 'Fuck you, Simon,' she said and slammed the door.

CHAPTER FORTY-TWO

Gardner climbed the stairs to his first-floor flat, his legs getting heavier with each step. It'd been a long day. They were all long days these days. Meeting Abby only made it worse. He always looked forward to their get-togethers, which made him feel guilty, but always came away feeling deflated. He'd arrive feeling like at least someone needed him, still trusted him, and then left knowing it was nothing but desperation.

He shuffled to his front door and closed it behind him, shutting out the argument his neighbours were having in the hall. He wished one of them would give in and just do whatever the other wanted – wash the dishes, take the bin out – but he knew it'd never happen. He'd been there. Anyone who'd lived with someone for more than six months had been there. But he wished one of them would just be the bigger person and shut up. His head was banging.

He checked his watch. Gone eleven. Maybe it was too late. Maybe he should do it tomorrow. He pulled his phone out of his pocket and dialled. It'd be pointless tomorrow. Just another empty gesture.

Gardner paced as the phone rang a couple of times and he wondered if it was too late.

'Hello?'

Gardner felt a twinge of disappointment. 'Hi, Dad,' he said. He could hear the TV on in the background but his dad said nothing. 'It's Michael.'

'I know.'

More silence.

'I just wanted to say happy birthday,' Gardner said. 'Sorry it's so late.'

'I'm up.'

'Right, well, just thought I'd ring and... see how you're doing. There's a card in the post,' he said and cleared his throat. 'You do anything today?'

'Like what?' his dad said.

'I don't know. Did David bring the kids?'

'Haven't seen him. Any of them.'

Gardner could hear the babble of changing channels and his dad muttering at the remote control. Some things never change. He could stay away from home for another five years and he'd still recognise his dad's grumbles.

'Anyway, what would I be doing if they did come? Having a party? Eating jelly and ice cream?' his dad said.

'Did he ring you?'

'No. Why would he? He never bothers any other time.'

Gardner sat down. David could be an absolute tosser at times. He used to get away with his selfishness with their mum. No matter how disappointed she was by his lack of visits she was always charmed into submission by David's kids. Put them on the phone for a few minutes and it absolved David of any responsibility. He doubted it worked on their dad. He wondered if Norman Gardner even cared whether he saw his kids or grandkids.

'I just thought he might've popped in,' Gardner said.

'He's probably busy,' his dad said. 'Same as you.'

They both let that hang in the air for a moment. Gardner wanted to argue that he actually was busy but somehow it didn't excuse the fact he rarely called anymore.

'I saw you on the news,' his dad said. 'Looks like you've got your hands full.'

'Yeah,' Gardner said.

'She's probably dead by now isn't she? Poor kid. Deserved better.'

Gardner bit his tongue. He knew that his dad didn't give a shit about Chelsea Davies. He probably hadn't even watched the full report. He'd have come to the same conclusion as everyone else. Michael Gardner's on the case, God help her. His dad didn't give a shit about any of the cases he'd solved, any of the people he'd helped. He just saw the failures and revelled in them. It proved his point. The police were the enemy. You were better sorting your problems out yourself. No son of his would be a pig.

'You still there?' his dad said.

'Yeah. But, look I've got to go.'

'How's Annie?'

Gardner froze. 'What?' he said.

'How's Annie?' his dad asked again, as if he was stupid.

'Dad, me and Annie haven't been together for years.'

He could hear his dad mumbling to himself. 'I know that,' he said eventually. 'I was thinking of whatshername.'

'Who?'

'The other one. The other girl you were seeing. I can't keep track.'

Gardner sat down. It'd happened half a dozen times now. The confusion and then the lies to cover it. A chimp could keep track of the girlfriends he'd had since Annie.

'Are you alright, Dad?'

'I'm fine,' he snapped. 'Thanks for ringing but I've got to go.'

'Alright. Happy birthday,' he said and listened to one last grunt from his dad before hanging up.

Gardner sat there and listened to the neighbours still going at it. He got up and headed for the fridge before turning back and finding the half-empty bottle of Southern Comfort from the cupboard. He looked at the pile of dirty dishes and doubted there was a clean glass in the place. He raised the bottle. 'Happy fucking birthday, Dad.' He took a swig and turned on the stereo. Perfect. Nick Cave.

Gardner held the bottle up to the light as the CD finished. Quiet suddenly overwhelmed him and he realised that the neighbours had stopped shouting. Maybe they're both dead, he thought. There was still a little left in the bottle. He found the lid and screwed it back on. Bedtime. He picked up his phone from the floor and stopped halfway to the bedroom. He found David's number and dialled. It was well past two in the morning. The voicemail kicked in. He should've rung the house phone. He'd wake the kids.

'David, it's Michael. I spoke to dad earlier. It's his birthday. Or it was. A few hours ago. You obviously didn't know that though or you would've been round to see him. Would've taken his grandkids to see him. Maybe even got him a card. But you obviously didn't know about it. Cause if you'd known and you didn't go and see him, that'd make you a selfish bastard. And you're not that are you, David? No, you're the perfect son with the perfect wife and the three perfect kids. Well, well fucking done on that, David. Well done.'

Gardner hung up and threw his phone on the bed before following it in.

Gardner woke up to a ringing phone. His mouth felt like a hamster had been hibernating in there. He grabbed the phone and prayed that it was work telling him all his cases had been solved. No one was missing, no one was dead, no one was in need of help. He could go back to sleep.

He looked at the screen. David. Gardner declined the call and lay there thinking he should get up. He needed to go to work. Needed to get some water and a bacon bun into him. And he needed to get a birthday card for his dad.

CHAPTER FORTY-THREE

The seating arrangements made it difficult to see anything. Despite the chaotic spread of families across the field, most of the children were facing towards the stage, eager to be entertained. Even if Abby sat at the front it would be difficult to see all the faces and her actions would be obvious, and, most probably, suspicious.

She decided to walk around the outside of the crowd on the pretence of looking for somebody, which wasn't really pretence when she thought about it. After two loops with no luck she took a position on the far side of the field nearest the exit and kept sweeping glances across the sea of faces during the performance. The sight of the children laughing and squealing with delight made Abby feel joy and pain in equal measure.

The sickly smells of toffee apples and hot dogs drifting from the various snack vans made her stomach turn.

As she half-listened to the words coming from the stage she wondered if Beth would really be there. Maybe it was a joke, a really sick joke. Or maybe she'd just read too much into that note.

She gazed at a couple of kids as they passed, one with blonde hair, one with brown. She guessed Beth would have dark hair. Both she and Simon did. But as the two girls stopped she started to wonder how she would know. How would she know when she saw Beth? Rising panic overwhelmed her. How would she know when she saw her daughter? She always assumed she'd just know, she'd feel it. She thought she'd been right before. She tried to recall what made her believe it before. What was it about those girls? But she'd been wrong those times. So what if she was staring at her daughter now and didn't know it?

Abby closed her eyes, drumming up the image of the girl she saw in her dreams. The little girl with the long hair. Somehow Abby had created this image and she was set in stone in her mind. Is that what she'd been looking for all this time? An imaginary girl?

She shook the thoughts from her mind. No. She would know her when she saw her. She would know her own daughter. And she would be here. She knew it. She just had to keep looking.

During the interval Abby got up and left her position to stretch her legs and get a reprieve from the overwhelming smell of greasy food. She hadn't slept the night before, thoughts of Beth, what would happen when she saw her, swirled around her head. She'd watched Simon sleeping and wanted to wake him, tell him that he needed to come, that they'd be getting their girl back. But she'd kept it to herself. He'd try to talk her out of it, tell her she was crazy.

She circled the field once more, her eyes scanning across the hundreds of faces, taking in each for the briefest of periods, long enough to discount them, not too long to make her conspicuous.

As she approached the back of the crowd a young woman with a small girl caught her eye. The woman was trying in vain to get the little girl to eat some candyfloss. The girl wriggled away from the woman, her face scrunched up, giggling as she fought. Abby smiled at the sight. She remembered having the same reaction to candyfloss when she was a girl. Even as a small child she couldn't believe that something with that consistency could possibly be edible.

Abby stumbled. She looked down at the outstretched legs of an unhappy-looking middle-aged man and managed to right herself before she tripped over.

'Sorry,' she said and walked around the man as he gave her a black look. She moved to the back of the crowd and kept watching the little girl fighting against the evil of candyfloss. The woman with her heaved a heavy, theatrical sigh and then started to pick bits off to eat herself. The little girl giggled again and the woman leaned over and brushed the dark hair from the girl's eyes.

Abby's heart stopped. She stepped forward a few paces, standing over the miserable man once again. Abby stared at the little girl and the rest of the world seemed to fade out. She was vaguely aware of the chatter and the presence of the crowd but they were so distant, so unimportant. All that Abby could see was the little girl.

The little girl was Beth.

CHAPTER FORTY-FOUR

Abby tried to control her breathing. She fumbled in her pocket for her phone. She had to call Simon. Or Gardner. Someone. Anyone.

As she took out her phone the performance started up again and the man behind her told her to get out of the way. Abby forced herself to move and found a spot a few feet away from the girl. The woman held her arm out and the girl snuggled up against her. Abby heard a cry escape from her mouth. The girl stared up at the stage, enthralled by Mr Toad. Abby couldn't take her eyes off her. She desperately wanted to go over and take hold of her. Hug her and never let her go.

The play seemed to go on and on. Abby shifted position and checked her watch; far more restless than the kids surrounding her.

Eventually the audience started to applaud and Abby knew this was her opportunity. She moved closer to the little girl and the woman. The woman stood up and started collecting up the remains of the picnic and the blanket. She told the girl to sweep the grass off her dress. She stood and swept her front and then, like a dog chasing its tail, she tried to clean her back. Abby laughed. The girl looked around at her and giggled back. The woman was concentrating on folding their blanket into a bag.

'Hi,' Abby said, her voice emerging as a croak. The girl looked at her and smiled. 'What's your name?'

'Casey,' the girl said. Abby felt tears sting in her eyes. She wanted to tell her, "That's not your name". But how was she to know? It wasn't her fault she'd been taken away and lied to.

'Hi, Casey,' she said. 'Did you like the show?'

Casey nodded. 'I like Mr Toad,' she said.

'Me too,' Abby said and glanced at the woman who was still shoving plastic cups and plates into a picnic basket. 'Is that your mummy, Casey?' Casey looked at the woman and shook her head. Abby felt her pulse race. She shifted her position. 'No?'

'No, that's Sara. She's my nanny.' Casey turned back to Sara and told her she needed to go to the toilet. Sara stroked Casey's hair and picked up her bags.

'Okay. Let's go,' Sara said.

As they passed Abby, Casey waved. 'Bye,' she said and Abby waved back pathetically before the tears started to fall. She'd been right. The red-haired girl wasn't something she'd conjured up; the message on the flyer wasn't her imagination. Someone wanted her to be there. Someone wanted her to know where Beth was.

But now what? All the thoughts that'd passed through her head last night, her dreams of finally finding Beth coming true, and she hadn't thought about what would happen when she did.

She watched as Sara led Casey across the field to the block of toilets and ignored the stares of people wondering why a grown woman was sitting alone in a field crying after a fairly average performance of *Wind in the Willows.*

Abby looked down to where Casey had been sitting and saw a small pink and white bag with a picture of a mouse on it. She picked it up and looked back towards the toilets. She stood and jogged across to the block. When Sara and Casey emerged she approached the woman.

'Excuse me?' Abby said and Sara turned to her. 'Did you drop this?'

Sara smiled and reached out for the bag. 'Thank you,' she said and handed it to Casey. 'Say thanks to the lady, Case.'

Casey smiled up at Abby and said, 'Thank you.'

Sara and Casey turned to walk away. Abby walked around them, blocking their path. Sara looked confused but remained smiling. 'I was just...' Abby looked down at Casey. 'What's the name of the woman you work for? Casey's mum.'

Sara's friendly expression evaporated. 'Excuse me?' she said.

'I just need to know her name.'

'I'm sorry,' Sara said and took hold of Casey's hand. As she tried to move past, Abby took hold of her arm.

'Please. Just tell me her name. It's important.'

Sara looked around for help but everyone was too busy monitoring their own brood and trying to escape the park to notice much of anything else that was happening. 'I'm sorry,' she said and pulled Casey away.

'You don't understand. I lost my little girl,' Abby said. Sara stopped and waited. 'And she...' Abby looked down at Casey. 'She looks like her. Please...'

Sara looked at Abby and swallowed.

'Someone told me she'd be here,' Abby said, fumbling in her pocket for the flyer. 'Someone gave me this,' she said, showing Sara the advert for the play. She turned it over. 'See? They said she'd be here. It was a girl with red hair.'

'I'm sorry but I can't help you,' Sara said, cutting her off. She tugged at Casey's arm and they left Abby standing alone amongst the pandemonium of parents trying to round up excited children and get them home. Abby stood helplessly and watched as Sara and Casey moved out of sight. She jumped as a small boy ran into her legs. His mother grabbed him by his sleeve and apologised to Abby. Abby stared through the woman and then suddenly took off at a run to follow Sara and Casey.

She weaved in and out of groups of people and muttered apologies as she knocked into them. As she approached the main gates she saw Sara and Casey crossing the road. Abby slowed down and followed at a distance. They got to another road and Abby hid behind a building as they looked both ways before crossing. When they'd got to the other side Abby moved away from the wall and followed. Her heart was racing. She could feel the sweat trickling down her back.

Fifteen minutes later Sara and Casey turned onto a residential street. Abby watched Sara talking on her phone and after a brief conversation she hung up and then turned around, looking straight at her. Abby stopped.

'Leave us alone,' Sara said. Abby looked down at Casey. She was no longer smiling and clung to Sara's hand. Abby felt her cheeks burning with embarrassment that she'd frightened her own child. What was she doing? She tried to think of something to say to Casey, to let her know it was okay, that she wouldn't hurt her but before she could, Sara turned and pulled Casey away, leaving Abby standing on the street. They disappeared out of view, turning down another road. Unable to control herself any longer, Abby collapsed onto a wall and cried.

Sometime later a police car pulled up.

CHAPTER FORTY-FIVE

'That her?'

Gardner looked through the glass into the interview room at Abby and nodded. She looked tired; somehow more fragile than when he'd seen her last. The old, ruddy-faced officer, Lane or Lang, he couldn't remember which, rolled his eyes.

'She said she knew you. She also said that someone had nicked her kid. She was harassing some woman and they called us.' He looked at Gardner for some sort of acknowledgement but Gardner kept his eyes on Abby. 'If you ask me, she's one sandwich short of a picnic.'

Gardner turned to the man and gave him a look which caused him to blush and look down at his shoes. 'Her daughter was abducted five years ago. She was attacked.' The old officer stared at his laces. 'She's not dangerous.' Gardner looked back at Abby. 'She's grieving,' he said, sighing. He opened the door. Lane or Lang attempted to follow him in but Gardner gave him another glare and the man cleared his throat and walked out, thinking better of it.

'I'll be out here if you need me,' he said.

Gardner shut the door with a scowl and took a seat opposite Abby. Abby looked up at him and tried her best to smile.

'Hi, Abby.' Abby just nodded in response. 'We meet again,' he said with a smile and crossed his arms, leaning on the table. It creaked under his weight. Abby shifted her eyes to her hands.

'I saw her,' she said, her voice barely a whisper. Gardner decided to let her talk. 'I can't believe that after all this time, all the time I spent... and now I've found her.' Abby looked up at Gardner expectantly.

He smiled back at Abby and felt a stab of guilt at what he was going to say. 'This isn't the first time you've thought you've seen her though, is it, Abby?'

Abby's smile didn't falter. 'I know. But this time I'm sure. I know it's her. I know it's Beth. Look,' she said and pulled out the flyer, pushing it towards Gardner. He looked it over and then his eyes met Abby's. 'The other side,' she said.

Gardner turned it over and looked at the writing on the back. He hated himself for thinking it, even though it was just a fleeting thought, but it was possible Abby had written it herself.

'Someone gave it to me yesterday, in the park. There was this girl with red hair,' Abby said. 'She gave it to me and said I should go. I just thought she was promoting the play but then I saw that on the back,' she said, nodding at the note. 'She wasn't handing them out to anyone else. It was meant for me.'

'She could've handed the rest out already,' Gardner said.

Abby shook her head. 'But what about that? She'll be there?' Abby took the flyer back and stared at it. 'It was meant for me. She knew Beth would be there and she wanted me to find her. And I did.'

'How did you know it was Beth?' he asked.

'I just knew. I saw her and I just knew.' Gardner's face was impassive. 'She reminded me of myself when I was a kid. She was just like I imagined she would be.' Tears ran down Abby's cheeks but she smiled. 'She was so beautiful. And smart. She seemed really smart.' Abby started laughing.

'You weren't sure the last time? Or the time before that?'

Gradually the smile faded. 'I thought I was at the time. But this is different. I know I made mistakes before but this time I just know. I know.'

'There was that girl two years ago. You swore she was Beth. You thought she looked like her.'

'I was wrong then. But I'm sure now.'

'Or the one before that. That girl in Scotland. What about her?'

'So I made mistakes.'

'There've been others. How many times?'

'Alright,' Abby said. 'Stop. Please.' She wiped her nose and took a few breaths. 'I know it's hard to believe and I know you have no reason to trust me this time but... I know it was her. This time, I really know. I can feel it. Why would she give me that if it wasn't Beth? Please, believe me. Please.'

Gardner looked away. He couldn't take the pleading look in her eyes. Despite knowing this was another false alarm, he couldn't bear to tell Abby to stop. The note was odd, and if you took it as Abby had it could mean something, but it didn't prove anything.

'Did you recognise the girl who gave it to you?' he asked, pointing at the flyer.

Abby shook her head. 'No. I tried to find her again but she'd gone.' She looked at Gardner, a light behind her eyes. 'But that doesn't matter now, does it? We've found Beth, we don't need her.'

Gardner blew out a breath. Though he'd been involved in dozens of cases since Abby's, many as traumatic, Abby's had never left him. Maybe that was his own fault, for indulging her, for giving her so much time, for listening every time she thought she'd found her daughter. He wanted Abby to get her daughter back, he really did, but it'd been five years and any hope he'd ever had had dwindled down to almost nothing now. He knew Abby would never stop, he knew this was her life, and as sad as that was, he knew it was all she could do. But how much encouragement could he give her? How much false hope was it fair to give? Maybe he'd been hurting her more than helping.

He looked back to Abby. Her head rested on her hands, elbows on the table. She almost looked as though she was praying. If only that would help.

'The nanny said you were harassing them,' Gardner said, breaking the silence.

'No, I wasn't. I swear. I just wanted to know her name.'

'The little girl?'

'No. The woman who has her,' she said. 'The one pretending to be her mother.'

'And what were you planning to do if you found out?'

Abby shrugged. 'She called her Casey.' She looked Gardner in the eye. 'She's not Casey. She doesn't even look like a Casey.'

Gardner stroked his chin with his fingers. He had no doubt in his mind that Abby truly believed that the little girl she'd seen was her daughter. Just as he knew that she'd truly believed it in the past. The flyer and the note only added to her conviction. He knew she would never do anything stupid, would never hurt the children she became attached to. He was more concerned with Abby herself, her mental wellbeing.

'She looked happy,' Abby said. 'Beth. She looked happy. So that's good, isn't it?'

Gardner forced a smile. 'Yes. It's good.' He waited for Abby to meet his eye again. Under the table his foot tapped and he made a conscious effort to stop it. 'This little girl. You don't want to upset her do you, Abby?'

Abby looked confused. 'No. Of course I don't. Why would I?'

'If she's happy. If you cause problems, follow them—'

'I wouldn't hurt her!' Abby said and pushed back in her chair. 'I just want her back. I just want my daughter back.'

'I know.' Gardner reached out for Abby's hand. 'I know you do. And I want that too. But we don't know that Casey is your daughter. You have no proof, no reason to think it's her.'

'I know she is though. The note proves it. It said she'd be there.'

'Abby, listen to me.'

'If you just go there and see her. You can do tests can't you? You can get proof.'

'Abby.'

'Please. Please. I need her back. I need...' Abby's voice dissolved into tears.

'I know. I know,' Gardner said and stroked the back of Abby's hand. After a few minutes Abby was silent again, her hair covering her face, but Gardner still saw the tears drip onto the tabletop. He heard the door open behind him and then close after a muttered apology. Gardner let go of Abby's hand. He wished there was something he could do or say to help her. 'Can I call Simon for you?' he asked. It was the best he could do.

Abby wiped her eyes and seemed to be considering her options. Finally she nodded.

He left the room and took out his phone and after several rings Simon picked up. Gardner told him what had happened and waited while Simon took it in, all the while listening to his calm, deep breaths. He sensed that Simon had been expecting this call for a long time.

'Is she alright?' he asked eventually.

Gardner wondered how best to put it. 'Not really,' he said. 'She's shaken up. She looks exhausted.'

Simon sighed at the other end of the phone. 'I'm in Leeds, working. It'll be an hour or so before I can get there.'

'I can take her home.'

Simon sighed again. 'Thanks, I'm on my way.'

Gardner hung up and went back in to Abby, taking his seat again.

'He's on his way back,' he said and Abby nodded. 'I can drive you home.'

'What's going to happen?' Abby asked.

Gardner took a deep breath. 'I don't think the woman is pressing any charges,' he said, avoiding what Abby really wanted to know.

'So you're not going to look into it?'

Gardner cleared his throat and looked at everything but Abby. 'To be honest, there's not much I can do. Can I keep this?' he said holding up the flyer. 'I can check for prints.' He shrugged. 'Even if we find this girl, I doubt it'd help.'

'What about the woman who has her? That's who you need to talk to.'

Gardner rubbed his eyes, knowing he'd be crossing a line. 'I can find out who she is. I can talk to her, maybe, but that's it. We need evidence.'

'But she's not going to admit it is she? How can I get evidence if you don't do something?'

Gardner felt his foot beginning to tap and leant back in his chair. 'I'm sorry, Abby, but I can't just go accusing people of things. I can't just walk in there and demand a DNA test,' he said and sighed. 'I'll try to talk to her. That's all I can do.'

CHAPTER FORTY-SIX

Abby opened the front door and Gardner followed her inside, wiping his feet on the mat. Abby walked through to the living room and turned to Gardner, wrapping her arms around herself.

'You don't need to stay,' she said.

Gardner shrugged. 'I don't mind.'

Abby walked past him, towards the kitchen. 'I'll make some coffee then,' she said and left him standing alone. She took her time making the drinks. She couldn't stand to go back in and make small talk. On the drive home Gardner had avoided mentioning what had happened. He asked whether she wanted to get something to eat; whether she'd found it colder today than yesterday; and finally if she'd heard the news

– someone had been stabbed in the twenty-four-hour garage around the corner the night before. She'd answered no to everything and was glad that the drive home was short for her sake as well as Gardner's. She wasn't sure he could come up with any more small talk or that she could be bothered to reply.

They'd said all they could say. He didn't believe her, didn't think that little girl was Beth. But how could he know? He hadn't even seen her. And how could he not think the flyer was relevant? So she'd been wrong before, she'd been convinced that she'd found Beth and been wrong. But this time she knew without a doubt. With or without the flyer she knew this time.

When she could no longer avoid it, she carried the mugs into the living room and handed one to Gardner. He nodded his thanks and they sat in silence. From time to time he pulled his mobile out and checked it.

Forty minutes later they heard the door and Gardner stood, mug still in hand. Simon walked in and looked at them both.

'You alright?' he asked Abby and she nodded. He walked over and pulled her towards him, embracing her briefly, until he pulled back and looked at her, his hands either side of her face. He said nothing but looked over his shoulder at Gardner.

'Thanks,' Simon said. Gardner nodded in acknowledgement and put his mug down on the table.

'I'll leave you to it,' he said.

Abby squeezed Simon's hand and then followed Gardner to the front door. She wanted to say something but didn't know what.

'I'll do what I can, Abby,' he said and then turned to leave. Abby watched him get into his car and drive away and then closed the door.

Abby came back into the living room and dropped into the chair, staring vacantly at her feet. Simon sat opposite her. 'You want to tell me what happened?' he asked.

'He didn't tell you?'

Simon let out a breath. 'He said you were harassing someone. A woman and her kid.'

Abby looked up at him. 'It was the nanny. Beth's nanny.' Simon let out a humourless laugh. 'It was her, Simon. It was Beth.'

'Okay.'

'It was Beth!'

'Okay.'

'It was our daughter!'

Simon looked at Abby, eyes narrowing. The words *our daughter* made him stop cold. Sometimes he felt like Abby thought he didn't care as much as she did. That he was over it and was happy to live his life without Beth. It was true that he managed to function day to day better than she did. He hadn't allowed Beth's disappearance to take over his whole life, like she had. He still worked. He still slept most nights. He still ate at least two meals a day. But it wasn't because he didn't care. He would've given anything to have his daughter back.

There were days when work was too much. Sometimes he'd photograph kids and his heart would break. At night he'd lie awake wondering where Beth was and why he wasn't out on the streets knocking on every door to find her. She'd come into his mind mid-meal and his throat would close and he'd have to walk away from the table. Sometimes he'd wonder what would happen if Abby were to fall pregnant again. Would she be happy? Would another baby ever replace Beth? Would it give her purpose? Or would she just fall apart even further?

He never told Abby any of this. He kept the illusion that he was strong and in control because one of them needed to be. It broke his heart to see Abby this way.

'It was our daughter,' Abby said again.

'How do you know?'

'Someone gave me a flyer yesterday,' she said, reaching into her pocket before remembering Gardner took it. 'This girl gave it to me, told me to be there, at the play, and then written on the back it said,

186

"She'll be there". You don't think that means something?'

'It does if you want it to,' he said.

Abby screamed in frustration. 'I'm not making this up. Why would I?'

'I didn't say you made it up. But being told to go to a play doesn't mean anything. She probably told loads of people they should be there. It's her job.'

'She didn't give one to anyone else,' Abby said.

'How do you know that? You could've been the last person she gave one to.'

Abby stood and dragged her fingers through her hair. 'God, you sound like Gardner.'

'Because it's probably true,' Simon said. 'You're giving it meaning because you want it to mean something.'

'No,' Abby said. 'I'm not. What about the note. It said she'd be there. And then she was. That's not a coincidence.'

'It is if the girl isn't Beth.'

'But it is her.'

'You don't know its Beth. You want to believe it because you were told to go there. You want it to mean something so all this fucking about isn't for nothing.'

Abby slapped him. 'Fuck you,' she said before walking out.

Simon rubbed his face where it stung and turned to follow her. 'I'm sorry,' he said and he heard the back door slam. Simon went through to the kitchen and looked out of the window. Abby stood at the end of the garden, her hands braced against the fence. He reached out for the door handle but let his hand drop back to his side. Leaning back against the worktop, Simon closed his eyes. Feeling in control again he lit a cigarette and levered himself up onto the worktop to watch over her until she was ready to come back.

CHAPTER FORTY-SEVEN

Gardner dumped the files onto the dining room table and watched as they slid off, one by one. He knew he should get on with it straightaway, but it had been a long day and seeing Abby hadn't helped. Nor had the promise he'd made her. Why did he say he'd talk to this woman? He had enough on his plate without going on wild goose chases and upsetting people by making suggestions that they might've stolen a child five years ago. He looked at the files and then turned and went into the kitchen, grabbing a beer from the fridge. He wanted to take the drink to the settee but the guilt was too much so he took it to the table and started to flick through the first of hundreds of pages of documents.

Chelsea Davies had been missing almost a week now. She'd been sent to the corner shop for a bottle of milk at four thirty p.m. When she hadn't returned after half an hour her mother, Jill Hoffman, became angry, thinking she must have met up with one of her friends and gone off to play. It wouldn't be the first time she'd done it; she was good at not doing as she was told. So Jill sent her son, nine-year-old Peter, to get the milk instead. It was only at nine p.m. that night that Jill realised Chelsea still hadn't come home. Jill was a single mother with five kids; she couldn't keep track of them all of the time. She'd called Chelsea on her mobile but it was switched off.

Leaving Peter in charge, Jill went out to look for her daughter. She called at as many of her friends as possible and asked some of the other parents to ring around. The corner shop was now closed so she was unable to find out if Chelsea had ever got there. At eleven p.m. Jill got home, hoping her daughter might be there when she arrived. When she discovered she wasn't, she called the police. A search began that night. Not one witness had come forward saying they had seen Chelsea leave the house that afternoon, nor had she been seen in the shop. No one had seen anything suspicious. No one had seen anything at all.

An appeal was made and Jill begged for her daughter to be brought back. She offered everything she had if only her daughter was returned to her. The local community started a collection to help bring Chelsea home.

The papers were loving it. It hadn't taken them long to dredge up Abby's case and compare it to the new one; suggesting Chelsea might never come home. She'd been gone five days. Beth had been gone five years. But it sold papers, something he knew all too well. Something his boss knew all too well. He'd been told in no uncertain terms to find Chelsea. They couldn't deal with the embarrassment of another high-profile unsolved case. Especially one with a missing kid. He was glad Atherton cared so much about the girls.

Gardner read through all the statements again. None of them were useful. He took another swig of beer and closed the folder. The investigation was at a dead end, he could feel it. It had barely begun but he just knew it. Though everyone reacts differently to stress and trauma, there was something about Jill Hoffman that bothered him. He couldn't say what. Or maybe he could, but his middle-class guilt stopped him. So what if the woman had five kids under the age of ten and all by different fathers? Middle-class families were rarely better in his experience. True, he'd bristled at the way she swore at her kids, and the state of the house made his skin crawl. But that's what poverty does. He couldn't blame Jill Hoffman for not being as well off as he was; it didn't make her a bad person. So what was it? Why did she bother him? Why couldn't he shake this feeling that something wasn't right?

He knew he should be focusing his attention on the Chelsea Davies case but he couldn't help thinking about Abby and what she'd said. What if she was right? What if one day, by some kind of miracle, she actually found her daughter, and he didn't listen to her? How could he live with himself?

Gardner drained the bottle of beer and stood to get another. As he walked into the kitchen he thought about Abby and Jill, about how different they were. He leaned against the fridge. It was his job to get these kids home and find out who was responsible for them being taken away. That was it. The rest didn't matter.

He took out another bottle and walked back to the table. He was going to find Chelsea Davies and get her back to her mother. What happened before or after that wasn't his concern. And he would help Abby. He would look into this woman she believed had her daughter. And he would look into the next one and the one after that. That was his job.

He sat down again and started re-reading the statements before noticing his dad's birthday card on the table, still unwritten.

CHAPTER FORTY-EIGHT

Abby came through the back door, stopping when she saw Simon perched on the worktop. They looked at each other for a while and then Abby closed the door. Simon slipped down and crossed the floor to Abby. He pulled her into an embrace and kissed the top of her head.

'I'm sorry,' he said. 'I shouldn't have said that.' Abby said nothing. 'But we need to talk.'

Leading Abby to the kitchen table he pulled out a chair for her and sat opposite, looking her over. Her hair was lank, her eyes sunken and dull. The clothes hung from her slight frame, making her look like a child dressed up in her mother's clothes. 'You're making yourself ill,' he said. Abby kept eye contact but said nothing. 'You can't keep on like this.

You can't spend the rest of your life like this.'

Abby shrugged. 'Like what?'

Simon let out a sigh and waved his hand in front of Abby. 'Like this. You don't eat properly. You barely sleep. You look like shit.'

'Well I'm sorry I repulse you but I've got more important things to worry about.'

Simon rubbed his eyes. 'You know what I mean. If you can't take care of yourself how would you ever take care of Beth?'

Abby looked at him like he'd slapped her this time. 'Fuck you,' she said, the chair groaning on the lino as she stood up to leave.

'I'm sorry,' he said, catching her arm. 'Please. Sit down.' Abby sat, staring past his head. 'I want Beth back as much as you do. I know you don't believe that, but I do.' Abby fidgeted with the buttons on her shirt. 'It's been five years, Abby. Five years.'

'So you think I should give up? Forget about her?'

'No. That's not what I'm saying. You shouldn't give up hope. But maybe it's time to stop with this.'

'With what?'

'With this charade. Pretending that it helps to go out there every day. It doesn't help. It doesn't help find Beth and it doesn't help you.'

'How do you know what helps?'

'Well does it?' Simon shifted himself into her eyeline, forcing Abby to look at him. The defiance drained from her face.

'What else am I supposed to do?' she asked.

'Move on,' he said and tightened his grip on her when she started to pull away. 'I'm not saying give up. I'm not saying forget about her. But you need to move on and start living again.'

'I can't.'

'Why not? Because you feel guilty? Because you think people will assume you don't care about Beth anymore? Do you think Beth will think that?'

Abby nodded through her tears. 'I need to know that I did everything. That I never gave up on her. I need her to know that.'

Simon cupped her face. 'You have done everything. I know that. Everyone knows that. And I think you know it too.'

'What about Beth? Does she know?'

Simon averted his eyes. There was no answer for that. He could tell her what she already knew but was unwilling to admit. Beth probably never knew that Abby even existed; that her real mother was out there searching for her. She never would.

They sat there for a long time, not speaking. When it finally became too dark to see Abby's face clearly, Simon made a move, certain that the conversation was over and his wish for a semi-normal life would never come true. At least not any time soon.

He released Abby's hand and stood. At first he was unsure who was speaking. Her voice was low but firmer and surer than it had been in a long time.

'Come and see her with me,' she said.

Simon froze. As he became used to the dark he could make out her eyes in the dingy light. They were no longer wet with tears but exhibiting a spark that had been long missing.

'Come and see for yourself. If you don't think that that little girl is Beth then I'll stop. I'll do whatever you want.'

'Abby–'

'Just look at her. If you can tell me truthfully it's not her, I'll stop. I promise.'

Simon sat again and studied her face as best he could in the dim light. 'How? How will you find her again?'

Abby sat forward. 'The street they turned onto was a dead end. They must live around there.'

'Maybe she was just trying to lose you,' Simon said.

'No, she must've lived in that area. If we go and wait we'll see her.'

Simon sighed. 'We can't just start following her again. You'll end up in bloody prison.'

'I'm not saying we follow them, I'm saying we just go there and you take a look for yourself. That's it.'

Simon leaned back in his chair and considered her proposal. He knew it was ridiculous and wasn't even sure he believed her promise of giving up. But if it was the only option he had to help her, then he'd have to go along with it. 'So if I think it's not Beth, you're just going to stop searching?' Abby nodded. 'And if I do think it's her?'

Abby smiled. 'Then we've found her.'

CHAPTER FORTY-NINE

Abby was waiting for Simon to come back from the studio. He said he'd be half an hour but it'd been almost forty minutes and she was itching to go. Maybe he wasn't coming back, and had no intention of going with her to see Beth. She couldn't understand why he didn't feel the excitement she felt, that they could actually be getting their daughter back.

The doorbell rang and Abby jumped up, thinking he'd forgotten his keys. She opened the door and found Jen standing there.

'Hey, babe,' Jen said and leaned forward to hug Abby. Abby moved out of the way to let Jen in and closed the door. Jen walked straight through to the living room and Abby slowly followed. 'Is this a good time?' Jen asked.

'Actually—' Abby started.

'It's been ages since we talked properly,' Jen said. 'I keep missing you.' Jen sat down and kicked off her impossibly high heels. Abby stayed by the door. Jen patted the seat beside her. 'I've got so much to tell you. I've got a new publisher. It's so exciting. I think this guy actually really likes my work. And he says I'll be his number one priority.'

'Great,' Abby said, still standing.

'And I've got something to show you. Where's your laptop? Paul's set up this website selling books but he also promotes writers he likes, so I'm thinking,' she said, framing her face with her hands. 'Perfect, right?'

'Look, Jen, I'm just waiting for Simon. He'll be back any minute. We've got an appointment.' Abby didn't want to tell Jen about Beth. Not yet. There was a time she'd be the first person she'd call about anything, big or small. But now?

'Oh,' Jen said. 'No problem, we can do it another time.'

The doorbell went again and Abby prayed it was Simon this time. 'Excuse me,' she said and left Jen sitting there.

Abby opened the door to Gardner and another man she'd never seen before. Her stomach tightened. 'Hi,' she said.

'Hi,' Gardner said. Abby glanced at the other man. 'Oh, this is DC Carl Harrington.'

Harrington stuck his hand out for Abby to shake. A thick, gold chain round his wrist rattled as he did. She looked at his hair as they shook hands and wondered if he'd used the full tub of gel or just most of it.

Abby looked back at Gardner and let them in. 'What's going on?' she asked.

'We were just in the area so I thought I'd pop in and let you know we checked the flyer for prints,' Gardner said, as Abby led them through to the living room. He stopped when he saw Jen. 'Sorry if we're intruding.'

'It's fine,' Jen said and stood up, slipping her heels back on. 'Can I get you anything? Tea, coffee?'

'No, thanks. It's just a flying visit,' Gardner said. 'Abby, can we?' He indicated towards the kitchen. Abby nodded and they walked away from the others.

'Did you find something?' Abby asked.

'We found some prints, two sets actually, other than yours, but nothing that matches anything in our database.'

'So what now?' Abby said.

Gardner cleared his throat. 'There's not much else we can do. We have no way of tracing this woman who gave you the note. I could contact the company who made the flyers, the promoters of the event, see if a woman with red hair works for them. But... it's a long shot. We don't even know if it's relevant.'

'But it could be,' Abby said. 'We have to try.'

Gardner nodded. 'I'll see what I can do.'

They walked back into the living room to find Jen giggling, her hand on Harrington's knee. She glanced at Gardner and moved her hand, standing up.

'I was just telling Carl about my new publishing deal,' Jen said and walked over to Gardner, putting her hand on his arm. 'I've got this great–'

'They need to go,' Abby said. No one said anything for a moment.

Finally Gardner nodded towards the door. 'Harrington,' he said and the other detective stood up.

'Nice to meet you,' he said looking at Jen, before walking towards the front door. 'Both of you,' he added as he passed Abby.

'Congratulations,' Gardner said to Jen before turning to Abby. 'I'll be in touch.' Abby went to follow him but he stopped her. 'We can let ourselves out.'

'What was that?' Jen said once the door had closed.

'What?' Abby asked.

'That!' Jen said. 'I was trying to talk to him and you practically pushed him out the door.'

'He had work to do. Important work. In case you hadn't heard there's a little girl missing. My little girl is still missing.'

Jen shook her head at Abby. 'Why are you being like this?'

Abby looked away, trying to count to ten. She got to three and turned back to her friend. 'Why did you come here? Why have you been here three times in one week when I haven't seen you for months?'

'*Because* I haven't seen you in months,' Jen said.

'But you came to see Simon, not me, the other day. Why?' Abby said. Jen looked stunned. 'You told him I was seeing Paul again. Why would you do that?'

'I never said that,' Jen said. 'I *asked* him. I thought I saw Paul the other day when I came to see you. I just wondered if you were speaking again.'

'So why didn't you ask me?' Abby said. 'I haven't seen Paul since the day he left me. Why would you go straight to Simon and say something like that?'

'You're right, I'm sorry. I should've asked you.'

'But you chose to tell Simon. It's like you're trying to get between us like you try to get between me and Gardner.'

Jen looked at her, eyes wide. 'Well, first of all, I'm sorry, I didn't realise there was a you and Gardner.'

Abby felt her face starting to burn. 'That's not what I mean and you know it. I mean he's a professional. He's trying to find my daughter and every time you see him you start fawning all over him like a teenager. It's pathetic. It's embarrassing.'

Jen looked at her with tears in her eyes and then bent down to pick up her handbag. 'Well I'm sorry I embarrass you,' she said. 'And I'm sorry I keep trying to be part of your life. I thought I saw him, that's all. It was just a mistake. A big mistake.'

Abby watched Jen stomp to the door and waited for it to slam before letting her own tears fall. Today was supposed to be a good day. She was going to find Beth. She was going to make Simon believe her. She was going to make Gardner believe her.

She wiped her face. She wasn't going to cry over Jen. She didn't deserve it.

Abby waited another hour for Simon to come home. The longer she sat there the more she thought she'd been too hard on Jen. Maybe she really did think she'd seen Paul. A while back she'd bumped into an ex-colleague in Tesco who told her she'd seen Paul with a kid. It'd hurt knowing Paul had moved on. That he'd rebuilt his life. That she wasn't a part of it anymore. Maybe Jen wasn't being malicious, wasn't trying to take Simon away from her. As long as she'd known Jen she'd flirted with anything that moved. It didn't mean she'd act on it. Maybe it was just a mistake.

And why should she care if Jen wanted to pursue Gardner? Maybe he wanted her to. He wasn't married. Didn't have a girlfriend. Why wouldn't he be interested in Jen? She was beautiful. She didn't have any baggage. What difference did it make to Abby?

CHAPTER FIFTY

Simon followed Abby's directions and parked at the end of the cul-de-sac Sara and Casey had disappeared down. The sun was slow getting started and the late-morning air was cool. A thin veil of wispy grey mist surrounded the car.

Abby sat silently, eyes focused on the small street, as she chewed on a fingernail. She'd been quiet since he came back. She was probably pissed off that he'd taken so long.

Simon leaned across the steering wheel and stifled a yawn whilst trying not to think too much about what he was doing there. He'd barely slept, the consequences of what he had agreed to playing on his mind all night. If the girl he saw wasn't Beth, would that be it? Would Abby really stop? Did he even have the right to tell her to? Maybe quitting would lead to Abby giving up on life completely. If he thought about it, her endless searching at least gave her a reason to get out of bed. Was he being naive to think she could move on just because he said she should? Pick up where she left off and get a job, live a normal life. Before she had Beth her career was everything. She loved her job, couldn't wait to get back to it. But that was then. A lifetime ago. Abby wasn't the same person, how could she be? Maybe he was just being selfish, trying to force Abby into a life that he considered normal.

But what was more frightening was the possibility he actually thought this little girl was his daughter. Then what? How would they prove it? If he agreed with Abby but they were unable to get her back, what would happen to Abby then?

And how was he supposed to know anyway? He didn't understand how Abby could be so sure about recognising her daughter. The last time they'd seen her she was just a baby, not even a year old. Was it possible to know her five years later? Maybe it was a mother's instinct. Simon worried that his lack of intuition could lead to serious consequences. If he wasn't sure, how could he say yes or no? His decision could either mean that he and Abby walked away from their own daughter or tore someone else's family apart.

What did he really want to happen today?

Abby's fidgeting in her seat shook Simon from his thoughts. The air was beginning to clear and the sun poked its head out of the clouds. A group of women with a gaggle of noisy children emerged from the street a little further down the road. The activity caused Abby to sit forward and search the group for Sara and Casey. Simon watched her, unsure of what or who to be on the lookout for. The sag of her shoulders told him everything he needed to know.

Simon wound down his window and shrugged off his jacket. He was just settling into his seat again when Abby shot forwards, eyes wide.

'That's her,' she said.

Simon sat up and followed Abby's gaze. Turning out of the cul-de-sac onto the main road, a young blonde woman walked leisurely along holding the hand of a little dark-haired girl. The girl was skipping and staring up at the woman, a grin spreading across her face. He stole a glance at Abby and noticed a single tear trickling down her face. He looked back at Sara and Casey, who were almost at the end of the road.

Without a word Simon opened the car door and got out. Abby opened her door and looked expectantly at him.

'I can't see her properly,' he said. 'I'll go after them. Wait here.'

'No,' Abby said and walked around to his side of the car. 'I want to come.'

'You can't,' he said, keeping an eye on Casey. 'If they see you, you'll get arrested.' He started to cross the road. 'Wait here, I'll call you and let you know where I am.'

Before she could argue, Simon crossed the road, following Sara and Casey, leaving Abby standing alone beside the car.

He barely noticed as Abby approached and sat down on the bench next to him. He could still see Casey twirling round and round on the roundabout but her face was a blur of movement and distance. Abby took his hand but he didn't avert his eyes to look at her. He was mesmerised by the sight of the little girl.

His head twisted around as Abby cupped his face. She wiped a tear from his cheek that he didn't even know had fallen. She was almost smiling at him.

'Well?' she asked.

Simon thought about everything that had crossed his mind the night before. He didn't want to rush into things. He made decisions with his head, not his heart. And yet the minute he'd seen that girl, he knew. He knew that he was looking at the little girl who was taken from him five years ago.

Simon looked into Abby's eyes. He opened his mouth and said, 'I don't know.'

Abby dropped her hand from his. 'What?'

Simon looked back at Casey as she jumped off the roundabout. She continued to twirl around and after several turns she fell to the floor in a giggling heap. An image of Abby drunk on cheap cider crept into his mind. Simon instinctively made a move to go to her but as Sara walked over and picked her up he stumbled back onto the bench and felt a stab of pain in his heart unlike anything he'd felt before.

He turned back to Abby and his breath caught in his chest. 'Yes,' he said. 'Yes.'

Abby reached out for him with shaking hands and stroked his hair, a smile peeking through the stream of tears like the sun through a rain-soaked window pane. Simon wrapped his arms around her and for the first time he felt like everything would work out.

Abby pulled away from Simon and turned around, leaning down and pretending to fasten her shoelace. Simon glanced to his side and saw Sara and Casey walking their way. As much as he felt he should, he just couldn't drag his eyes away from them. Grabbing his phone from his pocket he turned on the camera function and snapped a picture of Casey as she turned towards him. Sara stared obliviously ahead at the duck pond and tugged on Casey's hand, encouraging her to turn and look at the ducks and swans swimming carelessly through the muddy water.

Once they passed by, Abby turned back to Simon and followed his eyes down to the picture of Casey on his phone. She took the phone from his hand and lifted it closer to her face.

Abby and Simon walked hand in hand on the opposite side of the pond to Sara and Casey. They kept several paces behind them, but Sara never once looked their way and Casey was too concerned with distributing bread equally amongst the ducks to even notice she was the centre of their attention.

As Sara tried to lead Casey away she stopped and felt around in her jeans pocket. Pulling a phone out she answered while keeping an eye on her charge. After a brief conversation she hung up and shouted for Casey to follow her. Casey looked from Sara to the queue of ducks to the remaining bread in her hand. Making a quick decision she tore the bread into four and flung it into the water, laughing as the ducks raced to collect their prizes.

Sara and Casey headed towards the car park. Abby and Simon walked quickly in an effort to keep up. As they reached the car park a black Range Rover pulled in and Casey waved at someone unseen. Abby and Simon waited by the gate, trying to blend in with the incoming and outgoing groups of people.

Sara opened the back door of the car and ushered Casey towards it. As she did, the driver's door opened and a tall, red-haired woman stepped out. She walked around to Casey and bent down to give her a hug. Casey was speaking rapidly, probably regaling the woman with stories about ducks and swans and roundabouts. The woman smiled and stood up.

'That must be her,' Abby said.

Simon tore his eyes away from Casey and looked down at Abby. 'What?'

He followed Abby's eyes and saw she was no longer staring at Casey; instead she focused on the woman. As Casey was put into the car and the two women climbed into the front, Abby started to walk towards them. Simon pulled her back by the collar.

'Stop,' he said.

'I want to talk to her,' Abby said, trying to pull away.

'Abby, wait,' he said, his eyes still glued to the woman in the driver's seat. Abby turned and looked at him.

'What is it?' she asked.

'That woman,' he said, 'I know her.'

CHAPTER FIFTY-ONE

Gardner gave one last glance up at Marcus Davies' flat before getting in the car. It was the second time he'd spoken to Chelsea's father and he liked him even less now than before. Jill Hoffman had been adamant that he hadn't taken their daughter but only because they hadn't seen him for over four years and he didn't give a shit. Why would he want her? Jill had asked Gardner.

Why would he want her?

That got to him. Why *wouldn't* a father want his own child? He was sure she hadn't meant it that way, but to him it made Chelsea sound like a burdensome pet, or a piece of junk. But Davies' attitude was pretty much as Jill had made out. He couldn't care less about his daughter. He wasn't even aware she was missing the first time they'd visited and it didn't appear that he'd been losing much sleep since he'd been informed. He certainly didn't have her. He didn't have enough money to keep himself so why would he want a kid sucking up everything he had? Gardner left Davies' flat with no doubt that he was innocent; or innocent of abduction anyway. The man couldn't have abducted anyone; it would require half a brain cell and the drive to drag himself off the settee.

DC Harrington hadn't said a word the whole time they were there. He'd stood by the door, looking around the cramped living room in disgust. Gardner wanted to bring Lawton. He was trying to push her towards applying for the detective exam, trying to get her experience wherever she could find it, but though he had no doubt she had the intelligence and the commitment, she was still lacking in confidence. She was happy to continue knocking on doors asking old folks if they'd seen anything and listening to their life stories in return. He knew she was better than that. She could handle something bigger, Marcus Davies for example, he knew she could. *She* just didn't know it. So he was stuck with Harrington, who was actually a pretty good detective and had done some pretty good work on the case so far. Gardner just didn't like him. Couldn't say why. He just didn't.

As they drove through the estate, past the parade of boarded-up shops, Harrington wound down the window. Personally, Gardner would've waited until they were back on the main road. Less chance some kid would throw a brick at them.

'I think I'm going to need two showers after that. At least two,' Harrington said, lifting his shirt collar to his nose. 'Jesus. Maybe the kid is there.'

Gardner looked over at Harrington. 'What do you mean?'

'Maybe that's what smells so bad. The kid's rotting body,' Harrington said with a grin. Gardner didn't return it. 'What?' he said, laughing. 'It's a joke.'

'Hilarious,' Gardner said as he turned out onto the main road and finally wound down his window.

'So now what?' Harrington said.

Gardner shook his head. 'I want to speak to the mother again. See if you can get hold of Lawton. Tell her to meet me at the station.'

'Lawton,' Harrington said. 'You know, I think she's still a virgin.' Gardner resisted the urge to roll his eyes. 'She's just got that look about her, you know.'

'I think that could be construed as sexual harassment,' Gardner said.

'Not if she doesn't know about it,' Harrington grinned. Gardner just glared at him. 'Oh shit,' he said. 'You're not..? Are you?'

'No, I'm not,' Gardner said.

'Shame.' Harrington fell silent for a few blissful minutes. 'What about that blonde?'

'What blonde?' Gardner asked, his brain flicking through images of women they worked with.

'The writer. Jen.'

Gardner turned and looked at Harrington. 'What about her?'

'If you haven't already, she's well up for it. I thought I was in with a chance until you walked in, you bastard. She even gave me her number. Guess there's no accounting for taste.'

'What are you talking about?' Gardner asked, although if he was honest he had noticed it before. Every time they met she'd touched him at least once, though he wasn't convinced it was entirely personal to him. He got the impression Jen was pretty tactile, to say the least.

'Come off it,' Harrington said. 'You must've noticed.' Gardner just shrugged. 'Or is it the brunette you're interested in?'

'Abby?' Gardner said. 'I think that'd be inappropriate, don't you?'

Harrington leaned back in his seat, stretching. 'The heart wants what the heart wants. Or at least the dick does.' He grinned.

CHAPTER FIFTY-TWO

Abby and Simon watched as the car drove away. He led her back into the park and sat her down on the nearest unoccupied bench.

'Who is she?' Abby asked.

He stared at the ground for a while, unable to speak, unsure of what to say. He recognised the woman but couldn't think who she was or where he knew her from. Something about her triggered an uneasy feeling in his gut. Not just that she seemed to be posing as Beth's mother. Simon felt that he should know her, that she was significant in a way he couldn't recall.

'Simon? Who is she?' Abby said again, turning his face to look at her.

'I don't know,' he said, trying to pull a cigarette free from the pack. 'I recognise her but I can't think where from.' He rubbed his temples and closed his eyes. 'God!' He moaned in frustration. 'I know her.'

Simon looked at Abby, seeing the fear, the concern on her face, and moved closer, putting an arm around her shoulders. He wanted to say something reassuring, some innocuous words that he knew would really mean nothing but at least he would be saying something. But he couldn't do it anymore. Abby had been right all along. Her actions had been worth it after all. And sitting there by the playground less than an hour earlier he'd allowed himself to think that everything was going to be alright. That they'd work it out and Beth would be returned to them and they'd all live happily ever after. But now that feeling had evaporated and he was left with the stone-cold truth that they weren't really any closer to getting their daughter back. The fact that they'd seen her meant nothing. They had no proof, nothing to go to the police with, not really. If anything they were worse off. Now Beth was there, had been there right in front of them, but was completely out of their reach. But there was something he could do if only he could remember who that woman was.

Abby picked at the take-away with her fork but hadn't actually put anything in her mouth for more than twenty minutes. Simon had managed to eat something but she noticed that even he was struggling. Her mind was full of conflicting thoughts. On the one hand she was overjoyed that Simon had agreed with her. She wasn't going insane. Her daughter was within reach, finally. But then she knew that it wasn't that straightforward. How was she going to get Beth back? How would her little girl feel about it? She looked happy. Was Abby even right to want to take her away from that? How would Beth feel about being taken away from everything she'd ever known to be given to two people that were, to her, perfect strangers?

And then there was the woman. Ever since they'd seen her Abby hadn't been able to get her out of her mind.

Simon knew her.

She'd been pressing him, trying to jog his memory but it wasn't working and the more she pushed the more he retreated. She kept thinking about him and this woman, wondering how well they'd known each other. He wouldn't keep it from her, not something this important. But still it bothered her. She wondered if it was the thought of them together, a stupid jealousy. If only. No, what bothered her was the thought that kept sliding to the front of her mind that it was somehow Simon's fault. He knew the woman who'd stolen their daughter. If it hadn't been for him maybe she wouldn't have been taken.

She'd tried to call Gardner, keen to tell him the news and to find out the mystery woman's name; but she'd been unable to get hold of him. She wondered if he'd been to see this woman already, if he knew something Abby didn't.

Simon started clearing away the foil cartons. 'Finished?' he asked. Abby nodded, put her fork down and stood to help. They tossed the leftovers into the bin and went into the living room. Simon switched on the TV and flicked through the channels in a continuous loop. Despite having the most important event of their lives hanging over them, neither was able to talk. It was too much. Both knew the problems they faced and by keeping them inside hoped somehow they'd remain at bay.

Gardner slurped the last of his coffee in a vain attempt at staying alert. He glanced at Lawton. She hadn't said a word since they'd left Jill Hoffman's house. She was hardly talkative at the best of times, but he could understand the reason for her silence now. Hoffman was hard work. Working with anyone whose child was missing was hard, but it was more than that. Chelsea's mother seemed to resent the police at times. Maybe she thought they weren't doing enough, or she just didn't like the police anyway. Either way she was difficult, and Lawton, in her role as family liaison officer, seemed to take the brunt of it. Lawton was good at it. He'd been surprised just how good she was. She seemed to be able to bring comfort to victim's families, and usually they trusted her. But Hoffman was having none of it and he could tell Lawton was blaming herself.

'You sure you don't mind doing this?' Gardner asked.

Lawton shook her head. She hadn't asked him any questions when he'd told her he had one more stop to make. He couldn't decide whether he liked that about her or not. In this case it was probably a good thing. He knew he had no real reason to be there; that this probably had nothing to do with his case. And if you were going to be pedantic, Abby's wasn't his case, not really, not anymore. His case was the disappearance of Chelsea Davies. Yet here he was, sitting outside the house of what was most likely a normal family, an innocent family, and he was about to knock on the door and basically ask them if they'd stolen their child.

Maybe that's why he'd brought Lawton, so when these people inevitably complained about him she could back him up, explain he was just trying to prove to Abby once and for all that the girl she'd seen wasn't her daughter, that everyone's lives could go back to normal once he'd spoken to the little girl's mother.

Gardner could sense Lawton glancing his way every few seconds. 'What?' he asked.

'Sir?' Lawton said.

'You look like you've got something to say. So spit it out.'

She looked out the window towards the house. He waited for her to ask why they were there.

'You transferred from Blyth, right?' Lawton said, barely looking him in the eye.

Gardner felt the familiar twist in his gut. He didn't want to do this. Not now. And not with Lawton, of all people. He thought they had a connection. He thought she had some respect for him, maybe even looked up to him, however misguided that might be. He sighed and turned towards her. At least she had the decency to ask him directly.

'What about it?' he said.

Lawton looked down at her hands twisting on her lap. 'I just wanted to know how easy it was to move, to transfer down here.'

How easy? How could she possibly think it'd been easy?

'It's just,' she tried to make eye contact but couldn't quite do it. 'Lee's applied for this job in Birmingham and he thinks he's going to get it and that'd mean moving and I just wanted to know how it works, getting transferred.'

Gardner felt a brief moment of relief that this wasn't about him. That Lawton wasn't like the rest of them.

'You're leaving?' he said.

'No,' Lawton said. 'I don't know. He might not even get the job.'

Gardner felt a stab of sadness. He'd never really thought about it before but he'd miss Lawton if she went. They weren't really friends, didn't socialise outside of work, but of everyone he worked with she was the last person he'd want to leave. There were several others, on the other hand, he'd gladly see the back of.

'Do you want to go?'

Lawton shrugged. 'Maybe.'

'Maybe? How long have you been together?'

'Almost a year.'

Gardner was surprised. He'd never thought to ask her about her life outside of work. If he thought about it, he didn't know much about her at all.

'So what does this Lee do? What job's so important in Birmingham?'

Lawton shook her head. 'I'd rather not say.'

'Tell me.'

Lawton sighed. 'He's a motivational speaker.'

Gardner started to laugh. Lawton tried to look offended but couldn't help joining in with him.

'Don't laugh,' she said, eventually. 'He takes it really seriously.'

'I bet he does,' Gardner said, trying to compose himself. After a moment he turned serious again. 'Have you actually discussed it? Is it something you both want or does he just expect you to drop things and go with him?'

Lawton frowned. 'We've talked a bit,' she said. 'Listen, I'm not ready to pack up and leave just yet, I just wanted some advice.' She turned back to the house, clearly done talking about it.

Gardner looked down into his cup. He shouldn't have laughed at her. He took one last swig of cold coffee and tossed the paper cup onto the floor of the car with the rest before glancing over at the house.

'Ready?' he asked and Lawton nodded.

They walked across the street and Gardner knocked and waited. The door opened and a red-haired woman stood and looked at him. She ignored Lawton. She didn't ask who he was or what he wanted, she just waited. Gardner cleared his throat.

'Sorry to bother you. I'm DI Gardner,' he said, 'are you Mrs Helen Deal?'

CHAPTER FIFTY-THREE

The woman pulled her cardigan closed across her chest. 'It's Ms Deal,' she said, without altering her expression.

'I'm sorry to bother you this late but I was wondering if we could have a quick word?'

Helen finally glanced at Lawton before looking around the street. She stepped back, allowing them to enter. She looked down at Gardner's shoes as he wiped his feet on the mat. 'If you wouldn't mind taking your shoes off,' she said.

Gardner looked down at his feet and bent to do as she requested. Lawton, always prepared, slipped hers off easily. Helen stood in the doorway, leaning against the wooden frame as Gardner finally yanked off his second shoe. She led them into the living room and he noticed the pristine cream of the carpet and three-piece suite. Not that he was an expert but he didn't think light-coloured fabric and small children were a good mix. In the corner the TV talked away to itself. It took a moment for Gardner to realise that the reporter was talking about Chelsea Davies. For a second the three of them stared at the image of the little girl on the screen. Gardner looked away first and Helen switched it off before indicating that they should sit. Gardner was grateful that she hadn't slipped a plastic cover beneath him first.

'Can I get you anything?' she asked. Gardner declined and she sat down on the chair opposite him.

He looked around at the room. The decor was immaculate but the mantelpiece and every other available surface was covered in photo frames. Virtually every one displayed pictures of Casey.

When he turned back to Helen she was smiling. 'She's beautiful, isn't she?' she said.

Gardner and Lawton nodded and waited for the woman to turn her attention back to them. When that didn't happen, he reluctantly began. 'I'm sure you're aware of the incident a couple of days ago.'

'Of course,' she said turning to face him. 'Sara told me that some woman had been following them. She said her daughter had died.'

'Missing,' Gardner said.

'Oh. Well, I'm sure that's almost as bad. I couldn't imagine what I'd do if anything happened to Casey.' Gardner waited. 'She's not dangerous is she?'

'No. She's not dangerous. She's just... she never gave up looking for her daughter,' he said.

'Of course.'

'She thought that Casey looked a lot like her daughter.'

Helen shook her head. 'Poor woman.' Folding her hands she looked at the floor. 'How old was she? The girl, when she went missing?'

'Just a baby, eight months I believe,' he said although he knew precisely how old she was. 'Can I ask, do you think it's possible to recognise your own child after not seeing her for a long time? I mean if you last saw Casey when she was only a baby, would you recognise her now?'

'God forbid,' Helen said. She stared at the pictures on the table next to her and picked up the closest one. In it Casey was blowing out five candles on a birthday cake. Helen stared into the picture, eyes glazing over. Gardner thought she wasn't going to answer when finally she spoke again. 'Yes. I'd like to think I would.' She looked back at Gardner. 'But I suppose I can't be sure. I think it would probably be difficult. I imagine I'd see her face everywhere. I think everyone's a bit anxious at the moment.'

'Excuse me?' Gardner said.

Helen nodded towards the TV. 'With that girl missing. I think everyone's a bit on edge round here.'

A floorboard creaked outside the room and a small head peeked around the door. Helen's face lit up and she walked over to the little girl.

'This is Casey,' she said bending down to her. 'Casey, this is Mr Gardner. He's a policeman.' Again she ignored Lawton's presence.

Casey rubbed her eyes and smiled. 'Hello,' she said.

'Hello, Casey,' Gardner said. 'Shouldn't you be asleep?'

'I'm thirsty.'

Helen stood and smiled at Gardner. 'Excuse me,' she said and led Casey from the room. 'Come on then, let's get you some water.'

'Is he going to arrest me?' Casey said as she disappeared into the kitchen. Gardner laughed.

'Cute,' Lawton said.

Gardner stood to look at the rest of the photographs. Most of them were of Casey alone. Some showed Casey and Helen; a couple were of Casey and the nanny. One in the corner was too small for the frame. A closer look showed that the picture had been cropped. Gardner wondered if it had been Casey's father, a bitter break-up demanding he be cut out of all the family photos.

Gardner crossed to Lawton, standing by the mantelpiece. Most of the photos here were in frames but there were a few loose pictures piled at the far end of the fireplace. Gardner picked them up and flicked through. A couple were out of focus. One was obviously a couple of years old and had also been trimmed. At the bottom were three pictures of Casey when she was a newborn. One showed Casey in her crib, wrapped in a pink blanket. The other two showed Helen cradling her in her arms, looking both exhausted and ecstatic, the same look he'd seen on Abby's face in the picture at Simon's house. Gardner held them up for Lawton to see.

The floorboard squeaked behind them and they turned around. Helen was staring at the picture in his hand. Her eyes glistened and she reached out for it, stroking the image of the new baby with her thumb, mesmerised by the image. Gardner shifted his feet and broke the spell Helen was under.

'I'm sorry,' she said and wiped her eye. 'Just looking at this makes me... You'd think I'd have learned to control my emotions by now.' She clutched the picture to her chest.

'When was she born?' Gardner asked.

Helen stared at him for a few seconds before answering. 'The eleventh of November. 2004.' She crossed her arms. 'Was there anything else? I don't want to be rude but I don't really know why you're here. We're not pressing charges and it is getting late.'

'Of course,' Gardner said. 'I'm sorry to have bothered you.' He walked towards the front door, nodding for Lawton to follow, and started putting his shoes on. He could hear rustling and the sound of drawers opening and closing coming from the living room. As he finished tying up his shoes and stood, Helen came out brandishing a piece of paper. Gardner took it from her and looked down at Casey's birth certificate.

'Is that what you came for Detective Gardner?' she said.

Gardner let out a sigh. Casey Deal. Born eleventh of November 2004. Father registered as Alan Ridley. He handed the certificate back to Helen. She turned and walked back into the living room. Gardner waited for her to return but when it became clear she wasn't going to, he quietly let himself out without another word.

CHAPTER FIFTY-FOUR

Abby paced up and down the living room. Simon checked his watch. Still, the knock at the door startled them both. Simon stood but Abby was already in the hall pulling the door open.

She'd called Gardner at about six that morning. Miraculously he hadn't hung up on her but listened carefully to her frenzied, cluttered speech and promised to come by later to talk to her in person. Once she'd put the phone down Abby and Simon paced and tapped feet and pottered until he arrived.

Abby led him through into the living room and he acknowledged Simon with a slight nod of the head. Abby sat down beside Gardner and began asking questions at a mile a minute. Gardner waited for a pause in Abby's speech and then made his move.

'What made you think that the girl was your daughter?' he asked Simon.

'I don't know really,' he answered. 'I just knew.'

'She's our daughter,' Abby added, 'we know our daughter. If you saw her you'd know.'

'I've seen her,' Gardner said.

For a few brief moments the world seemed to stop. Abby and Simon looked at each other, both knowing what was going through the others mind.

'I spoke to her mother.'

'Who is she? Simon recognised her. The woman, he knows her from somewhere.'

Gardner looked at Simon, who nodded. 'I can't remember how I know her but I definitely recognised her.'

Gardner seemed to process the information but it obviously wasn't enough. He dug his fingers into his eyes, unable to look at her. 'She's not your daughter, Abby. I'm sorry.'

Abby dropped back from Gardner and shook her head. 'How do you know? How can you be sure?'

'I saw her birth certificate. I saw the pictures of her holding Casey when she was born.' He shook his head. 'I'm sorry.'

'But...' Abby looked to Simon for help. Simon just dropped his head to his hands, his eyes tightly closed.

'I am sorry,' Gardner said again.

'What was her name?' Abby asked. 'The woman, what's her name?'

'I can't tell you that, you know that.'

'But he knows her from somewhere. It might be important, it might help.'

Gardner watched Abby intently, and for a moment she thought he might relent. Instead he rose, apologised once more and left Abby and Simon sitting there, all hope lost once again.

Gardner sat in his car outside the house and leant back against the headrest. He was starting to wish he hadn't gone to Helen Deal's house. Not only was she likely to put a complaint in about him turning up and all but accusing her of child theft but now he'd left Abby broken-hearted again. He hadn't really expected that Casey would turn out to be Abby's missing daughter; he knew it was a fool's errand from the start, just like all the others, but he had to admit he was disappointed. There was no way the pictures of Helen with Casey just after she was born were faked. Lawton saw them and agreed. The way Helen had thrust her daughter's birth certificate at him was odd but then again he had all but accused her of being a criminal; what would he have done if their positions had been reversed? Helen Deal had seemed a little peculiar, a little tightly wound, but he had no doubt in his mind that the girl was in fact her own daughter.

CHAPTER FIFTY-FIVE

Abby had barely said a word since Gardner had given her the news. She left the house early in the morning, telling Simon she needed time alone, and returned hours later, red-eyed and mute. She knew Simon had guessed she'd been to see Casey again.

The deal they'd made hadn't been mentioned. She didn't know where things stood. The deal was if Simon didn't agree the little girl was Beth then she would give it up. As things stood though, Simon *had* agreed with her. It was only Gardner that disagreed and it was possible Gardner was wrong. Still, the deal wasn't mentioned so she continued.

Simon wasn't there when she'd come home. He hadn't left a note saying where he'd gone or what time he'd be back. For all she knew he'd gone away on one of his trips.

The front door opened and Abby caught a glimpse of Simon before he disappeared up the stairs. She found him in the back bedroom pulling down a box from the top of the shelves, rummaging through photos and papers. Abby stood in the doorway watching.

'I remembered,' he said, not looking up. 'I remembered who she is.'

Abby stood up straight, her mouth suddenly dry. 'Who is she?' she asked. Simon pulled out a tatty book and furiously flipped through the pages. 'Simon?' she said.

He looked up from the book. 'Her name's Helen. Helen something. I took her photo.'

Abby frowned and crouched down beside him. He was checking an appointment book from 2005 – the year Beth disappeared.

'I remember her now. She came and had portraits done. She came twice, I think,' he said, his finger tracing down the page. He stood up and looked over the shelves to the photo albums. He kept copies of lots of the photos he took, samples of what he could do for potential customers.

Abby watched him and felt her heart beating hard against her chest. If Simon could prove he knew this woman, that she had some connection to him, then surely the police would have to look more deeply into her.

Simon pulled an album off the shelf and flicked through it. When he reached the end he tossed it aside and pulled another one out. Halfway through he stopped.

'That's her,' he said.

Abby took the album from him and stared at the picture. That was her alright. The woman who drove away with her daughter. The woman who stole her daughter. Abby's fists curled into the plastic album cover.

'I remember her now,' Simon said and Abby looked up at him. 'She was really demanding, a total pain in the arse, insisted on this and that, wanted everything exactly how she said.' He took the album back from Abby and stared at the picture. 'She was weird. She asked loads of questions. She told me about her kid...' Simon closed his eyes. 'Shit,' he said.

'What?' Abby asked. 'She *does* have a daughter?' Abby felt her heart sink.

'No,' Simon shook his head. 'She had one. She told me her daughter died.'

Abby felt a chill run down her spine. 'What? When?' she asked.

Simon checked the appointments book again. 'Her appointment was in February 2005. I can't remember when she said. Maybe a few months earlier. She just kind of blurted it out. She seemed, I don't know, shocked that she'd said it. Like she wasn't used to talking about it. She'd been asking about Beth.'

'Wait,' Abby said. 'You told her about Beth?'

Simon nodded. 'I'd just seen my daughter for the first time; I was desperate to tell someone about her.'

Abby felt sick. Was that why she'd taken Beth? She'd lost her own daughter and wanted a replacement?

'I didn't think it'd matter telling a stranger,' Simon said. 'She didn't know us, didn't know about you being married.' Simon staggered back. 'Is this is my fault?'

CHAPTER FIFTY-SIX

Gardner sat at his desk, scribbling on the same patch of his notebook until the paper wore through. Chelsea Davies was still missing and he had absolutely no leads. One neighbour remembered seeing a car outside Jill Hoffman's house the afternoon Chelsea went missing but was only partly sure of the colour and had no idea of the make. She was positive that it'd been there from about lunchtime until possibly around the time Chelsea disappeared. Jill Hoffman confirmed that it'd been a friend visiting but she had left long before Chelsea came home from the park with her brother. The friend, Louise Cotton, confirmed this and a search of her house had come up empty. The girl had just vanished.

Five grand had been raised by the local community and one of the national papers had whipped up its readers into a frenzy and got the reward to thirty thousand. It had also made it clear that the police were not doing their jobs. Gardner wondered if they were right. Was he doing his job? By rights he should've been concentrating fully on the Davies case but his mind kept slipping into thoughts of Abby and the woman she believed had her daughter. Something was niggling him. Something about the woman. Simon Abbott thought he knew her but couldn't remember how. Was that it?

He tried to focus on Chelsea Davies. There had to be something he was missing.

He checked his watch and decided to pay Jill Hoffman another visit. Plenty of time to get there and speak to her again before having to face his boss. And maybe then he'd actually have something to tell him.

Simon had gone out, Abby didn't ask where. He obviously needed space. So did she. She'd dialled Gardner's number with the intention of passing on the information about Helen but had hung up before he could answer. She checked Simon's appointment book after he'd left and discovered the woman's full name. Helen Deal. Something clicked in her mind when she read it but she didn't know what. Maybe she could find a number for her, or an address. She'd gone through the phone book but the number wasn't listed. She'd tried Googling her but came up empty. She could go back to the street where she'd seen Beth and the nanny. Maybe she'd see them again, follow them home.

Gardner said he'd seen evidence that Casey was Helen's child. He'd seen pictures of her holding the baby just after she'd been born, he'd seen a birth certificate. That didn't mean anything. It didn't mean that the girl she had now was the girl in the pictures. Abby dragged her handbag across the floor and pulled out her purse. Inside was a frayed picture of Abby holding Beth minutes after she was born. Abby stroked the picture. What if she was wrong? Simon was sure about this woman; sure she'd said her daughter had died but was it possible she'd had another daughter since and this was all coincidence? That she was seeing links because she wanted to see them? Had she been mistaken again? She'd been so sure the little girl was hers. Was it just desperation?

But Simon had agreed with her, hadn't he? Could she have convinced him somehow with her own insistence?

Abby reached for the phone again and called Gardner.

Gardner pulled into the station car park and watched as the wipers tried to keep up with the rain. Turning off the engine, he sat in the car listening to the rain pelt against the windows. The visit to see Jill Hoffman had been a waste of time. He'd arrived to find her watching some American reality TV show and she'd barely taken her eyes off the screen long enough to acknowledge his presence, never mind answer any questions. He'd asked how she was coping and she'd turned and said, 'I can't talk about it. It's too hard,' and then refused to answer anything else. One of the smaller kids had come in and asked where Chelsea was and Jill looked at him, shrugged and said 'We don't know,' before looking back to the TV. The boy waddled back outside and Gardner found him playing alone in front of the house as he left. So much for having something to tell the boss.

Gardner checked his phone and discovered a message from Abby. He sighed and the phone rang, still in his hand, and he answered his boss straightaway. The meeting he was meant to be in was about to start. Gardner promised DCI Atherton he'd be there in ten minutes and hung up. He climbed out of the car and ran towards the building as the raindrops fell, fat and grey. Moving into the cigarette-littered doorway of the police station he listened to Abby's message.

'Hi, it's Abby. I'm sorry to keep hassling you about this but Simon remembered who the woman was. Her name's Helen Deal. Simon took her photograph not long before Beth was taken.' She sighed. 'He said she asked him about Beth, and she told him she'd lost her daughter. Her daughter died.' She paused again. 'And I know that doesn't mean she couldn't have had another baby but... But I thought you should know. Anyway. I guess that's it. See you...' The message cut off.

Gardner leaned against the wall and stared out across the car park.

The blackening clouds moved quickly as the wind gathered speed. Plastic bottles and wrappers spun around in circles, debris forming miniature tornadoes.

'Shit,' he said and pushed himself upright. Simon had been right. He did know Helen Deal. Obviously not well but still, it could be relevant. He looked at his watch and attempted to clear all thoughts of Abby and Simon from his head. He could always go back to Helen Deal's house later. But for now he had to keep his mind focused on other things. Keeping his job for one.

CHAPTER FIFTY-SEVEN

Helen gathered up her things and put them in a bag. Casey was busy deciding which shoes to take with her, Sara patiently letting her try each pair.

Since Sara had told her what had happened the other day Helen hadn't been able to settle. So now she was going to have to leave for a while until things blew over. She couldn't risk someone coming after Casey, couldn't risk losing another child. The story all over the news about the Davies girl was getting to her. You couldn't turn on the TV or look at a newspaper without seeing her face. And that it happened here, in Redcar, just made it worse. Is that what had started all this? Is that why that woman had suddenly come after Casey after all this time?

She went out into Casey's room and took the small suitcase from Sara's hand. Casey twirled around in front of them, giggling and holding her fairy tiara in place.

'You can go now,' Helen said to Sara. 'I'll take over with the packing.'

Sara looked at Helen, surprised. 'I don't mind staying.'

'That's okay,' Helen said. 'My things are packed. I just need to sort this little monster.' She tickled Casey, causing her to squeal, and then she walked towards the door. 'Casey, say goodbye to Sara and then choose your clothes. Don't pack too much,' she said.

Casey ran to Sara and hugged her. 'Bye, Sara,' she said and then turned to look at her wardrobe again.

'Bye, Case,' Sara said and followed Helen downstairs. 'I really don't mind staying to help.'

Helen ignored her and took some money out of her purse. 'We'll be fine,' she said, handing Sara the money. 'That's for this week and next. If you could come by and water the plants, pick up the post, and so forth.'

Sara put the money in her pocket. 'When will you be back?' she asked.

'Oh, probably a week,' Helen said. 'Depends when we outstay our welcome.'

Sara nodded. 'Well, just ring me and let me know.' She put on her jacket and walked to the door.

'I'll see you next week.'

'Okay. Have a good time,' Sara said and stepped outside. 'You too, Case,' she shouted up the stairs.

'Thank you, Sara,' Helen said and closed the door. She watched Sara disappear down the street and then checked in on Casey, telling her to choose a couple of toys to take. Leaving Casey to make a decision she carried her bag downstairs and put it by the door.

'Don't be long, Casey,' she shouted up to her daughter as she climbed the stairs. 'We're going to see Daddy.'

CHAPTER FIFTY-EIGHT

Gardner stopped outside Helen Deal's house and checked his watch. It wasn't too late to visit, though she would probably disagree. Anytime was probably a bad time for him to call again, but he needed to know if she remembered Simon. Not that that would prove anything. But Abby said that her daughter had died. It was all he'd been thinking about during the meeting. Helen's daughter had died. Yes, she'd probably had another baby, like Abby said, but wouldn't she have mentioned it when they talked about losing a child? He'd tried contacting the registry office but, of course, they were closed by the time he'd come out of the meeting with Atherton and he didn't have the energy to argue with the jobsworth on the emergency service line. He'd have to check first thing in the morning.

Gardner got out of the car and ran up the steps. There was no sound coming from the house. He knocked and waited. Leaning back he looked up at the windows. No lights were on upstairs but then it was barely dark yet. He wondered what time Casey would go to bed, what was normal for a kid that age, and looked at the window next to him. Curtains were drawn but he couldn't see any light peeking out. He knocked again, harder.

Gardner checked his watch once more, before leaning impatiently, with his hands on either side of the door. He went to knock one more time but thought better of it. There was no one home. He sighed and walked back to his car. He'd try in the morning. He was too exhausted now. Some reporter had ambushed him on his way out of the station asking him pretty much the same questions as his boss had. He'd been slightly less polite in his responses to the reporter. But he didn't care about that right now. He just wanted to go home and sleep and try not to think about Abby or Helen Deal or his boss or Chelsea Davies. He needed a full six hours and maybe then he'd be able to think straight and even come up with some answers.

As he pulled up outside his flat he glanced down at his phone, wondering why Abby hadn't checked in with him. Usually she would've been chomping at the bit, urgently needing to know what had happened, what had been said. Climbing out of the car he decided that he should enjoy the silence and take the opportunity to kick back with a much-needed beer and a proper night's rest.

Gardner chucked his jacket on the back of the settee and watched as it slid off onto the floor. He left the old files from Abby's case on the table, too tired to start looking through them tonight. He opened the fridge and ignored the unopened food, instead pulling out a bottle of beer. Opening it on the edge of the table he walked into the living room, turned on the TV and collapsed onto the settee. Too tired to reach for the remote, he let some bad sitcom play, leaned back and took a long sip. He looked around the flat. There wasn't a single photograph up in there. No family snaps from good times. He laughed to himself. What good times? He didn't have anyone in his life that he wanted on his mantelpiece. He had a few prints that could go on the walls but he'd been in the flat for almost six years now and he still hadn't finished decorating, never mind putting pictures up. He closed his eyes and listened to the TV talking to itself.

He woke with a start as tepid beer pooled in his lap. 'Shit,' he muttered and stood up, leaving the almost empty bottle on the table. Heading for the bathroom he stripped off his clothes and left them in a heap outside the door. He climbed into the shower and stood under the warm water for a long time.

CHAPTER FIFTY-NINE

Helen opened the door to the Yellow Sands Bed and Breakfast. The place was barely still standing but it would do. As long as she had Casey nothing else mattered. She approached the desk and rang the bell. An elderly man shuffled through the door, smiling as if she was the first visitor he'd had in years. Maybe this wasn't the best place to be.

'I'd like a room, please,' Helen said. 'For a week.' She wasn't sure she'd be there that long, but it was best to keep her options open. The less she had to deal with anyone, the better.

'Just for yourself?' the old man asked.

'Yes. But have you got a double room?'

'Of course,' he said and turned the guest book around for her to sign in.

Helen filled it in and paid in cash. The old man handed her a key and told her to give him a shout if she needed anything. She waited until he'd disappeared before going outside to the car and bringing Casey in.

Casey stood in the doorway of the room holding her mouse bag close to her chest. She looked up at Helen. 'I thought we were going to Daddy's house,' she said.

'We are, honey,' Helen said and led her inside.

'When?' Casey asked.

'Maybe tomorrow. I'm not sure yet.'

Casey yawned. 'I'm tired,' she said and Helen nodded. She took Casey's hand and sat her on the double bed.

'You'll have to sleep in here with me tonight, honey,' she said to Casey. 'Is that okay?'

'Will Daddy come and stay here with us?'

'I don't know, honey,' Helen said and pulled Casey's shoes off. 'But we'll go and visit him soon. Why don't you put your pyjamas on and brush your teeth?'

After Casey was asleep, Helen sat staring out across the harbour watching the ships far out at sea, dim lights on a black landscape, thinking about what to do next. She wanted to feel settled, wanted to be at home. But how could she when that woman was after her daughter? She liked it in Whitby, she'd spent a lot of time there as a child, but she'd moved back to Redcar for a reason. It's what she knew. What her family knew. This was just a place for holidaying, not for living. But she had no choice now. She couldn't go back. Not ever.

CHAPTER SIXTY

Opening his eyes, Gardner looked at the clock. Five thirty a.m. He rolled over and pulled the sheet across his body.

He stared out into the dark room, sleep escaping him, thinking he'd let Abby down. He felt as though he was letting everyone down at the moment – Abby, Chelsea, his boss. Maybe it was him. He was the weak link. The newspapers were right. He shoved the pillow behind his head. Perhaps he should stop feeling sorry for himself and just get on with it. Get on with speaking to Helen Deal again.

He knew that it may come to nothing but still, something was nagging him. And what if it came to something? Then what? What if the girl was Beth Henshaw and it was over? He tried to ignore the little voice in the back of his head that told him he'd probably never see Abby again. So what? That was irrelevant. He turned over and faced the other wall as if it would help.

Eventually he got up and went into the living room. He could start flicking through Abby's files. Maybe something would click.

The sun was just coming up as he scanned each page, unsure what he was looking for. Memories formed, inspired by the notes, some his own, some from other officers. He kept turning the pages.

And then he saw it.

'Shit,' he said.

Helen Deal. One of the witnesses from the doctor's surgery.

Helen Deal had been there. Why hadn't he remembered this before? He read through the page again. PC Cartwright had interviewed her. She'd known nothing. End of.

'Shit,' he said again and walked into his room to get dressed.

And then a jolt. His heart was thumping against his chest.

Her daughter died.

Gardner paced up and down the small patch of floor in his room.

Her daughter died.

He sat down on the end of the bed and rested his head in his hands, focusing on what Abby had said. Simon had taken her picture a few months before Beth disappeared. Helen told him that her daughter had died. When? Had she said?

He stood up again. What had Helen told him? Casey was born on the eleventh of November 2004, two months before Beth. Helen had told Simon her baby had died shortly before Beth was born. That must've been Casey. If she'd had another kid by then she would've mentioned it to Simon, wouldn't she? So even if she'd had another baby, even if she'd called her Casey too, it would've been after Beth was born. So the birth certificate Helen showed him couldn't belong to the little girl he'd seen. It wasn't possible. There was nothing in Cartwright's notes about a baby either.

'Shit,' he said and scrambled around on the floor for his clothes. In less than two minutes he was out of the front door and on his way.

Gardner checked his watch. Only just gone six forty-five. He parked across the street from Helen Deal's house and debated whether he should make a move yet.

At seven he got out and went and knocked on the front door. There was no answer. The street was empty, as you'd expect at that time of the morning. As he looked along at the surrounding houses, he noticed that each was identical. Curtains drawn upstairs and down. No lights. Even the street lights were virtually all out.

Gardner knocked again and looked at the upstairs windows of Helen's house. No signs of twitching curtains. No one checking who was calling so early in the morning.

He turned around and went back to his car and headed for the station, file in hand. Lawton was at her desk when he got there. She probably had less of a social life than he did. She looked up as he rushed through the office.

'Sir?'

'Is Cartwright in today?'

'I think so,' she said. 'What's going on?'

'I need you to do something for me,' Gardner said. If he was going to do this he should at least have concrete evidence that the little girl wasn't Casey Deal. 'I need you to contact the registry office and find out about Casey Deal. Her date of birth was 11 November 2004. I need to know when she died. It's urgent.' He started to walk away but then turned. 'And if you see Cartwright, let me know.'

Gardner pushed through the doors and started searching for Cartwright. He should've known he'd be loitering around the canteen, talking shit. He shouted him from across the room. Cartwright stood up and took his time walking over.

'Sir?' he said. 'I was just–'

'The Beth Henshaw case,' Gardner said, not caring what excuses Cartwright had for not actually doing any work. 'You interviewed Helen Deal. You remember that?'

Cartwright looked blank so Gardner thrust the file at him. 'She was in the doctor's surgery when Abby Henshaw was there. You interviewed her afterwards to eliminate her. Ringing any bells?'

'Yes,' Cartwright said, eventually. He glanced at the notes. 'Why?'

'Did she have a baby? Helen Deal?'

Cartwright shrugged. 'I don't know.'

'You can't remember or you didn't check?'

'I don't know.' He looked at the notes again. 'I asked if she'd seen anything, if she'd seen the van, if she knew Abby Henshaw. But she didn't so that was it.'

Gardner was losing patience. 'But did she have a baby? Was there a baby in the house when you questioned her?'

'I don't know. I didn't see a baby. We were sat in the kitchen, I didn't see-'

'You didn't check?'

'No, I... There was a baby's car seat in the hallway. I didn't think-' He stopped and looked at Gardner who was breathing heavily. 'What's going on?'

Gardner walked away, too angry to speak. He was furious at Cartwright. How could he have been so stupid, so incompetent? But why hadn't he checked too? Why hadn't he gone over every single witness himself?

He could've found Beth Henshaw five years ago.

CHAPTER SIXTY-ONE

A few phone calls later Lawton informed Gardner that Casey Deal died on the 15th of December 2004. Helen Deal had never had another child; at least she hadn't registered another birth.

That girl couldn't be her daughter. Abby had been right. And he'd ignored her.

Gardner sat in his car, watching Helen Deal's house. He hadn't told anyone yet. Not even Lawton. He couldn't. Not yet. He couldn't face that he'd made such a huge mistake. He needed to find Helen Deal and make things right.

Just after eight, a young blonde woman approached the house and climbed the steps. She rummaged in her bag and pulled out a set of keys.

Letting herself in she closed the door behind her. Gardner climbed out of the car, his legs stiff. He crossed the street and knocked at the door. A few moments later the woman answered it.

'Yes?' she said.

'I'm DI Gardner,' he said, showing her his warrant card. 'I'd like to speak to Helen Deal, please.' He suddenly realised how much of a mess he must look in his clothes scraped up off the floor.

The woman looked startled. 'She's not here. What's wrong?'

'You are?' he asked.

'Sara Walters. I'm her nanny.'

'Do you know where she is?'

'She's on holiday.'

Gardner felt his heart sink. He tried not to show the panic he was feeling. 'When did she go?'

'Yesterday.'

Gardner nodded. 'Do you know when she'll be back?'

Sara shrugged. 'She said next week. She wasn't exactly sure.'

Gardner sighed. 'Has Casey gone with her?'

'Of course.' Sara looked past Gardner, up and down the street. 'Is something wrong? Has something happened to Casey?'

'No,' he said. 'Can I come in?' Sara paused and then stepped back. 'Do you know where they went?'

'Devon,' she said. 'Somewhere in Devon. She has relatives there.'

'Did she leave a contact number or an address?' Gardner said, looking around.

'No. I mean, I have her mobile number.'

'Okay, I need you to give it to me.'

'I don't understand. Is she in trouble? Is it about that woman? The one who followed me and Casey? Has she done something?' Sara asked, her face creased with concern.

'Sara?' She stopped and took a breath. 'Casey's okay but I need to get hold Ms Deal as soon as possible.'

Sara nodded and bent to get her phone out of her bag. Gardner walked into the first room at the top of the stairs. It looked like a guest room. He quickly scanned the drawers and cupboard and then moved on. The next room was Casey's. It was bursting at the seams with toys and games. They hadn't cleared out when they left. He checked the wardrobe; there were a lot of empty hangers. He looked around at the rest of the room. It would be impossible to tell how much had been taken. It appeared that Casey had at least one of everything.

He moved on to what was obviously Helen's room. There were a couple of photos, possibly of her parents, but nothing compared to what he'd seen in the living room. He checked the drawers and wardrobe. Like Casey's there were a lot of spaces. Of course he couldn't know how many clothes Helen had to start with, but she obviously had money and kept up appearances. He was willing to bet that she had taken more than was necessary for a week's holiday.

He went back down the stairs and found Sara with the phone to her ear. As he approached her she held it out to him.

'It's not ringing,' she said.

Gardner took the phone and listened. He hung up and then found Helen's number in Sara's contact list and tried again himself. He rubbed his eyes and wondered what to do next. He looked up; about to tell Sara to call him if she heard from Helen, when something caught his eye. Or rather the lack of something caught his eye.

He walked past Sara into the living room. The mantelpiece and tables were completely empty.

CHAPTER SIXTY-TWO

Gardner sat outside the house and tried to rehearse his words. After several failed attempts he gave up. It didn't matter how he said it, it would sound the same in the end. He'd made a huge mistake. Abby had been right and instead of helping get her daughter back, he'd let her slip through his fingers. Abby trusted him. She put all of her hope and faith in him and he had let her down, utterly and completely.

When he could put it off no longer, he took a deep breath and walked up to the front door. Knocking three times, he prepared himself to break Abby Henshaw's heart once more.

Simon led him through to the kitchen, calling out to Abby as they approached. Abby turned around from the dishes and smiled at Gardner. The smile quickly faded as she noted the seriousness of his expression and she wiped her hands on her jeans and went over to the table. He could see her hands shaking. Simon put an arm around her shoulders and they both waited for Gardner to speak.

Clearing his throat he pulled out a chair. 'Why don't we sit down?' he said. Abby and Simon looked at each other and then sat, their legs touching.

'Did you get my message?' Abby asked. Gardner just nodded. 'Her name's Helen, right? Helen Deal?'

'Yes,' he said.

The room was quiet except for an insistent dripping tap and the white noise of normal life continuing on the street outside. Gardner wished he was anywhere but here. He wished he had something else to tell them. At least if Beth was dead it would be an ending; some closure for them. But this, it just re-opened the wounds that had never really closed, and this time poured a good helping of salt on them.

'Michael, please,' Abby said. The sound of his first name was jarring. He rarely heard it at all these days but coming from Abby it was painful. She'd only ever used it once or twice before and now he knew why. It was too personal. The barrier that his profession allowed him meant he could remain at a distance. He hadn't always achieved that but it gave him the option all the same. Now he was completely part of this family's hell and he had no choice but to see it through.

Gardner swallowed. 'I decided to go back to speak to her after I got your message. I thought maybe she remembered you too,' he said, looking at Simon. He could see Abby's hands twisting on her lap. He didn't want to tell her about Helen, about her being there that day. Not yet anyway. 'I stopped by last night but there was no answer. Then later I thought about what you'd said in your message. About her daughter dying.'

Abby and Simon looked at each other. 'And?' Simon said.

'She told me that Casey had been born in November 2004. The birth certificate verified it. Casey Deal was born then. And you were right; she died on the fifteenth of December that year. She was five weeks old.

I thought maybe she'd had another kid, like you said, that if she got pregnant again straight away, if she named her Casey too...'

'But she didn't though, did she?' Abby said.

Gardner shook his head. 'There's no record of her having another baby.' Abby gripped Simon's hand. 'I went back this morning,' Gardner continued. He could see Abby's chest rise and fall in rapid breaths. 'She's gone. Helen and Casey. They're gone.'

'Beth,' Abby muttered. 'Her name's Beth.'

Gardner looked away from Abby and Simon. He saw her stand out of the corner of his eye and the shattering sound caused him to jump. Simon tried to pull the second glass from Abby's hand but she tore away from him and released it, letting it sail into the kitchen window.

Gardner could no longer separate the sound of smashing glass from the noise emanating from Abby's throat. Simon held onto her.

'This is your fault,' Abby screamed at him. 'This is your fault. Why didn't you stop her? She took my baby and you just let her.' She pulled away from Simon and ran at Gardner, her hands swinging at his face and chest. Simon grabbed hold of Abby, forcing her arms to her sides while Gardner looked on, powerless. 'We told you it was her and you didn't listen,' she screamed at him.

Abby sunk to the floor and howled. Simon lowered himself to her side and rocked her. Gardner watched, feeling as though the last five years hadn't happened. They were back to that same place. Abby on the edge of her sanity, Beth still out of reach, and he was just as useless as he had been back then.

CHAPTER SIXTY-THREE

'Alright, try and get hold of whoever's in charge and ask if anyone fitting her description works for them. It could be tricky, we don't exactly have much to go on other than "red hair" but I suppose it makes her stand out,' Gardner said, balancing his phone on his shoulder. 'We need to know who this woman is. How she knew Beth would be there. And why she told Abby. And I want to know as soon as anyone finds anything on Helen Deal. Phone, car, anything.'

Gardner could hear someone talking to Lawton in the background. 'Are you listening?' he asked.

'Yes, sir,' she said. 'DC Harrington's here. He wants a word with you.'

Gardner sighed. 'Put him on.'

'Where are you?' Harrington asked. 'I thought we had a date with Ms Hoffman's coven.'

Gardner rubbed his eyes. He wasn't going to lie, he hadn't forgotten about Jill Hoffman's friends. He'd planned on another round of interviews with everyone in her inner circle. But what happened with Abby had changed his priorities. He knew he should've passed it on to a colleague, that his focus should've been with Chelsea, but he couldn't think about anything but Abby and how much he'd let her down. Besides, Harrington was capable of interviewing a few women.

'Something came up,' Gardner said. 'You're on your own.'

'What?'

'I'm in Manchester.'

'What for? Has there been a sighting down there?' Harington said.

'No. Just start without me. I'll speak to you later.' Gardner went to hang up.

'Wait. There's something else,' Harrington said, almost whispering. 'You know Jen, the writer.'

Gardner tried to get his brain around the leap in conversation. He had better things to be thinking about. 'What about her?'

'We went out last night.'

'And?'

'And... She's hot. I'm telling you, you should've taken your chance when you had it.'

'I've got to go,' Gardner said.

'Are you pissed off?'

'What? No. I just don't have time for this. I'll speak to you later.' Gardner hung up and then regretted it. Had he given Lawton everything she needed? He'd found out himself who ordered the flyers for the performance of *Wind in the Willows*. He just needed Lawton to find the girl with the red hair. It couldn't be that hard, could it?

He got out of the car and looked up and down the street. He didn't trust the sat-nav for one minute. He was looking for a flat but all he could see was what looked like an industrial estate. But the robotic woman kept insisting he'd arrived at his destination so he parked at the kerb and got out. The looming buildings blocked out any sunlight there was and the place was eerily quiet. It wasn't an industrial estate. It was an abandoned industrial estate.

After a couple of minutes of wandering about he noticed a door with four buzzers. He walked up to have a look; maybe someone could give him directions. And then he saw the name on the third plate. Ridley.

This was it. Gardner pressed the buzzer and waited for a reply. After a few seconds a man answered, a well-spoken voice that he recognised from their phone conversation. The door clicked and Gardner went in, ignoring the ancient-looking lift, taking the stairs instead.

He'd gone to a lot of trouble tracking down the man he was about to meet. Had called in a lot of favours, and owed a lot of pints in return for the dozens of calls made by his colleagues. But it was worth it. He'd finally managed to track down the one person who might be able to shed some light on Helen Deal. Since he'd left the house after breaking the news to Abby he'd barely stopped. He was going to find Helen Deal if it was the last thing he did.

Gardner went to knock on the door to the flat but it opened before he had a chance, and the man in front of him held out his hand. 'DI Gardner, come in,' he said. 'I'm Alan Ridley.'

The man was older than Gardner expected. His hair, though still thick, was grey and he moved with the stiffness of a man who'd been around a long time. He tried to work out his age. Maybe mid-sixties? Almost twice Helen's age anyway.

Ridley let Gardner in and led him across the open-plan loft. There were plenty of exposed brick and aluminium surfaces. It probably cost a fortune to live in an abandoned industrial estate. What was wrong with a normal house?

'Can I get you anything?' Ridley asked, stopping at the kitchen area. 'Tea, coffee?'

'Water would be great, thanks,' Gardner said and looked around. Maybe Ridley and Helen were from different generations, but there was one thing they had in common – money. He'd looked into Helen's background and discovered she was from a wealthy family. Her grandfather was some kind of big-wig in the steel industry. Maybe that was how they met, some sort of rich person's event where they celebrate just how much money they have.

Ridley handed Gardner a glass of water and then led him to the sofa. 'Sit down,' he said and took a seat opposite. Gardner took a sip of water and watched Ridley over the top of the glass. When they'd spoken on the phone the man had been taken aback by the mention of Helen's name but hadn't been particularly reluctant to talk about her. Gardner got the feeling things hadn't ended well between them. He wondered if Ridley blamed her for the death of their daughter.

'So what can I do for you, Detective Gardner?' Ridley asked. 'You said it was about Helen?'

'Yes,' Gardner said and put his glass down on the stained wood floor. If Ridley cared he didn't show it. 'You and Helen were in a relationship. You had a baby together.'

Ridley sighed and leaned back into the plush leather chair. 'Yes, we did,' he said. 'Casey. She died not long after she was born.' He looked at his feet.

'What happened?' Gardner asked, wanting to get Ridley talking about his daughter but also about Helen.

Ridley shook his head and coughed. 'Cot death.' He looked Gardner in the eye. 'It was no one's fault. They hadn't picked up on any underlying problems. She just...' He shrugged and blew out a breath. 'Helen took it very hard. I did too, but Helen...'

Gardner waited for him to go on but when he didn't he pressed him. 'Tell me about you and Helen. How did you meet? How long were you together?'

Ridley let out what might've been a laugh. 'We met in a bar in...' He shook his head, trying to recall. 'I think maybe the November. 2003 it must've been. She was beautiful but kind of a mess. She was drunk, telling me that her fiancé had broken it off with her a few weeks earlier.'

'Do you know his name?'

'I don't.'

'So you started a relationship with her despite her being a mess?'

Ridley looked at Gardner. 'It doesn't make me proud but I took her home that night, thinking it was a one night thing. But...'

'But?' Gardner asked.

'Helen is the kind of woman who gets what she wants. She worked her way into my life.'

'How?'

'Persistence. She was actually quite charming when she wasn't drunk. She kept calling again and again and in the end I kind of fell for her. I thought I was lucky that a beautiful young woman like her would be interested in an old fart like me.' He laughed. 'And it's not what you're thinking.'

'What am I thinking?' Gardner asked.

Ridley looked around the apartment. 'That she was after my money. Firstly I didn't have any then. This is all quite recent. And secondly, she had plenty of her own.'

'Or her family's, anyway,' Gardner said and Ridley smiled.

'Quite,' he said. 'I'm not sure Helen's worked a day in her life.'

'So you started a relationship with her,' Gardner said, wanting him to continue.

'Yes,' Ridley said. 'We had quite an intense relationship. Like I said, she always got what she wanted. And what she wanted most was a baby. And apparently I was the man for the job.'

'What about the fiancé?' Gardner asked. 'You said *he* broke it off. She didn't get what she wanted there did she?'

Ridley shrugged. 'I can't really say what happened there, detective. I only know what Helen told me.'

'Which was what?'

'That she'd been with this man for a while. She'd moved here to Manchester to be with him. Uprooted her life, as she put it. And then he wasn't willing to commit.' He smiled at Gardner. 'To be honest, I'm not entirely sure there ever was an engagement.'

'You think she made him up?' Gardner asked.

'No,' Ridley said and shook his head. 'No, I think he was real but I don't think he ever asked her to marry him. I think that's what she wanted. I think she wanted to marry him and have children and obviously he thought otherwise.'

'So she found someone who wanted what she did?'

This time Ridley did laugh. 'No. She found someone she could manipulate. She talked about children frequently; anyone could see she was baby mad. But I made it clear from the start I wasn't interested in being a father. She assured me it was fine. That we could have fun without making commitments. But a few months later she was pregnant.'

'And you don't think it was an accident?' Gardner asked.

'I know it wasn't an accident. She admitted later that she'd never been on the pill. I'm just surprised it didn't happen sooner.'

'So when she told you she was pregnant, what happened? She wanted you to marry her? You thought she was trapping you?'

'Quite the opposite,' Ridley said and Gardner frowned. 'I know I said I didn't want to be a father but when I found out she was pregnant I couldn't just walk away. But that was exactly what Helen wanted me to do.'

'I don't understand,' Gardner said. 'If she didn't want you to be involved, why bother telling you? Why not just leave?'

'And there lies the essence of Helen Deal,' Ridley said, smiling. 'She enjoyed it. She enjoyed hurting me, letting me know she'd won. She wanted me to know that she'd got what she came for.'

'But you didn't walk away.'

'No. Once I found out she was carrying my child I knew I couldn't walk away. I wanted to be a part of the child's life. I doubted that Helen and I would continue having a relationship but she couldn't completely exclude me.' Ridley leaned over and pulled a pack of cigarettes from his pocket. 'Do you mind?' he said, holding them up to Gardner, who just shook his head. 'I assume because of what I'd said previously she thought I'd just agree to it. She told me she was moving back to the north-east and that was it. In the end I told her I would move there too, that she couldn't stop me being a part of our child's life.' He took a drag of the cigarette. 'I followed her, left my life here,' he said. 'I found a B&B, stayed there a little while. In the end she allowed me to move into the house, it was quite large, but she made it clear she wanted little to do with me. I think she saw me more as the help than anything else. To be honest I thought she'd met someone else. She didn't have friends, not that I knew of. She wasn't one for socialising really. She was often in her room, reading, ignoring me. But all of a sudden she was spending a lot of time out of the house.'

'Do you know who it was?' Gardner asked. 'This mystery man?'

'No idea,' he said. 'I didn't care that much to be honest. I had no interest in Helen anymore. I was only concerned about the baby.' He stubbed out the cigarette and frowned. 'At one point I thought she was sleeping with one of the builders. She seemed very friendly with them, but I imagine they were beneath her. Manual workers. I think she just enjoyed having them there, intimidating me.'

Gardner felt something stirring in his gut. 'She had the builders intimidate you? In what way?'

'She'd made it clear to them that she didn't want me there, despite her inviting me to move in, I might add. I suspect that was just another one of her games. They were mostly just unfriendly towards me, but a few months after I moved in one of them physically attacked me. Pushed me against the wall, said he'd hurt me if I touched Helen again. I don't know what she'd told them but I left shortly after. Moved back to the B&B.'

Gardner swallowed. He had a pretty good idea where this was going. 'What do you remember about them? The builders? Do you know where they were from?'

Ridley nodded. 'They were Czech,' he said. 'I remember trying to talk to one of them about Prague once; I'd spent a little time there when I was younger. You can imagine the response.'

Gardner felt his pulse racing. 'What else can you remember? What the business was called, maybe?'

'I can do better than that,' Ridley said. 'I can tell you their names.'

CHAPTER SIXTY-FOUR

Miklos Prochazka and Damek Hajek,' Ridley said and Gardner sat staring at him. 'Hajek was the one who threatened me. Horrible little man.'

Gardner took out his notebook. He was about to start writing when he realised he had no idea how to spell the names. He handed the notebook to Ridley. 'You remember their names after all this time?' Gardner said and watched him write them down.

'I made a point of finding out their names. I saw the other one rummaging about in Helen's handbag one day, no doubt looking for money. He claimed he was looking for a pen. And then when they started acting aggressively towards me I made sure I got their names. I thought they might be useful to know at some point. I really thought one of them might do something more than push me,' Ridley said and handed back the notepad.

'So you reported them to the police?'

'No,' Ridley said. 'Like I said, I moved out and didn't have any more trouble from them. But I'm good with names. I tend not to forget them.'

Gardner raised his eyebrow. He wished he had the same ability. 'So how did Helen know them? Did she have a relationship with them before they started working for her?'

'I don't think she knew them until they turned up at the house to start work. I have no idea where she found them. She appeared to be quite brusque with them to begin with but after a couple of weeks they seemed quite chummy. I don't know if that was a real friendship or if she was just trying to get to me.'

'So you moved out, then what? How much did you see of her? What was your relationship at that point?'

'We didn't really have one. I moved out and barely saw her until Casey was born. I attempted to make contact but she didn't want to know. I asked to be involved, or at least informed of any anything regarding the baby, but she blew me off. I dropped by the house from time to time. I didn't expect she'd invite me in; it was more to keep tabs, make sure she didn't run off. Although I don't think she would've left Redcar. She seemed obsessed with the place. Her ancestors were in the steel business. I think she was under the illusion that they'd built the town,' Ridley said. 'Anyway, it was pure luck that I was there at the birth. I saw a taxi pull up to the house and Helen get in. I followed her to the hospital and was allowed in.'

'Helen didn't put up a fight about it?' Gardner asked.

Ridley shook his head. 'No. She didn't want the hospital staff to see what was really going on. So she pretended we were the happy couple.' He snorted. 'She wouldn't have called me though, I know that much. If I hadn't have been outside the house that day she wouldn't have told me she'd had the baby.'

'What about afterwards? Did she give you access to Casey?'

'Yes. She even let me move back in after a few days. I'd been looking for somewhere more permanent to stay but hadn't found anything. I suggested moving back in to help with the baby and she agreed. Who knows why? She was so overjoyed about Casey that I think she forgot everything else. It was all about her and the baby. I think I was there to run errands,' he said. 'But I didn't mind. All the other stuff seemed to fall away.'

'What about Hajek and Prochazka?' Gardner asked, referring to his notebook. 'Where were they after the baby was born?'

Ridley shook his head. 'No idea. I didn't see them again after that.'

'So what? You and Helen were happy?'

'Maybe not with each other. But with Casey,' he shrugged. 'Everything was about that little girl. And then she died,' he said. 'Helen lost it. We were both devastated, of course, but Helen lost control. This was a woman who was so good at controlling things, at getting what she wanted, and when she lost the most important thing in the world, she couldn't cope. I felt terrible for her. She didn't have any family or friends to turn to. She was so vulnerable,' he said, shaking his head. 'I wanted to help her, wanted to be there for her, but Helen,' he said and rolled up his shirt sleeve. 'Helen wanted me there even less than before.'

Gardner looked at Ridley's arm. The scar was long, from his elbow to his wrist, and looked like it had been cut deep. 'She did that?' Gardner asked.

'Yes.'

'She blamed you for Casey?'

Ridley ran his finger along the scar. 'She blamed me. She blamed God. She'd been screaming and shouting for hours, telling me to go. I didn't think I could leave her like that so I went into the other room. I thought she'd calm down. But the next thing I know she's there with a kitchen knife. She swiped it at my face,' he said, running his hand along his cheek. 'Fortunately it just scratched me. I tried to reason with her, tried to get the knife and she did this.' Ridley swallowed. 'You wouldn't believe the amount of blood. Helen just stood there watching. I told her to call an ambulance. I said I'd tell them it was an accident but she refused. I tried to get to the phone but she pushed me away from it. Eventually I managed to get past her and I left.'

'You didn't report her?' Gardner asked.

'No,' Ridley said and let out a deep breath. 'Maybe it was guilt about Casey, maybe I felt sorry for her. But I didn't tell the police. Perhaps I should have. I really don't think she was safe to be around.'

He was right. If Ridley had reported Helen maybe she wouldn't have had the chance to take Beth.

'Did Helen have another baby?' Gardner asked.

Ridley looked surprised. 'Not that I'm aware of. Though I wouldn't be the best person to ask. After the incident with the knife I got my things and left. But I'm sure she'd have wanted to have another child though. She was quite desperate.'

Gardner nodded. 'How far do you think she'd go to get what she wanted?'

'To have a baby you mean? I think she'd be quite comfortable manipulating some other poor sap.'

'Do you think she'd be capable of abducting a child?'

Ridley looked at him, surprised by the question but not shocked by the insinuation, probably realising why Gardner was there asking questions. He swallowed and nodded. 'Unfortunately I think that's entirely possible.'

CHAPTER SIXTY-FIVE

Gardner took the stairs two at a time. He was itching to get to his desk, to find more information on Miklos Prochazka and Damek Hajek. If he could find out about the men who had attacked Abby he'd have something concrete to take to his boss. To take to Abby.

As he went through the door he ran into DCI Atherton, almost knocking him over. Atherton frowned at him. 'I hope your haste means you have a lead in the Chelsea Davies case,' he said.

Gardner stopped and turned. 'No, sir,' he said, 'but I have a lead on the Beth Henshaw case.'

Atherton frowned again and then realisation seemed to dawn. 'Henshaw's a cold case, is it not?' Atherton said.

'Yes,' Gardner said. 'It was. But new evidence has come to light.'

'Such as?' Atherton said and raised his eyebrows.

Gardner sighed. He didn't have time for this. 'Abby Henshaw saw a girl she believed was her daughter.'

'Hasn't that happened before? On several occasions?'

'Yes, but this time was different,' Gardner said and Atherton looked slightly more interested. Gardner gave him the abridged version.

Atherton pulled the face he always did when sizing something up. Gardner waited him out. 'Alright,' he said. 'And what about the woman? Helen Deal. Have you brought her in?'

Gardner took a breath. 'No, not yet' he said. 'She's gone.'

'Gone?' Atherton said as if he'd never heard the word before.

'Yes,' Gardner said. 'She told the nanny she was taking the girl to Devon to visit relatives. I think she's gone for good.'

Atherton crossed his arms and looked at Gardner for what felt like an age. 'Well it sounds like you're going to be extremely busy,' he said. 'I want this sorting as quickly and quietly as possible. The papers are all over us about Chelsea Davies, I don't want this getting out as well.'

'Yes, sir,' Gardner said. 'I'm going to follow up this lead on the builders and speak to the nanny again.'

'Good,' Atherton said and started walking away. 'You do that.'

Gardner's jaw clenched. He didn't need Atherton to tell him he'd screwed up. He already had the media telling him. Abby telling him. And the little annoying voice inside his head telling him. Another voice really wasn't necessary.

CHAPTER SIXTY-SIX

They were just finishing dinner when the doorbell went. Simon got up and answered it and when Abby heard his voice as he made his way up the hallway she wished that she was still in bed.

Simon led Gardner through into the kitchen and Gardner and Abby's eyes met.

'I'm sorry to interrupt,' Gardner said, noticing the dinner plates.

Abby could see Simon staring at her, probably trying to judge her mood. 'It's alright,' Simon said, 'we're finished anyway.' He picked up the plates, put them into the sink and started to rinse them.

'How are you?' Gardner asked Abby. She raised her head and allowed the briefest of smiles to pass her lips.

'I'm fine,' she said. Her face was red and she knotted her fingers. 'I'm sorry.' Gardner looked to Simon for a clue but he just shrugged. 'I was out of line,' Abby continued. 'I should never have lashed out at you.'

'Abby,' Gardner started.

'No. Please. I was wrong. This wasn't your fault. You couldn't have known what would happen. I shouldn't have said all those things.'

Gardner looked at the floor. 'I think you had every right,' he said.

Simon brought Gardner a drink and they moved into the living room. There was still an atmosphere of tension in the room and for a while no one spoke. Finally Gardner broke the silence.

'I have some news,' he said.

'About Helen?' Abby said. 'Have you found her?'

Gardner shook his head. 'No, I'm afraid not. But we contacted the company who distributed the flyers. They confirmed a woman matching the description you gave does work for them. Her name's Alice Gregory. Unfortunately she's on holiday. But she's due back in a few days so I'll speak to her then.' He could see the disappointment in Abby's face. 'I also tracked down the father of Helen's baby. I went to speak to him earlier today. I asked if he thought Helen was capable of taking a child and he believed it was entirely possible.'

Abby let out a ragged breath. 'So where does that get us?' she asked.

'Did he tell you if she'd had another kid?' Simon asked.

Gardner chose to field Simon's question. 'He didn't know if she'd had another baby. He left under difficult circumstances shortly after Casey died.'

'Difficult?' Abby said. 'How?'

'Helen attacked him. Stabbed him,' Gardner said.

'Jesus,' Simon said. 'And she's got Beth.'

'I don't think she'd hurt her,' Gardner said. 'But he told me something else.' Gardner cleared his throat. 'Helen had builders working on the house before Casey was born.'

Abby felt her stomach tighten.

'He said they were Czech. Helen had them intimidate him,' Gardner said. 'He also remembered their names.'

Abby took a breath and Simon took her hand. 'Have you found them?' she asked. 'The man who raped me?'

'I found them in the system,' he said and picked up the file he'd brought with him. 'Miklos Prochazka and Damek Hajek. They were cousins.' He looked at Abby whose chest was moving quickly. He opened the folder and took out a photograph, handing it to Abby. As soon as she looked at it she dropped it like it was burning her hand. 'You recognise him?' Gardner asked and Abby nodded. 'He was one of the men who attacked you?' Gardner asked and Abby nodded again. 'Abby, was he the man who raped you?'

Abby started to cry and through her shallow breaths she managed to say, 'Yes.'

Gardner waited for Abby to drink the glass of water Simon had given her. She had stopped crying but sat staring at the floor, stunned. He gave her a few more minutes before he moved on, before he told her what he'd found.

'Abby?' he said and waited for her to focus on him. 'His name is Damek Hajek,' he said pointing at the photograph that was still on the floor. 'He was murdered last year in a dispute over money.'

Abby looked at him and he waited for a response. He wasn't sure what to expect. Would she be glad he was dead? Or would she feel like he'd escaped justice. He wasn't entirely sure himself.

'He's dead?' Abby said.

'Yes.'

'How? What happened?'

'He was stabbed in the neck. Apparently he owed money to some people who didn't like waiting. His cousin found him.'

'And what about him? His cousin,' Abby said. 'What happened to him?'

'Nothing,' Gardner said. 'He found the body, reported it to the police. So far no one has been convicted of the murder.'

'So he's still out there?' Abby said.

Gardner shook his head. 'Not anymore,' he said. 'He was still living at the same address as when he reported his cousin's murder. He was arrested this afternoon in connection with your rape and Beth's abduction.'

Abby let out a laugh, somewhere between relief and disbelief. 'So you've got him?' she said. 'Have you spoken to him?'

'No, not yet,' Gardner said. 'He was arrested in Leeds. I'm going to go down first thing to question him.'

Abby looked at Simon and he pulled her towards him, hugging her. Gardner felt a little bit of the weight from his shoulders slip away.

Abby turned back to Gardner. 'Will he tell us where Beth is?' she asked.

He shook his head. 'I don't know,' he said.

CHAPTER SIXTY-SEVEN

Abby closed the door and waited for the laptop to fire up. Her hands shook as she typed in the web address. She needed to talk to someone, needed to tell them what she felt. Simon had tried to talk to her after Gardner left but she needed a faceless audience. She couldn't stand the look in Simon's eyes as she bared her soul.

She sat on the bed, her legs tucked beneath her, and watched as the page loaded. She logged in and ignored the latest posts from the others. Today she had her own story to tell.

She had dreamed of killing him. Or at least of hurting him, making him suffer, wiping that smirk from his face, making him beg her for mercy, plead for his life. Sometimes she wondered what would happen if they caught him and she came face to face with him. She had this one dream where the judge told her she could do what she wanted to him and they opened up the courtroom into a ring and all the judges in their wigs and the jurors with their little notepads were standing around in a circle egging her on. He'd be there in the centre and he'd cower beneath her and she'd feel like finally justice was being served. She'd pull back her arm to land the first blow but then her arm would suddenly feel so heavy, like lead, and she couldn't move it, and the people watching were silent wondering why she was so weak. She'd scream out and with every bit of her she'd manage to pull her arm up, ball her hand into a fist and swing it at his face but when she made contact it was so slight, almost tender, a little tap was all she could muster and then he'd smirk at her and light a cigarette and the judge would set him free. She woke up crying because she knew she could never do what she wanted to. Knew she'd never have the chance and that she wouldn't have the strength even if she was given the opportunity.

And now she would never get to him, he would never be punished for what he did to her. To her daughter. There was a part of her that was pleased he was dead. She hoped he had suffered. Hoped it was long and painful and that he was alone. She wondered if he thought about her as he lay there in his last minutes. She doubted it. She was probably just another face in a sea of people, of women, he'd hurt.

Her hands paused over the keyboard. She didn't want to read it back, didn't want to know if it made sense. It was a release. Only she didn't feel any freer. Didn't feel like justice had been served.

She thought about telling the police it was the other one, the living one, who'd done it. Then at least someone would be punished, something would be done. But they'd be able to do tests and they'd know she was lying. Besides, he didn't do it so how could she lie about it? He hadn't raped her. He'd just allowed it to happen.

Abby closed the laptop and realised she hadn't actually posted the message. It didn't matter, whether she did or not it wouldn't change anything. It wouldn't close any doors. She'd still see his face when she closed her eyes. Only now she'd see a ghost.

CHAPTER SIXTY-EIGHT

Gardner put the leftovers in the fridge knowing that they'd probably sit there for a week or so before being thrown in the bin. The fridge was full of perfectly good fresh food that could be made into something edible but mostly it was just easier to get a take-away. Cooking for one seemed pointless. Depressing even.

For the past few hours he'd been trying to find someone who knew Helen around the time Beth disappeared. The house she lived in now - or had done until he'd spooked her - wasn't the same house she lived in with Ridley in 2005. He'd been to her old address but the neighbours on one side had only been there a year and the woman on the other side only vaguely remembered Helen. She remembered her being pregnant.

She remembered her moving out, baby in tow. But she knew nothing about Helen losing her baby. She hadn't even known her name until Gardner had told her. The neighbours further down and across the street were even less help. No one knew a thing about Helen Deal. And, he guessed, that was just how she liked it.

Eventually he got up and looked at the files stacked up. He needed to go over the stuff on Miklos Prochazka, to prepare for the interview tomorrow. He had more background stuff on Helen Deal to sift through. But he also had another missing girl needing his attention. Atherton had promised him some extra pairs of hands but those promises were frequently broken and, besides, he felt like he had to see them through himself, felt responsibility for them all. He couldn't remember feeling this tired and alone for a long time. And that was saying something.

He reached for the case file, and wondered if Chelsea Davies was alone. They were no closer to finding her. *He* was no closer to finding her. The media had been speculating that the girl must be long dead by now but Gardner knew that wasn't always the case. True, the longer a missing person went unfound the more *likely* it was that they were dead but it didn't mean that they *were* dead. Look at Beth Henshaw.

He flicked through the notes, trying to find something he'd missed. Another search of houses was due to start in the morning; unfortunately he wouldn't be there to coordinate it. Hundreds of properties were to be looked at again, and the perimeter was to be widened to include many more. So far they hadn't had any resistance from residents about going through their homes. For lack of a better lead, Gardner would start interviewing key witnesses again. They'd start with Chelsea's family and friends, and on from there for as long as it took.

Closing the folder, Gardner yawned and stood up. He was kidding himself that the answer was there and, anyway, he was so tired that even if there was a full confession in there somewhere he doubted he'd even see it.

He went into the bedroom and lay down on the bed, fully clothed. The guilt was eating away at him. Part of him wanted to admit the truth to Abby, that he'd fucked up, that one little mistake had led to five years of misery. Why hadn't Cartwright been thorough? Why hadn't he followed up? If they'd looked closer at Helen back then, Beth would've been returned to her parents. Abby's life wouldn't have been ruined.

He turned onto his side. But what good would the truth do her now? It would destroy her. It would make her lose all faith in him. They were on the right path now, that was all that mattered. He'd start fresh tomorrow and maybe then something would happen. They'd search more properties for Chelsea. He'd speak to Miklos Prochazka and maybe he'd lead them to Helen Deal. Something would happen tomorrow.

As he drifted off to sleep he thought: something *has* to happen.

CHAPTER SIXTY-NINE

Gardner looked through the window at Miklos Prochazka. He looked nothing like his cousin, there was no family resemblance. Where Damek had been tall and slim with dirty blonde hair, Miklos appeared shorter, stockier, with hardly any hair at all. He sat slumped forward in the chair, his fingers gripping the table edge. As Gardner entered, the man looked up like a startled animal. Gardner stifled a yawn and took the seat opposite Miklos.

'Who are you?' Miklos asked.

Gardner watched him carefully. He was clenching his fists, quickly and constantly. He'd already been told that Miklos had confessed. When they'd picked him up from his flat he'd cried and nodded his head like

267

he'd been expecting them to come. But Gardner wanted to hear it himself, wanted to know the whole story. He'd admitted being involved in the assault on Abby and the abduction of Beth, but he'd yet to give any real details.

Gardner took out his notebook and pen and watched Miklos squirm. For a man who'd already confessed he seemed awfully jittery. A confession led to a strange calm in most people.

'I'm DI Gardner,' he said. 'I was in charge of the investigation into the rape of Abby Henshaw and the abduction of Beth Henshaw.'

Miklos nodded. 'I'm sorry,' he said and looked Gardner in the eye briefly before returning his gaze to the table.

'Sorry for what?' Gardner asked.

'For what I did. For that little girl and her mother.'

'I'd say it's a bit late for sorry,' Gardner said and Miklos bowed his head further. Abby had confirmed that it was Damek who had raped her, she'd even admitted that Miklos had helped her out of the van afterwards, had seemed less sure of what he was doing. And yet Gardner could feel no sympathy for the man, had no time for his apologies.

'Did she get her back?' Miklos asked.

'What?'

'Did the woman get her little girl back?' Miklos asked again.

'No,' Gardner said and wondered why he wouldn't be aware of that, whether he was lying. Miklos closed his eyes, his mouth moving as if he was praying. Gardner didn't want him to have the comfort of prayer so he moved on. 'I want you to tell me what happened. Why you did it.'

Miklos opened his eyes. 'She asked us to do it. She paid us. I didn't know about the baby. She didn't tell me about the baby,' he said.

'Who paid you?' Gardner asked.

'The woman from the house. Helena,' he said. 'She made us do things for her. She paid us money so we did it. But I didn't know about the baby. I swear.'

'What was her second name? The woman from the house?' Gardner asked.

'I don't know,' Miklos said, shaking his head. 'I swear I don't know.'

Gardner nodded and moved on. It didn't matter, he already knew her name. 'You said she made you do things, like what? How did she make you do them?'

'She hired me and Damek to do work on the house. She caught me going through her things. She said she would call the police and I begged her not to.'

'You were stealing from her?' Gardner asked.

'Yes,' Miklos said and looked away again. 'She told us to leave but then the next day she called again and told us to come back. She didn't like being alone with that man she lived with.'

'Alan Ridley?'

Miklos shrugged. 'I don't remember his name. But when she had her baby, we stopped going there for a while. Then one day, weeks later, maybe more, Damek told me to go and get in the van. Said she had another job for us to do. I thought we had to go back to finish decorating but we went to a house and we just sat there. I asked Damek what we were doing but he wouldn't say. Then after a little while he got out and went and slashed the tyres of the car at this house.' Miklos looked at Gardner. 'I said why did you do that but he wouldn't tell me.'

'Did you find out whose car it was? Gardner asked.

'He never told me but I recognised it later. The day... it happened.'

'The day you attacked Abby Henshaw you mean? It was Abby's car he damaged.'

Miklos nodded and then shrugged. 'I don't know why she wanted it done. She didn't say who this woman was.'

'So why did you agree to it?'

'She said she'd call the police about the stealing. She never told me the things she wanted us to do. Always Damek. He didn't care what he did if she paid him money.'

'What else did she have you do?' Gardner asked.

'We broke into a house. I don't know who lived there; it was another house, not the woman's–'

'Abby's,' Gardner said and Miklos nodded.

'She told Damek to break in and to make a mess. He broke a window in the back; we went in and he took something. He started to break things but then I saw a neighbour and told him we should leave. He told Helena that we'd done it anyway,' he said.

'What else?' Gardner asked and Miklos shook his head. 'That was it?'

'Yes,' he said.

'What about Alan Ridley?' Gardner asked and Miklos looked down. 'You never did anything to him?'

Miklos shook his head. 'No.'

'What about Damek? He do anything?'

'No,' Miklos said again.

'That's funny because Mr Ridley claimed you intimidated him, threatened him. He said he thought Helen had asked you to do it, that she'd told you lies about him.'

Miklos looked at the floor. 'She didn't like him. She said he wasn't nice. I couldn't understand why he was there, why they were together. They shouted all the time. But I never did anything to him. Never.'

Gardner thought about it. He'd already admitted what'd happened to Abby and Beth, to damaging Abby's car, to breaking into Simon's house. Why lie about threatening Ridley?

'What about Damek? You said he didn't care what he did? Maybe he threatened him when you weren't around,' Gardner said and Miklos shrugged.

'Maybe. I don't know,' he said. 'I didn't see anything.'

'Alright,' Gardner said, 'let's move on. Helen had already got you to slash Abby's tyres, to break into the house. You agreed because you didn't want her to call the police about the stealing, is that right?' Miklos nodded. 'So when she came and asked you to attack Abby and take the baby, why did you agree? You must've known you could've ended up in more trouble than you would about stealing a few pounds from her purse.'

'I didn't know,' Miklos said, his eyes pleading. 'She never told me things. She always went to Damek. He came to me and said we had another job to do. This was a few months later. I asked what it was and he wouldn't tell me until the day. He told me to drive and we stopped at the pub. I kept saying "what are we doing here?" but he wouldn't tell me. Then all of a sudden he tells me to start driving again. He said that we had to follow someone and we had to frighten her.'

'And you just went along with it?' Gardner said.

'I didn't want to,' he said. 'But Damek showed me the money she'd given him. It was a lot. I thought we could take the money and leave.' He shrugged. 'I didn't want to work for her anymore.'

'How much was it?' Gardner asked.

'Five thousand pounds,' Miklos said. 'A lot of money.' He wiped the sweat from his top lip. 'Damek said it would be easy. All we had to do was wait for the woman to drive past and then follow her. I was driving and Damek said to follow, to drive close to her and then he said to go past her and knock her.'

'To force her off the road?'

Miklos nodded. 'I knew it wouldn't hurt her. Just scare her. When I started following her car I remembered it was the one Damek had slashed the tyres on. I thought this woman had done something to Helena and she was getting her back.' He shrugged. 'No one got hurt before so I thought that would be it.'

'And you didn't think that five thousand pounds was a lot of money for something so easy?'

Miklos took a deep breath. 'Yes, maybe,' he said. 'But I was greedy. I just wanted the money.'

'So then what happened? You'd forced her off the road, why did you get out? Why not just drive away?'

'He told me to stop. I was confused at first. I thought we were done but he shouted at me again to stop. I thought maybe something had happened, that she was hurt. I thought he'd seen it and was going to check on her.' Miklos shook his head. 'I should've known he would never do anything like that. He was selfish. He didn't care about anyone but himself.'

Gardner waited. He was trying to work Miklos out. He seemed sorry. He seemed to have been carrying guilt around. So why hadn't he come forward earlier?

Maybe because people always look out for themselves.

'I stopped the van and Damek said we had to go and get her. I asked what he meant and he said we were supposed to get her and put her in the van. He said we'd drive her away and leave her somewhere. She'd be scared. That was what we were supposed to do. I didn't want to, I tried to argue but he got out. I stayed in the van and I saw the woman get out of her car. She walked towards Damek and said something and then he hit her.' Miklos winced at the memory. 'He knocked her to the floor and then pulled her towards the van. I got out and I was shouting at him. I heard her say something about a baby, I thought she was pregnant. I told him to stop but he wouldn't listen. And then I saw the baby in the car.'

Miklos looked Gardner in the eye and his face crumpled. 'I shouted at him and said she was there. The woman was screaming and telling him that her baby was in the car but he wouldn't stop. He shouted at me, told me to get her in the van. He didn't acknowledge the baby at all.' Miklos looked at the floor again. 'I didn't know what to do. I helped him get her in the van. I thought someone might come. Someone might see us.'

Gardner saw a tear roll down Miklos' face. 'We got her in and I waited for Damek to climb out but he didn't. I knew what he was going to do and I just shut the door and drove away. I didn't try to help her at all,' he said.

'He'd done it before?' Gardner said and felt his stomach tighten. 'He'd raped someone else?'

'Yes,' Miklos said, his voice coming out as a whimper. 'Back home.'

'He wasn't convicted?' Gardner asked.

Miklos shook his head. 'No. He always got away with it. No one would go to the police, they were scared of him.'

'So you knew he was a rapist. You knew what would happen when you put Abby in that van and yet you did nothing.'

Miklos started crying. 'I know I deserve to be punished. I'm as bad as him.'

Gardner stood up; he needed to be away from Miklos for a few minutes, to leave him to wallow in his own guilt for a while. He walked out of the interview room and into the toilets. The window was open and a cool breeze blew through the small space. He splashed some water on his face. Why was this so hard? He already knew what had happened to Abby, why was it so difficult hearing it from Miklos? Hearing this shit was never easy but he could usually distance himself, always step back and take in the facts, keeping the emotions separate.

Miklos' tears, though he believed the emotion behind them, made it worse somehow. He pitied himself, was opening himself up for redemption, forgiveness. But as far as Gardner was concerned he wouldn't be getting any. He'd wondered how Abby had felt when he'd told her about Damek. He wondered if she felt cheated. He knew he did. And yet, here was the other culprit, offering himself up for punishment, for everything the law could throw at him and all he could think was he wished Miklos had been murdered in a squalid flat too.

CHAPTER SEVENTY

Gardner went back into the interview room and took his seat. Miklos had stopped crying but he didn't acknowledge Gardner's return. He sat still and only when Gardner spoke did he move.

'Who took Beth Henshaw?' Gardner asked and Miklos looked at him as if he didn't understand. 'The baby? Who took her from Abby's car?'

'I don't know,' he said. 'We didn't take her. I guess Helena took her but...' He shrugged. 'I never knew.'

Maybe that was true. It made sense that she'd do it herself. She'd want as few people involved as possible. And a woman taking a baby from a car would look less suspicious than two builders.

'Maybe it was the man,' Miklos said and Gardner's head shot up.

'The man?' he said. 'What man?'

'The father.'

'Alan Ridley?' Gardner said and Miklos shrugged again. 'You said, maybe it was the man. Who were you talking about?'

'After we left, when I saw on the news that the baby had gone missing, I told Damek we should call the police. We could call anonymously, tell them about Helena. But he wouldn't. He'd told me that he didn't know about the baby in the car, that Helena hadn't told him about her. But later Damek said he'd heard Helena talking to a man about their baby. Something about them going away together. They were moving I think. She was saying "you're her father". She was upset,' Miklos said. 'Damek thought she was trying to get back together with him.'

'Ridley?'

'I guess,' Miklos said. 'Damek said the baby in the car must've been hers. Damek said maybe she wanted Ridley to get her and they would move away. But I saw on the news. It wasn't her baby. So I said to Damek: why would they take someone else's baby? They had their own baby.'

'Helen's baby died,' Gardner said, trying to make sense of what Miklos was telling him. By the time Beth was taken, Ridley was long gone. So who was she talking to? Would Helen have asked him to come back? She said that he was the father. Helen may well have been delusional enough to think that Beth was really her daughter; she'd named Beth after her dead baby like some kind of replacement. Was it possible she thought that Beth really was Casey, that Ridley was her father?

In which case why didn't Ridley mention that call when he spoke to him? Unless he and Helen hadn't really ended things at all?

CHAPTER SEVENTY-ONE

Gardner had called Abby and told her about Miklos Prochazka. That he'd admitted everything, that he'd be charged with conspiracy to commit a sexual offence, assault, and possibly conspiracy to kidnap. He'd be punished for what he'd done to her. She seemed grateful to him and that little piece of gratitude stuck in his throat. Maybe it was something, a part of the puzzle, some closure on part of her ordeal. But it hadn't helped him to find Beth. And that was what Abby wanted more than anything else.

He hadn't asked her about Damek Hajek, about how she felt. It was none of his business. Maybe someday she'd tell him, when it was all over. But for now it didn't matter because it wasn't over. He still needed to find Helen Deal before he could bring Beth home.

'You don't think it's odd?' Gardner asked. 'I mean, I hardly get on with my boss but I know he has a wife and three kids. He found out when my mother died and he made a point of asking me about her funeral. People who work together, especially closely like you and Helen, they usually talk. Get to know each other.'

'She's private,' Sara said. 'Other families I've worked for have been more chatty.' She shrugged again. 'Helen's different. She's kind of...'

'Kind of what?' Gardner asked.

'I don't know. She keeps a distance and that's fine. Sometimes she's a bit odd, she gets angry.'

'With who? You? Casey?'

'No,' Sara said. 'She never shouts at Casey. Ever. And that's weird,' she said, smiling. 'All parents shout at their kids. But Helen never does. Not that I've seen anyway. She treats her like a princess. Like she's some kind of precious object that can't be touched.'

Gardner thought this was an odd way to describe a kid. But then if Helen had lost one baby, maybe she was paranoid about losing another.

'She get angry with you?' he asked Sara.

'No, not really. A couple of times, mostly when I first started, she got a bit upset with me. Like, if I brought Casey back a few minutes late or if she came back with dirt on her or something. She's a little over-protective.'

No shit, Gardner thought. She probably thought that Sara had run off with her or was going to kill her with mud poisoning. He had to wonder why she'd allow anyone else near the girl, let alone look after her all day.

'I've heard her shouting on the phone though,' Sara continued. 'A few times. I think maybe she was talking to Casey's dad. I don't think they have a very good relationship. I guess it ended badly.'

'What do you know about him? Casey's dad?' Gardner asked.

'Nothing really,' Sara said. 'I've never met him. I know sometimes they'd go and visit him, not often but now and then. But he never came to the house,' she said. 'I guess Helen didn't want him there.'

'So they're still in touch though,' Gardner said and wondered how honest Alan Ridley had been.

'I guess. I think maybe Helen would prefer it if they weren't but I suppose she does it for Casey's sake.'

'Do you think maybe Helen would've taken Casey there now?' he asked. Sara frowned but didn't say anything. She had to know by now that Helen wasn't really in Devon. 'Do you think she would've gone to see Casey's dad?'

'I'm not sure. Like I said, I don't think they got on well. I remember coming in one day and Helen was surrounded by photos. I don't think she even knew I was in the room. I picked a photo up and asked who the man was and Helen jumped up, snatched it off me and told me to get out. The next day she seemed in a better mood so I asked her if he was Casey's dad. She said yes but she wouldn't go into it anymore. I guess it was a sore point.'

'So you know what he looks like, Casey's dad?' Gardner asked. Sara nodded and Gardner stood up. 'I'll be right back,' he said.

He returned with a file, flicking through it, and pulled out the driving licence photo of Alan Ridley.

'That him?' he said pushing the photocopy at Sara. She leant forward and squinted at the picture.

'No,' she said. 'This guy's way older. Paul was maybe a little younger than Helen, kind of skinny.'

'Paul?' Gardner said and felt every muscle in his body tense. 'His name was Paul?'

'Yes,' Sara said and pushed the piece of paper back towards him. 'I remember Helen saying "Paul's no longer part of this family". Then she wouldn't talk about it anymore.'

Gardner blinked and tried to form some words. He looked down at the file and sifted through the sheets. It had to be in there. At the bottom he found another photograph. One that had been used a long time ago. One that showed what a happy family Beth had been taken away from. He pushed the picture of Paul, Abby and Beth Henshaw towards Sara.

'Is that him?' he asked, his voice shaking. 'Is that Casey's dad?'

'Yes,' Sara said. 'That's him.'

CHAPTER SEVENTY-TWO

Helen heard the door close and she stood up to go into the kitchen but Casey beat her to it. 'Daddy!' Casey shouted and Helen saw her run to Paul and hold her arms up for him to hug her. She stared at Paul. He looked like he'd seen a ghost and for a moment she thought she was looking at one. He was gaunt and pale. More than usual.

She'd been there for hours, waiting for him to arrive, making herself at home although she was hardly at home there. They weren't exactly the normal family. Helen had only been there a handful of times. She hated it there. There was no one around for miles. It was like a ghost town. She understood why he chose to live there, he had secrets. But it was so boring.

There'd been no sign of life, no cups left on the drainer, no bowls of porridge on the table. She walked through to the living room and turned on the light. Nobody home. She saw the phone on a table beside the sofa and recognised the blinking light. She guessed he hadn't got her message.

For a second Paul held her gaze until he looked down at Casey and smiled. 'Hey princess,' he said. 'What are you doing here?' He picked Casey up and kissed her.

'Me and Mummy came to see you. We got here ages ago but you weren't here.'

Paul looked at Helen. 'What are you doing here?' he asked her.

'Casey told you. We came to see you, Paul,' she said and smiled. 'Didn't you get my message?'

'What message?' he asked and put Casey down.

'I left a message for you letting you know we were coming,' Helen said. 'Where've you been?'

Paul walked past Helen into the living room. He looked at the answering machine, saw the blinking light.

'Can we go and look at the horses again,' Casey asked, following them into the room. 'We could take some carrots. Horses like carrots, don't they?'

'Maybe.' Paul nodded and smiled at Casey and then looked at Helen. 'How long have you been here?' he said.

'Just a few hours,' Helen said, before turning to Casey. 'Go upstairs, honey.'

'But I want to see Daddy.'

'Upstairs,' Helen repeated. 'Daddy and I need to talk about something. About a present for you.'

Paul rolled his eyes and Casey's face lit up. 'Is it a pony?' she asked. 'Or a puppy.'

'Wait and see,' Helen said and watched Casey skip out of the room. When she heard her walk across the creaking floorboard upstairs she smiled at Paul. 'So where have you been, Paul? I was getting worried about you.'

'I'm sure you were,' Paul said. 'I was always your top priority.'

'She came looking for her,' Helen said. 'She frightened Casey half to death, chasing after her.'

She saw Paul's jaw clench but he just shrugged. 'Who?' he said. Helen laughed. He was a terrible liar. To her anyway.

'She was trying to take Casey away,' Helen said. 'Somehow she knew that she'd be at that play. You know, the one you were supposed to go to? That you were meant to take your daughter to.'

'I couldn't go,' Paul said. 'I had to work. I told you that.'

'Well, looks like you were right not to go. She would've seen you. Think how that would've looked.' She watched him for a reaction but he kept his head down. 'You still haven't told me where you were.'

'Away. There was a book fair,' Paul said. 'I don't need to check in with you, Helen, we're not together anymore. You can't control me.'

'What if there'd been an emergency? What if something had happened to Casey?'

'When have you ever needed me for anything?' Paul said. 'You told me that yourself. You don't need me. Casey doesn't need me.' He stood up and walked past Helen into the kitchen. Helen followed him and leaned against the doorframe while he pottered about. 'Is that why you're here? You need somewhere to hide?' he said.

Helen stood up straight. 'Where else would I go? We're in this together, remember?' Paul leaned against the worktop and closed his eyes. 'We did this together.' Helen could see his hand shaking as he turned to her.

'If they're looking for you–' he started.

'Why would they look here?' Helen said. 'I haven't given them any possible reason to suspect you. What possible reason could they have for looking here?'

Paul swallowed. 'None. They wouldn't,' he said quietly.

'Then we'll be okay won't we?' she said and went to the bottom of the stairs. 'Casey?' she called up. 'Come down now, honey. Come and talk to your daddy.'

Casey came bounding down the stairs and ran at Paul. 'Can we go and see the horses? Please?' she begged.

The knock at the door caused them all to turn. When neither Helen nor Paul moved, Casey started running to the door. Helen ran after her but was too late. Casey pulled open the door. A blonde woman looked at Casey and then up at Helen before tossing a cigarette butt across the garden.

'Yes?' Helen said.

'Is Paul there?' the woman asked.

'Who are you?' Helen said, her arm going around Casey's shoulders, pulling her close.

CHAPTER SEVENTY-THREE

Gardner sat in the car, still in shock. He wasn't sure he was capable of telling Abby that her ex-husband had been the one who'd taken Beth from her.

After Sara told him, he'd been in denial himself. She must've been mistaken. Maybe the man Helen claimed was the little girl's dad just looked like Paul Henshaw. And happened to be called Paul too. Maybe Helen and Paul got involved with each other in the years after she'd taken Beth and Paul had no idea who the girl really was. He thought he was being a step-father to Casey Deal, none the wiser about her real identity. Maybe it was some awful coincidence.

No, Helen must've known who Paul was, known he was Abby's

ex. She'd practically stalked Abby, sending Miklos and his cousin to sabotage her car. She would've known who Paul was. Maybe it was another of her games. She'd taken her time and found Paul Henshaw, seducing him, getting him involved, playing him, making him an accessory to her crime. If only.

He knew Abby hadn't had contact with Paul since the divorce. Bitter wasn't the word for it. He'd called Lawton to find an address for Paul, hoping that Helen and Beth would be there, unaware that he'd found out about their connection to Abby's ex.

Gardner rubbed his hand across his face and looked at the house again, wishing he was elsewhere. He could sit there all day coming up with conspiracy theories but he knew that's all they were. Paul Henshaw had been involved from the start. How could he have missed it? He tried to think back to the early days of the case, how he'd dug into Abby and Paul's lives. There was nothing that linked Paul to Helen Deal. Was there? There were no calls to anyone they hadn't checked. No CCTV footage of Helen in the shop.

CCTV. Gardner remembered showing Abby and Paul the footage from the doctor's surgery. Paul saw Helen on the tape. He covered it up, said he thought he'd recognised the man in the video. But it was there all along and he'd missed it. Missed something else.

This was a nightmare. In a way it was something; a new lead, a way to find Helen and Beth. But still. He could think of a million better ways for it to happen.

When he found out Simon remembered Helen he thought that'd been the link. That Helen, grieving over her own daughter, had seen an opportunity, found a baby girl and decided to take her. He thought Simon was the catalyst. His emotions about seeing his new daughter leading him to tell Helen about Beth and events spiralling from there. Helen had followed him, seen him with Abby, followed Abby with Beth and ultimately set things up to take Beth away.

But it wasn't Simon at all. It was Paul. He must've known about Abby and Simon and planned his revenge. And who better to steal a child with than Helen Deal?

He took a deep breath and opened the car door. As he walked up to the house Abby opened the door.

'We need to talk,' he said.

CHAPTER SEVENTY-FOUR

Gardner sat facing Abby and Simon. He wished he'd come up with something before arriving, so he'd at least be prepared instead of sitting looking at them, their faces growing more and more concerned with every second.

'What is it?' Abby asked. 'What's happened?'

Gardner cleared his throat. He remembered the day he'd arrived to tell her and Paul that the body of a baby had been found. That had seemed so much easier. Or maybe that was just hindsight. He'd probably sat there trying to rehearse his words just the same. He recalled the sadness he'd felt when he'd first been informed, the bitter disappointment that the case had ended that way, with the death of Beth Henshaw. But as the details had come in he'd felt a rising hope that it wasn't Beth at all, that there was still a chance she'd be found. The fact it meant it was a different baby, another mother's child that was dead, didn't weigh too heavily. It was always someone's child, someone's parent, someone's friend. There would always be victims and they always had someone who cared for them. It was sad, yes, but if he was going to do his job he had to keep a distance from these things and if he had to feel then it was better to restrict it to his own cases.

He remembered Paul answering the door, asking what was wrong, refusing to get Abby. Paul had reacted exactly how you'd expect a father to react after being told his daughter could be dead. Except he wasn't a father. And he already knew Beth wasn't dead. He didn't want Abby to know about the dead baby. He insisted he would do the DNA test. He was forcing Abby's hand. Making her admit the truth.

'Michael, what's going on?' Abby said and Gardner let out a breath.

'I spoke to Sara Walters today, the nanny,' he said. 'I wanted to know if she had any idea where Helen could've gone. The thought had crossed my mind that she'd have gone to Alan Ridley.'

'I thought he hated her,' Simon said. 'I thought they had nothing to do with each other.'

'They don't,' Gardner said. 'I asked about Casey's father. She didn't know a great deal. He only saw Casey occasionally. What she did know was his name,' he said and Abby sat forward holding her breath. 'She said he was called Paul,' he said and he saw Abby stiffen. 'I showed her a photo of your ex-husband and she identified him as Casey's father.'

Abby couldn't tell if it was her or the room that was spinning but she knew that if it got any faster she'd wake up. She'd had these dreams, or rather these nightmares, before. Gardner would tell her that he'd found Beth but she couldn't have her back because someone better had her. Or tell her that she'd never had a baby and then lock her into a room and leave her there. Or Simon would come into the bedroom carrying Beth and tell her that he was sorry, that she'd been punished enough and that she could finally have her back if she promised to be good. But she always woke up just when she thought she couldn't take it anymore.

But this time she didn't. She could hear Simon's voice but she couldn't make out the words. He sounded angry and was standing, his arms waving around. But in front of her Gardner was still sitting, watching her, looking concerned.

'Abby?' he said and she tried to focus on his face. She'd never noticed before that he had green eyes. Or maybe she had. She couldn't remember. 'Abby?' he said again.

She stared at him and tried to understand what and why and how. Her hands shook as her thoughts fought with each other, trying to push their way to the front of her mind. There *had* to be an explanation. Maybe Paul had just met Helen and the nanny was confused. Or she'd been completely wrong and it wasn't Paul at all. It must've been a different Paul, there are lots of Pauls.

She could hear her heartbeat so she closed her eyes and concentrated on it, trying to amplify it and make it drown out the thought that Paul was guilty. There *had* to be another explanation.

Gardner's hand on her shoulder made her jump. 'Abby?' he said.

Unable to speak, she turned to Simon. He was quiet now, standing there with his hands linked on top of his head. He was staring at her too. He was waiting for an explanation from her, they both were. Maybe she was supposed to have known all along that it was her husband who'd betrayed her, who'd torn her life apart. Or she was supposed to be coming up with an excuse for him, defending the man she knew could never do something like this. But she still couldn't speak. She opened her mouth to try just in time for the vomit to hit the carpet.

Kneeling on the floor she could see their feet rushing towards her. Abby wiped her mouth and turned to Gardner. 'Is it true?' she asked.

Gardner bowed his head. 'Sara identified him-'

'She could be lying,' Abby said. 'Helen could've told her to say that. She could be trying to fuck with me some more.'

'We don't know anything for sure yet but I don't believe she was lying. I don't think she knew anything about what was really going on.'

'You didn't believe that she was my daughter either,' Abby said and saw Gardner wince at her words. 'She could be lying, trying to make him look guilty when he's not.'

'Are you sure he's not?' Simon said and they both looked up at him.

'What?' Abby said.

'Are you sure he's not guilty? Are you positive he wouldn't do this?' Simon said.

'Of course he wouldn't,' Abby said. 'He wouldn't,' she muttered and looked at Gardner for confirmation.

'Look, we don't know anything for certain yet but Sara claimed that she saw the photographs of Paul with Helen and Casey. Helen was cutting him out of them. I'm getting an address for Paul,' Gardner said. 'We'll find him and get to the bottom of this.'

'I think we're already at the bottom of it,' Simon said.

Abby closed her eyes and pictured Paul in her mind. He was a good person. This was all wrong. 'We need to find him,' Abby said, opening her eyes. 'We need to know why the nanny thought it was him.' When Simon shook his head Abby spoke again. 'Simon, we need to find-'

'I know why she said it was him!' Simon said and slammed his fist into the wall. Abby recoiled as he raised his fist for the second time. Abby reached over for him but Simon pulled away.

'Simon...' Abby tried through her tears, 'maybe she's confused.'

'What? You think she found the picture of him in a photo frame she bought from fucking Woolworths?

'Simon, please.'

'Wake up,' Simon said. 'He did it. He took Beth away from us. It makes sense. How else would they have known where you'd be that day? How else could they be sure? Because Paul told those fuckers to wait for you there. He told them to-' Simon stopped and looked at her. She could see the blame in his eyes. *Why didn't you know your husband was capable of this?*

'You're the one who told her about Beth,' Abby said. 'You started this.'

'No,' Simon said. 'He started it. He was so fucking angry at you he wanted to hurt you.'

'Alright,' Gardner said. 'Enough.' He moved between Abby and Simon. Abby turned away from them both. 'We don't know anything yet. We don't know that he was definitely part of it.'

'Yeah right,' Simon said.

'We don't know anything,' Gardner repeated. 'But blaming each other doesn't help. We're going to find Paul and talk to him. Alright? Abby?'

Abby let out a shaky breath and turned back to him, nodding. Gardner looked at Simon. 'Alright?' he said, as his phone rang. 'Gardner.'

Gardner stepped outside to take the call, eager to get some air. 'You got the address,' he said as soon as he picked up.

'Yes,' sir,' Lawton said. 'But there's something you should know.'

'What is it?' Gardner said. Lawton didn't speak immediately. 'What?' he said. 'What's going on?'

Lawton sighed. 'I asked PC Wilson to do it because I was trying to deal with something else.'

'And?' Gardner said, feeling his patience running out.

'And he said that I should ask DC Harrington because he'd heard him mention Paul Henshaw earlier.'

'Harrington? Why would he be looking for Henshaw?'

Lawton sighed again. 'Someone asked him to find an address for him. It was off the record, I think.'

'Who asked?' Gardner said.

'I don't know. He wouldn't say. But he gave me the address.'

'Is he there?'

'Yes, sir.'

'Put him on.' Gardner paced up and down until Harrington came on the line. 'Who asked you for Paul Henshaw's address?'

'Look, I'm sorry, I wasn't thinking-'

'Who was it?'

'Jen Harvey,' Harrington said. 'She was at mine last night, she asked for a favour.'

'A favour? What the fuck were you thinking?' Gardner said. 'Why did she want it?'

'I don't know. She said she needed to see him. Said it was important.'

'So you just handed it out?' Gardner rubbed at his eyes. 'We'll discuss this later. Send me the address.' He disconnected and walked back inside Abby's house. 'Why would Jen Harvey be looking for Paul?'

'What?' Simon said. Abby sat there, clearly still dazed.

'Jen Harvey asked one of my team for Paul's address. Any idea why?'

Abby shook her head. 'I don't know. She thought she saw him here a few days ago. I thought she was lying, causing trouble.'

'Is she part of this?' Simon said.

Gardner turned his attention back to Abby, his expression asking her the same question.

Abby started to shake her head. 'I don't know,' she said, her voice barely more than a whisper. 'She wanted a favour from him, I think. Something to do with a website or her book.'

Gardner saw Simon calling someone. 'What are you doing?'

Simon turned away, his breathing coming out like a snorting bull. 'Jen? It's Simon. I need you to call me back. It's important.' He hung up. 'I'm going.' He started to walk out of the room. Abby reached for him only for him to shrug her off.

'Get off me,' he said.

'Where're you going?'

'I'm going to find out where he is and fucking kill him.' He pulled away from Abby and opened the door.

'Simon-'

'Fuck,' Gardner said and went after Simon. 'Hold on,' he said, reaching out for Simon's arm but he pushed him away. Gardner stumbled back as he watched Simon climb into the car. Gardner pounded on the window but Simon ignored him, driving away. Gardner called Lawton back. 'I need you to get someone to Paul Henshaw's address now. Get onto the locals. I'm on my way to get you, we're going over there. And find someone to come to Abby Henshaw's. I want someone with her.'

CHAPTER SEVENTY-FIVE

'Paul's not here,' Helen said and started to close the door but Jen put her foot in the way.

'I saw him through the window,' she said. 'I know he's in there.'

Helen held onto Casey. 'What do you want?'

'I just want to talk to him.'

Helen glanced through the doorway into the kitchen. Paul stood there, frozen like a frightened child. Helen turned back to Jen.

'He's not here,' she said and tried to close the door again.

'I just want to talk,' Jen said, her voice rising as Helen tried to shut her out. 'I know I'm probably the last person you want to see but I saw your website. I thought we could talk about maybe working together.'

She paused. 'And I know you want to see Abby. We could all get together. Like old times.'

Helen lost her grip on the door and it swung back.

'I know you were there, Paul. I know you went to see her. So I know you still care. And I'm sure she'd want to see you. I can pass on a message if you like,' Jen said, craning her neck, trying to see past Helen.

'He's not here,' Helen said and pushed the door shut. She could hear Jen banging on the door. 'Upstairs,' she said to Casey. 'Get your things.'

'But I want to stay with Daddy.'

'No, Casey. We're going,' Helen said.

'Ohhh,' Casey said, dragging out the word before stomping up the stairs.

Helen walked back into the kitchen. Through the window she saw Jen walk away and get into her car.

Helen stared at Paul. 'I hope you don't mind me not inviting your friend in. But I'm not really in the mood for guests.'

'I don't know why she was here,' Paul said, swallowing hard. 'I haven't seen her in five years.'

'But you've seen your ex-wife.'

'No, I haven't.'

'I should've known you'd break. That you'd go running back.'

'You're the one who went back there,' Paul said. 'If you were so concerned with someone seeing you, that Abby might see you, why did you go back to Redcar in the first place? You could've stayed away. But you can't help yourself, can you? It was like that from the start. You couldn't even stay away from the doctor's. What kind of fucking psychopath goes and sits there in front of cameras, knowing it's the first place the police will look? You could've stayed hidden but it wasn't enough, was it? You have to play your mind games, don't you? Was it to keep me away from Casey? Or just to make me sweat? Because, I don't know about you, but there hasn't been a day since it happened that I haven't expected someone to find out. That someone will come and knock on the door and that'll be it. Game over.'

Helen shook her head, ignoring his words. 'You couldn't do it, could you? Not face to face. You don't have the guts. You never did. Plenty of ideas but never the courage to actually follow through. So what? You put a note through her door? Anonymous phone call? What else do cowards do?'

Paul shook his head. 'Helen...'

'Why would you do that? Why would you destroy your own family?'

'Family?' Paul said. 'You think we're family now? You used me. You manipulated me, turned me against my own wife.'

'Manipulated?' Helen laughed. 'I told you the truth. I told you she was sleeping with Simon Abbott. I told you her baby wasn't yours. I told you she'd be better off with us.'

'And how did you know all that, Helen? How come you just stumbled across it all? You knew what you were doing from the start. You set out to destroy our lives because you wanted Beth.'

'I wanted you!' Helen said. 'I wanted to drive you apart so I started following her. I wanted to find a way to get between you but in the end I didn't have to. She did that for me. I saw it all, all the secret meetings with him. She was making a fool out of you. They both were. He even *told* me the baby was his. He was gloating about it like he'd done nothing wrong.'

'And you just couldn't wait to tell me about it. Couldn't wait to put your plan into action while my life was falling apart.'

'It was all true, wasn't it? And don't try and tell me you were forced into anything. You wanted this as much as I did. Whose idea was it to follow her? Who was the one that said we'd have to get her out of the way?'

She could see Paul shaking. 'And who let things get out of control? Who let those animals do what they did to her?' he said.

'I never wanted that to happen. That wasn't my fault,' she said. 'But you knew what you were doing, Paul, let's not deny that.'

'No, you knew what you were doing. You saw an opportunity and you took it. I meant nothing to you. I was just a way of getting what you wanted.'

'We were family,' Helen said.

Paul laughed. 'Bullshit. As soon as you had Beth you were trying to find ways to get rid of me. You wouldn't let me near her. You wouldn't leave me alone with her. You couldn't get rid of me fast enough.'

'You were the one who walked away. You were the one who wouldn't even come near her for months on end. We were supposed to be together. That was the plan.'

'How could we be together? How could I just walk away from Abby and then start playing house with you? If I hadn't stayed away, you wouldn't be here now, you'd be in prison. We both would,' Paul said. 'And you knew that. I think that was the idea from the start. You got what you wanted, Helen. You always do. I'm just surprised you stuck around long enough for me to find you at all.'

'You really think that? I loved you. I did what I did for you. For both of us. I saw what she was doing to you and I saved you. You deserved better. We both deserved more and I got it for us and then you just walked away.'

'The only reason I still see you is because I'm the only person who has the power to take her away from you. You think I'm weak, but I have the power here. I can take everything away from you.'

'You *are* weak,' Helen said. 'If you weren't such a coward you would've already gone to the police instead of tip-toeing around your ex-wife.' She turned to walk away. Paul was a fool. He was pathetic. 'I have the power here. You might've led her to me but I know you'll never give yourself up. Which means I just walk away and you and your ex-wife will never see me or Casey again.' Helen started up the stairs. 'Casey, are you ready to go?'

'I'll call the police, Helen,' Paul shouted after her. 'You'll lose another child.'

Helen froze. It felt as if her heart has stopped for a moment and then with every second that passed her breathing quickened. Her throat closed up. She turned around and looked at Paul standing there, phone in hand.

CHAPTER SEVENTY-SIX

Simon drove towards the beach, his heart hammering in his chest. He hadn't realised it was raining until he'd been driving for a few minutes but as he pulled up and looked out over the sea he couldn't ignore the rain anymore. It thundered down onto the roof of the car and he closed his eyes trying to use the sound to blank out his thoughts.

He sat with his head against the window, listening to the rain. Paul was Abby's ex. Her responsibility. How could she not have realised something was wrong?

Opening his eyes, Simon wiped at the steamed-up window. The rain was coming down hard and he realised he'd been crying. He should go back and talk to Abby, talk to Gardner like a grown up, find out where

Paul was and bring Beth back. It hurt him to think it was someone so close who'd taken their daughter, God only knew how Abby felt. But it was another step forward. He had to think of it that way. Another step closer to getting Beth back. And Paul would be punished for what he did. He'd go to prison.

Simon slammed his hand against the steering wheel. He didn't want him to go to prison. He wanted to hurt him. Make Paul feel everything that he'd felt, that Abby had felt, over the past five years. He felt his throat close up, choked with tears, and punched the wheel again and again. He just wanted to hurt Paul. For Beth, for Abby, for himself.

He wished he'd brought his cigarettes; he could really do with one. Or ten. He went to put the car in reverse when his phone rang. Jen.

'Why were you at Paul's?' he said before she could speak.

'How did you know?' Jen said.

'Just tell me. Why were you there?'

'I needed to see him,' she said. 'I wanted to prove to Abby I wasn't lying about seeing him hanging around.'

Simon sighed. What had he been expecting her to say? That she'd been in on it all along? That she was going to warn him they were onto him?

'And alright, I wanted to see him about this website he's got too - which I know is selfish of me but he might be able to help me,' she said. 'But I did want to prove it to Abby. I know she's angry with me. But he wouldn't talk to me.'

'He's there? Now?'

'Yeah,' she said. 'Why? What's going on?'

'I need the address,' Simon said. He scribbled it down on an old parking ticket and hung up before Jen could ask any more questions. The address was less than thirty minutes from where he was. In half an hour he'd have his hands on Paul Henshaw.

The tyres screeched as he pulled away.

CHAPTER SEVENTY-SEVEN

Gardner was on the way to Paul Henshaw's when the call came.

They'd found her.

He pulled over to the side of the road and closed his eyes, feeling his heart sink, wishing he could be there. 'Where?' he asked.

'At Louise Cotton's house,' Harrington told him.

Gardner opened his eyes. 'Jill Hoffman's mate?' He could feel Lawton's eyes on him.

'Yes. She-'

'Is she..?' Gardner asked, gripping the steering wheel. 'Is she alive?'

'Yes. She's alive. She was in the loft. She seems fine but she's been taken to the hospital to get checked over.'

Gardner let go of the breath he'd been holding in. She was alive. He let out a little laugh and felt relief wash over him. He turned to Lawton.

'Chelsea Davies. She's alive,' he said and Lawton smiled.

Of course it wasn't over yet. The investigation was really just beginning but the girl, the girl was safe. At least there was that.

Gardner took some more details and asked Harrington to keep him informed. He leant forward, resting his head on the steering wheel.

'Her friend had her?' Lawton said. 'Was her mother involved?'

'I don't know,' he sighed. 'Maybe. It wouldn't be the first time.'

'Why now? We searched Cotton's house. We searched everywhere.'

'Harrington said police saw her entering the property but she refused to answer the door, which aroused suspicion. She got Chelsea to climb into the loft, pretending to play hide and seek. When they found her, Cotton swore that Chelsea had just turned up and she was about to call the police. Maybe she was partly telling the truth, she could've just moved her from somewhere else. I don't know,' he said, rubbing his eyes.

Lawton shook her head. 'I should've seen it. I spent more time with them than anyone.'

Gardner turned to her. 'No one saw it, Dawn. You can't blame yourself.'

Lawton stared out of the window. 'But-'

'Look where we're going now. I had no idea Paul Henshaw was involved. Not a fucking clue.' He sighed. Maybe the papers were right about him.

Lawton wiped her nose. 'Should I get back there? I'm the liaison.'

Gardner looked at his watch. Lawton was right. She should be there. But they were halfway to Paul Henshaw's and he wanted more than anything to have him in custody. He started the car and pulled away.

'We'll get Henshaw first. It won't take long.'

CHAPTER SEVENTY-EIGHT

Simon drowned out the voice of the sat-nav directing him to the address he'd been given, instead thinking about the first time he had seen Beth. She had been nineteen days old. It had been torture waiting that long but he'd made an agreement with Abby and he had to abide by it. It was no surprise that Paul stuck to Abby and Beth like glue for those first few weeks. He would've too, given half the chance. But each hour that passed when he didn't see his little girl was agony. He wondered what little landmarks would've happened in the time before he'd even clapped eyes on her. Abby called him a couple of times, teary and overjoyed, and she sent a picture to his mobile but the image was blurry; it could never do his girl justice. Phone calls and pictures were fine, but not what he really wanted. Not the real thing.

Eventually Abby called and said he could see her. Paul had gone to meet someone, a business thing that couldn't be avoided, and would be gone all day. When he'd come off the phone he'd panicked. He was going to see his daughter. He'd spent an inordinate amount of time choosing something to wear and then picking a gift to take from the mountain of toys he'd been stockpiling in the spare room for months. He'd finally chosen a soft pink toy that was either a cow or a dog; it was kind of hard to tell. When he was finally ready, he'd gone to Abby's house and knocked at the door.

It was the first time he'd ever been inside her house. They'd always met at his place or somewhere neutral. It felt wrong to be there but when Abby led him through to the living room and he peered down into the bassinet at his beautiful little girl, he forgot about all that. Nothing else mattered in that moment. He didn't care if Paul came home and saw him. Then as if she had sensed he was there, Beth woke and Abby picked her up. Settling himself on the settee, he reached out for Beth and as he held her in his arms for the first time, he cried. He cried at the simple joy of Beth; at the thought of him being a father; at the way Abby looked at him and their daughter; and at the foolish decision he'd made to let them go.

If only he had spoken up back then. If only he had never let her go then none of this would have ever happened. He and Abby and Beth would still be together; a family.

As he got further and further off the main roads, his speed increased. He'd probably be stopped by the police before he could get to Paul. He'd miss his chance.

The mix of anger and excitement he'd felt earlier was beginning to wane. Why hadn't he told Abby or Gardner he'd got the address?

Because they'd stop you. Because you wouldn't get your chance to hurt him.

CHAPTER SEVENTY-NINE

Abby paced up and down trying Simon's phone over and over. Where was he? Maybe he needed time alone to process what they'd heard about Paul. But how much processing did he need to do? It was *her* ex-husband. Surely she should be the one having trouble with it.

Maybe that was it. It *was* her ex-husband. But how could Simon blame her?

Easily, she thought. Easily. Because she blamed him when she found out he'd talked to Helen Deal about Beth. That was the first thing that came to mind. *This was your fault.*

Only it wasn't.

She collapsed onto the settee and tried his phone again. It kept on ringing but there was no answer. She hung up and held the phone to her chest. She could try Gardner. She didn't even know where he was going so couldn't be sure if he'd be there yet. She hadn't thought to ask where Paul was. She blinked away the tears. He promised to call when he got there. He couldn't be there yet.

She stopped pacing and closed her eyes. Why had Jen been looking for Paul? She tried Jen's number.

'Hello?' Jen said.

'Why were you looking for Paul?' Abby said.

Jen sighed. 'I already told Simon. I was trying to prove to you that he was there. That I wasn't lying to you.'

'You've spoken to Simon?' Abby asked, her stomach tightening. 'What did you tell him?'

'Just what I told you.'

Abby felt sick. 'Did you tell him where Paul was?'

'Yeah,' Jen said. 'Why? What's going on?'

'I have to go,' Abby said and cut Jen off. Simon knew where Paul was. He was probably headed there now. What was he going to do to him? What would she do?

She called Gardner. 'Simon knows where Paul is,' she said.

'Shit,' Gardner said. 'I've got a local going over there. Don't worry,' he said but Abby wasn't convinced. 'Is someone there with you?'

'He's outside,' Abby said.

Gardner sighed. 'Okay. I'll keep you posted.' He disconnected and Abby threw the phone down.

She was angry at him for leaving her there, for not letting her go with him. She knew she couldn't go. It was a police investigation; of course she couldn't go and start asking her own questions. But she was angry with him for leaving her there alone with her thoughts. She'd allowed herself to think there'd been a mistake, that the nanny was either being malicious or just simply wrong. But now she was alone she couldn't help but dig deeper and everything she thought she knew seemed tainted. Every memory she dredged up of Paul, of the things they did, the life they shared, it all seemed wrong.

Thoughts of the day it happened, of the days that followed, of the weeks leading up to it, they all took on new meaning. Everything she believed was wrong. Her husband had betrayed her. She knew it. She just knew it. The nanny wasn't wrong, she wasn't being malicious. It was him. It had been him all along.

CHAPTER EIGHTY

Gardner drove through the little village and wondered why anyone would want to live out in the middle of nowhere. It was like a setting for a horror movie, all eerily quiet and deserted. But then if you were trying to hide it was probably ideal.

'You think Abbott's already here?' Lawton asked, glancing around the tree-lined road.

'I hope not,' Gardner said. Simon Abbott had a temper, a history of violence. He'd kicked the shit out of guys before over a comment about his girlfriend. Who knew what he'd do to Paul Henshaw? Gardner turned into the narrow lane where Henshaw lived. Maybe Abbott had every right to hurt him. For what he'd done to Abby, he deserved it.

He noticed the police car outside the house he'd been told was rented by Paul Henshaw. Simon's car was parked at an angle a few metres away.

He ran from the car, Lawton a few feet behind him. As he made his way up the path he saw the door was wide open, splinters of wood scattered across the kitchen floor. He stopped as he approached the officer, giving him a confused look and then he saw Simon sitting on the kitchen floor, his head hanging, blood on his hands and shirt. Gardner looked over his shoulder at the officer who just stood there saying nothing. He looked about seventeen.

Gardner looked back at Simon and it was only then he noticed Paul Henshaw, lying on his back on the kitchen floor, blood pooled around his body. His eyes were open, staring blankly at the ceiling.

When he could tear his eyes away from the body he looked back at Simon who didn't appear to notice he was even there. He bent down beside him and saw the cuffs around Simon's wrists.

CHAPTER EIGHTY-ONE

'Oh my God,' Lawton said, turning to go outside.

'What the hell happened here?' Gardner asked, looking at the young officer standing by the door. He stood gawping at Paul's body, unable to turn his eyes away.

'Who are you?'

Gardner turned around and saw an older officer coming into the kitchen. He looked like he was ready to draw a weapon, if only he had one.

'DI Gardner,' he said and the older man relaxed slightly and walked around the edge of the kitchen, being careful not to go too near the body.

'PC Ernie Fletcher,' he said. 'We arrived approximately fifteen minutes ago. Door had been forced open. Found the body and this one sitting here, staring at it.'

Gardner looked at Simon, who hadn't moved a muscle the whole time. He was still staring into space.

'He was crouched over the body,' Fletcher said. 'I restrained him and checked the rest of the property.' He looked at Gardner like he wanted a pat on the back. 'It's empty,' he said to finish.

Gardner put his hands on his head and looked at the ceiling. This couldn't be happening. It could not be happening. 'Have you called this in?' he asked Fletcher.

'They're on their way,' Fletcher said. He stepped closer to Gardner and bent to pull Simon up by the arm.

'What're you doing?' Gardner asked.

'He's a suspect in a murder investigation,' Fletcher said. 'Get up.'

The movement seemed to shake Simon free of the trance he was in and he allowed himself to be pulled to his feet. For the first time he looked at Gardner, his face lined with panic.

Gardner wanted to go after them but he knew he could do little for Simon now. He was found at a murder scene and they were going to take him in regardless. He could follow them to the station and request to speak to Simon but it would be down to the locals to decide in the end.

He looked down at Paul's body and quickly turned away, walking to the door for some air, ignoring the look the young officer gave him. Hopefully Fletcher was right and the techs were on their way. Until then all he could do was wait.

He knew he had to tell Abby what had happened but it wasn't something he was going to do by phone. Besides, what was he going to say? It would be hard enough telling her Paul was dead. But that Simon was chief suspect too? He could tell her things would be okay, that he'd work it out, that he'd get Simon home to her. But he didn't know if he could do that. Because he had no idea if Simon was innocent.

CHAPTER EIGHTY-TWO

Gardner sat in his car waiting for the cavalry to arrive. Lawton sat beside him. He couldn't decide if she was silent out of respect or if she was too caught up in her own thoughts. What happened with Chelsea Davies hit her hard. She blamed herself and she wanted to be there. Instead he'd made her come out here. Dragged her into another mess.

He could see Simon sitting in the back of Fletcher's car, while Fletcher leaned against the door as if he was waiting for the RAC to turn up. Gardner stared at his phone. He was surprised Abby hadn't tried to call him already, desperate to know what was happening, whether Paul was really involved, or to tell him Simon still hadn't returned home. Maybe she was still pissed off with him for not letting her come along but if he was glad of anything it was that he'd stood firm on that. Having Abby with him when he walked into this shit-storm was the last thing he needed.

He turned the phone over in his hands. He wasn't going to call her, wasn't going to show that little respect for her by telling her like that. It had to be done face to face.

'They're here,' Lawton said.

Gardner looked in his rear-view mirror and turned around. Three cars were pulling up in a line behind Fletcher's car and the man himself was holding out his arm, flagging them down as if they wouldn't know what they were looking for. He watched four men climb out of their cars and head towards Fletcher. Two of them ducked their heads and looked at Simon in the back of the car.

He saw Fletcher point towards his car and one of the men, dressed like a lawyer in an expensive looking suit, looked over. The other three headed back to the cars. He guessed they were the SOCOs and hopefully the pathologist.

Gardner got out of the car and walked to meet the man coming towards him, the one dressed like a lawyer. He stuck out his hand. 'DS Carlisle,' he said and shook Gardner's hand.

'DI Gardner,' he said. 'Fletcher fill you in?'

Carlisle gave him a smile. 'He gave me the highlights but I'd like to hear it from you,' he said.

They walked towards the house. The young officer at the door moved out of their way without a word. Gardner wanted to ask him if he'd actually had any training in scene preservation but as he'd already trampled through the scene himself he couldn't really point fingers. They stood in the doorway so that Carlisle could take a look at the scene. A couple of seconds later he nodded and walked back towards Gardner's car to make room for the SOCOs.

'So, I'm guessing this isn't just a nice and simple domestic or B&E,' Carlisle said.

'If only,' Gardner said. 'Basically, it's connected to an ongoing investigation, a rape and abduction case. Henshaw?' he said, waiting for Carlisle to recognise the name. 'The kid's still missing. She was taken five years ago.'

Carlisle nodded. 'Yeah, I remember that.'

'To cut a long story short, evidence was found earlier today that the man your guys are currently poking at, Paul Henshaw, was involved.'

'So who's he?' he asked and pointed at Simon.

'The kid's real father,' Gardner said.

'So he'd have good reason to off this guy then?'

Gardner blew out a breath. 'He certainly has a motive.'

'And he was found at the scene crouching over the body,' Carlisle said.

'That too,' Gardner said.

'Listen, I'm going to see what's happening in there and I'm going to tell Fletcher to take your guy in. You're more than welcome to stick around and listen to the interview.'

'Thanks,' Gardner said pulling his phone out again. He watched Fletcher do a three-point turn and drive slowly past the line of cars. In the back seat Simon turned and looked at Gardner, his face unreadable.

CHAPTER EIGHTY-THREE

Abby sat by the window, hugging her knees to her chest. The rain was coming down hard and she wished Simon would come back. She needed to talk to him. Needed to know things were okay. She held her phone in her hand and wished Gardner would call her too. He promised to let her know when he found out anything. He must've had something to tell her by now. She tapped the phone on her knee and it started ringing, causing her to jump. She answered on the first ring.

'Hello?' she said.

'Abby, it's me,' Gardner said.

'What's happening? Have you found Paul? Is Simon there?' There was a silence on the line and she looked at the phone's display to check if they'd been disconnected. 'Hello?'

'Abby,' Gardner said and sighed. 'I need you to listen to me. Is an officer still with you?'

'No, I told him to go. What's going on?'

Gardner sighed. 'I wanted to come and tell you in person but I can't get there right now. And you need to know...' He stopped again and Abby felt the nausea rising.

'What's happened?' she asked. 'Is it Beth? Is she there?' More silence. 'Michael, please. Tell me what's happened.' She could hear him breathing.

'I'm at Paul's house now. There's been an-' he stopped. 'Paul's dead.' Abby could hear a faint buzz on the line. All she could think was, is it always there, that buzz? 'Abby?' Gardner said.

'Yes,' she said, her voice flat. 'I'm here.'

'I'm sorry.'

'Simon?' she said. Gardner didn't answer. It felt like the world had stopped.

'I arrived at Paul's house and found police already at the scene. Paul had been stabbed,' he said and Abby sunk into the chair. She could hear movement, voices in the background. 'Simon was here when I arrived. They've arrested him on suspicion of murder. I'm going to go down there now for the interview.' He paused. 'Abby, I'm sorry I had to do this over the phone but I need to be here and I didn't want someone else calling you-'

'Has he asked for me?' she asked and Gardner was quiet for a minute. 'Simon?'

'I don't know,' Gardner said. 'Look, it might be better for you to stay put. I can't see them releasing him for a while. I can come by on my way home but it'll be late.'

'Okay,' she said, her head spinning. 'Was there any sign of Beth?'

'No, I'm sorry.'

Abby closed her eyes. She could feel any hope slipping away. She could feel herself slipping away. There was nothing she had faith in anymore.

'Another thing,' Gardner said and sighed like he couldn't bring himself to say whatever it was. 'Paul's body will need to be formally identified. I know he didn't have any family...'

'Okay,' she heard herself say.

Someone spoke to Gardner in the background and he replied but she couldn't make out the words. 'I have to go,' he said. She could hear him walking, a car door slamming. 'I'll let you know as soon as I hear anything.'

'Okay.' She was about to hang up when she suddenly thought of something else to say, something she needed to know. 'Did he do it?' she asked and Gardner didn't say anything at all. 'Did Simon kill him?'

Gardner let go of his breath. She could picture him running a hand across his face like he did so often. 'I don't know,' he said.

CHAPTER EIGHTY-FOUR

Gardner got home after midnight and collapsed onto the settee. He couldn't even be bothered to get a beer, despite it being all he'd thought about the entire drive home. He wanted to drink until he'd forgotten this day had ever happened and then climb into bed and stay there for a month.

The interview with Simon had gone as well as could be expected. He'd denied killing Paul Henshaw, of course, but the fact that two police officers had found him crouching over the body with blood on his hands wasn't good. That he'd stated to Gardner himself that he was going to kill Paul was a whole other matter. It didn't prove he was guilty. But it didn't help.

But there was still the lack of a murder weapon. The entire house and surrounding gardens had been searched and no weapon had been retrieved. From Gardner's calculations, Simon couldn't have arrived at Henshaw's much earlier than the police. Gardner wasn't that far behind him. And then there was the time of death. It was never precise but the pathologist suggested Paul had been dead for approximately two to four hours. It didn't quite add up.

He peeled himself off the settee and made his way to the kitchen. Instead of grabbing the beer he'd been hankering after he just stood at the sink, staring out of the window at the night sky. He wondered what Abby was doing. He'd called her on his way back, offering to go round, but she'd refused. She wanted to be alone, said she was tired and would speak to him tomorrow. He doubted she was sleeping. He doubted he'd sleep himself even though he was exhausted.

If there was one thing that could be said for the day it was that Chelsea Davies was fine. Physically, anyway.

Chelsea hadn't been harmed and from the little information they'd got from her so far she'd been treated well and had even been given some cool new toys. Louise Cotton was alright, a bit bossy like her mum, but alright. Anything else Chelsea had to say would have to wait for the next day. She had to rest.

Cotton had been taken into custody and was to be charged with false imprisonment and kidnap. Harrington said she'd cried and insisted she hadn't harmed Chelsea and had only done what Jill Hoffman had asked her to do. She hadn't wanted to get involved but needed the money. Jill Hoffman was being questioned. A third woman was being looked for in connection to the conspiracy.

Gardner walked out of the kitchen, back to the settee and lay back and stared at the ceiling. It wasn't quite the happy ending he was after.

CHAPTER EIGHTY-FIVE

Abby sat at the window. Her back was hurting from sitting in the same position all night. The only time she'd moved was to lean over to pick up the phone. Gardner had called with an update on Simon's situation. He didn't mention Paul's name at all.

For the rest of the night Abby had been sitting there by the window just thinking. When the numbness had worn off she found herself crying and wondered who she was crying for. She hadn't seen Paul for almost five years but to know he was dead didn't seem right. She couldn't imagine him not being in the world somewhere. And then she cried some more except this time she was angry because the man she'd devoted her life to had betrayed her. Except she didn't really devote her life to him and that was why he'd done it. But he still did the worst thing imaginable and she wanted to hurt him, make him suffer like she had. Only now she couldn't because he was dead, someone had got there first. And the police thought Simon had done it and maybe they were right. Maybe he did do it.

And I don't blame him.

Only thinking about killing someone and actually doing it is totally different and she didn't really believe she could do that, not even to Paul. Especially to Paul. But Simon? She didn't know what he was capable of. She'd seen his temper before. She'd seen what he did to that man outside that nightclub when she was a teenager. But that was different, wasn't it? He couldn't kill.

But she never thought Paul could do what he'd done either.

She sat there looking out into the dark street, watching lights turn on and off in the houses across the road, and all she could think was: I just don't know anymore. None of you know. All of you across the street saying goodnight to your husbands and sons or mothers and wives. None of you know. The people you sleep next to every night, they're not the person you think they are. Your brothers and sisters and friends and neighbours, none of them are who you think they are. You think they're good people and they're not.

None of us are.

CHAPTER EIGHTY-SIX

'What did he say to you?' Abby asked as Jen curled up in the chair. She'd called her wanting, or needing, to know what Paul had told her. Whether he'd seemed guilty. If he had any regrets.

'I didn't speak to him,' Jen said, still looking dazed. 'I can't believe he's dead. I just can't get my head around it.' She wiped a tear from her cheek. 'I can't believe he was involved at all. I just...' She shook her head. 'It's my fault, isn't it? If I hadn't told Simon where he was, he'd still be alive.' Jen wiped her nose. 'I guess now I know why he didn't want to see me. She was blocking the door. She said he wasn't there but I knew she was lying.'

'Who?' Abby asked, her heart suddenly in her mouth. 'Who was with him?'

Jen shrugged. 'Some woman. His girlfriend or whatever. She just kept saying he wasn't there and then slammed the door on me.'

'Was there a little girl there too?'

'Yeah,' Jen said. 'She answered the door.' Realisation dawned on Jen's face. 'Oh my God.'

Abby grabbed the phone. Gardner picked up on the third ring. 'It's me,' she said. 'Helen and Beth were at Paul's house. Jen saw them.'

Gardner arrived twenty minutes later. 'Paul was alive at that point? You saw him?' he asked Jen.

'Only through the window, but yes, he was definitely alive.'

'Did you see Helen leave?'

'No. I left after she slammed the door on me. There was no point staying. He wasn't going to talk to me.'

'Did you notice her car?'

Jen shook her head. 'No, I'm sorry.'

'Okay,' Gardner said. 'DS Carlisle will want to speak to you too.'

Jen nodded. She looked at Abby. 'I'm sorry, Ab. I didn't know. I didn't know it was her.'

'I know,' Abby said.

'We're checking CCTV around the area. Unfortunately, there isn't any that close to Paul's house so we can't see her coming and going. But we are checking the surrounding areas. I still think Whitby is our best bet. Her mother's house is there, she must know the place well, and I think she sticks to what she knows. She came back to Redcar for a reason.'

'What if she's not there? She's not stupid. She could go anywhere.'

Gardner nodded. 'We're still looking nationwide, Abby. We will find her.' He pulled his phone out. 'I need to make a few more calls and then we'll get going, alright?'

Gardner turned up the radio that was helping to maintain a comfortable atmosphere in the car, hiding the silence that sat wedged between him and Abby. He didn't think small talk was appropriate considering what they were going to do, and got the feeling Abby didn't want to talk anyway.

Abby leaned against the door, half closing her eyes. A few minutes later the news came on the radio and Gardner's fingers tightened around the steering wheel. Chelsea was safe and sound. His boss was telling anyone who'd listen what a good job his team had done. But there were still people asking why it had taken as long as it had to find her. Especially when she was so close by. Why hadn't they checked there before? Why didn't they notice something was wrong with that woman, with the girl's mother? The same woman they'd been supporting until a day ago.

The case had been passed on to someone else to sort out now the hard work was over. And he was back here sorting out this mess. Again. The media hadn't got hold of it yet. Thankfully. But it wouldn't take too long. There'd been reports of a murder but the victim hadn't been named so no one had connected the dots. He hoped that it would all be over with before anyone picked up on it, for his sake as much as Abby's. But he doubted it.

Abby leaned over and switched off the radio. He gave her a half-smile but said nothing. He didn't know if she was doing it for his benefit or her own. He'd never really considered how the Chelsea case made her feel. He wondered if she'd started to question him. How many cases he'd been involved in. How many he'd solved. Maybe she thought the papers were right. That the police, that he, had made a mess of this case. That it was his fault Chelsea Davies had not been found. That Beth had not been found.

CHAPTER EIGHTY-SEVEN

Helen watched Casey playing on the floor of the bedroom in the B&B, making the doll and the purple octopus have a conversation. All she wanted was for her daughter to be happy, to be safe. To be a family. All Paul wanted was to destroy it.

He was always the weak one. She should've known he couldn't be trusted. Just because he wasn't getting his own way, he was willing to destroy all of their lives. He didn't care about Casey, about how it would hurt her. How could he? He wasn't her father. She should've known when he backed out of taking her to the play that something was wrong. He was always whining about how he never got to see Casey anymore and then when he had the chance he walked away.

Helen wondered how she had been so blind. Right from the start he'd faltered. He wanted to send notes, let his wife know the baby was alright. How stupid was he? She'd put a stop to that. And what right did the woman have anyway? She'd proved she wasn't worthy of a child. Paul had told her himself how she'd put herself first. How she planned to abandon the baby as soon as she could so she could get back to her own life, her career. He'd told her all about his selfish wife.

Helen closed her eyes, picturing Paul beside her, his hand brushing lightly against her skin. There was a time when she loved him, truly loved him. The day she told him that his wife had cheated on him, that his daughter wasn't his own, he'd wept. They'd been walking through the park, still just friends. He broke down and begged her to say she was wrong. She wiped his tears and held onto him like a child. He'd been so vulnerable then. They both were.

She wanted him even before her world fell apart. She'd seen him in the shop, talked to him, tried to seduce him. But he was so loyal. He even wanted to introduce her to his wife. The woman who had everything she wanted. Who didn't appreciate any of it. He imagined they'd be friends, share the joy of motherhood. She didn't take pleasure in destroying what he had. He needed to hear it, needed to know the truth. And once he did, they could be the family they both craved.

Helen blinked as tears stung her eyes.

'Mummy?'

Helen turned and saw Casey standing beside the bed, clutching the purple octopus, fear in her eyes.

'What's wrong?' Casey asked.

Helen took a deep breath and wiped her eyes. 'Nothing, honey,' she said. 'Mummy's fine. Go back and play.' Casey remained standing there, staring at Helen. 'It's alright, Casey. Everything's fine. Go and play.' When Casey still didn't move Helen screamed, 'Go!'

Casey ran into the bathroom and Helen tried to control her breathing. Look what he'd done. Look what he'd made her do. She slumped onto the bed, her head in her hands. She could hear Casey crying and she felt a pain in her chest. *He made me do this.*

Helen got up and went into the bathroom. Casey was curled up under the sink, the octopus held against her face. Helen bent down and put her hand on Casey's head.

'I'm sorry I shouted at you, honey,' she said. 'Mummy isn't cross with you.' Casey didn't move. 'Mummy's just upset. Will you give me a hug?'

Casey looked up at Helen. 'I want to go home,' she said. 'I want to go and see Sara.'

'We'll go home soon, honey,' Helen said.

'When?' Casey asked. 'I don't like it here. I want to see Daddy.'

Helen held onto Casey. How could she tell her she wouldn't see her father again?

CHAPTER EIGHTY-EIGHT

Abby stood over the body. She was supposed to say yes, this is Paul Henshaw, but she couldn't. He didn't look right. She couldn't tell if it was because he was dead, if it was his waxy skin and closed eyes that made him seem wrong; or if it was because she realised she didn't know who he was anymore.

The man who'd shown them in, the pathologist she guessed, was standing opposite her, hands crossed respectfully in front of him, probably waiting for her to say something so he could cover Paul up again and get on with the rest of his day. Gardner stayed close to the door, giving her space.

She kept staring at Paul's face. She could feel tears stinging her eyes but she didn't want to cry. He didn't deserve her tears. She wondered if the pathologist wasn't standing there whether she'd touch him, slap him in the face. But she couldn't touch him now. No one could. He'd got away with it, without ever having to face her and admit what he'd done.

A phone rang behind her and she looked up at the same time as the pathologist. Gardner excused himself and stepped outside. She could see him through the little window, pacing as he talked. He was nodding and then suddenly he stopped. Abby wondered what he was being told. Whether Simon had admitted killing Paul or if they'd found Beth and Helen, or if it was nothing to do with her at all. Gardner held the phone against his shoulder and pulled a notebook from his pocket, to scribble something down. He caught Abby's eye and she turned away, back to her dead ex-husband. The pathologist was watching her now, getting impatient.

She gave Paul one last look and then said 'Yes.' The pathologist seemed surprised by her voice and dropped his pose. 'It's Paul,' she said and the man nodded and covered him over.

That's the last time I'll see him, she thought. She hadn't seen him for a long time but it seemed strange that she couldn't anymore. But more than anything it meant she would never know why he did it.

Abby opened the door and stood behind Gardner.

'Has he seen her today? She hasn't checked out?' Gardner said to whoever was on the other end of the phone. 'Alright,' he said eventually. 'Thanks.' He turned to Abby. 'Are you alright?' he asked.

'Who was that?' Abby said, ignoring him. He looked at the phone and notebook in his hand. 'Was it about Helen?'

Gardner guided her out of the way as a porter wheeled a trolley, covered with a dark blue tarp, into the morgue. 'Yes, we may have a lead on Helen.'

'Where is she?' Abby asked.

'Some old guy who runs a B&B in Whitby saw her picture on the news. He thinks she's been staying there.'

'And Beth? He's seen her?'

Gardner shook his head. 'He claims she didn't have a kid with her. I'm going to check it out anyway.'

'I want to come with you,' Abby said and Gardner started to argue. 'Please. Please, I can't just sit and wait.'

Gardner sighed.

'Please,' she said again, her hand on his arm. 'We're closer to Whitby than home anyway.'

'Fine,' he said. 'But you stay in the car.'

CHAPTER EIGHTY-NINE

As they drove along the winding roads towards Whitby, Abby listened to half of Gardner's conversations, trying to work out what the other people were saying. He'd said things about coordinated efforts and investigations and yes, back up from the police in Whitby would be useful but, no, he couldn't be sure Helen would be there, it was just a lead he was following up. He never mentioned the fact that Abby was sitting next to him in the car and every time he was asked about Abby or Simon, Gardner gave her a sideways glance and tried to talk about her without talking about her.

Abby tried to ignore his voice and concentrate on what they were doing. She had been praying that Helen would be there and that this would be over. Having an end in sight was all that was keeping her sane.

She couldn't think about Simon and Paul and how long she'd been living this nightmare. She just wanted it to end. She stared at the road ahead, watching it disappear under the car. She counted the seconds between road signs or trees. She didn't let her mind slip into other, darker areas.

'Abby?' Gardner said and she turned to him, realising he was no longer on the phone. He looked concerned and she wondered what had been said to him, what she'd missed when she zoned out. 'Are you alright?' he asked and she felt the dampness on her cheeks.

'I'm fine,' she said and wiped her face. 'How long until we get there?'

'Ten minutes, maybe,' he said. 'We've got all units looking for her car. A black Range Rover. That should be easy to spot in the country,' he added and Abby tried to smile. 'Several cars have been stopped in the area but none with the right registration. I doubt Helen would've changed plates but still...' Abby could feel him watching her but she couldn't respond. She wanted him to keep talking even if she wasn't really listening to the words. At least then she didn't have to listen to her own thoughts.

Abby stared out of the window and noticed a sign for Whitby. The pain in her stomach worsened and she started wondering if she really wanted to be there. What if she came face to face with Helen Deal? She didn't know if she could handle it.

A black Range Rover pulled up alongside them at the lights and Abby thought her heart would stop. A kid in the back pressed his face into the window and Abby turned back to the road ahead.

Gardner leaned forward, like he was looking at street names. They were getting close. He'd told her she'd have to stay in the car and she'd wanted to argue but now she didn't think she'd be able to stand anyway. She would just sit and watch and wait for something to happen.

Abby looked around her at the tall houses looking out over the harbour, surrounded by fish and chip shops and tacky souvenir stands.

Gardner slowed the car outside a soft-brown brick house with a "Vacancies" sign in the window. Gardner pulled up in front. 'Wait here,' he said and Abby nodded. She watched him walk to the door, and then got out, following him inside. Gardner approached the desk. An old man came out and shook his hand.

'Mr Carter?' Gardner asked and the old man nodded, glancing at his warrant card. Gardner took out a picture of Helen and Beth and showed it to Carter. 'She's been here?'

Carter took the picture, holding it close to his face. 'Definitely her,' he said. 'She didn't have a kid with her though.'

'When did she check in?'

Carter shuffled back behind the desk and turned the page of the guest book. His finger traced down the page, slowly. Abby wanted to shake him.

'There,' Carter said and pointed to a neatly written name. Catherine Portman.

'Her mother's name,' Gardner said. 'She hasn't checked out yet?' he asked Carter, who shook his head. 'Can I see her room?'

Carter found a key and trundled back round to Abby and Gardner. 'This way,' he said.

Carter opened the door and Gardner stepped inside, holding his arm up to prevent Abby from following him. The bed was unmade. A few items of clothing were thrown on a chair. A toiletry bag sat on the windowsill. Gardner bent down, looking at something under the bed. He stood up. In his hand was a pink and white bag with a mouse on it.

Abby sat in the lobby as Gardner made call after call. He wanted someone to come and take prints in the room. Another man had called with another alleged sighting of Helen in his B&B so he wanted every B&B and hotel in Whitby checking. He wanted someone at Helen's mother's house.

Gardner hung up the phone and went to put it back into his pocket when he did a double take. Abby turned to follow his gaze and she saw it. A black Range Rover stopped outside.

CHAPTER NINETY

Abby ran after Gardner as he jumped into the car. She climbed in as he reversed, watching as Helen's car sped off, swerving around parked cars. They followed her onto the main road; she was heading out of town. Gardner swerved in and out of traffic, trying to overtake Helen. Abby tried to see into the car, see if her daughter was in there.

Gardner slammed his foot on the brakes. 'Shit!'

He ground to a halt an inch behind an SUV, which had backed out onto the road. He slammed his fist onto the horn and the SUV pulled back in, letting Gardner pass. The gap between them and Helen widened. 'Fuck,' he muttered and turned on his siren.

They could see Helen's car up ahead before it turned off, swerving violently around a corner, barely missing oncoming traffic.

The Range Rover seemed too far away. The road was fairly narrow but otherwise empty as far as she could see. She held onto the door handle, her fingers white. Gardner put his foot down, the gap closing. For the first time Abby thought they might catch her. Maybe things would be okay.

It didn't seem real at first, like something off the TV. Helen's car seemed to drift sideways before tipping over onto its side, sliding across the road on its roof and rolling over, upright again, before stopping at the edge where the tarmac met the grass. Abby lurched forward as Gardner slammed the brakes. She could hear Gardner talking, asking if she was okay and then saying something about an ambulance and she was going to say she was fine and didn't need it until she realised he was on the phone again and it was probably for Helen and it crossed her mind that they should just leave her there.

And then she thought about Beth in the back of the car.

Gardner tried to grab hold of Abby and stop her but she pulled away from him, running towards the car, calling Beth's name. Gardner took her arm and pulled her back. He could see Helen slumped over in the front.

'Abby, I need you to go back to the car,' he said but Abby just stood there, staring at the car. 'Abby,' he shouted. 'Go back.' She finally looked at him and stepped back onto the road. She made no attempt to get into the car but at least she was out of the way. He took a deep breath and walked along to the driver's side. He had no idea if Helen was alright. The car didn't appear to have too much damage.

He looked through the window to the backseat. He saw the vague shape of something but it was impossible to tell what it was. He realised that he was holding his breath as he stepped to the front of the car. He edged along so he could see Helen in the front and saw her eyes flicker open.

Gardner and Helen looked at each other and then Helen's mouth began to move. He couldn't hear her from outside the car but it seemed like she was repeating something over and over.

'Helen?' he said, his voice raised enough for her to hear but hoping it wasn't aggressive enough to spook her. 'It's DI Gardner. Do you remember me?' She showed no sign that she had even heard him let alone recognised him. Gardner swallowed. 'Can you move?'

Helen's mouth kept moving but her body stayed motionless. He wiped his hand across his mouth, noticing how dry it felt.

'Helen?' he tried again, his voice raspy. He stepped towards the door and her hands moved to the wheel. 'I'm going to open the door, alright?' Her eyes followed him to the door. He focused on her hands and pulled it open. The interior light blinked on. Gardner checked her lap and the passenger seat but couldn't see a weapon of any kind. Helen looked at him. She was still speaking but he had to strain to hear her.

'You can't have her. You can't take her away. You can't have her...' she said.

Gardner looked to the back seat. A blanket was thrown across it. He looked back to Helen.

'Who, Helen? Who can't I have?' Helen's eyes flicked behind her. Gardner looked at the backseat again. 'Do you mean Casey?' he said. Helen's voice cracked and her chant sped up. 'Is she here, Helen?' he asked. 'Is Casey with you?' He watched as Helen's hands slid down the wheel. 'Helen?' he said. 'I want you to keep your hands on the wheel.' She stopped moving. 'That's right. Just keep them like that.'

He shifted his weight to his other foot and tried to peer into the backseat. He needed to know where the girl was. It was possible she could be under the blanket but surely she would've moved by now unless she was seriously injured. He looked at the blanket but saw no movement. Whatever was under the there was completely still.

Gardner turned his attention back to Helen. She was still sitting with her hands in front of her but she was no longer speaking. 'Helen?' he said. 'I'd like you to come out of the car. I'd like to talk to you. Can you do that? Can you move?'

Helen kept her eyes straight ahead. 'You can't have her...' she started again.

'Helen, please. I just want to talk. Just for a little while-'

'You can't have her. You can't take her away.'

'Helen,' Gardner said and moved to the back door. 'I'd really like you to come out and talk to me.' He reached out to the handle and saw Helen shift in her seat. 'But I can get in here if you'd prefer.' He pulled the handle and heard the click as the door opened. Gardner paused, the door was barely open an inch. Helen stopped speaking. He eased it open another inch and she span around in her seat.

'Leave us alone,' she said.

'Who?' he said and pulled the door wider. Helen jumped from the car. Gardner slammed the back door shut and reached for Helen at the same moment as he saw the knife.

He grabbed hold of Helen's arm as she swung the knife towards him. He pushed her arm up and heard the clatter of the knife hitting the tarmac. Helen screamed and clawed at his face. He grabbed her other arm and turned her around, pushing her up against the car.

'You can't take her,' Helen said, furious tears rolling down her face.

Gardner pulled his cuffs out. 'Helen Deal, I am arresting you on suspicion of the abduction of Beth Henshaw, and the conspiracy to rape and assault Abigail Henshaw. You don't have to say anything but it may harm your defence if you do not mention, when questioned, something you later rely on in court. Anything you do say may be taken down and given in evidence.'

'No. You can't. She's my baby. She needs me.'

Helen struggled against Gardner and fell to the ground. She brought her knees up to her chest and cried. Gardner bent down in front of her. 'Do you understand?'

Helen shook her head. 'You can't take her.'

Gardner stood and went to the back door of the Range Rover. Helen screamed as Gardner opened it and grabbed the blanket, pulling it back. There was nothing there.

CHAPTER NINETY-ONE

Helen closed her eyes. So this was it? This was how it would end? Paul was right. She'd lost another child. Only she didn't lose her. He'd taken her away. He'd forced her hand, he'd driven her to it. But even in taking his life she'd been too late. Even as she'd felt the blade going in, the warm caress of his blood on her hands, she knew it was too late. They were going to take her away. She tried to stop it, tried to get away. But in the end she knew what would happen. They'd find her. She knew what she had to do.

You can't take her. I'm her mother.

Helen slumped on the floor by the car, still muttering to herself, seemingly oblivious to Gardner's presence. Gardner leant against the door frame and took a breath. He'd been sure Beth was there, in the car. He was sure he'd found her. He checked the rest of the car while Helen sat there staring into space. But he found nothing. Abby stood there, watching. She took a couple of steps towards Gardner and then stopped again, looking from him to Helen and back again.

'She's not here,' he said to Abby and then turned back to Helen. He needed her to tell him where Beth was, what had happened to her. He'd seen what she was capable of and he was beginning to get that feeling he'd had five years ago. That Beth Henshaw was no longer alive. He felt that this was nearly over, that this was the end. He really wished Abby wasn't there. 'Where is she, Helen?'

Helen stared through him and continued muttering under her breath. Gardner crouched down in front of her and took hold of her chin, pulling her face up, forcing her to look at him. 'Where is she?' he said.

Helen stopped and stared into his eyes. A smile spread across her face. 'I'll never tell,' she said and started laughing. 'I'll never tell.' She pulled away from him and turned towards the car, blood trickling down her forehead. Gardner grabbed her again and turned her around, slamming her against the car.

'Tell me where she is!' he said.

She started laughing louder and tears rolled down her face. 'You'll never find her.'

Gardner let go of her. Helen kept laughing and he stepped back. He wanted to hurt her. He wanted to hurt her until she told him what he wanted to know. He walked away and took a deep breath. Abby was standing there, frozen. When he turned around Helen had stopped laughing and was staring at him.

'You don't have children, I can tell,' she said and smiled at him. Gardner started walking back to her, his fists clenched when he felt Abby's hand on his arm. She walked past him and stopped.

'She won't tell us anything,' Gardner said.

Abby bent down and smacked Helen across the face with the back of her hand and Gardner flinched.

'Where is she?' Abby asked. Helen didn't blink, just stared out across the road, blood trickling down her nose now. Abby took Helen's face in her hands. 'Look at me,' Abby said. Helen kept her eyes on the road. Abby shook her but she still refused to meet her eye. 'Do you think you're helping her?' she said. 'You think she's happy wherever she is, on her own?' She paused, waiting for some reaction, but got none. 'What happens when you're locked up and she's left alone? Then what? What kind of mother would do that?' Helen finally turned her eyes to Abby. 'You have to tell us where she is. You're hurting her. Where's Beth?' she asked.

'Who?' Helen asked.

Abby swallowed and bit her lip. 'Casey,' Abby tried. 'Where's Casey?' She watched as Helen's face changed from confusion to a strange sort of serenity and then to anger.

'What do you want with her? Why won't you leave us alone?' Helen said.

'I just want to know she's okay.'

'She's my daughter!' Helen shouted.

Abby flinched and moved back, glancing at Gardner. Her hand curled into a fist. 'I know,' she said.

'He made me do it,' Helen said. 'I had to stop him. He was going to take her away.'

'Who? Paul?' Gardner said, looking at the knife Helen had dropped.

'I knew he'd betray me. He was going to tell on me.' Her eyes focused, first on Abby and then Gardner. 'You're trying to take my baby. That's what you want. You couldn't look after your baby so you want mine,' Helen said, spittle shooting out of her mouth.

Abby shook her head. 'That's not true.'

'You're a terrible mother. You didn't want a baby. He told me. You got rid of your baby. And now you want mine.'

'That's a lie.'

'I deserve her. I'm a good mother. You're not a mother. You're not *her* mother.'

Abby's head kept shaking. 'That's not true.'

'Helen, look at me,' Gardner said.

'I'm a good mother,' Helen said. 'You didn't want your girl. *He* didn't want her. He gave her away.'

'You took her from me,' Abby screamed, unable to take it anymore.

'Helen, listen to me,' Gardner said.

'She's not yours,' Helen said.

'We know that Helen. We just want to-' Gardner started.

'Where is she? Where's my daughter?' Abby shouted.

'Abby, calm down. Helen, look at me.'

'You can't have her. You don't deserve her,' Helen said. A tear ran down her face and she tried to speak but her voice came out as a croak. Abby leaned closer.

'What?' she asked.

Helen started giggling. 'She'll be okay. I took care of her,' she said.

Abby looked over her shoulder at Gardner. He crouched down beside Abby. 'How did you do that, Helen?' he asked.

'She'll be okay now,' Helen said again. 'She'll be okay. It's all okay now.'

Abby stood up. It wasn't going to work. She'd never tell them where she was.

'She's sleeping now. My angel's sleeping now,' Helen said, no longer laughing. Abby looked at Gardner and he saw her face change. And they both knew.

Abby walked across the road and sunk to the floor.

Her daughter was dead.

She bent over, like she'd been punched in the gut, tears streaming down her face.

Gardner pulled Helen to her feet; he could hear an ambulance siren in the distance. Helen fell back against the car, a drowsy smile on her face. Abby ran back across the road, screaming at Helen, not even words, just screaming at the woman who had taken everything from her. Gardner grabbed hold of her, pulling her back, even though

340

he wished he could just let her have this. Let her have this one small justice after everything Helen had done to her.

Abby kicked against him but he kept tight hold until she gave in, falling against him. He held onto her and told her it'd be alright even though they both knew it was bullshit.

He looked down at Helen, still muttering to herself as the ambulance pulled up beside them. Abby pulled away from him and crossed back to the other side of the road, falling to her knees, her hair covering her face. The paramedics looked from one woman to the other and then to Gardner for guidance. He pointed at Helen and they walked to her, checking her over before putting her into the ambulance.

CHAPTER NINETY-TWO

Abby sat on the cold grass at the side of the road watching them load Helen into the ambulance. She turned away; she couldn't look at her. Gardner was on his phone again. He looked from Helen to Abby and said, 'Are you sure? We're on our way,' before hanging up.

Another police car arrived and Gardner ran over to them, pointing at the ambulance and then back along the road they'd come up. One of the officers climbed in the back of the ambulance with Helen and it drove away. The other officer got back into his car and did a three-point turn. So that's it, Abby thought. That's all there is to it?

She put her head down. She could hear Gardner's shoes on the tarmac. He stopped in front of her, his scuffed shoes just in front of her own. He bent down to her but instead of saying the kind words he was probably trained to say he took her hand and pulled her up.

'We've got to go,' he said and led her back towards the car. Abby stopped halfway and waited for him to say something. He opened the door and looked back at her, waiting for her to move.

'No,' Abby said. 'I can't. I can't do it anymore.'

Gardner closed the door and came back. He took her arm and led her to the car and this time she let him because what was she going to do out there? As he started the car and drove back towards the town she wondered what she would do at home. What happens now? She closed her eyes.

When she finally opened then, they'd stopped outside another B&B. Another police car was parked ahead. Is this where Beth was? Where Helen had left her?

People were staring, wanting to know what was going on. In the distance she could hear a siren and it was only when the blue lights hit her eyes that she realised that it was behind her. An ambulance to take her daughter away.

Abby threw the car door open and ran up the steps into the B&B. She needed to see her. Just one more time. Just to touch her hair and tell her how sorry she was that she wasn't there for her, that she couldn't save her. She pushed through the door and heard voices upstairs. As she got to the top a uniformed officer tried to stop her.

'Let her in,' she heard Gardner say and as she ran into the bedroom she saw a paramedic crouching over Beth. She could see her dark hair spilled across the pillow.

'She's alive,' the paramedic said. 'Unconscious, but alive.'

Abby felt a surge through her body. Her daughter was alive. Beside her she saw Gardner's hands cover his face. She pushed her way to the bed. The paramedic stepped out of the way and Abby knelt down in front of her daughter, her hands shaking as she tried to touch her face. Behind her she heard movement and Gardner took her arm as the paramedics tried to get in.

'Will she be alright?' Abby asked but no one answered.

CHAPTER NINETY-THREE

Abby and Gardner ran down the hospital corridor, almost colliding with a porter as they turned the last corner. As they ran through the doors to A&E, the staff looked up, en-masse.

'Can I help?' a nurse asked them, stepping forward.

Gardner flashed his warrant card. 'A little girl was just brought in, unconscious. Where is she?'

The nurse looked over her shoulder and another, older, woman came around the desk. She looked at Gardner's ID and then addressed him. 'Doctor Padel is with her now,' she said, nodding towards a cubicle.

'Is she in there?' Abby said. 'Is Beth in there?' She stepped forward but Gardner held her back. 'What's wrong with her?'

'They're just checking her out,' the nurse said. 'She was unconscious when they brought her in. I don't know...' She looked from Abby to Gardner and then stepped back as Doctor Padel emerged from behind the curtain. He stopped short as Abby reached for his arm.

'Is she okay?' Abby asked.

The doctor looked at them and Gardner stepped forward. 'I'm DI Gardner,' he said and reached for his ID again but the doctor waved it away.

'She'll be fine,' he said. 'She'd been given a sedative. She's awake now but still very drowsy. We'll keep her in for observation. We're just seeing if we can find her a bed on the children's ward.'

Abby pressed her hands up to her face and swept them back over her hair. Relief washed over her. She was okay. Beth was okay. 'Thank God,' she said. 'Can I see her?' Abby asked.

The doctor looked at Gardner again and then walked away without a word. Abby waited for Gardner to speak.

'There are certain... procedures we have to go through,' he started.

'What do you mean?' Abby asked.

Gardner sighed. 'We can't just let Beth go home with you... you know that.'

Abby swallowed. She had never really thought about what would happen if she ever got Beth back. Not all the logistics and bureaucracy involved.

'As far as Beth is concerned Helen is her mother,' Gardner said. 'And I know it's hard. I know all you want is for your daughter to be back with you, but it's not as easy as that. There'll be a period of transition.'

'What does that mean?' Abby asked.

'Beth will be placed into care.'

'What?' Abby said.

'She will come back to live with you eventually.'

'When? How long?' Abby said.

Gardner shrugged. 'I can't say. This is a difficult situation.' He shook his head. 'A social worker will work with both you and Beth. You'll get to know her over time and then when the time's right, she'll come and live with you.' Gardner looked at the floor.

Abby felt like the world had stopped. After everything she'd been through, after all this time she had finally found her daughter and still she couldn't take her home.

Gardner touched Abby's shoulder. 'I'm sorry,' he said.

'Can I at least see her now?' she said. 'Just for while? The doctor said she was drowsy, she won't even remember it.'

Gardner nodded and pulled back the curtain. The nurse stood and watched, keeping a distance. As Abby stepped into the cubicle, she started to cry.

Beth lay beneath the sheet on her side, legs pulled up to her stomach. Her eyelids fluttered open and closed again as Abby approached her. Abby reached out and brushed the hair from Beth's face, her hand shaking.

Beth opened her eyes and blinked a few times before smiling. 'I remember you,' she said to Abby.

Abby let out a sob and then smiled at the little girl. 'You do?'

'You were at *Wind in the Willows*. You found my bag,' she said and her eyes drooped closed again.

'That's right,' Abby said and smiled. 'How are you feeling?'

'I'm tired,' Beth said.

Abby turned and saw the doctor behind her. 'We're taking her up to the ward,' he said.

Abby turned back. She wished she could stay with her but it was impossible.

'Night, sweetheart,' Abby said and stroked Beth's hair once more. As she turned to leave Beth spoke.

'Where's my mummy?'

Abby started to cry. Gardner led her out of the cubicle. A nurse smiled and went in, followed by a porter. The doctor opened the curtain and they pushed Beth's bed away.

CHAPTER NINETY-FOUR

Gardner thanked Detective Carlisle and hung up. Simon had been released, he was on his way to the hospital. Carlisle had been questioning Helen Deal regarding the murder of Paul Henshaw but she'd been less than co-operative. They had the knife Helen had dropped. It was the weapon used to kill Henshaw but she wasn't saying a word.

Gardner wanted to stay put in Whitby, not only to speak to Helen, but for Abby's sake too. But he'd been informed that Alice Gregory, the woman who'd given Abby the flyer, had finally been in touch and he wanted to speak to her himself. He wanted to know how she was involved. She was waiting for him when he arrived back at the station.

'Take a seat,' he said and sat down across from her.

'What's this about?' Alice asked. 'I just got back and had like a million messages saying you wanted to talk to me.'

'It's nothing to worry about,' Gardner said. 'I just wanted to ask you about some flyers you were handing out last week.' He pulled out the plastic bag with the flyer inside. 'You were handing them out at a fun day in Locke Park.'

'Yeah?' she said.

'You gave this one to a woman called Abby Henshaw. You handed it to her and said, "You should go." Do you remember that?'

Alice sat forward and pulled her sleeves down over her hands. 'I hand out loads of flyers. It's my job.'

'Okay. Do you always speak to people when you hand leaflets out? Do you always tell them they should go to something?'

Alice shrugged. 'Sometimes. I don't know. Sometimes it helps, like they feel guilty for ignoring you.'

'Okay. The woman you gave this flyer to said she thought you didn't have any more flyers with you. She thought you'd given it to her specially. And I think she was right because this was written on the back.' Alice looked at the writing on the flyer before looking down at the floor. 'Alice, this is linked to a very serious crime.' Alice's head shot up. 'Now, I think you may be covering for someone and if you decide not to tell me anything it makes me think you have something to hide.'

'I didn't write that. He must've done it.'

'Who?'

'Some bloke gave me twenty quid to give it to her. I saw him lurking about the park for ages. I thought he was some sort of paedo or something, hanging around where all them kids were. He came up to me and handed me the flyer, and I thought the last thing I want is one of the bloody things back. He wanted me to give it to this woman. And I said I was done but he gave me twenty quid so I thought alright then.' She shrugged and stopped for air. 'So he pointed out this woman who was sat on the bench. And I asked him if he fancied her. He was all nervous and sweaty and he had gloves on, like driving gloves or

348

something. And he said it was really important she got it. I thought he wanted to ask her out or something. He looked like a bit of a loser. So I went over and gave it to her and that was it. Then I went home.' Alice stopped for a second before looking Gardner in the eye. 'He didn't kill her did he?'

'No, he didn't,' Gardner said. 'Do you remember what he looked like?'

Alice shrugged again. 'Skinny. Tall.'

'Is this him?' Gardner asked and showed her the photo of Paul Henshaw.

'Yeah, that's him. Freak.'

Gardner thanked Alice Gregory and headed out to get back to Whitby.

His head was banging. Why would Paul Henshaw suddenly tell Abby where Beth would be? Why would he wait so long? They may never know that but at least he had done the right thing in the end. And at least they now knew why Helen had killed him. That was something.

'Sir?'

Gardner turned to find Lawton jogging towards him.

'I just wanted to know how the little girl was. Beth,' she said.

'Looks like she's going to be fine,' he said.

'And Abby?'

Gardner shrugged. 'Who knows. But she's found her. That's what counts.' He turned to walk away but stopped. 'How did the interview go?'

'Sir?'

'The motivational speaker.'

'Oh,' she said. 'He didn't get it.'

Gardner smiled. 'Glad to hear it.'

Lawton smiled at him. 'Anyway, I'd better get back to it,' she said, and he watched her walk away.

Gardner walked along the corridor towards the children's ward. He knew Abby had stayed outside, waiting to hear how Beth was. She knew she couldn't see her but still she waited. She'd been waiting for a long time, she was used to it.

Gardner looked through the small window to where Abby was sitting. She looked exhausted but at the same time more full of life than he'd ever seen her. He wished he'd seen more of her that way, wished he'd been able to make her happy before. But that wasn't his place. It never would be. He'd done what he'd promised. He found Beth. What else did she need him for?

He saw Simon get out of a lift at the other end of the corridor. He should've said something but instead he turned away. He'd go and see them both soon. See how they were holding up. But first he had something else to do.

CHAPTER NINETY-FIVE

Abby turned as she heard footsteps behind her. They slowed as she caught Simon's eye. He glanced towards the door of the children's ward.

'Is she alright?' he asked.

Abby stood and nodded. 'She'll be fine,' she said and smiled at Simon. She saw his shoulders drop in relief and he walked towards her, smothering her with a hug. Abby held on tightly, her face buried in his chest.

Simon pulled back after a while. 'Are you alright?' he asked.

Abby smiled. 'Yes,' she said. She felt a lightness she hadn't felt in five years. She felt almost like a real person again.

Simon led her to the chairs outside the ward. He sat with her hand in his. 'Have you seen her?'

'Last night,' she said. 'She was still drowsy but she recognised me. From the play.' She looked towards the ward. 'They won't let us see her again for a while. This is going to be so hard. Not just for us, but for Beth.' Abby swallowed hard. 'She thinks Helen is her mother. How's she going to get past that?'

Simon shook his head and pulled Abby close to him. 'I don't know,' he said. 'But we'll work it out.'

They sat in silence for a while, watching life happen in the microcosm of the hospital corridor. Doctors rushing around. Parents pacing up and down. Children crying.

'I thought it was you,' Abby said, eventually.

Simon kept his arm around her shoulder. He didn't look at her face. He didn't speak, just nodded.

'I thought you killed Paul,' she said. 'I'm sorry. I should've had more faith in you.'

Simon still didn't look at her. 'It's alright,' he said. 'I should've told you I was going there. But I knew you'd stop me.' He finally looked at Abby briefly before turning back to the door. 'I don't know what I was going to do. Maybe things would've ended the same either way.'

CHAPTER NINETY-SIX

The officer outside the door nodded at Gardner as he walked into Helen's room. She was on her side, facing the wall, but he noticed her eyes move towards him when he walked in. For a moment he stood at the foot of the bed looking at her. She was quite a tall woman but lying in that hospital bed she seemed tiny. Maybe hospital had that effect on everyone, making them seem vulnerable and small. But staring down at her it seemed impossible that this woman had caused so much pain to so many people.

He walked to the side of the bed to face her and she closed her eyes, blocking him out. After a while he pulled up a chair and sat beside her like he was just another visitor. The room was quiet. There were no monitors beeping or other patients crying out for help. Just the sound of movement outside the room and the both of them breathing inside of it, waiting each other out.

'Where is she?' she said.

Gardner was surprised she'd given in first but he'd guessed what her first question would be. He didn't think she'd intended to cause Beth any harm. She was the only person he believed she wouldn't harm. Maybe she thought keeping her sedated would mean she was safe while Helen left her alone. She'd booked them into several B&B's, trying to keep them all guessing. He didn't know how long Beth had been left by herself. He debated whether he should tell her anything about the girl; maybe make her suffer like Abby had all these years, but he needed her to talk. 'She's being taken care of,' he said. 'Kids aren't supposed to be given sedatives.'

'I know how to take care of my daughter,' Helen said and opened her eyes. 'Is she here?'

'No,' Gardner lied. 'She's at another hospital.'

Helen eyed him up, probably knowing he was lying. Not that it mattered, she wouldn't be allowed anywhere near her. Gardner thought he should feel good about that but when you thought about it from the Beth's perspective it wasn't as sweet. For better or worse, Beth thought that Helen was her mother. She was all she'd ever known and that was going to be ripped away from her.

'I want to see her. She'll be scared on her own,' Helen said. 'When can I see her? I'm her mother. They have no right keeping me away from her. She should be here with me.'

He wanted to tell her to stop lying, that it was over. But he wondered how much of it she truly believed, whether she'd convinced herself that Beth was really her daughter. 'What happened Helen?' he asked her.

'We were in an accident,' Helen said.

'Who?'

'Me and Casey.'

'She was in the car with you?'

'Yes. Of course she was. Where else would she be?' Helen said and Gardner sat back.

'Why were you out on that road? Can you remember?'

'We were going out for the day. A trip to the seaside,' Helen said.

'Sounds fun,' Gardner said. 'And what about the day before? Did you do anything?'

Helen narrowed her eyes at him, pausing before answering. 'We saw Casey's dad,' she said eventually.

Gardner gave her a little smile. Oh she was good. Keeping it close enough to the truth but not admitting anything. The perfect way to play the insanity card. But Gardner could see the light behind her eyes, the calculating. He had no doubt she was crazy but she wasn't totally unaccountable.

'How was he?' Gardner asked. 'Did you have a good time?'

She paused again. 'He was fine,' she said.

'Did you kill him?'

Helen's eyes hardened. 'Of course not.'

'The eleventh of November,' Gardner said. 'Does that mean anything to you?'

'It's Casey's birthday,' Helen said.

He paused. 'What about the fifteenth of December?' Helen froze and he knew he'd struck a nerve. 'That was the day she died, wasn't it?'

Helen threw herself from the bed, clawing at his face, screaming. Gardner grabbed her wrists, trying to restrain her. The door swung open and a nurse and the officer who'd been outside ran in. Between the three of them they got Helen back onto the bed and managed to restrain her. Helen was still screaming and for a second Gardner felt a stab of regret. But at least he now knew that Helen hadn't blocked out the death of her child. She knew what had happened, what she'd been doing. And she would be held accountable.

Gardner walked out into the corridor and felt his phone vibrating in his pocket. 'Gardner,' he said, turning away from the disapproving looks of a passing nurse.

'Where are you?' Atherton said.

'Whitby. I've just spoken to Helen Deal. I think-'

'I need you back here.'

'What for? Chelsea Davies?'

'No. The mother admitted her part in it this morning. She's been charged. DC Harrington spoke to her,' Atherton said. 'There's a girl missing. No one's seen her for three days. Dad thought she was with mum, mum thought she was with dad.'

'How old?' Gardner asked.

'Fourteen,' Atherton said.

'History?'

'Nothing they've cared to share so far,' Atherton said. 'I want you on this one. This Henshaw story will be all over the news shortly. We could use a little positive press even for just a little while. Get back up here.'

'On my way,' Gardner sighed but Atherton had already hung up. Gardner leaned back against the wall. It's over, he thought. Time to move on. So why wasn't he happy?

He slid his phone back into his pocket and headed down to the children's ward.

CHAPTER NINETY-SEVEN

Abby lifted her head from Simon's shoulder as Gardner walked into the waiting room.

'Have you heard anything?' Abby asked.

Gardner shook his head. 'Not about Beth. Helen's been charged though,' he said and got himself a cup of water from the cooler.

Abby just nodded. Whatever they did to Helen wouldn't be enough. 'Where is she?' Abby asked.

Gardner took a long sip and looked over the rim of the plastic cup at Abby. He didn't seem surprised by her question, as if he'd been waiting for it. 'She's here,' he said. 'She'll be taken into custody as soon as she's fit to leave the hospital.'

'Have you spoken to her?'

'Yes,' he said. He leaned his head back on the chair and closed his eyes. 'She didn't say much but she's been charged with abducting Beth, what she did to you, Paul's murder.' Gardner shook his head at it all. 'They're getting a psychiatric consult.'

'I'm sure she'll pass it with flying colours,' Simon said.

Abby watched Gardner. He looked shattered. She wondered if he had to stay with them. If he was legally obliged just in case they tried to take Beth with them. Just in case she tried to steal her own daughter. She laughed briefly to herself. No one noticed.

Standing, Abby got some water from the cooler. She looked at Simon; he'd closed his eyes again. She wondered how long it would take him to drop off. For some reason she felt wide awake. More awake than she had felt since... She couldn't remember when.

She leant back into her chair and looked up at the pictures on the walls. Various cartoon animals and characters from books and films adorned them. She wondered what Beth was into. What was her favourite story? What was her favourite film? Food? Game? Would they have all changed by the time Abby was allowed to take her home?

Abby knew in her head that the system was right, but in her heart? She didn't know what to expect from the next few weeks, or months, but it didn't seem fair. It *wasn't* fair. None of it was fair. Having her daughter stolen from her. Her husband betraying her in the worst way imaginable. Being unable to take her daughter home now they'd found her at long last. Having her own daughter ask her where her mummy was.

She pinched her eyes shut to stop the tears from falling. She thought about that day. About how she'd lied. About how she'd betrayed Paul first. She thought about what Helen said. That she was a terrible mother. That she never wanted a baby. It wasn't true.

But was she to blame? If only she hadn't cheated on Paul. If only she'd told the truth. But "if only" never works. We make our choices and live with the consequences. Maybe no one is to blame.

She thought about Paul. She always regretted what she'd done to him. She wondered how life would have gone if he'd never found out about the affair and none of this had happened. Could she have gone on lying forever? She wondered if she'd ever forgive him. She still hadn't quite taken it in that he was gone.

She thought about Jen. She hadn't done anything wrong. She *had* seen Paul that day. She wasn't being malicious. She should know they'd found Beth. Abby took out her phone but stopped. She'd tell her in person. She owed her that. No matter what had happened she was still her friend. In her own way she'd stuck by her through it all. Maybe now this was over there'd be room for Jen in her life again.

Abby looked at Simon and touched his hand. She loved him. In the end maybe she would have gone to him anyway. How could she ever know? Life had pushed them down a different path.

She thought about Helen. Helen who'd lost her baby. She would never forgive her. She thought about the tragedy of losing a baby. She didn't need to imagine what it was like. Helen had shared that with her. But in the end Abby would get her daughter back. What would Helen get? She deserved to lose everything after what she did. What kind of person would take someone else's child away? She didn't know. Maybe everyone was that kind of person. If you were pushed enough, who knew what you could do? What you were capable of.

She thought about Beth. She was the only truly innocent one in all of this and however hard this was for her and Simon it'd be worse for Beth. How do you tell a child that her mother *isn't* her mother? How do you tell her that her name *isn't* her name? It was enough to break her heart all over again. And yet... she would have her back. That was all that really mattered.

Abby looked at Gardner and wondered how she could ever thank him for what he had done for her. She wondered if she would see him again when this was all over and done with. She hoped she would. She still needed him to guide her through what was ahead.

The door opened behind her. Abby stood up and faced the nurse. Gardner opened his eyes.

'Just to let you know that she's being discharged soon,' the nurse said.

Abby turned to Gardner who stood. Simon rubbed his eyes and looked about the room before noticing the others were standing. Gardner left with the nurse. Abby looked through the narrow pane of glass at Gardner as he talked to a middle-aged woman in a tartan skirt. The woman looked up at Abby and smiled before Gardner turned and opened the door, stepping back through.

'Abby, Simon,' he said, 'this is Margaret McLachlan. She's the social worker who'll be taking Beth. She'll be working with you a lot over the next few weeks.'

Margaret held out her hand and Abby and Simon shook it. 'It's nice to meet you,' she said. 'I'm about to take her home.' She coughed as she said this. 'It'll be a few days at least to get her settled. Feel free to call me,' she said and handed over a card to Abby. 'I'm afraid you won't be able to see her just yet but I can keep you up to date. I'll have to come and speak to you both sometime over the next few days. I realise how hard this is, but go home and get some rest and we'll take it from there.'

She smiled again and turned to Gardner. Gardner smiled at Abby and then held the door for Margaret.

'Can we see her before she goes?' Abby asked.

'I'm afraid not,' Margaret said and turned to leave the room.

Abby nodded. 'But she's okay?'

Margaret smiled again. 'She's just fine.'

'Hang on here and I'll give you a lift home,' Gardner said.

He left Abby and Simon alone. Abby stood by the door and felt Simon step close to her. He rested his chin on her head. They both gazed through the window. Eventually the door to the ward opened. Gardner held it open as the nurse wheeled Beth, who was sitting in a tiny wheelchair, out towards the lift, Margaret by her side.

The nurse turned backwards, pulling Beth's chair into the lift. Abby felt Simon's breath in her hair. She put her fingers to the glass.

Seeing the movement, Beth looked up. She smiled at Abby and, just before the lift doors closed, she waved hello.

You couldn't know what it felt like to have something stolen from you. The one thing that meant more to you than anything else. One minute it was there. The next it was gone.

Think of your most prized possession. Think of the one thing you love more than anything else. Think of the one thing you would die for. And then think of losing it.

Think of the words of comfort given by others and how useless they are. Think of how the world keeps going on and on but how yours would stop, just like that. Think of the emptiness and the gaping hole where love once was.

Maybe you'd feel numb. Maybe it hurt too much to even contemplate. Maybe you couldn't bear to think about it and so you buried your head in the sand and pretended everything was okay.

I couldn't do that. I couldn't let it go. I couldn't grieve and move on. I didn't want to face the rest of my days with that emptiness.

I chose to do something. I chose to be a mother. Her mother. I chose her. I wouldn't stop until I had a daughter again.

ACKNOWLEDGEMENTS

I'm extremely grateful to everyone who helped make this happen, but especially to: The team at Moth Publishing, in particular Andrea Murphy and Sarah Porter, for their faith in me and my writing. Everyone at New Writing North for all their help and support over the years, in particular Claire Malcolm and Olivia Chapman. Will Mackie, my brilliant editor, who worked so hard and made the book so much better. Camilla Wray and Sallyanne Sweeney for the advice early on. Paula for promising to read this one. Cotton for taking me on long walks when it just wasn't working. My family for supporting my dreams of being a penniless writer, especially Mam for being my manuscript guinea-pig; Dad for the encouragement despite not reading "that kind of thing"; and to Donna and Christine for sharing the weird crime-obsessive genes. Stephen, for keeping me going; for putting up with all the mountains and molehills, and just about everything else.

Thank you.